*Jeff had b.......................se
about wom...*

He knew instinctively when he had appealed
to a woman, and he also knew just what that
woman desired of him. Usually, it was one
thing: she wanted to go to bed with him. He
had come to realize that most women he met
wanted this even though they would not admit
it to themselves. There was a certain electric
something which passed from them to him,
communicating their secret desires. And this
was the wordless message he got from this
erstwhile stranger, this Mrs. Latimer.

Helen Latimer was going to be the key that
would unlock doors which would otherwise
have been shut for him. What would she do, he
wondered, if she ever discovered he was black?

GOLDEN STUD

Lance Horner

A FAWCETT GOLD MEDAL BOOK

Fawcett Publications, Inc., Greenwich, Connecticut

THE AUTHOR GRATEFULLY ACKNOWLEDGES THE IN-VALUABLE EDITORIAL ASSISTANCE OF LAWRENCE BLOCHMAN.

GOLDEN STUD

Printed in the United States of America

First Printing: August 1975

1 2 3 4 5 6 7 8 9 10

To my long-time friend
CAL ST. CLAIR

CHAPTER I

BRICKTOP whoaed his horse to a stop in the shade of an enormous live oak whose trailing banners of tattered gray moss cast undulating cross-hatchings of light and shadow on the dirt road. Bricktop? No. He must never again think of himself as Bricktop. Now that he was once more a free white man rather than a fugitive slave, he must think of himself only as Jefferson Carson. Despite the hair-raising events of the last ten days, he must never forget that he was the same "Jeff Carson" who had set out from Philadelphia so many dangerous months ago.

His memories of life as Jeff Carson were pleasant, unlike his tragic recollections of life as Bricktop, the white-skinned nigger slave of Willow Oaks Plantation. By the curious operation of the genetic laws of Mendel (who had not yet been born), the son of a beautiful octoroon had come into the world with red hair and a white skin. Nothing could have made him more despised by Bax Simon, owner of Willow Oaks. Bax ardently believed that no damned nigger had the right even to look like a white man, let alone pass as one. A nigger was a nigger, no matter what the color of his skin. Simon had further reason for hating Bricktop: his red hair confirmed Simon's suspicion that a red-headed itinerant tradesman had abused the hospitality of a night's lodging at Willow Oaks by secretly humping a virgin teen-age wench, an honor Simon had been reserving for himself.

Growing up, Bricktop instinctively sensed Simon's animus and returned it in kind. He was a rebel by nature, and took preverse pleasure in defying plantation rules. Early puberty and a prodigious sexual endowment drove him frequently to the offlimits women's quarters. When he was caught, he was strung up by the heels in the barn and lashed until his buttocks streamed blood down to his neck. When he ran away, he was soon recaptured and

7

Baxter Simon personally and gleefully burned a large WO —for Willow Oaks—into his back. Struggling during the branding operation, Bricktop had pushed away the red-hot iron; the burn left a scar across the palm of his right hand.

Well, those days were gone forever. At least he hoped so. For the second time—no, the third—he was about to start a new life, thanks to Minnie. Minnie was Philomena George, the poor little rich bitch he had seduced aboard the Ohio River side-wheeler. Poor Minnie! She had certainly been in love with him, and he hated having to abandon her. Even after he had been exposed as "a damned nigger," he could have persuaded her to run away with him, though they couldn't have married because she was white. Hadn't she helped him escape by unlocking his spancels and stealing a horse for him? He might regret her deep in his loins, but one thing was certain: he was never going back to Willow Oaks Plantation where he had grown up as a Negro slave and where he would finish his days in bondage if he were ever caught and returned to Mississippi.

He felt something crawling under his shirt, and scratched. There must have been bedbugs in the tavern he had just left. He had slept so soundly that he had not noticed them during the night, but a few were still feeding on him this morning. He should strip off his clothes and get rid of them, but he was on the public highway and there was no privacy. By nightfall he should be near New Orleans. Thank God for that! Once there, he would no longer have to keep looking over his shoulder to see if by one chance in a thousand he was being followed. There was still the off-chance, he reasoned, that Walter George, Minnie's father, had learned of his daughter's defloration and was hot on his trail. But since Minnie would certainly not tell her father about her unmaidenly fling, Jeff felt safe on that score, at least for the present. Of course, if Minnie should give birth to a black baby within the normal term. . . .

Well, that had been a hellish few hours to live through, but he had survived, and here he was almost within spitting distance of New Orleans, where he was confident neither Papa George nor Baxter Simon would find him. He was used to city ways and there would be a thousand places to hide in New Orleans. He could even dye his hair, but he didn't think that would be necessary.

While he was not grieving over his separation from Minnie George, he had to admit to himself that he had briefly toyed with the idea of marrying her and setting himself up as heir to The Georgics, her father's plantation. What a bit of irony that would have been—an ex-slave becoming owner-boss of an aristocratic plantation! And nobody would have known of the brand between his shoulder blades that made him as black as the crudest *bozal* just out of the hold of a slave ship from Africa.

He finished his scratching—damn those filthy bedbugs! —and sat up straight in his saddle, the better to ease the tightness of his pantaloons around his back pocket. He took out his worn leather wallet and, glancing up and down the road to make sure nobody was coming, opened it to count his money. Nearly two thousand dollars. That was certainly enough to give him a stake in New Orleans, to keep him until he made the right connections and started something profitable. He had no doubts about his abilities; it was just a matter of deciding what he would do. Should he set up a stable of whores like the ones he had had in Pittsburgh and Louisville? No. There was no great amount of money to be made in prostitution unless a man had twenty or so on his string, and it would take time to acquire that many. There must be some other way to make big money in a hurry. Just what it might be, he did not know, but something would turn up. It always had.

The soggy pone and the watered-down chicory coffee that had comprised his breakfast had left him feeling hungry, but he would have to stifle his appetite until he reached another tavern or an ordinary. Probably the food there would be no better—it never was—but at least he might get some ham and eggs for his midday meal. Ham and eggs were the staple diet in this part of the country. He had already sickened of them and hoped he would be able to change his menu once he got to New Orleans. He should; New Orleans was a French city, and the French were noted for their culinary art.

He stood up in his stirrups again to ease the wallet back into his pocket, carefully buttoning the protective flap. He would willingly have sat in the cool shade for an hour, but if he wanted to get to New Orleans, he could not spend time daydreaming along the road. He pulled up on the reins, started the horse with a few peremptory clucks, and trotted off. He even whistled a tune, timing it to the clop-clop of the horse's hooves.

It was a glorious day, the sky a true cerulean blue with not a cloud to be seen. He had heard that New Orleans held a carnival to usher in Lent, and he hoped he would be in time for it. In his present euphoria over his escape and freedom, he would welcome a few days of carnival. It would be a good occasion to make the important connection he needed—everyone would be gay and carefree and drunker than hooting owls. That was one thing, he warned himself, he must not do: he must not get drunk. Perhaps it would also be a good idea, difficult though it might be, to swear off women. The telltale brand on his back was far more dangerous in the South than it had ever been in the North, and, he again reminded himself, it had been a combination of drunkenness and that brand that had nearly caused his death—or even worse, his living out the rest of his life as a Negro slave. But damnit, that was all behind him now. It was clear traveling ahead.

He was now passing people on the road. They were mostly blacks going to the cane and cotton fields. Each of them, as he passed, looked up, grinned, and greeted him with a "Mornin', mastah suh." Even the few white men whom he met doffed their hats and greeted him affably. And why not? He was young and handsome, and most important of all, white—at least as far as they could see—and he had a go-to-hell smile and a bantering reply for all their greetings.

Some distance down the dusty road he saw a carriage and horses drawn over to the side. Sensing something wrong, he slapped his horse's neck and spurred the animal into a gallop. He rode up alongside the carriage in a cloud of dust, and quieted his horse.

A woman was the only occupant of the carriage. A stocky young Negro coachman was in the road examining one of the horse's hooves. Whenever Jeff Carson saw a woman, regardless of her age or appearance, he assumed a dashing personality. He was able to assay this woman in a glance. She was handsome, dressed in the height of fashion, and probably between thirty-five and forty. With a sweeping lift of his hat and a smile that displayed his white, even teeth, he spoke to her.

"Jefferson Carson, ma'am, at your service. You seem to be in need of some assistance and I was wondering if I could provide it."

Nobody could resist Jeff's smile, particularly when he stoked the charm into his voice, which in all his dealings with women took on a particularly rich and vibrant timbre. The woman in the carriage smiled back at him and laid her hand, heavily encrusted with rings, on the side of the carriage. Jeff checked that hand; it was white and well cared for, although it showed signs of age that were not apparent in the carefully powdered face. Equally important, the diamonds were costly, so she must be rich, a fact underlined by the elegant carriage and the fine pair of horses. A thought flashed through his mind: he might be able to delay his arrival in New Orleans by one night.

"I believe that one of the horses has a loose shoe. Solomon"—she pointed to the black who had the horse's hoof between his legs—"is seeing if he can fix it," she replied, continuing her smile.

"Then let me see if I can help him. I'm not too experienced in shoeing horses, but I've seen it done and perhaps we can repair the damage sufficiently for you to get home, provided, of course, you do not live far from here."

Again she smiled. "Only about half a mile. I was just returning from an overnight visit to my married daughter, who lives a few miles down the road. I live at Poinciana Plantation, which is the next big house on the right. I'm Mrs. Latimer."

Jeff slid from his horse and walked to the carriage. He reached for the hand on the damask arm of the side bar

11

and slowly lifted it to his lips, carefully appraising the diamonds as he did so.

"And I am Jeff Carson of The Georgics, Mississippi on my way to New Orleans." His kiss lingered for a moment on her hand, which she did not withdraw. "I hope I may be of some slight assistance to you."

She nodded in the direction of the coachman, who was remounting the box. "It would appear that Solomon has already solved the difficulty, but my thanks just the same." She glanced at a tiny jeweled watch that was pinned to the lilac silk bodice of her gown. "It is going on midday, Mr. Carson. May I invite you to have a bite of lunch with me? As a matter of fact, the only other place where you might eat is some ten miles down the road, and I'm certain that the food you would get there would be most unpalatable."

Again Jeff bowed. "Thank you, Mrs. Latimer. I've been on a steady diet of ham and eggs. But I would welcome a chance to clean up and change my clothes before I appear at your table. Would that be possible?"

"More than possible, Mr. Carson, it can become an actual fact. Why don't you hitch your horse to the rear of the carriage and take the rest of your short journey to my house on the seat here beside me? If you have ridden horseback all the way from Mississippi, I'm sure you must be as sickened of the horse as the beast is of you."

"An excellent idea." He could sense there was more to this woman's invitation than she had revealed in her speech. He led his horse around and fastened the reins to the rear spring of the carriage. Then he opened the little door in the side, took down the flight of steps that were folded inside, and climbed up to sit beside her. It was a shallow landau and he had to sit with his long legs straight out in front of him. The whole interior of the carriage further proclaimed the wealth indicated by the woman's clothes and her jewelry. Here was an unexpected fillip, and he was certain he could turn it to advantage. He eased his body from the strained position it was in, conscious of his soiled trousers so near the whispering lilac taffeta of her dress.

"Do put your hat back on, Mr. Carson." She smiled at him. "The sun is hot and I would not want you to invite sunstroke. Besides, you have a pale complexion which burns easily, and a sunburn would be painful."

"Thank you." He replaced his hat and she adjusted the bit of black lace that served as her parasol. The coachman started the horses. With a glance backward to see that his horse was following, Jeff turned full attention to her.

"Just one thing troubles me, Mrs. Latimer, and that is what your husband is going to think when you arrive back home with a strange man beside you."

She made a little *moue* of disapproval. "I happen to be a widow, Mr. Carson. My husband has been dead for several years, and now that my daughter is married, I live alone and run my own plantation with the help of my overseer. We raise cotton, and as our land is still fertile, we produce good crops."

"You are a courageous lady to have taken over the management of a plantation." He smiled sideways at her, heart quickening. Her hand, which rested on her knee, was fascinatingly near his thigh.

"I managed it for several years before my husband died. He was an invalid, and little by little he became more and more incapacitated and I took over the reins of management. So it was no very difficult thing for me to do it all when he died. You may not believe it, but I am as accomplished at getting a field plowed and planted as I am at serving afternoon tea to my friends. It's all in the getting used to."

"My admiration, ma'am. It isn't every woman that could do it." He realized that her eyes were appraising the length of his stretched-out legs, finally coming to rest on the bulge at his crotch. They lingered there a moment and then sought his.

"It isn't every woman that is free to do what she pleases, as I am." Her hand slipped just a fraction of an inch closer to his leg. It was so near now that he could feel its warmth through the light drill of his trousers. "Believe me, I'm no namby-pamby woman who faints at the least provocation. No, Mr. Carson, I'm not. I couldn't manage a big plantation with some two hundred slaves if I were."

He did not answer. They were turning at the gates of a

13

long avenue of live oaks leading to an imposing villa. The mansion was perhaps not quite as impressive as the Greek-revival Mississippi manors, which boasted porticos of classic pillars. It was more in the French colonial style—one-storied, with a wide veranda. He watched young blacks sweeping the gravel driveway with twig brooms; the whole appearance was one of absolute tidiness resulting from constant care.

The coachman stopped under the shelter of a covered *porte cochère,* and when he had quieted the horses, sprang from the box to open the door and assist Mrs. Latimer down the tiny flight of steps. Jeff jumped down beside her and together they ascended the steps of the long gallery. The thick, ornate oakwood front door was opened by another handsome young black in livery who bowed low to Mrs. Latimer and welcomed her home with a "Good day, mistress ma'am. I trust yo' found Miz Eliza in good health."

"She is fine, Pompey."

Inside the house, in the cool of its semidarkness, Jeff needed a moment to adjust his eyes, but he could see shining floors, rich rococo furniture, and filigreed gold frames around oppressive ancestral portraits.

"I'm going to give you an hour to tidy up," Mrs. Latimer said, removing her hat and passing it with her sunshade to the servant. "Then you will come down and we shall lunch. I must tell the cook that I have a guest and that we shall be eating in the dining room rather than from the usual tray she prepares for my luncheon."

"I hope I'm not inconveniencing you."

"Laws no! Having a guest is always a welcome break in the monotony of my days." Her hand touched his arm lightly. "I just hope there'll be enough food to satisfy a big man like you."

"I'm sure there will be." Jeff bowed slightly. "And I'll have your charming company along with the food."

Again her hand touched his arm and he was aware of the warmth of it. And he was also aware of the slight tumescence she'd roused on him in her carriage.

"You have a delightful manner, Mr. Carson. And now

I shall have Pompey take you to one of the guest rooms. He will bring plenty of hot water and towels, so do perform your ablutions, and when you have finished, ring for him. He will show you to the dining room where I shall be waiting for you."

"My sincere thanks, Mrs. Latimer. You do not know what a luxury it will be to feel clean again. Believe me, I shall not take too long, because I anticipate lunching with you and getting to know you—much better."

She glanced at him from under her long lashes. "You do flatter me, but I love it. I've lived here alone so long that a compliment from a man is enough to set my head a-spinning. *Au 'voir.* I'll see you a little later."

There seemed to be nothing more that Jeff could say. She made no move to depart, and to cover up the momentary awkwardness of silence, he reached for her hand and conveyed it to his lips. Yes, he'd unerringly made the right move again; the hand was not withdrawn. He felt that fullness in his groin, which he knew must be evident through the tight material of his trousers. Again he felt her eyes appraising him. Well, he had nothing to be ashamed of, so with a confident swagger he followed Pompey down the polished floors of the hall to the guest room.

CHAPTER II

JEFF luxuriated in the tin tub of warm water, the scented soap, and the fleecy towels Pompey brought him. It was the first opportunity he had had for a real bath since he had been grooming for his last ill-fated dinner at The Georgics —so rudely terminated by the appearance of Baxter Simon. At most of the taverns along his escape route he had been forced to satisfy himself with hasty ablutions under the pump at the horse trough or with a minuscule basin brought to his room.

As he poured suds over his scarred back, Jeff reflected that his chance meeting with Mrs. Latimer was the first real break he had had since the Carsons had found him hiding in a barn outside Natchez. He had raised such a rumpus as a lad when Baxter Simon decided to sell his mother that Simon had included Jeff, then Bricktop, in the coffle he was taking to the vendue table in Natchez.

This time Bricktop–Jeff's escape attempt was successful. The staple with which his spancels were attached was embedded in a decaying beam. With patient work he managed to pull it loose during the night. He made his way to a barn behind an inn on the outskirts of Natchez, climbed into an empty carriage to hide, and fell asleep. The carriage was one in which Henry Carson and his wife were driving back to their home in the North after attending a secret Abolitionist meeting in the heart of slave country. Carson, a kindly old retired schoolteacher, was happy to be able to put his philosophy into action. When he had recovered from his surprise at finding manacles on what he thought was a white boy, Carson bought a file to free the boy's wrists and decided to take him along to freedom.

The husky redhead repaid his benefactors when the Carson carriage was attacked by bandits who thrived along the Natchez Trace. He sprang from the vehicle, grabbed one highwayman from the rear, and broke his neck. The other robber fled in panic when Jeff picked up his fallen companion's pistol.

The Carsons took Bricktop to Philadelphia. They gave him a name and a basic education—his native intelligence enabled him to cover a surprising range of studies in five years—and when pneumonia killed them within a few days of each other during the bitter winter of 1816, they left him the few hundred dollars of their savings.

Jeff's inheritance fueled a monumental binge that lasted from Philadelphia to Pittsburgh, where he woke up broke and in bed with a charming slattern named Veronica. Veronica had hustled to keep them in eating money as they traveled down the Ohio in search of warmer climes. They picked up another girl in Cincinnati and a third in Louisville, where Jeff decided he'd settle for a while. He found the life of a pimp a pleasant and easy one. His women went eagerly out to hustle for him as long as they were permitted to enjoy his extraordinary and inexhaustible virility. River sailors always had plenty of money after their long trips in keelboats and barges up the rivers from New Orleans. But Jeff's career as a fancy man had been cut short by the intervention of Blue-eyed Mike, the king pimp of the Louisville riverfront.

Veronica had warned him about Mike. Good old Veronica! She probably loved him in her way. She'd brought Jeff a pistol when she reported Mike's threat to kill him unless he kept his girls out of the Shippingport district—which was where the sailors hung out. So when Mike showed up to repeat the threat in person, Jeff shot him dead.

Mike just happened to have more than four thousand dollars on him, so Veronica and Jeff split half and half, and Jeff bought a ticket for New Orleans on the new-fangled double-decked steamboat *Washington* that was sailing that night. Veronica wouldn't set foot on that fool contraption, which was a block long and spouted sparks out of both of its tall smokestacks. Not on your life! It was bound to blow up, and she didn't want to be on it when that happened.

It was aboard the side-wheeler that Jeff met the Walter George family. The Mississippi plantation owner and his wife had come for their two daughters, who had been in a girl's school in Louisville. Charlotte, the elder sister, was quite plain, but Philomena, the younger one, was a stunner. Jeff seduced her before they were past Owensboro. It had been simple enough. The "staterooms" were merely partitioned sections of the general cabin and the sexes were segregated—women aft and men in the forward quarters—but the upper deck under the stars was not. And Philomena—Minnie, she called herself—was just as eager as he was. In fact, by the time the *Washington* had entered the Mississippi at Cairo, Minnie had persuaded her father to invite Jeff to stay at The Georgics, and Jeff broke his journey at Natchez to ride overland with the Georges. . . .

Better stop thinking about that part of his life, he warned himself. He stepped out of the tub and toweled himself roughly. True, those first few weeks had been pleasant. Minnie had been an exciting lay. But why dwell on the past when a bright future was just about to open up? Now that he felt clean all over and every inch the gentleman, it was time to start concentrating on making himself irresistible for his imminent conquest of Mrs. Latimer.

Jeff opened his saddlebags and took out a change of small clothes, a clean shirt, and the reserve pair of white pantaloons he had been saving for New Orleans. Well, one afternoon would not ruin them for future wear. They were badly creased from packing, but they were clean.

He opened a small leather case and took out his razor, shaved himself easily with the still-warm water, and viewed his face in a tripod shaving mirror which he could tilt to just the right angle to catch the light. The clean clothes felt good against his scrubbed skin. And when he had combed his still-damp hair he felt a wicked sense of anticipation, ready for any occasion, not the least of which would be luncheon with Mrs. Latimer.

Jeff had been born with a sixth sense about women, just as he had been born with red hair. He knew instinctively when his appeal had reached home to a woman, and just what that woman desired of him. Usually she wanted to go to bed with him. He had come to realize that most women he met wanted this pleasuring, even though they sometimes didn't admit it to themselves. A static spark passed from them to him, communicating their unspoken desires. And this was the wordless message he had got from Mrs. Latimer. Perhaps her desire would never be uttered in words, but he knew she wanted him. As for his wanting her—he shrugged unconsciously—one woman was about the same to him as another. Perhaps Minnie George had been something special, but she had gone out of his life. Now almost any woman would do. Sure, the young and beautiful were more exciting, but unless she were old and repulsive, practically any woman could rouse him. He grinned. He raped so easily! Mrs. Latimer was older, but she was certainly a beautiful woman, and—he remembered the diamonds on her hand—there was the fringe benefit of great wealth.

He surveyed himself from head to foot in the long pierglass mirror. Despite the wrinkled shirt and pantaloons he was quite pleased with the rakehell reflection. He wished he might have been an inch or so taller so he would exceed six feet, but that couldn't be remedied. He admired the way his muscular body was delineated by the thin garments he was wearing. He was well satisfied with his good looks: his strong neck that so powerfully supported his head, the clear whiteness of his skin, and the brightness of his eyes. He smiled at himself and was proud of the sensual curve of his moist red lips. He nodded in approval at his image in the glass, then ran his comb again through his auburn hair, setting a wave in its dampness. Yes, he was thoroughly satisfied with himself.

What a shame that when he undressed, those telltale scars on his body branded him as a Negro slave. Well, he didn't have to show the brand marks to anyone. Nobody would ever again know about them. This was a vow he had made to himself. Even in his most intimate moments in bed with a woman, he always made certain that the candles were blown out. Many women had begged him to leave them lighted the better to enjoy him. He was adamant. If it was impossible to protect himself with darkness, he kept his undershirt on, and long practice had made him adept at reciting many reasons why. His favorite explanation was that this particular fettish enabled him to perform better as a lover. And he had never had any complaints about his performance. He had yet to meet a woman he could not satisfy. Sure, the scars branded him, but, goddamnit, they did not detract from his appearance with his clothes on. He leaned closer to the mirror and winked at himself rakishly. Then he smiled and nodded to his reflection, which nodded back to assure him that he was all he thought he should be.

He wished he had brought some scent with him, but this was a luxury he could not carry in his crowded saddlebags. His gaze touched a bottle of Florida water on the dressing table. He broke the seal, splashed the liquid on his hands, and slapped his newly-shaven face with it. Now he was prepared for Mrs. Latimer. Quite!

She had said to summon the butler, Pompey, when he was ready. He looked around the room for the bell pull and found it beside a French gilt étagère which contained a collection of dainty porcelain bibelots. He examined them more closely and smiled. They all sounded the same key-note. Some were pornographic—dainty Dresden nymphs and fauns disporting themselves most licentiously. Quite a collection for a widow lady! He wondered if they expressed some hidden desire of hers to be pursued and raped, as was surely happening to one of the little nymphs. He imagined he could do better than the half-ram who clutched that nymph so tightly in his lecherous embrace.

Jeff was still smiling as he pulled the bell cord. On further thought, he returned to the mirror and carefully adjusted his trousers so that the bulge in his crotch was even more apparent. Might as well leave no doubt in Mrs. Latimer's mind of his capabilities. If she enjoyed the gambols of china fauns and nymphs, it was not only possible but probable that she would enjoy the real thing far more. He now saw secondary roles for the young and handsome coachman, and the equally young and vigorous butler. He nodded to his image. Indeed, Mrs. Latimer might turn out to be a woman after his own heart.

He heard steps in the hall. When the butler opened the door to his room, Jeff appraised him with new interest. Yes, he fitted very well the role of sporting bedmate for the lady of the house. He was tall, as muscular as a field hand, and undoubtedly a mulatto because his face was finely featured and his lips not too thick.

"Yo' rang, mastah suh?" The butler was properly obsequious.

"Yes, Mrs. Latimer said that when I was ready, you would show me to the dining room."

"This way, mastah suh." Jeff welcomed the "mastah suh." It showed he was accepted as a white man by a black, and he knew that the eyes of a black man were far more experienced in detecting passers than any white man's. Simon had warned him, "There are nigger fingernails, and roots of nigger hair you ain't ever going to hide." To hell with Simon.

Jeff followed Pompey down the long windowless corridor. Doors opened on both sides. They crossed a large elegantly furnished drawing room and walked into an equally large dining room. At a long table set for two Mrs. Latimer awaited him. He felt her eyes appraising him as he walked across the room, and instead of seating himself immediately at the table he walked around it to her side and once again lifted her hand to his lips.

"This is indeed a boon to a weary traveler," he murmured, holding her hand, which she made no effort to recover. "You will probably never know how really pleasant it is to sit at a table like this after so many hit-and-miss meals in roadside taverns. But, of course, the pleasantest thing of all is the pleasure of your company." Her hand still rested in his. "It is not often that a mere wayfarer is given a taste of heaven."

With seeming reluctance she withdrew her hand slowly and indicated the high-backed chair across the polished table.

"But it is so far away, dear lady." He drew down the corners of his mouth in mock injury. "A whole expanse of walnut between us. I should have to shout to make you hear . . ."

"A fact which we can remedy. Pompey!" She beckoned to the butler. "Please change the table setting. Mr. Carson is going to sit here, just around the corner from me." She indicated a place at the table, then looked up at Jeff and smiled. "How perceptive of you, Mr. Carson. It is really not necessary that we be so formal, is it?"

"And doesn't that apply to our names as well?" His smile was a physical caress. "Everyone calls me Jeff. I hardly know whom you're addressing when you say 'Mr. Carson.' Couldn't it be just Jeff?"

"How very nice. But you must reciprocate by calling me Helen."

"Thank you, Helen. See, isn't it already much easier and pleasanter?" He leaned back to let Pompey place a cup of bouillon before him. He tasted it with the silver spoon and found it delicious. He wondered if his hostess had a male cook, too, and if so, if he were as young and virile as her butler and coachman.

The meal progressed. Pompey deftly removed plates and

substituted clean ones. There followed a slice of fish, delicately poached in wine, a thin slice of veal with a sauce of tomatoes and onions, a ragout of beef, a salad of crisp greens, and, to top it all off, a molded pudding which Mrs. Latimer served herself.

"I was determined you would not have ham and eggs again." She placed the dish of pudding before him. "You see I remember."

He tasted the pudding before he answered her, his gaze holding hers. "The only difficulty, Helen, is you are going to spoil me for that time when I must go back to ham and eggs." He felt a slight pressure against his knee. It was immediately removed, and it had been so fleeting that he did not know whether or not he imagined it; but when he put his hand down under the table, it encountered hers. He looked at her and she seemed to nod at him. It was an almost imperceptible movement of her head, but it implied a tacit understanding between them. Her nod to Pompey was certain and emphatic.

"Thank you, Pompey," she said. "Now, if you will bring seegars and a light for Mr. Carson, you may be excused. You can clear away after Mr. Carson has finished smoking." She straightened, freed her hand from Jeff's grasp, waited until Pompey had brought a silver-mounted mahogany box, and opened it to release the delicate odor of fine Havana cigars. Jeff selected one, clipped the end, and accepted a light from a candle burning in a silver candlestick which the butler held for him. With a discreet bow to Mrs. Latimer, Pompey disappeared behind a green baize door and Jeff was alone with his hostess.

As soon as the door had closed, Mrs. Latimer put her finger to her lips, tiptoed over to the door, and quietly opened it. Seeing nobody, she smiled and returned to the table. "Servants," she said, "have a way of eavesdropping. I wanted to be sure nobody was there." She sat down once more while Jeff drew the aromatic smoke into his lungs and expelled it in floating blue rings. Once more her hand sought his lap. He squeezed it, and moved it higher on his thigh. She did not take it away. Her lips parted slightly, as if she were breathless.

"You might think me very forward, Jeff." She blushed. "Sometimes something happens between two persons. It immediately sweeps away all hesitation and any formalities. Haven't you experienced that? You see, I wanted you from the moment you stopped your horse to rescue a lady in distress. We have no time for long and wordy discussions, so I have come directly to the point. I want you. Do you want me?"

Without answering, he moved her hand along his thigh until it encountered that throbbing hardness.

"Isn't that your answer?" he whispered.

His hand searched for her heated flesh under the multitude of petticoats and the whalebone stiffness of her hoop skirt. He finally encountered the moist warmth he sought. His fingers moved in a rhythmical caress. She gasped and edged her chair closer to his. His lips covered hers, and his tongue thrust hard between her teeth, exploring the hot, liquid depths of her mouth.

Her hand on his thigh trembled with anxiety, struggling with buttons and frantically undoing them. After a moment it was his turn to gasp and arrest her hand.

"You're flirting with danger," he murmured in her ear.

"But it is a danger I don't fear," she said, breathless now.

"But perhaps I do," he answered. "It is something that will be all the more pleasant if it is delayed a bit."

"You mean . . . ?"

"I do not consider New Orleans so pressing that I could not remain overnight. Surely, that would be better than some half-consummated affair here at your table."

She withdrew her hand and freed herself from his fingers.

"Then you don't have to mount your horse and leave immediately after our luncheon?"

He shook his head, laughed, and kissed her again. Slowly, they stood up. He rebuttoned his trousers and pressed close against her.

"There are things," he promised, "that are better at night when all the house has retired and there is no danger of servants walking in."

She waited until he had kissed her again.

23

"Pompey will not come back until I ring for him."

"But for all you know, he may be listening on the other side of the door. One needs to be free from all fears to enjoy love to the utmost."

"Then you will stay?"

"If I am asked."

"And oh, I do ask you. Will you stay, Jeff?"

"I'll stay."

"You'll not regret it."

She sagged, limp in his arms, while he counted the diamonds on the hand resting on his shoulder.

"And I promise *you* won't either." Then he left her standing alone while he crossed to the wall and pulled the bell cord.

Linking his arm in hers, he slowly left the dining room. They went out onto a small, leafy patio where vines sheltered them from the sun and a small fountain splashed liltingly into a turquoise pool.

"Now that I am to be here all day and all night," he said, "why don't you have our horses saddled? We will ride, look over your plantation, spend the whole afternoon in anticipation of what lies before us tonight. Maybe we can find a shady spot under some tree where we can lie in the grass and explore each other further. Our final discovery of each other, however, must wait until tonight. Believe me, it will be more enjoyable."

"Is that what you would like to do?" She clung to him. "The curtains in my room could be pulled, and we could enjoy ourselves all afternoon there."

His grin challenged her. "After an afternoon of anticipation, we'll enjoy the night that much more. If we do as you suggest, tonight will be only an anticlimax. Let's draw the full joy of each other then and not now."

"Can I wait?" She pulled him closer. Her heart thudded against his chest.

"We can wait," he answered. "We have much to look forward to."

"I already know what I look forward to." She stroked him urgently along his fly.

"Perhaps you have more to anticipate than you realize

now." He grinned at her. "Now go and change into your riding clothes, and I shall be waiting for you here."

She was unwilling to let him go, but he gave her a gentle shove. "Remember, you'll be glad you waited." He smiled down at her, almost mocking her naked hunger.

Finally, unhappily, protesting, she was gone. He sat down on a wrought-iron chair and drew deeply on his cigar. It had been easier than he had thought it would be. It had not been necessary to make advances. She had done it all. Perhaps he should spend more than one night with her. No, one would be enough. Moreover, it should provide some reward for him, in addition to pleasure, even though his little job would not be too difficult. She was an attractive woman and he was confident he could satisfy her. Somehow this chance encounter was going to stand him in good stead.

He flicked an ash from his cigar and then stamped it out on the tiled floor. At least he would not have to perform in daylight. But then, he wondered, thinking of the strength and muscularity of Pompey and Solomon, perhaps she would not be enraged to discover he was a Negro. No, it was better to stay on the safe side. A ride around the plantation, dinner, and moments passed in the evening cool on the balcony, and she would be more anxious—provided, of course, that he could hold her off that long. He was confident he could. Women always did what he wanted. This woman would be no exception.

Good God! Was he glad he was Jeff Carson and not Bricktop! Life was suddenly good, and the prospects for tonight even better.

CHAPTER III

FAINT pink light fragmenting the eastern sky awakened Jeff, and he became slowly aware of his surroundings. He tried to extricate himself from the tight embrace of Helen's arms. She, too, awakened and drowsily pulled him closer to her, but he demurred and gently removed her hand.

25

"It is nearly daylight," he whispered. "It's far better for us both that I be found sleeping in my own bed and you in yours when your Pompey arrives with his morning tray of coffee. I'm leaving you now, my dear, and it will give us both time for forty winks before the household day begins."

She clung to him, hoping to arouse him again despite his resistance, but he gently pushed her away. He stood up and his feet groped around on the floor for the clothes he had tossed aside carelessly the night before. He donned shirt and trousers, but encountered some difficulty in buttoning them. Then, with underpants, socks, and boots in one hand, he leaned down to implant a swift kiss on Helen's eyes. Quietly, he tiptoed across the floor, opened the door slowly so that the hinges would not creak, and crept down the hall to his own room. Once there, he heaved a sigh of relief, took off his trousers, and sought the chamber pot which he needed badly. He welcomed the comfort of his bed but could not immediately sleep.

He congratulated himself. It had been a successful night. He had thoroughly enjoyed it. But more important, Helen had enjoyed it a great deal more. He was a consumate actor—he knew that—but last night he had not had to resort entirely to acting. He had not had a woman for a long time, and Helen's perfumed body had responded to every nuance of lovemaking he inaugurated. She had been insatiable; but he had sated her. He had matched her hungry summons not once or twice, but at least three times, if he remembered correctly. And she was obviously desirous of more when he left her this morning.

Enough was enough! He liked to leave his women wanting more. It made them more amenable afterwards. All in all, yesterday had been a pleasant day, an eventful night. They had gone riding in the afternoon, found the shady spot he had suggested, and rested on a smooth bed of leaves under a canopylike live oak. They tantalized each other almost beyond endurance, but he had been adamant that they must leave the dénouement until night. So they had torn themselves away from each other, her face pale, hands visibly trembling, sought their horses again, and rode back to the mansion. Here each had had a short nap alone—she would have had it otherwise, but he was stubborn—and then dinner together by candlelight and a long evening on the cool gallery, where they had talked of many things—her husband, her life in New Orleans before she had been married, and his life in Philadelphia, which he had embellished with much detail of his own invention.

He had told her that he had left his uncle's plantation in Mississippi to live in the city. He was not, he said, cut out for plantation life. It lacked the excitement of the day-by-day changing scene of a city. He was bored with a plantation full of niggers; he longed for company. She admitted that it had been difficult for her, too, to adjust to the isolation of plantation life. Now she was accustomed to it and did not want to return to the city. Jeff wondered if her brawny butler and coachman had anything to do with her reconciliation to rustic living. Probably.

They had watched the moon come up, its silver light casting black shadows under the trees. Then they had entered the house. She would have lighted a candle, but he persuaded her not to, and they made their way down the long hall to her room clasped in tight embrace. Once inside, she would again have lighted a candle, but he did not give her an opportunity. His hands stripped her bare. He then shed his own clothing—all but the protective undershirt.

The rest of the night was like so many other nights that he had spent in so many other beds. It had been pleasant and he had enjoyed it, but now that it was over, he wanted to sleep and forget all about it. Despite the great mental activity of plotting a golden future, it was not long before he was snoring.

A knock on his door awakened him a few hours later. Sunlight streamed through the jalousies. He clutched at his body to reassure himself that he was wearing his shirt before he gave permission to enter. It was Pompey, as he had suspected, bearing a silver tray with a pot of coffee and the information that Mrs. Latimer would be awaiting him for breakfast in half an hour. He gulped down a cup of coffee and had barely time to wash his face and dress before presenting himself, refreshed and renewed to his hostess.

She was seated at the table behind a dully gleaming silver coffee urn, and when she looked up at him and smiled, he noticed sooty circles under her eyes. Well, it had been a strenuous night. He considered the circles under his own eyes as a badge of courage, a reward for meritorious service and all-night endurance.

"Jeff dear," she greeted him, "I imagine you are ravenous this morning."

"Ravenous indeed," he answered, glancing around the room to make sure that Pompey was not there before he kissed her lightly on the cheek. "And you?"

"Equally so, although I doubt if I shall be able to eat anything."

"And why not?"

"Because something tells me that you are about to leave me today."

"I must." His half-smile implied that he regretted his departure as much as she. "I should not have delayed here overnight, but it was a temptation I could not resist."

"Why must you hurry to New Orleans, my dear? Surely you could spend a week or two here?"

He shook his head. "I must go, dear lady. I have so much to accomplish, I must start at once. You see, I have got to find a place for myself in the city. I have no friends there, and I do not know what I am going to do. The small amount of money I have with me will not last. I am entirely at sea, and the sooner I find a safe harbor, the better."

She turned the spigot on the coffee urn, refilled his cup, and passed it to him. "Black?" she asked.

Jeff nodded. Pompey came through the green baize door with a covered silver serving dish. He helped Mrs. Latimer to scrambled eggs, then served Jeff. While Pompey was fussing, Jeff could communicate with his hostess only by meaningful glances and secret smiles. Pompey went out for a platter of bacon, then once again for hot biscuits, honey, and butter. During this time there was no chance to talk, but Jeff was sure that Pompey was looking at him with a baleful eye. Undoubtedly, Jeff thought, the man was jealous. He certainly must have suspected what had gone on during the night despite their efforts at secrecy. Jeff was glad he was leaving. He would not put it past Pompey to put arsenic in his coffee should he remain. The man looked capable of it.

Finally, however, the butler could find no further excuse to linger in the dining room. Whether or not he was eavesdropping behind the door, Jeff could not tell. Mrs. Latimer did not take the precaution of checking his whereabouts.

"I'm desolated that you cannot stay." She buttered a hot biscuit and spooned honey on it.

"And so am I. I can think of nothing more delightful than being here with you, but you can understand why I feel I must go. I have to establish a place for myself in the city."

She nodded halfheartedly.

"Perhaps I can help you in some small way," she volunteered.

These were the words he had been waiting for. What form might her assistance take? Would she offer him money? He hardly thought so, but if she did, he would willingly take it. He wondered for a fleeting second just how much she valued his stud services for a night. Highly enough, he hoped, to show true appreciation. But if she didn't pay him, he would don a role of gentility and say nothing, although he felt recompense was due him.

"How," he asked, and then added, "dear lady?"

"I have friends in New Orleans. As you know, I lived there before I married Mr. Latimer. I was thinking of giving you a letter of introduction to someone who is very important in New Orleans. It might open a door that you could not possibly enter otherwise."

Inwardly he considered a mere letter pretty poor payment for his services of last night, but he smiled back at her as though she had given him one of the rings sparkling on her fingers.

"You think a letter might be of use to me?"

"The letter I propose would surely be. You would not quibble about what it might represent?"

"Dear lady, I shall accept it most gratefully. I'm sure any friend of yours would be most worthwhile and most helpful, too. May I ask to whom the letter would be addressed?"

"To Captain Dominique You," she answered. Then, noting the blank look on his face, she added, "Do you know who Dominique You is?"

He shook his head, woefully ignorant.

"You have heard of Jean Lafitte?"

Again he shook his head.

"Then you are entirely unacquainted with New Orleans and the people who matter there."

"Perhaps you can enlighten me."

"It's a long story." She poured him another cup of coffee. "So long, in fact, that I hardly know where to begin." She hesitated a moment and then talked as he finished his breakfast.

She began by telling him about the brothers Lafitte, Jean and Pierre, who not only owned a blacksmith shop on the little street called St. Philip which ran alongside the cathedral, but also owned a large store on Royal Street stocked with the finest merchandise in New Orleans.

There were those, she said, who regarded Jean Lafitte as a pirate, but this, she assured him, was not the entire truth. Yes, he was a pirate of sorts, but he operated legally under letters of marque from the Republic of Cartagena that permitted him to prey on all Spanish ships. To be sure, he did not take them to Cartagena to claim them as prizes. That was too far away, so he brought them to Barataria, near the mouth of the Mississippi.

Of course, he admitted, sometimes he mistook a French or English ship for a Spanish vessel, and captured those as well, but it hardly mattered to him; he was not too particular. These ships, too, were brought to Grand Isle, which was located on Barataria Bay some sixty miles south of New Orleans. Here he maintained a settlement which was the home port of the privateers, and this was his base of operations. He had changed it from an unlawful community of pirates to a respectable community (if any such community could be said to be respectable). In fact, the leading merchants of New Orleans were accustomed to going there to buy merchandise and were treated with respect and all considerations of safety.

Now, the merchandise of captive ships, profitable though it was, represented only a small part of his business. Since Congress had passed the law forbidding the importation of slaves into the United States, Lafitte had branched out and was doing big business selling contraband Negro slaves who had been confiscated from slavers plying the route from Africa to Havana. Plantations of the South were avid for slaves, and they didn't care where they got them. It was impossible to supply the market, and Lafitte was making more money selling slaves than he had ever made trading in fine laces, satins, and other European goods which he had brought from Barataria to his shop on Royal Street. He maintained huge barracoons at Barataria, but the fancier slaves were brought to New Orleans to be sold through his blacksmith shop. Fine specimens, even though they were rough *bozals* straight from Africa, were bringing around eight hundred dollars each.

Without exception—she emphasized the point by bringing down her dainty fist forcefully on the table—Jean Lafitte was the most important personage in New Orleans. He was openly accepted there, if not socially, at least among the leading businessmen of the city. Yes, she knew him well, but she didn't know him as well as she did his principal lieutenant, Captain Dominique You, and it was to this Captain You that she was giving Jeff a letter of introduction. You was a good friend of hers, and if she asked him to pay particular attention to Jeff, she was certain he would.

After hearing this, Jeff changed his mind about the letter. Perhaps this introduction would be even better than one of her rings. He would sell the ring, spend the money, and be right back where he was now. If this Dominique You was as important a person as she said he was, and if the brothers Lafitte were the ruling men of New Orleans, the letter would prove more valuable than any diamond ring.

31

He questioned her. "Do you think there might be a place for me in their organization?"

She nodded. "I'm sure they would be glad to have your services. You're a most delightful person, Jeff, and I would be only too happy if you were to stay here with me for a while. I think I know you pretty well, even after this short acquaintance. You see, I know men. You are, I am afraid, something of a rogue. No, no, I do not mean that in a disparaging way, but I can see you'll do anything to get ahead in this world, and I'm sure you would have no conscientious qualms about working for the Lafittes. Would you?"

He smiled back at her and nodded agreement.

"Then I'll ring for paper and ink and write the letter." She pulled the bell cord. When Pompey appeared, she instructed him to bring her writing case. He returned with the leather box and she spread the silver ink horn and quills out on the table.

Jeff watched, listening to the quill scratch across the sheet of fine note paper. He wondered what she was writing, but was confident she would report only good about him. When she had finished, she shook sand over the paper, read it over, and passed it to him. A smile crossed his face as he read it. He was more than satisfied.

M. Dominique You
c/o M. Jean Lafitte
The Blacksmith Shop
St. Philip St.
New Orleans

Dear Friend Dominique:

The bearer of this letter, Jefferson Carson, Esq., is a very good friend of mine and he is coming to New Orleans to seek his fortune. It occurred to me that you might have a place for him in your organization.

I am sure you will be delighted with him and I know that he will be a good man for you. Anything

32

that you can do for him will be appreciated by your
old friend,

HELEN LATIMER

. . . who sends you her best wishes and hopes that
you are in good health and enjoying yourself.

When Jeff handed the letter back, she folded the sheet
of paper and sealed it with a blob of red wax, into which
she pressed a gold seal bearing her initials. She stood up
from the table. He followed suit and moved to stand close
beside her.

"This," she said as she handed him the letter, "is something I am only too happy to do for you. You have made
me very happy. But there is something more—something
more personal—that I would like to do for you." She
reached into the bodice of her dress and fumbled for a moment until her fingers drew out a fine chain of gold, at the
end of which hung a large golden cross of intricate work-
manship set with small diamonds. She unclasped the chain
and cross and handed them to him.

It was still warm from her body.

"Please accept this as a talisman from me. Wear it
always, Jeff, and it will remind you of me. Perhaps it will
bring you the good luck it has brought me. Don't part with
it ever. May I put it around your neck?"

He bowed his head, and she took the chain from his
palm and circled his neck with it. Then she unbuttoned
his collar and tucked the charm under his shirt. He felt
the warmth of it against his skin. He could also feel her
hand creeping down over his chest, seeking and tweaking
his paps.

"How can I thank you?" he mumbled, seeking her lips.

Her fingers slowly undid the buttons of his shirt, and
then, when they met the obstruction of his heavy belt,
undid the brass buckle, and crept still lower. He pushed
himself into her clutching hand, thrilling as it clasped him
tightly and moved slowly and rhythmically.

"You don't know?"

He shook his head.

"I can tell you, but I hoped you might guess!"

"How?" he repeated.

"Delay your departure by one hour . . ."

He kissed her. "Small payment for all you have done for me."

"I disagree." She smiled up at him. "I would consider it an extravagant payment." Without releasing him, she took a step, but he did not follow.

"Let's not waste any time." Her voice trembled.

"But, dear heart," he demurred, "something inside me makes it impossible to do what you want in the light of day."

She pressed the fingers of her free hand against his lips to silence him. "Remember what I told you yesterday. Curtains in my room can be drawn. They are so heavy that no light can enter."

He swung her up in his arms and carried her through the door.

"Just one hour," she whispered, "then you *must* be on your way. Don't stay longer or I could never let you go."

He carried her down the hall, kicked open the door of her room with one foot, and lowered her to the still-unmade bed. Going to the window, he pulled the cord and the heavy draperies closed. It was as dark as night in the room. He shed his clothes in a heap on the floor. As he bent over her, the golden cross dangled in her face and she kissed it.

"See," she whispered, "it always brings me good luck."

"And me, too." His weight pressed against her.

CHAPTER IV

JEFF found it difficult to leave Helen. She had asked for only one hour, but their enjoyment carried them well beyond two. After his second climax, he was exhausted. He would willingly have napped for a third hour, but he was anxious to be on his way, and besides, at the end of another hour, the whole performance would start again and he would not have the strength to quit the house. He dressed reluctantly, opened the draperies wide to let in the sunshine. He kissed her as she lay sleeping among the sweaty sheets, and went to his room to gather his saddlebags. Going out to the barn, he found his horse had already been saddled. He rode past the front gallery where they had sat the night before, half expecting to see her waving to him. She was not there. He turned his horse down the long avenue of trees to the main road.

Instead of focusing on the day ahead, which he hoped would be his last on the road, his thoughts turned back to the woman he had just left. Although surrounded by all the accouterments of respectability, she was not inherently what her Southern peers would call a respectable woman. In fact, according to his experience, she knew all the tricks of a trained harlot, and he wondered where she might have learned them. Surely no woman reared in the respectability which her surroundings indicated would have permitted herself to become such an avid and tempestuous bedmate. Usually he was able to satisfy, thoroughly, any woman he was with, but, he had to admit to himself, this woman was more adept than any professional, and more demanding than a sex-starved amateur. Surely she had not learned her technique from an invalid husband. But then, he considered, perhaps her husband had not always been an invalid, and he might have demanded such erotic dexterity in their lovemaking. On the other hand, perhaps her very avidity had made him an invalid! He had heard of such things.

He wondered if she practiced all her tricks on her butler and coachman. It was well that she had two of them, for certainly no one man could stand a nightly diet of her insatiable vagaries. Well, she would not be able to sap *his* manhood, and no matter how delightful the prospect of staying with her—at least until the novelty wore off—he was glad to be on his way.

Perhaps her golden talisman would bring him good luck. He transferred the reins from his right hand to his left and unbuttoned his shirt to pull out the cross. It was a beautiful thing, although he would have been happier had the diamonds been larger. Still, he would never go broke as long as he had it. It must be worth at least a thousand dollars; not bad for a night's labor. It was better than hoeing cotton.

His way led through flat and swampy country. The sun beat down upon him unmercifully. He was glad he had eaten a substantial breakfast because as noon approached he was getting hungry, yet saw no signs of any tavern. When he passed a fairly substantial house with a well sweep in the front yard, he stopped to ask for a drink of water. The woman of the house smiled at him hesitantly, while two small children tugged at her skirts. She accompanied him to the well and drew up a dripping bucket of water for him. It was cool and quenched his thirst. Afterwards he elicited the information from her that there was a tavern a few miles down the road.

On arrival, Jeff ordered feed for his horse and went into the slatternly public room where he ate a hearty bowl of gumbo, thick with tomatoes and okra. It was surprisingly good, so good, in fact, that he had his bowl refilled before starting on his way again.

A few miles down the road he rode beside a large body of water which, a passerby told him, was Lake Ponchartrain. The city of New Orleans, the traveler informed him, was just "a short piece yonder."

Jeff arrived in the city late in the afternoon. Merchants were putting up the iron shutters across their shop fronts. After several stops to inquire about rates, he finally found a small hotel on Bourbon Street where he could stable his horse and get a room for himself for a dollar. For another dollar he could buy three meals a day. It was a halfway decent room, he discovered after the proprietor had taken him up and raised the jalousies to let in the light. The thing Jeff liked most about it was the balcony furnished with chairs and flowering jasmine and roses.

Before the man left, Jeff ordered a bath. A slender black boy came in with a tin tub and buckets of water. Jeff asked him if there was a tailor shop nearby. The boy, who seemed alert and intelligent, nodded in assent but informed him

36

that, if he needed clothes, it would take at least two weeks to have them made. There was no place, he assured Jeff, where he might find new ready-made clothes.

"If'n yo' a-needin' trogs in a hurry, mastah suh," he said, pouring water from the cans into the tub, "whyn't yo' go to Congo Square? It mostly for black people, but they have second-hand clothes that sometime mighty good. If'n yo' asks my mastah, he 'low me to go with yo' 'n' show yo' de way. Reckon yo' never find it yo'self. Kin I help yo' wash?"

Jeff denied the second request but promised that he would avail himself of the first. The boy told him he had only to ask for Ramon and Mr. deVeau would fetch him. Jeff finished washing off the dirt of the road and put his travel-stained clothes back on. He went down to arrange with the proprietor for the boy to accompany him. The fee for this, he was told, would be two bits, and Jeff changed one of his dollar bills. The man then rang the bell on his desk for Ramon.

The boy and Jeff set out together. Jeff was enthralled with the narrow streets and the iron lacework balconies of New Orleans, which was quite different from any city he had ever seen. As they walked along the narrow sidewalks —Ramon informed him they were called *banquettes*—he caught glimpses of tropical greenery—camellias, fern, azaleas—through doorways they passed. Jeff wondered what more fascinating delights might be hidden from the eyes of passersby.

It was a long walk to Congo Square and it was nearly dark when they got there. The square was illuminated by torches outside temporary booths erected around it. Several minutes elapsed before Jeff realized he was the only white person there. The square teemed with blacks, promenading up and down the *banquettes,* eating and drinking at the stands, gossiping in small groups, or examining merchandise for sale in the stalls.

"Thinkin' mayhap yo' a-goin' to find somethin' here." Ramon stopped before a stand displaying various articles of clothing and presided over by a wizened black man with a kinky white wool cap of hair. "Ol' Père Antoine, he gits the best clothes in all N'Orleans. He a-makin' the rounds o' all the rich folkses every mornin'."

He nodded to the old man and then presented Jeff.

"This yere young mastah, he a-lookin' for somethin' special in the way of clothes. He a-wantin' only the best. Ain' a-lookin' for no cheap nigger trogs."

The man came out from behind his kiosk and measured Jeff with his eyes, smiling and nodding his head in approval.

"Mighty fine-lookin' young gentleman. Yes suh! He shore is one handsome man. Got somethin' jes' for yo', mastah suh. Jes' got it this mornin'. Belongin' to young Mastah Trouville, it did. He got hisself killed in a duel yisterday mornin' so I right on hand to git his clothes. His folks a-sayin' it ain' bin worn never."

He disappeared inside the stall and came forth with a bundle carefully wrapped in an old sheet. His gnarled black fingers undid the cloth to disclose a suit of bottle green broadcloth which he held up proudly for Jeff's inspection. It appeared, as the old man said, to be brand new. While he held it, Jeff fingered the sleek broadcloth and caressed the satin lining. It was a far more wonderful suit than any he had ever possessed, and he hoped it would fit him. It appeared it would as Père Antoine held it up, measuring the shoulders, but Jeff wanted to be sure. Where could he try it on? That was easy, the old man informed him. He had only to slip behind the kiosk where it was dark, take off his old clothes, and try on the new ones.

How much would it cost if it did fit and Jeff decided to buy it? The old man scratched his white wool with a bony finger and hesitatingly quoted a price of twenty-five dollars. Jeff shook his head in denial. He was certain that this was not the final price and that old Père Antoine was merely starting high so that he could come down if necessary.

Jeff passed the coat back to Père Antoine. It was roughly shoved back into his hands with an offer to sell for twenty dollars. Once again Jeff shook his head and made a counteroffer of ten, which nearly drove the old man to tears. He stroked the material, exclaiming on the high quality of the cloth and the excellence of the tailoring, then finally came down two dollars. But the bargaining continued until a price of fifteen dollars was reached. Jeff agreed to take the suit if it fit.

Following Père Antoine's gesturing hand, he stepped behind the booth, accompanied by Ramon. Stripping off his white trousers and jacket, he handed them to Ramon to hold while he struggled into the fashionably skin-tight pantaloons, made to hug the legs so snugly that a strap under the shoes was necessary to keep them down. With Ramon's help, Jeff squirmed into them, smoothing the cloth like sausage skin around his legs. He found all the necessary buttons and had only to suck in his stomach a little to fasten them. Ramon rubbed his fingers over Jeff's legs and exclaimed at the perfect fit. He passed Jeff his boots and promised to spit and polish them next morning. The coat strained against Jeff's broad shoulders, but it fit well, and the sleeves were the right length. Taking his wallet from the trousers Ramon was holding, he stepped out in front of the kiosk in the glare of the torch while Père Antoine held up a shard of mirror for him to see. Ramon and Père Antoine were unanimous in declaring the suit fit perfectly. Père Antoine bobbed his head up and down on his pipestem neck as much as to say that he knew all along it would.

"Yo' a-goin' to need a weskit," he informed Jeff. This was true. The short-waisted coat with long tails called for a waistcoat. Jeff waited while Père Antoine rummaged through a pile of clothes on the floor of the booth, which was nothing more than trampled earth. He finally unearthed a brocade waistcoat and brushed off the dust with a stubby whiskbroom. The vest was of apple-green brocade with filigreed gold-and-amber buttons, but when Jeff removed his coat and tried it on, it was somewhat too large —a condition the old man remedied by pinning in the back. He then threaded a long needle with coarse white thread and stitched up the back so that it fit Jeff snugly.

His boots were new and, considering Ramon's offer to polish them, they would serve. He did need a decent white shirt, however, with the fashionable high collar that came up under the ears, and a stock to go with it. Père Antoine was unable to supply either of these, but he asked Jeff to wait while he slipped into the neighboring booth. He was back in a moment with a freshly laundered shirt of white lawn and a black satin stock. He measured Jeff's broad neck with a greasy tape measure and then measured the neckband, grunting his satisfaction when he found the shirt would fit.

He made a neat parcel of Jeff's old clothes and the several pairs of silk socks Jeff had chosen, wrapped them in a smoothed-out newspaper, and tied them with a knotted length of twine, handing them to Ramon. Jeff carefully counted the bills from his wallet and passed them to Père Antoine.

While waiting, Jeff had noticed a shirt of lavender silk supported on a stick at the side of the booth. He called Ramon's attention to it. "How'd you like to have a new shirt, boy?"

"That one?" Ramon pointed to the lavender silk, his eyes growing large. "If'n that the one yo' means, ain' never had nothin' so elegant like'n that in my whole life."

"Then it's yours if it fits you." Jeff motioned to Père Antoine to take it down, and Ramon quickly stripped off the soiled and sweaty tow-linen shirt he was wearing. His fingers lingered for a moment on the softness of the silk and tweaked at the pearl buttons. He slipped it on over his milk-chocolate skin. It was too big for him, and he had to turn up the cuffs, but he assured Jeff this didn't matter. It was so far superior to anything he had ever owned that he would have worn it even if it fit him like a tent. Père Antoine made a bundle of Ramon's soiled shirt, and they were finally ready to leave.

They paused in the square to drink a cup of coffee served by an enormous black woman who had a pot boiling over a fire of twigs at a tiny wayside stand. The coffee was hot and black and bitter with chicory. Jeff followed Ramon's example of sweetening it liberally with sorghum, which the woman passed in a stoneware jar. When Ramon discreetly retreated a few feet behind Jeff to drink his coffee, Jeff made a mental note: the black boy was well trained.

40

He appraised the lad. Ramon was somewhere between eighteen and twenty, not overly tall, with strong muscular shoulders. He was good-looking, with an intelligent face, somewhat more Latin than negroid. He had wide-set brown eyes, a straight nose with flared nostrils, and his lips were thick, but not blubbery.

Any young man of Jeff's pretensions should have a black boy to attend him, and this might be the right one. It would be easier to buy him directly, rather than going to some vendue house and bidding on someone with unknown qualities. All the fingering in the world could give no more than an idea of a slave's physique; no amount of fingering could determine his disposition or character.

He was reluctant to expend the capital necessary to buy a slave, and there was the subsequent expense of feeding and housing him, but his new status demanded one. He thought with regret of the many servants at The Georgics he might have had if he and Minnie had inherited the plantation, but all that was far behind him now. Jefferson Carson without a black servant would be just another young man in the big city, but with a Negro attendant, particularly a fine-looking black like Ramon, he would instantly acquire prestige. He was tempted; if Ramon were for sale, he'd make an offer for him.

It was late when they returned to the hotel from Congo Square, but Mr. deVeau was still sitting behind the desk in the minuscule lobby. He bowed to Jeff when he came in and signaled to Ramon to leave by the door that led to the servants' quarters.

"Thank you for loaning me your boy." Jeff was anxious to start a conversation with the man.

"Might's well be doin' that as sittin' on his ass all day long. Right smart boy, he is." DeVeau nodded. "He been with us some spell. Matter of fact, he was birthed right here, 'n' been with me always. His dam died a spell back, and I been thinkin' o' sellin' him 'cause ain' rightly got much use for him round here, but it hard to part with a boy what was borned here."

Jeff walked over and sat on the counter, dangling one tightly-encased trouser leg. "Thinking of selling him?"

DeVeau nodded.

"How much you planning to ask for him?"

The man got up from his chair and came around to the front of the counter. "He a likely buck. Strong and ain' got nary an imperfection on him. Biddable, too. Comes from good stock, he does. His dam, she purentee Fanti, 'n' his sire a Cuban free mulatto which I hired to stud her, so the boy, he ain' all black. Sire a damned good-looking man." He suddenly looked up at Jeff. "How come yo' askin' me all these questions. Yo' thinkin' mayhap to buy him?"

"Mayhap." Jeff nodded. "Just a passing fancy, that's all. I like the boy, and he certainly was a help to me. Seems bright and intelligent."

"Shore is. Jes' got one bad fault. That boy shore is wench crazy. Jes' let a wench pass by in the street 'n' he a-poppin' the buttons right off'n his pants."

Jeff smiled. "Well, that's natural for a young buck like him. I like a boy with spirit. How much you asking for him?"

DeVeau hesitated, watching Jeff's foot as it moved back and forth. "Likely young bucks like'n him a-bringin' round eight hundred dollars at vendue these days."

Jeff shook his head. "That's too much. He's not big enough or strong enough to be a field hand, and he's not light enough or pretty enough for a house servant. If he was about six inches taller and about thirty pounds heavier, he might fetch that much, but as he is, I doubt you'd get more than six hundred for him on the vendue table, and then there'd be your commission to pay."

"He's a right likely boy." DeVeau was loath to concede any of his slave's bad points.

"Let's say he's a fair specimen. He ain't no Fancy, but I've taken a sort of notion to him. Don't want to get me some ornery boy that's hard to get along with, and this boy of yours seems biddable. Tell you what. I'll offer you five hundred dollars spot cash and, as long as I stay here—which may be for some time—he can continue working for you."

DeVeau pondered the offer for some moments, stroking his chin. "How about five-fifty?"

Jeff shook his head. "Five hundred cash."

Again deVeau was silent for some time, and Jeff could almost hear him thinking.

"Might jest take yo' up on it. Been thinkin' o' gettin' shet o' him 'cause they ain' much here what he can do. Got us enough help 'n' he sometimes underfoot."

"Then call him in here."

"What for?" DeVeau scowled.

"Don't want to buy any buck less'n I go over him and finger him. He appears all right, but I want to see him with pants down."

"Tol' yo' he right sound."

"Prefer to finger him myself, and besides, I'd like to know how the boy would like me for a new master."

DeVeau grunted in disgust. "Don' make him no never-minds if'n he do or if'n he don'. He up for sale. He a-goin' to git solt, 'n' that's that. All foolishness."

"But that's the way I do business." Jeff nodded vigorously to emphasize his point. "Finger him first and then ask him."

"Better step back with me." DeVeau indicated the door. "Cain' have yo' a-fingerin' no nekked buck here in the lobby. Got us some womenfolks a-stayin' here, 'n' don' want 'em to see it. Come this way."

Jeff followed him through the door into a dark open courtyard and across it, cautiously picking his way over rubble until they came to another building on the far side. Inside, a tallow dip burned in an iron candlestick, showing the meager furnishings of the room. The boy Ramon sat on one of the chairs, an arrangement of string between his fingers as he studied the next move in the intricate cat's cradle which was occupying him.

"This man here a-thinkin' o' buyin' yo', Ramon," deVeau said.

Jeff saw a smile spread across the boy's face. "How'd you like me for a new master?" he asked.

"Shore like it fine, mastah suh, if'n Mastah deVeau, he kin spare me."

"Mastah Jeff, if you're going to belong to me."

"Yas suh, Mastah Jeff suh, shore like to be yore boy,

though Mastah deVeau, he a right fine mastah."

"Then come over here and strip off your trogs."

The boy took a nimble step and stood beside Jeff. At another nod of Jeff's head, he carefully undid the pearl buttons of the silk shirt, took it off, and hung it on a chair. He hesitated a moment, a question in his eyes before he undid the buttons of his pants. Jeff's nod was encouraging, and he let the pants slide to the floor, standing naked before Jeff.

It was really a waste of time to examine the boy. Jeff could see that he was physically perfect. Nevertheless, he let his hands wander over the smooth satin of the boy's skin. Then he bade him kneel so that he could spread his buttocks. At a prod from Jeff, Ramon stood up and faced him. Jeff ran his hand over the hardness of the boy's belly and down into the wiry hair of his genitals. Then, cupping his genitals in one hand, he pulled the foreskin back and examined the purple glans. He was surprised at the automatic erection.

"Quick on the trigger, ain't you, Ramon?"

Ramon grinned self-consciously. Jeff expressed surprise at the smallness of the boy's genitals. "Ain't never going to make much of a breeder," Jeff said to deVeau. "He's pretty small."

"Yo' a-buyin' him for a breeder?" deVeau asked.

Jeff shook his head. "Funny, though, that he isn't hung heavier."

"Sometimes I think that's poppycock 'bout all niggers a-bein' hung heavy. They jes' like white folks, they are. Some hung heavy 'n' some not. This one jes' ain'."

Jeff nodded in agreement, thinking as he did so that he was among the favored ones. He told Ramon to put his clothes back on.

"Planning on buying you, Ramon."

"That shore fine, Mastah Jeff, suh."

"You'll continue to work here for a while, but remember, when I want you, you're to come when I call you."

"Shore will jump to it, Mastah Jeff suh."

"And another thing, I want you to make yourself a pallet in front of my door and sleep on it."

"Kin do, Mastah Jeff suh."

Jeff and deVeau passed out of the room and across the courtyard. Once in the lobby again, deVeau sat down behind the counter and wrote out a bill of sale for Ramon and Jeff carefully counted out five hundred dollars in bills from his wallet. He handed the paper money to deVeau, took the bill of sale in exchange, and bade him good night.

He climbed the stairs to his room slowly, candle in hand. Ramon was already before his door, spreading a torn blanket on the floor.

"You're my boy now, Ramon." Jeff produced his key and unlocked the door.

"Shore am glad to be, Mastah Jeff suh. Likes yo' a lot, I do. Sick o' staying here. Bin here all my life 'n' want to go places."

Jeff smiled at him. "God alone knows where we're going, boy. Let's hope it will be to a lot of good places."

"Shore do hope so, Mastah Jeff suh." He waited until Jeff opened the door. "Bed myself right down here, mastah suh. Ain' no boogers nor hants a-goin' to git in."

"Watch out, Ramon. I'll see you in the morning. Remember, you're my boy now."

"Ain' fergettin'. Thank yo' for the shirt, Mastah Jeff suh. Bestest shirt I ever had in my life."

Jeff smiled and closed the door behind him. He stood for a moment in the room, candle in hand, before he walked over and placed it on the stand beside his bed. Well, he had five hundred dollars less than before, but he had bought a fine young buck who, he was sure, was worth more than he had paid for him. It was like having money in the bank. Ramon was a good investment; he could always sell him if he had to. Maybe he should have hinted to Mrs. Latimer that he would rather have had a black boy than the trinket she had given him. He pulled out the golden cross and looked at it, letting the flame of the candle send the diamonds into irridescence. No, the diamonds in the cross were worth more than Ramon. And the cross could be kept in reserve.

But Ramon was a good investment. Of that he was sure. The boy was as good as cash any time. Besides, he couldn't

cut any figure in New Orleans without a black boy. He'd
have to get some new clothes for him, though. Couldn't
have him around in linen tow pants. Well, there was always
Congo Square and Père Antoine. He'd make another trip
there so Ramon would be a credit to him.

All in all, it had been a good day. He was safely in New
Orleans, where neither Walter George nor Baxter Simon
would find him. He'd already fitted himself out with a
decent suit of clothes, and he had a fine-looking slave to
follow him around. Not bad for one day—not bad at all for
the illegitimate offspring of an octoroon wench and a
passing stranger with red hair.

CHAPTER V

ANXIOUS as he was to present his letter of introduction
to Captain Dominique You (and he reminded himself how
very fortunate he was to have even this feeble connection
in a strange and friendless city), Jeff felt a desire to get
acquainted with New Orleans first. He had seen only a
sample the night before on the way to Congo Square, but
what little he had seen had intrigued him. He stretched
his legs in the comfortable bed and was tempted to turn
over and go back to sleep, but regretfully decided against
it. Inspired by his awakening sensuality as he got out of
bed, he wished for a moment that he were back with Helen
Latimer. Man! What a woman she was! But when he saw
what merely thinking about her was doing to him, he forced
her image from his thoughts, donned his shirt and under-
drawers, and unlocked the door. He half expected to see
Ramon curled up on his torn blanket, but both were gone.

Back in his room he discovered a dangling wire with a
white porcelain knob on the end, pulled it, and listened to
a faint jangle down in the courtyard. While waiting, he
slipped on his old trousers and stepped out onto the balcony, parting the thick green jasmine plants to peer down
into the street. Already the streets were awake, but with a
languid activity far different from the bustle of Philadel-

phia. A Negro walked by, his person bristling with brushes and a clutch of brooms over his shoulders, sleepily calling out his wares. He was followed by an immense black woman in starched white with a red bandanna tied in a perky bow on her head. She held a tray suspended by a strap around her neck and was calling out "Pralines," probably the waferlike confections in her tray. A well-dressed man walked by with a somewhat faster step as though he had some important business in mind, and an attractive young lady, frothy in blue silk and lace, strolled by, accompanied by a stern elderly woman all dressed in rusty black. Her chaperon, he supposed. He hoped that every attractive young woman was not so attended, but he reminded himself of the recent French and Spanish background of the city and feared that this might be the accepted custom. However, in a city this size there must be many houses of prostitution. He would inquire of Ramon, who seemed to know everything. Just now, after thinking of Helen Latimer, he felt in need of a woman, although he disliked having to spend money for such a service. Even when his prime equipment found no paying customer, there was always plenty of volunteer talent about. All of which reminded him of Helen Latimer again, and in his present condition he cursed himself for having left her so soon.

A rap on the door took his mind off his present exigency and he left the balcony to open the door. Instead of Ramon, it was a most attractive mulatto wench, slender yet curvacious, with a piquant heart-shaped face around which clustered ringlets of dark brown hair.

"Yo' a-ringin' for me, mastah suh?" She inventoried him quickly, then smiled at him provocatively. "I'se Zelda, 'n' what can I do for yo', suh?"

He wanted to tell her there were a number of things she could do, but hesitated because he did not know in what capacity she was there to serve him. By her smile and her glance from under long lashes, however, he suspected she would not be averse to helping him in any way.

"No." He hated to let her go, but it seemed better not to become embroiled in something that might cause trouble.

He would ask Ramon about her status in the household before he started anything, but he was glad someone attractive was close at hand. "No, Zelda." He smiled at her. "Nothing you can do for me right now except to see if you can find Ramon and send him up here."

She appraised him again with a little cluck of approbation as she allowed her glance to sweep over his body, then lifted her eyes and looked at him directly. "Ramon, he shore a lucky boy to git hisself such a fine new mastah like'n yo'. Wishin' yo'd have bought me instead. Kin serve yo' better'n Ramon, 'cause he jes' a boy, less'n yo' the kind what likes boys best."

"No, it's not that, Zelda, and I imagine you could serve me in many ways better than he could." Jeff grinned back at her. "But it wouldn't look too good to have you following me up and down the streets. Have to have a boy for that."

"But a boy, he no good at nights, 'n' yo' say yo' ain' one of those men what's a-likin' boys better'n gals."

"I'm not—most certainly not—but now, Zelda, if you'll send Ramon to me, I'll appreciate it. Perhaps we can arrange something for some night. Yes?"

"Shore kin if'n yo' ask Mr. deVeau. He don' like me a-messin' round with the guests less'n he know."

"Then I'll ask him." Jeff could hear running footsteps on the stairs, and Ramon's head appeared.

"Yo', Zelda, what yo' all a-doin' here a-sweet-talkin' my mastah?" he demanded between gasps for breath. "Whyn't yo' a-tellin' me his bell's a-ringin'? He my mastah 'n' I don' want no wench like'n yo' a-foolin' round with him. He quality, my mastah is, 'n' if'n he wants hisself a gal, he kin go to Madame Hortense's 'n' pay her five silver dollars for one. I don' want no wench a-foolin' round with him like'n yo', what spreads her legs for any man what pays Mastah deVeau two bits."

"Whoa there, boy." Jeff grabbed him by the shirt collar and swung him around. "Can't have you talking like that to this pretty little Zelda. Could be that I'll be needing her sometime, and if so, two bits is a right likely sum to pay. Now, there are things for you to do. First of all, I want you to fetch me a pitcher of hot water. Got to shave and you've got to learn how to do it for me. It's going to be your first lesson, so get back here. And as for you, Zelda, come into my room for a minute. We've got a little business to attend to also."

She waited until Ramon left and then sidled in the door beside him. He closed the door and locked it. Slowly he approached her and lifted her face to his and kissed her, feeling the warm wetness of her tongue penetrating between his teeth. Her hand slipped to his crotch, and he helped her unbutton his trousers while she exclaimed in surprise and ecstasy.

"We haven't got time this morning," he whispered hoarsely. "Ramon will be back in a minute."

"Won' take me no whole minute," she said, sinking to her knees before him, her arms clutching his thighs.

He felt the warmth of her body and the pressure of her breasts against his legs, and he retreated a step to make sure he had turned the key in the lock. Her arms tightened around his body, drawing him closer to her. Her mouth was warm and wet and sweet and, before he knew it, his body arched in spasm. He clung to her, as the weakness of his knees endangered his footing. He went limp all over, then straightened up and pushed away her still-questing lips while he rearranged his trousers. When he could get his breath, he felt in his pocket and found two bits, which he gave to her. With a faltering step, he went to unlock the door. Ramon was standing in the doorway.

"How she do, Mastah Jeff suh?" Ramon stood aside while Zelda slithered through the doorway.

"Fine." Jeff had scarcely regained his breath.

"She do it for everyone else, but she won' do it for me, even if'n I offers her money. She a-sayin' I'm too young 'n' too little, but I'm a-tellin' her that I'm mighty potent, I am."

"Well, let's forget about it. You talk too much, Ramon. Too damned much. Better learn to keep quiet, or I'll take a strap to you. Now I'm going to teach you to shave me, and if you give me a single nick, I'm going to have you whipped. So you'd better pay attention and be careful."

49

Jeff showed Ramon how to prepare lather, than sat down in a chair and taught him how to put a towel around his neck and spread the lather on his face. Then he pointed to the leather case that held his razors and had Ramon select the one with the ivory handle. Jeff told him where to find the strop and showed him how to strop the razor and apply it to his face.

Ramon's hands trembled ever so slightly, but he was all care as he proceeded to shave Jeff according to his master's instructions. Although unused to such work, he did it deftly and quickly and did not even nick the skin. Jeff had feared he would emerge a mass of bloody cuts. When he was finished, Ramon admitted that he shaved himself occasionally and was not a complete tyro.

His face now smooth and glowing, Jeff showed Ramon how to help him dress, although he warned him, without giving any explanation, that he was never to remove his shirt. So, according to Jeff's instructions, Ramon removed the soiled white pants and the drawers. Then, still according to Jeff's instructions, he held the pair of clean linen drawers while Jeff slipped them on. The boy unbuttoned the sausage-tight pair of new trousers, then eased them on his master.

"Yo're a-needin' galluses," Ramon informed him. "Kin git those 'thout'n goin' to Congo Square for 'em."

"And handkerchiefs, too," Jeff mentioned. "Reckon I'll go out later, after I've had my breakfast, and see what we can find." He regarded Ramon quizzically. "You're a boy who seems to know everything. Reckon working around a hotel has taught you a lot. Tell me, where does a man go in this town if he wants to get laid?"

"Laid, Mastah Jeff suh? Don' rightly know what yo' means by gittin' laid."

"Where does a man find a woman in this town? I need one. Haven't had one in a long time."

"Yo' jes' had Zelda, Mastah Jeff suh."

"That doesn't count. I want a woman."

"Yo' mean a whore—someone yo' pays?"

Jeff nodded and winked at Ramon. "Exactly."

Ramon grinned back at him. "Well, they's a lot o' 'em

right here in N'Orleans. First off, they's the cribs, but they not too good. They not for a gentleman like'n yo'. I go there when I kin save up 'nuff money. Fo' bits it is, 'cause them two-bit whores ain' so good." He sighed. "Ain' had 'nuff money to go there for a long time."

"And would you like to go?"

"Jes' a-rarin' to go, Mastah Jeff suh, but only got me three bits. Bin tempted to take a two-bit hussy though, I a-needin' it so bad."

"So outside of the cribs, what would you recommend for me?"

Ramon scratched his head. "Reckon yo' a-wantin' the best."

Jeff nodded again. "Best ain't none too good for me."

"Well, then, that's Madame Hortense's place. She got a whorehouse, tho' she ain' a-callin' it that. She a-callin' it the Ridin' Academy, though they ain' no horses there. All the young bloods 'n' a lot o' older men go there. Right fancy place it is, Mastah Jeff suh, 'n' right costly it is, too. She got white gals in there, 'n' some octoroon gals for them that fancies 'em. Heard tell she a-puttin' on a show if'n a man got 'nuff money to pay for it. They a-sayin' she got a nigger boy there by the name o' Lancer what puts on a show with the colored gals 'n' it costs twenty-five dollars jes' to watch it. Shore do wish I could get me a job like'n that, but reckon I'm too picayune. They a-sayin' that Lancer, he the heaviest-hung nigger in the world. Shore do wish I could be like'n that Lancer—or yo', Mastah Jeff suh."

"Guess that's something you can't do anything about, boy." Jeff motioned for Ramon to hand him his stock, which Jeff tied himself, and then pointed to his boots, which Ramon eased on, not forgetting to put the strap of the pantaloons under the heel. Then Ramon held Jeff's coat for him and stood back to admire his master.

"Yo' shore looks scrumptious, Mastah Jeff suh. I do declare, yo're downright handsome."

"Need a new hat, I do." Jeff had in mind a wide-brimmed Panama hat such as he had seen the men of New Orleans wearing.

51

"Kin show yo' where to git it. Yo' a-wantin' that I bring yore breakfast up here to yore room 'n' then yo' won' have to go down to the dinin' room?"

"A good idea. Do I have any choice for breakfast?"

"Yo' gits ham 'n' eggs 'n' grits 'n' hot bread 'n' coffee. Everyone here gits the same. Kin put a li'l table out on the balcony for yo'. Be right back."

Jeff went out on the balcony and once again became engrossed with the teeming life of the street below while he waited for Ramon to bring up his breakfast. His short encounter with Zelda had been interesting, but it had been over almost before it had begun and had not satisfied him. Perhaps he would try this famous house of Madame Hortense's that Ramon had mentioned. At least he would have Ramon point it out to him so he'd know where it was. Poor Ramon! Jeff felt sorry for him. He was a likable boy, and it was a shame that he had been so woefully short-changed when genitalia were given out. Well, everyone could not be as generously endowed as he himself, he mused. He was grateful; it had stood him in good stead all his life.

He heard the door of the room open, and Ramon entered with a big tray covered with a napkin. He set up a small table on the balcony, placed the tray on it, and removed the napkin. Jeff sniffed eagerly at the savory aroma. It looked and tasted delicious. No more wayside taverns for him from now on. He guessed that there must be something to the reputation of French cooking because the ham was delicately pink and tender, the eggs white and golden with a crisp brown border, the bread hot and oozing butter, and the coffee savory with chicory. When he had finished, Roman took the tray. Jeff went inside to comb his hair. He decided to go bareheaded until he could buy a hat, as the one he had worn on the road was soiled and the band sweat-stained. He went downstairs to the lobby where he found Ramon waiting for him. After bidding Mr. deVeau a good morning, they went out together into the street.

Ramon took him to a shop on Bourbon Street where he found a hat to his liking. No wonder the men here wore straw hats—they were so much lighter and cooler than a heavy beaver.

After wandering the streets for a while and looking at the displays in the windows, Jeff sat on a bench in the park in front of the cathedral. The sight of this imposing edifice brought to mind Mrs. Latimer's instructions as to how to find Dominique You. She had said to go to the blacksmith shop of the brothers Lafitte near the cathedral. Ramon knew where it was, and Jeff wanted to see the shop. Ramon took him past the place, but they did not stop.

When Jeff asked Ramon if he had heard of Captain Dominique You, Ramon's eyes widened. He told Jeff that after the brothers Lafitte, You was probably the most important personage in New Orleans and that he was now engaged in building a house especially for the Emperor Napoleon, whom he and the Lafittes planned to rescue from some island where the English had imprisoned him. Ramon seemed to know almost everything of interest that happened in the city.

Jeff stopped at a sidewalk café for lunch while Ramon ate in the alley in back of the kitchen. The afternoon wore on. They had covered most of the city by foot, when Ramon suddenly took an abrupt turn and led Jeff around a corner.

"This here's Condé Street," Ramon explained. Jeff looked at him blankly.

"Yas suh, Mastah Jeff suh, this here's where Madame Hortense have her whorehouse. See, it that one." Ramon pointed to an iron-latticed, bay-windowed house where several girls laughed together on one of the balconies, abloom with potted plants. They walked slowly by, ignoring the smiles and welcoming gestures of the aggressive young females. Jeff took note of the street and the door so he could find his way back alone.

Ramon asked Jeff if he would like to see the cribs. Jeff was curious to compare cut-rate commercial sex in New Orleans with his own experience in Louisville. Ramon led him through a series of narrow streets to an even narrower alley that paralleled one turn of the river. The one-story buildings each had a narrow doorway and one iron-barred window.

It was a sordid street. Gutters beside the narrow *banquettes* were black with filth and offal, and the thoroughfare itself was a dusty stretch of hard-packed earth, scarcely wide enough for a chaise to pass through. As it was not yet dark, there was not much activity on the street —a few men, both white and black, peering at the prostitutes, one of whom sat behind each window. Some women wore bedraggled finery, but others had on only carelessly draped robes which gaped conveniently to display their fading charms. One side of the street, Ramon informed him, was for blacks, and the other for whites. As far as Jeff could see, the black girls were younger and far more attractive than their white sisters, who were, all in all, a pretty tired and shopworn lot, who had come down to the cribs on their way to something lower.

Ramon's whole manner changed from the moment he entered the street. He bubbled with excitement, his erection evident, and he fairly danced along as he pointed out the occupants of the cribs. He admired them all, particularly the white ones, who were forbidden to him. Several times he stopped to wave at occupants on the black side, explaining to Jeff that he had patronized them in the past.

The women were too sordid for Jeff's taste, but their squalid appearance did not disturb Ramon. They might have all been beauties as far as he was concerned, for he gazed upon them with fascination and desire. After the two had gone through the street once on the white side, he begged Jeff to repeat the trip again on the black side. Here he pointed out the wenches he had been with, extolling their virtues.

Jeff stood Ramon's slavering lust as long as he could.

"How'd you like one of those women this afternoon?" he asked.

"Like it fine, Mastah Jeff suh, but ain' got no money with me." He pointed to a girl in one of the cribs. " 'N' if'n I did have, I'd take that one. Ain' never bin with her, and they a-sayin' that she shore somethin' special. Shore been a-hankerin' to try her out."

Jeff looked in the direction of Ramon's pointing finger. The girl, seen through the iron bars, was younger and more attractive than her sisters. Moreover, she looked clean. Her peignoir of sleazy pink silk boasted an edging of tattered marabou, and when she caught Jeff and Ramon staring at her, she stood up, opening the gown to display a lithe young body. Cupping her breasts in her hands, she beckoned with her head.

"You like her?" Jeff asked.

"Shore do, Mastah Jeff suh. Yo' a-likin' her, too?"

Jeff shook his head. "She's pretty for a nigger wench, and she's far above the rest on the street, but I've no taste for this sort of place." He hesitated a moment. "I'll wait outside." Then he had a second thought. "Remember what you told me about that boy who works for Madame Hortense?"

"Lancer? He mighty heavy hung. Why?"

"I'm thinking about the show he puts on. Wondering how you'd like to put on a show for me if I paid for the girl. I could go in and sit at the foot of the bed and watch you. Something new for me. I'd be willing to pay to see you humping."

"Don' know if'n I could do anythin' with yo' a-watchin'. A fly in the room, I gits upset."

"But you say this Lancer does it. Reckon you can do anything he can. Looks to me as though you're ready right now." He looked down at Ramon and laughed.

"Gotta see what de gal a-sayin'. Mayhap she not a-wantin' a white man a-lookin' on."

"Then go in and ask her."

Through the open barred window he watched Ramon talking to the girl, who at first appeared indignant but became more interested as Ramon continued to cajole her.

"What did she say?" Jeff asked. He wanted the vicarious pleasure of watching Ramon perform.

"She a-sayin' that even if'n she is a whore, she's a decent girl. She ain' puttin' on no show for anyone less'n she gits paid double. She a-wantin' a whole dollar to let me pester her whilst yo' a-lookin' on, 'n' she say no funny business

55

like'n yo' done with Zelda this mornin'. Jes' straight pesterin', that's all."

A dollar seemed reasonable enough, so Jeff prodded Ramon ahead of him into the single room. The girl, over-awed by Jeff's presence, closed the door and drew the curtains at the window. The room was in semiobscurity, but Jeff could still see.

"White mastah a-goin' to give me a dollar?" she asked.

Jeff produced the dollar and handed it to her, whereupon she let the flimsy robe slip from her shoulders and stood naked before Ramon. Her two fully rounded breasts with dark reddish-brown nipples seemed almost too heavy for her slender body. She crossed the room to where Ramon stood. Slowly she started to undress him. She paused after removing each garment to let her hands slide over the newly exposed part of his body. Jeff saw that Ramon aroused was not as puny as he had believed. He stood rampant under the gliding caresses of the girl. At length, when she had stripped him of all his clothes, she eased herself onto the bed, patting a place beside her for Jeff. Ramon knelt on the bed, spreading her legs apart, and without any preliminaries entered her.

It was the shortest performance Jeff had ever seen. No sooner had Ramon entered the girl than a spasm shook his body, and he fell inert across her. He lay there for some moments, gasping for breath, and then gathered himself together and stood up. His erection was gone, and he glanced apologetically at Jeff.

"Jes' couldn't hold it in, Mastah Jeff suh. No sooner I gits in her 'n' I explodes."

"Well, it wasn't much of a show," Jeff had to admit. "Think I could have done better myself. Maybe someday I'll show you just how it should be done." The girl stood up and he smiled at her. She came closer to fondle him.

"Now if'n the pretty white mastah like to show this worthless nigger boy jes' how a girl should be pestered, ain' a-goin' to be no extra charge. Uh-uh, shore like to have yo' pester Jinny, mastah suh. Ain' never had no white man, 'n' like to see how it is."

Jinny's stroking hands tempted Jeff. Reluctantly he

pushed her away. If she persisted, he would have to have her willy-nilly, and he had no desire to follow Ramon. What the hell? In this place, you always followed *somebody*.

"Not today, Jinny." The utterance of her name brought rushing memories of Minnie George. Suddenly the whole scene became distasteful to him—the panting, open-mouthed girl, her seeking hands, the muskiness of her body—and he could not wait to leave the narrow crib. Rather than offend the girl, he took another two-bit piece from his pocket and gave it to her. While she was thanking him, he pushed open the door, signaled Ramon to follow, and walked out into the street. He ignored the noisy succubi trying to attract his attention with joggled tits and sucked fingers.

Ramon hurried to catch up.

"Whereat we a-goin' now, Mastah Jeff suh?"

"Back to the hotel." Jeff was curt with him. "Take the shortest way there."

His thoughts were muddled as he strode toward the hotel, but not his feelings. The brief contact with Zelda had not satisfied him. Seeing Ramon and the girl, even for the few seconds they had been together, had aroused him. Then there was the sudden and exciting memory of Minnie George. Had he really loved her? There must have been some personal emotion involved besides his desire to own The Georgics because he could not get her out of his mind. Whatever it was, there was only one thing that could calm his restless nerves now: a woman. He needed one; he must have one.

When he entered the hotel, he dismissed Ramon, saying he would ring for him if he wanted him. He stopped at the desk and spoke to Mr. deVeau.

"You have a bed-wench named Zelda?"

"Shore do, Mr. Carson."

"I can use her. Send her up to my room, at once."

"But Mr. Carson . . ."

"No *buts,* sir. I'll pay the regular charge, or more if you desire. I know she's available. Ramon told me so. Just hurry."

"Yes suh, Mr. Carson. Know how yo' feels. Gets to the point sometimes when a man cain' hold it no longer. Zelda, she be right up, 'n' ain' a-goin' to charge yo' more'n two bits."

Jeff reached into his pocket and threw the money on the desk. Before Mr. deVeau had a chance to thank him, he was on his way to his room. This time, he was certain, Zelda would earn her money.

CHAPTER VI

JEFF allowed two days to pass before he presented his letter to Dominique You. As long as he held that letter with its potential of employment, he felt halfway secure, but he dreaded meeting You in case he should be told there was no opening for him in the Lafitte organization. After all, why should an important man like Captain You take an interest in Jeff merely because of a letter from a woman who, for all Jeff knew, he might well have forgotten? Except, Jeff reasoned, that Helen Latimer would be difficult to forget, especially if Dominique You had known her as intimately as Jeff had.

On the morning of the third day he resolved to take the bull by the horns. He made Ramon take particular pains when dressing him in his new clothes. He also had Ramon don his own new outfit so that when they left the hotel they could be mistaken for prosperous young planter in fine clothes and Panama hat, followed by his fittingly accoutered servant.

By now the narrow streets and the overhanging iron balconies were so familiar to Jeff that he wasted no time admiring them. When they reached the small green park in front of the cathedral, they halted. They had walked slowly to avoid dampening the armpits of their coats with dark crescents of sweat. Here, Jeff thought, is the famous blacksmith shop of the Lafitte brothers. He paused for a moment to adjust his clothing, tighten the black satin stock around his neck, and permit Ramon to wipe his shoes and brush the dust from his trousers. Then, glancing around to see if anyone was watching, he straightened Ramon's clothing so that the boy would reflect the status of his master.

It was only a few steps to narrow St. Philip Street, and the smithy was not difficult to find. Wide double doors were open, and in the semiobscurity of the shop, wheezing bellows stirred the fires in the forge to flare angrily to life, painting the interior with rhythmic flashes of red and orange. They heard the resonant clang of iron against iron and smelled the acrid odor of scorched horses' hooves. They heard the subdued hum of conversation from the small group of men sitting on the *banquette* in front of the door; the men all looked up as Jeff and Ramon approached. None of them rose, but they regarded the two strangers with undisguised interest when they entered the gloomy interior of the shop.

When his eyes became accustomed to the darkness of the smithy after the bright sunlight of the street, Jeff noticed a formidable-looking man standing at the anvil, his hammer ringing against the horseshoe he was shaping. Jeff advanced a few steps as the man put down his hammer and with a pair of long tongs embedded the horseshoe in the coals. He pumped the bellows until the horseshoe became red and malleable. He next transferred it to the anvil again and delivered a few more hammer blows. Then he plunged it into a tub of water, listened with some satisfaction to the prolonged sizzling, and finally recognized Jeff's presence.

He was a short, stocky man with powerful bulging biceps under the rolled-up sleeves of his rough blue cotton shirt. He regarded Jeff warily, but looked him directly in the eye. Even in the obscurity of the shop, Jeff could see that his eyes were a light, clear blue. Jeff was immediately attracted to the man.

"Pierre Lafitte, at your service, *m'sieur.*" The man's lazy drawl and slight accent showed only nominal interest in his caller. "What can I do for you?"

"Mr. Lafitte?" Jeff was startled that this man he had heard so much about, the brother of the great Jean Lafitte, should be engaged in physical labor. "Allow me to introduce myself. I am Jefferson Carson of Philadelphia. I am most happy to make your acquaintance. I have here"—he produced the letter from an inside coat pocket—"a letter to Captain Dominique You. It is a letter of introduction, and I was told to present it to him here."

"Ah, the good *capitaine*." Lafitte hesitated a moment. "Was the name Carson, *m'sieur*?"

Jeff nodded.

"Then, M'sieur Carson, had you been here but ten minutes earlier, you would have found my friend Dominique You sitting in that chair." He pointed to the only armchair in the doorway. "But, alas, he has left."

"It is a matter of much regret to me," Jeff replied. "I was most anxious to have him read this letter."

"Ah, but it is not an occasion for any great degree of despair, *m'sieur*." Lafitte shrugged his shoulders and smiled. "You see, I know where the good *capitaine* You was going, and I also know that he will be pleased to see you because a letter introducing a stranger is always welcome. Dominique just left for the house of Madame Hortense in Condé Street. He is to have his *petit déjeuner* with her, and I know that he would be only too happy to have you interrupt his visit, especially with a letter."

"If you believe I would not cause him inconvenience. Naturally I would not want to annoy Captain You."

Lafitte smiled again. He was, Jeff thought, a truly engaging person.

"The good Dominique is an old friend of Madame Hortense's. He occasionally patronizes her house as a customer, but even more often he goes there merely to visit with his *bonne amie,* Madame Hortense. Between the two of them they know enough scandal to overthrow the whole city, and each one is avid to hear some juicy tidbit from the other. No, you will most certainly not cause any inconvenience. Since you are a newcomer, both Madame Hortense and Dominique will be happy to lay eyes on you." Lafitte picked up the horseshoe he had been making, looked at it intently, and turned it over in his hands before placing it back in the coals.

Jeff realized that he had been politely dismissed, but so tactfully that he felt nothing but warmth for the man. This was indeed a city of courtesy. He took his leave of Lafitte, walked out of the shop into the bright sunshine, passed the curious stares of those about the door, summoned Ramon, and walked up the street.

It was only a short distance to the cunningly named Riding Academy, and he asked Ramon to take shortcuts. He hesitated to break in on You's *tête-à-tête* with the famous (or infamous) Madame Hortense, but, on the other hand, he was delighted that his first visit to her house was on business rather than pleasure. Being officially introduced to the place as a person disinterested in Madame's wares was much better than knocking at her door some evening as a stranger come to see and sample her merchandise. In the very near future, however, he would indeed be a patron of hers, and now that he thought about it, the sooner the better. He had already been too long on short rations.

With Ramon following him, Jeff turned the corner into Condé Street and had no difficulty finding the door of Madame Hortense's house. It was a most formidable door of oaken planks studded with iron spikes; its very grimness accentuated the promised delights available within. A chain with a metal knob dangled on the outside. Jeff had been hoping that some of Madame Hortense's beauties might adorn the balconies above; he was disappointed. It was too early, he told himself, for any such tantalizing display. Perhaps later in the afternoon, when offices closed and men had the leisure to stroll down the street with lecherous eyes for the lovelies above.

He pulled the chain, listening to the high-pitched jangle of a bell in the interior courtyard. Moments later he heard the rasping of bolts being withdrawn, and the door was opened by a young black, so strikingly muscular that he was indeed outstanding. Jeff considered him the finest-looking Negro lad he had ever seen.

"Good mornin', mastah suh." The black was soft-spoken and polite. "Kin I do somethin' for yo'?"

"You must be Lancer. I've already heard about you

61

from my boy here." He gestured over a shoulder to Ramon behind him.

"Yas suh, I'm Lancer."

"The one who put on the famous shows?"

"Yas suh. We calls 'em *partouses*."

"I understand you are to be congratulated on your performances. Perhaps I'll see one sometime. But for the moment, will you kindly convey my good wishes to your mistress and tell her that I come here from Mr. Lafitte, who sent me to see Captain You?"

Lancer bowed and flourished his hand in a welcoming gesture. "Yas suh, mastah suh, will you kindly come inside and I'll tell Madame Hortense. Captain You is with her."

Jeff stepped through the grim doorway into a courtyard lined with balconies surrounding a compact and verdant garden where broad banana fronds cast fringed dark shadows on the sun-splattered interior. Lancer motioned him to a seat on a marble bench, then skipped lightly up a flight of stairs to the first balcony. He rapped softly on a door opening on the court. At a word from inside, he opened the door, only to reappear a moment later and return light-footedly down the stairs.

"Captain You 'n' Madame Hortense mighty happy to see yo', mastah suh." He beamed at Jeff. "Yore nigger boy kin wait for yo' out'n back with me, but yo' tells him to keep his eyes on the ground. He ain' supposed to look up at the girls if'n they walk along the balcony. They's for white men only 'n' cain' have no nigger a-eyin' 'em. Specially now, 'cause sometimes they ain' all dressed at this time o' day."

Jeff told Ramon to accompany Lancer and to follow the instructions to keep his eyes on the ground. He knew, of course, that Ramon would do no such thing, but at least he had been instructed. Ramon would be wise enough not to get caught staring open-mouthed at the girls. And if he did steal a look, he was doing only what came naturally.

Jeff followed Lancer up the stairs, noting as he did so how the thin pantaloons shaped themselves to the powerful muscles of the boy's legs and how the tow linen of his shirt stretched across his massive shoulders. This young black was indeed a handsome man, and Jeff wondered where the lady of the house might have bought him. Seeing Lancer in the flesh, Jeff could understand how his mistress could easily charge a high price for one of her spectaculars. Surely he would be exciting to watch, provided his partners were equally good-looking. Of course, the partners would be black, but Jeff supposed that any black girls *chez* Madame Hortense would be extra Fancy.

Jeff followed Lancer along the balcony. The black boy rapped at the door again. A voice inside asked him to enter. The first thing that caught Jeff's eye in the gaudy overfurnished room was the figure of a woman of uncertain age on an elaborately carved and gilded chaise longue. She was so painted and bedizened that Jeff couldn't even hazard a guess as to how old she was. Nor could he judge her age from her hair, which had been dyed a bold and brassy yellow. Her ample figure was tightly corseted and she was dressed in a froth of laces and satin. Jewels sparkled at her throat, her wrists, in her ears, and on her hands. She looked a question at Jeff and then answered the question herself by pointing to the occupant of a chair with one hand and with the other patting a chair near her for Jeff's occupancy.

"Captain Dominique You," she said. Her words were slightly accented, but her lovely voice was so low and controlled that the accent made it even more enchanting. The cultured voice issuing from this wrinkled harridan surprised Jeff. Despite her brassy appearance and her profession, he recognized that she must, at one time in her life, have been a lady of some quality.

Dominique You half rose from his chair and nodded perfunctorily at Jeff. The size and corpulence of the man, his round red face and his deep-set, almost black eyes, combined with the fringe of white hair, gave him a forbidding appearance.

"I am Jefferson Carson," Jeff said. "I have a letter for you, and although I much dislike breaking into your *tête-à-tête* with *madame,* I would much appreciate it if you would read it."

63

Her stays creaked as Madame Hortense reached over and tapped Jeff lightly on the wrist with her fan.

"Tut, tut, young man." She smiled at him, and he could see that, like most women, she was intrigued by him. "Nothing could interrupt our *tête-à-tête*. We have already ruined quite half the reputations in New Orleans, and now we shall have a new subject to talk about after you leave. Yourself! And that, I am sure, will make a most interesting bit of conversation, *n'est-ce pas?*"

"I hope it will be entertaining, even though you do not know me." Jeff smiled his most engaging smile at her.

"Who needs to know you?" She opened her fan with a click of the ribs and fanned herself vigorously for a moment. "You are young. You are extremely handsome. That is your *carte blanche* to any situation. In addition, I would not be surprised if you are an unprincipled rascal. Otherwise why should you have a letter for Dominique You, who is the veritable prince of rogues—aren't you, Dominique, *mon ami?*"

"I like to think so, my dear Hortense, but each day I am getting older, and the profession of rogue is only for younger men like our friend here. However, my dear"—he nodded to Hortense—"with your permission we shall see what this young man's letter contains."

"I'm even more curious than you, so hurry, Dominique. I can scarce contain myself. We shall have so much to talk about after M'sieur Carson has gone."

While You broke the seals on the letter, Madame Hortense again pointed her fan to the armchair near her chaise longue. Jeff distrusted the spindly gilt legs, but the chair managed to support his weight when he sat down. Captain You flipped open the silver-handled lorgnette which he wore on a black ribbon around his neck, adjusted the paper at arm's length, and read the letter. When he had finished, he dropped it in his lap and winked at Hortense.

"You'll be surprised when I tell you who wrote this letter," he remarked. "Someone we both know very well."

"*Hélas!* You have piqued my curiosity. Don't keep me in suspense any longer."

You delayed a moment in answering her, a knowing

smile on his lips. Finally he spoke. "It's from Helen."

"From Helen Gordon? Who married the rich Latimer and is now a widow? Damn! She must have led him a merry way to the grave. Well, well! From Helen Latimer."

"The same, my dear."

"And what does my dear Helen want?" She waggled an admonitory finger. "Don't tell me, I already know. She has taken a fancy to this young man—Helen always did like handsome young men—and she wants you to help him. Right?"

"Quite right. How did you know?"

"Because I know Helen. Any handsome man would interest her, and this one particularly."

"Yes?" You raised his eyebrows.

"Oh, for heaven's sake, Dominique, you never notice things the way I do, but when M'sieur Carson walked across the floor, I knew immediately that he would satisfy any woman. And how is my dear Helen?" Madame Hortense asked Jeff.

"In the best of health when I saw her a week or so ago."

"And still a widow, if I am not mistaken?" You asked.

"A very rich widow I am sure." Madame Hortense smiled. "And so, Dominique, what are you going to do for Helen's protégé?"

"I think possibly we could use him."

"Not possibly—probably, or rather certainly. I told you he is a rogue, and this is the kind of man you are looking for in your business. Yes?"

"Most assuredly."

"I shall be happy if I can be of any service to you," Jeff broke into their conversation.

"Don't be too happy, young man," Hortense warned him. "Anything to do with the Lafittes may well cost you your neck, especially if you are connected with Dominique. But then, we are all no better than we should be."

Captain You heaved himself up from his chair and took several steps to stand before Jeff.

"Report to me at the blacksmith shop tomorrow morning at ten. We'll try to find something to keep you out of mischief."

"Better say to keep him *in* mischief," Hortense interrupted. "And speaking of mischief"—she smiled archly—"I think we should do something to celebrate this young man's entry into your business."

"A glass of champagne?" You suggested.

"Tut, tut, Dominique. What does a young man want with a glass of champagne, except perhaps to quench his thirst? I ask you, Dominique, what did you think about when you were M'sieur Carson's age? Certainly not champagne. *Jamais!* You had other more important things on your mind. Women, if I remember correctly, and I most certainly do."

"*Madame* is a wise woman." Jeff smiled at her.

"After years spent in this business one has to be wise, particularly in knowing men. At this moment I'm wishing I were as young as you are, M'sieur Carson." Instead of tapping him with her fan, she let her fingers rest on his arm. He could not help noticing that her diamonds were even larger than Helen Latimer's.

She sighed. "But I am not as young as I would like to be, so I must find a worthy substitute for myself. Dominique, ring the bell for Lancer."

Once again Jeff listened to the distant jangling of a bell. After a moment running steps sounded on the stairs, then a knock on the door. At Madame Hortense's word, the door opened and Lancer stood framed there. "Lancer boy, go to the top floor and tell Chloe I want to see her here." She waved him out of the door.

"Chloe?" Dominique asked, breaking the silence. "Perhaps our young friend does not care for black girls."

Hortense sat bolt upright on the chaise. "Any man should appreciate Chloe. Despite a touch of the tarbrush, she is the loveliest girl I have ever had, except perhaps Helen Latimer."

Jeff smiled to himself. So he had not been wrong. The elegant Mrs. Latimer had indeed been a professional, and right here in Madame Hortense's house. He knew it; she was far too practiced in ways to please a man to be an amateur. Now he was already anticipating this unknown

Chloe. He could feel the incipient swelling in his groin at the very thought of her.

"I yield to *madame's* choice." He spread his hands palms up. "I am sure she knows."

"You can be damned glad you didn't add 'after years of experience.' I would have resented that." She turned toward the door, responding to the soft tapping. "Here she is now."

The door opened and Jeff sucked in his breath. Never before had he seen such a beautiful girl. She was the color of a tea rose with a vibrant pink showing through the pale ivory of her skin. Her long dark hair was gathered in a clasp at the nape of her neck and fell nearly to the floor behind her. Her eyes, deep and luminous like the eyes of a sacrificial virgin at the ancient Egyptian corn festival, peered out from under long lashes, first at Madame Hortense, then briefly at Dominique, and finally at Jeff, where they lingered. Her red lips parted in a half-smile, showing perfect teeth.

"Chloe," said Madame Hortense, who was all charm, "we have here M'sieur Jeff, who is going into business with Dominique You. We felt that a celebration should be forthcoming to mark the occasion, and I know of nobody with whom M'sieur Jeff could celebrate better than yourself. Do you think you could help him celebrate?"

Again Chloe looked at Jeff and her admiration for him was apparent in the little in-drawing of breath that she made. The tip of her coral tongue circled her lips.

"Most certainly, *madame*." She hesitated a moment and then added, "Between Mr. Jeff and myself, we shall be able to make fireworks. Skyrockets and Roman candles will be set off to celebrate."

"Don't be so damned poetic, *ma chérie*. We'll take the fireworks for granted. And now, if you will conduct M'sieur Jeff upstairs to your room . . ."

"With pleasure, *madame*."

Jeff was so enraptured with Chloe that he had scarcely paid attention to Madame Hortense. Compared to Chloe, Minnie George was not fodder for wet dreams. He finally came back to earth and added his own, "With pleasure."

Together they walked out of the room.

Madame Hortense waited for the door to close, then smiled at Dominique You.

"You have a new recruit," she said. "And if I am not mistaken, this young cockalorum will prove valuable to you."

"I would have said that myself, my dear, but now that I know you approve of him, I am doubly sure. Yes, he will prove valuable."

"And," she added, "I am sure that tomorrow morning Chloe will brag that he is a man among men. *Hélas, mon ami,* there are many times when one wishes one were younger, but never in my life have I wished it more than I do now."

"And I! I've reached that time in life when most of the addresses in my black book are physicians!" You laughed.

"Hush, *mon ami.* Let us observe. Let us both tiptoe quietly upstairs to the linen closet on the floor above, to the peephole there which looks into Chloe's room. I have charged as much as fifty dollars for a man to stand at that peephole, but for once I shall be magnanimous and charge you nothing at all, provided . . ."

"What?"

"You will give me equal time at peeping as you preempt for yourself."

CHAPTER VII

JEFF left Madame Hortense's Riding Academy in a world of his own. The overhanging balconies, the glimpses of verdant courtyards, the people passing in the hot street had no existence for him. Within his new horizon there was only the exciting memory of Chloe's lips, the perfumed softness of her hair, the tea-rose smoothness of her accommodating body. He had never been happier in his life.

The unforgettable image of unbelievably beautiful Chloe had completely displaced that of Philomena George. Could he ever have been really in love with Minnie? No, he decided as he strode back to his hotel with a sweating Ramon panting to keep up. Minnie must have been a passing fancy. Her shining prettiness would surely fade as the years progressed, and she would become a stout second edition of her mother, with all the cloying cuteness inappropriate to her age. He was lucky—even though she had helped him escape with his life—that Minnie belonged to the past. Otherwise he might never have met Chloe, who was the most important thing that had ever happened to him.

His experience with Chloe had been unalloyed rapture. He did not know, of course, that he had also been performing for the delight of Madame Hortense and Dominique You, who sought vicariously to recapture their youth. Even if he had suspected that there were eyes beyond the wall, he would have been so completely absorbed by Chloe that it would have made no difference.

When Jeff reached the hotel, deVeau was slouched behind the desk, yawning as he again offered Zelda to him. However, Jeff was so completely satiated that he desired nothing more than to wash the sweetness from his body and relax alone with his thoughts of Chloe. After sending Ramon to fetch hot water, he dismissed the boy for the day, stripped off his clothes, bathed himself with a soapy rag, and collapsed on the bed, luxuriating in his physical exhaustion and his vivid recall of the most perfect woman he had ever had. Yes, he continued to assure himself, he had finally encountered complete feminine perfection.

Although he thought himself both physically and mentally exhausted, he found that his thoughts of Chloe were beginning to arouse him. As the mental images persisted, he became so rampant that he would have welcomed Zelda to his arms just to find physical release. He was far too tired, however, to get up and ring the bell to summon her. There was an easier way, and he resorted to it. When release came, he relaxed, at last able to leave his mind a blank. Sleep was the answer, because he needed to renew his strength and clear his thoughts before his appointment with You in the morning. Ignoring the sun that was still shining through the jalousies, he turned over on his side and within moments was dead to the world.

He was awakened once during the night by hunger; he had had nothing to eat since breakfast. He struggled from the bed and groped his way to the door to find Ramon curled up on the blanket outside. He woke the boy and dispatched him to the kitchen to forage for food. Ramon returned with a cup of warmed-over coffee and two stale croissants, which Jeff ate. Back in bed, he slept until the morning sun, streaming across the sheets, awakened him.

His first thoughts on awakening were of Chloe. He remembered how she had insisted on his removing his shirt and how piqued she had been when he had refused. He could not know that both Madame Hortense and Captain You were also puzzled over his curious behavior, though they accepted his explanation to Chloe that it was an idiosyncrasy affecting his virility. Yes, Madame Hortense had assured You, some men had strange quirks. She had known those who could perform only with their shoes on, some who could not remove any clothes, and others with even weirder wonts. One man she had known was impotent unless he wore a coonskin cap. Another had to don women's pantalets. . . .

Reluctantly Jeff got out of bed and summoned Ramon, who stared in amazement at the state of his master's anatomy until a soft cuff on the ears reminded him to start helping Jeff to dress. Ramon then ran to the kitchen to order a huge breakfast. Jeff realized reluctantly that man cannot live on love alone—that bread is also necessary. And when the bread is served toasted, with ham and eggs and grits and a pot of steaming coffee, the whole world seems brighter.

On this day Jeff decided to leave Ramon at the hotel while he visited the Lafitte blacksmith shop. He knew the way now, and it was only a short walk. Moreover, he had already established his status as a slave owner. Ramon would only be in the way. He walked slowly on the shady side to avoid arriving bathed in perspiration.

Dominique You awaited him in an armchair on the *banquette* before the smithy. Sitting beside him was a man who bore such a striking resemblance to the humble blacksmith he had met the previous day that Jeff was sure he must be Jean, the more famous of the Lafitte brothers. Captain You lifted himself ponderously a few inches above the seat of his chair and made the presentation, explaining that this was the young man who had come with a letter of introduction from Helen Latimer.

Jean Lafitte smiled in recognition of her name, rose from his chair, made a sweeping Old World bow, and welcomed Jeff with outstretched hand.

"My friend Dominique tells me that you would like to join our organization," he said. His smile showed a row of perfect white teeth, contrasting with the deep mahogany tan of his face.

Jeff returned the bow with equal courtesy and extended his own hand. Lafitte grasped it with fingers like steel clamps. Jeff winced inwardly but did not betray his pain. This was evidently a test: Lafitte seemed satisfied.

"Indeed I would, sir," Jeff answered. "I've been in New Orleans only a few days, coming here as a perfect stranger. But since I arrived, I have heard nothing but praise for you and your brother, as well as for Captain You. It seems that I could not have come to finer people. I am eternally grateful to Mrs. Latimer."

Lafitte smiled. "The fair Helen is a good friend, but there are some who might counsel you against joining our organization. Believe me, we are not all that popular in New Orleans. Some even call us pirates, though I can assure you we are not. We operate legitimately under letters of marque from the Republic of Cartagena. Our business here at the smithy is legitimate. Otherwise why would my brother wear himself out daily shoeing horses? And our store on Royal Street is patronized by the finest and most respectable women in New Orleans. As to our base of operations in Barataria . . ." Lafitte did not finish the sentence, but added as an afterthought, "You will find out about that later."

He paused to stare thoughtfully at Jeff. Then: "Our business has recently taken a new turn, which may not be to your liking. The silks and laces, the brocades and gewgaws at our shop on Royal Street, are all profitable.

But we are engaged in a far more productive enterprise at present. I'll be the first to admit that it is not entirely legitimate, but it is infinitely more profitable."

"May I ask what it is?" Jeff interrupted, sensing that Lafitte wanted the question.

"Indeed you may," Dominique You answered, "seeing as how we have both agreed that we want you in this business."

"I shall answer in one word." Lafitte smiled at Jeff. "And that word is—slaves. Yes, black men and women— more particularly, black men. That is the great demand today, Jeff. We can no longer import slaves into the United States legally, and yet the demand for them is greater than ever. Fine *bozals* just off the ship from Africa will bring eight hundred dollars or more, and the market is ever expanding. Negroes are sold on sight. Plantation owners can't get enough slaves."

Jeff thought of Baxter Simon and his great slave-breeding operation at Willow Oaks Plantation. He asked, "Why can't the market be supplied with slaves bred locally? I had a friend who kept a stud book, raised his stock carefully, and made a fortune." The statement was true except for the word "friend."

Both Lafitte and You shook their heads. "It will be a long time before that sort of breeding will catch up with the expanding market. Some few places in the South are already breeding slaves, true, but their output is only a drop in the bucket," Lafitte said. "Figure this: it takes about eighteen years for a slave to develop fully. We can't wait that long. Perhaps in another twenty years the supply problem will be solved, but the demand for slaves is today."

"So where are you going to get them?" Jeff asked.

"There is only one place," You answered. "Cuba. Or more specifically, the city of Havana."

"It is the only legitimate slave market left today," Lafitte added. "Spain has not outlawed slavery."

"And Havana is only a short sail from here," You continued. "We bring the slaves here from Cuba. In Cuba a likely *bozal* just off the ship from Africa sells for around three hundred dollars. Here we sell him for eight hundred dollars or more and there are no questions asked."

"You smuggle them in?"

"It is not a word we like." Lafitte shrugged. "But, alas, we have to accept it. We bring them here to meet the demand, which mounts every day. There's not a plantation owner in the country who doesn't bless us. We are really helping the prosperity of the nation because slaves are needed to produce more cotton and cane. The more we raise, the richer the country gets. And after all, isn't national prosperity everyone's business?"

Jeff nodded. If smuggling was the only way to get needed slaves into the country, who could do it more efficiently than the Lafittes, Captain You, and company? They could get away with it as practically legal. Men who walked the streets of New Orleans with prestige and respectable reputation, the Lafittes were no furtive smugglers.

The two men watched Jeff intently, waiting for him to speak.

"Then, gentlemen," Jeff said, smiling as though agreeing to a proposition that had not yet been offered, "what is it that I can do for you? Is there a way that I can be of service to your organization?"

You heaved himself out of his chair and waved his hand at Jeff to remain seated. He entered the wide door of the blacksmith shop and reappeared in a few moments, followed by a huge black whose velvety skin glistened from liberal applications of oil. A fine specimen of manhood— tall, muscular, his head shaven, his features flat, rigid—he was naked except for the leg irons on his ankles.

"This is what we mean." You had the man stand before Jeff on the *banquette*. "You can help us round up stock like this. Our business in slaves is growing rapidly. We need more men to help us. We need men to go to Havana and bring these critters here. We need men to take care of them, to contact our customers. We need help in every direction. And good men are hard to find."

Jeff moved his gaze away from the black and looked from You to Lafitte. His mind was already made up. First, he was being offered entry into a lucrative profession

73

which, if not entirely legal, was at least tolerated. Second, he admired both Jean Lafitte and Dominique You. They were his kind of men. He belonged with them. As to what happened to men like this *bozal,* that was up to God.

"I'm flattered, gentlemen, that you consider me good enough to join your organization. You know very little about me except for a letter of introduction from a mutual friend. But if you offer me a job, I'll attend to it to the best of my ability, and I promise to give you one hundred cents worth of labor for every dollar you pay me."

You nodded in silent approval. Lafitte said, "It may take a little time before you are valuable to us. You have a lot to learn. Later we'll discuss final monetary arrangements. For the present we'll pay you ten gold dollars a week and found. Ultimately we will offer you a share in our profits, but meanwhile accept ten dollars a week while we are training you."

"Agreed." Jeff shook hands in turn with Lafitte and Captain You.

"We have a ship sailing tomorrow evening for our base in Barataria, sixty miles to the south. We want you aboard, prepared to spend considerable time down there. There you will become acquainted with the way we do business."

Lafitte led the big black into the shop, his leg chain clanking on the *banquette,* and Jeff was left alone with Dominique You. The captain laughed.

"So enjoy yourself, lad. All of today and tomorrow until sundown to do exactly as you please. You're going to find plenty of work at Barataria, and you will need time to learn the ropes. However, you will find ways to enjoy yourself there. Our settlement is by no means spartan. There will be much to entertain you."

"Thank you, Captain You. Are women there?"

"Women a-plenty, young cockerel. I can't guarantee rare hothouse blooms like Hortense's Chloe, but you'll find serviceable wenches. Women play an important part in your life, yes? A woman's letter introduced you to us. Yesterday my good friend Madame Hortense entertained you with one of her loveliest young women. Tell me, how did you like Chloe?"

"The most exciting hump of my whole life, Captain You! I've thought about little else since I was with her."

"You'll have more to think about from now on." You winked at him. "There'll be time for women, too. But"—he hesitated—"tell me one thing, young cockerel . . ."

"Yes?"

"Do you always perform with your shirt on?"

"You mean . . . ?"

"Don't get your balls in an uproar. News travels fast in an establishment like Madame Hortense's. You had scarcely left the house before Chloe started raving about you. She was eminently satisfied with you and wanted everyone to know it, but she did find that one tiny fault with you."

"The shirt, you mean?" Jeff laughed.

You nodded, joining Jeff's laughter.

"Well, put it down as an idiosyncrasy, Captain You. I can't explain it to you with a straight face except to say that I am more comfortable that way. In fact, otherwise I can do nothing."

You brayed his laughter. "Well, young cock, if a shirt helps you, by all means wear it."

Jeff smiled. "I think I shall walk down Condé Street and pull the chain in front of Madame's door. Then when Lancer answers it, I shall ask for the services of Chloe . . ."

"Then good luck to you . . . a pleasant time."

"Thank you, Captain You. And I shall continue to wear my shirt."

Lafitte appeared in the doorway and crossed the *banquette*. "Tomorrow at five," he said.

CHAPTER VIII

NEXT morning Jeff dragged his feet reluctantly through the sunshine of Condé Street. Several times he had to step into the gutter to avoid being splashed by black women scrubbing down steps and sidewalks in front of houses. The women always looked up at him with smiles that displayed rows of gleaming white teeth. To their murmured "Good morning, mastah suh," he responded only with a wan smile, for he was still remembering his tearful farewell to Chloe. She had clung to him, reluctant to let him go, her hands trying to seduce him into another hour's stay with her. But he was truly spent, and, much as he might wish it, was physically unable to respond to her caresses. He had left her weeping and felt like weeping himself as he descended the stairs from her upper room to the first-floor gallery.

He had to pass Madame Hortense's door and was surprised to see it open. She called out to invite him in for a *tête-à-tête* over a cup of chocolate, confessing that she had had Lancer leave her door open.

She had been all smiles, lounging against a hillock of small lacy pillows on her huge bed. She motioned him to sit in the chair beside her, rang for Lancer, and ordered chocolate and brioches for Jeff. "Can't have an important guest of mine leaving on an empty stomach," she had informed him, patting his hand, then letting her fingers slip down to rest on his leg.

Jeff counted the little breakfast as charged against the fifty dollars he had handed over to her the night before. Not that he regretted the money—not a single copper penny of it—but he had other ideas in his head as he sat beside the wrinkled harridan who, he could recognize, had once been an extremely handsome woman. He hoped that her talonlike fingers would not start moving up his leg. To forestall any provocative fondling he picked up the hand and kissed it, placing it back gently on the satin sheets. It was a matter of business that he wanted to discuss with her, and he could not allow his thoughts to be diverted. Besides, if he had been unable to respond to Chloe earlier, he certainly could not react here.

Yes, his business had to do with *madame*. He wanted Chloe for himself alone. Would *madame,* when he had accumulated sufficient money, sell Chloe to him?

She delayed answering for several moments while she

sipped her chocolate and crumbled a brioche into tiny balls. It would take a great deal of money to buy Chloe, she finally said. Why buy her? He could enjoy her whenever he wanted, and if his taste leaned toward tea-rose octoroons, she would find one for him, one she would guarantee to be a virgin. He shook his head. It was Chloe alone he wanted. She might be expensive. She was no ordinary octoroon, but an extremely beautiful and accomplished one. Still, he was quite unprepared for the figure of five thousand dollars which *madame* quoted. He wondered whether if he had allowed *madame's* fingers to inch their way to his crotch (where they had most certainly been headed) her price might have been lower.

Yes, five thousand dollars was a lot of money, said Madame Hortense, but not an unusual price to ask for an octoroon. Young bloods of the town often paid that much for a mustee at the Octoroon Ball and then set her up in a house on Rampart Street. This would be little enough for Jeff to pay for Chloe if and when he accumulated a fortune, as he surely would.

So he had left Madame Hortense frustrated, but with her solemn promise not to dispose of Chloe to any other person. She would reserve Chloe for him. Then, as though she sensed the intensity of his desire for Chloe, she added a kindly word of encouragement. If he was successful with the Lafitte organization, as she was sure he would be, it would not take him long to accumulate such a sum. "Something tells me, young man, that you usually get what you aim for. True?"

"Not always, *madame*." He shook his head.

"But there is one thing of which I am sure." She smiled up at him, and despite her lack of paint, powder, and rouge, she had an intriguing face. "You usually get any woman you want, don't you?"

His compressed lips smiled back at her.

"And, I'll venture to say, you have never disappointed a woman yet." She waggled a forefinger at him.

"Never, *madame*," he admitted somewhat proudly.

"Now get on with you. Dominique tells me you are going to Barataria, and I don't want you to be late."

He squeezed her hand, then impulsively reached over to kiss her on the throat. He walked out the door without turning back to look at her. At least he had her solemn promise not to sell Chloe to anyone else. Well, if his job under the Lafittes went the way he hoped, it would not take him too long to accumulate the money. True, any time at all would be too long, but he had to accept *madame's* word, and leave Chloe behind for the present. He walked along the gallery, down the flight of stairs, and into the courtyard where Lancer was waiting to let him out.

His footsteps dragged automatically. His mind was still in the scented room where he had, at least for a few hours, owned his Chloe. What an artist she was! He mentally reviewed all the women he had ever known. Only one, Helen Latimer, had approached Chloe. Helen Latimer was an older woman, quite old enough to be Chloe's mother, and all her sophisticated tricks in bed could not outweigh Chloe's youth and beauty.

It hurt him to leave Chloe, knowing that other men would lie with her as intimately as he had, and that she would fondle them as professionally and perhaps as lovingly as she had fondled him. No, that could not be quite true! There had been more to her embraces than mere commercial pantomine. She cared as much for him as he did for her, yet what could she do about it? Or what could he? Five thousand dollars! She was worth it, but would he ever really have that amount of money to buy her? The ten dollars a week would not go on forever. He must work hard to begin to share soon in the profits Lafitte had promised. Hurry the day when he could place the money in Madame Hortense's hand and lead Chloe away so that she would belong to nobody but him forever and ever!

Ramon was in the tiny lobby of the hotel when Jeff entered, and he gestured the boy to follow him. Maybe, he thought, Ramon had been a foolish investment. He was just that many dollars further away from buying Chloe. But even if he had not purchased Ramon, he would not have enough to buy Chloe, so why torture his mind? He must concentrate on the great opportunity for gain ahead of him. Here he was only a few days in New Orleans, and he had already been accepted by the Lafittes. Chloe would have to wait. His immediate purpose was to succeed in this chance Helen Latimer had provided. His thoughts turned again to Helen. Should he have stayed longer at her plantation? She had been infatuated with him, he mused, as his fingers unconsciously sought the golden cross at his neck.

But enough of these thoughts of females! Women had always been his greatest source of trouble, although they were also his greatest source of pleasure. What a mess he had gotten himself into over Philomena George! Forget them all—forget Minnie George, Helen Latimer, and even Chloe—at least for the time being. Concentrate on the job he had to do for the Lafittes. There must be another woman whose lips were as beguiling as Chloe's, whose skin as petal-soft, and whose murmurs in his ear as passionate as hers. And yet—he allowed himself one fleeting second of doubt—if there were, he had never found her. He tried to convince himself if such a woman existed, she would not be a professional whore in Madame Hortense's Riding Academy. So forget Chloe. Concentrate on the business at hand!

He needed a valise. He couldn't travel with his saddlebags now that he had accumulated more clothing, so he sent Ramon out with instructions to buy one for less than the five dollars he gave him.

When Ramon had closed the door behind him, Jeff sat down on the edge of the bed. He must think clearly, but he still had trouble getting Chloe and her embraces out of his mind. After all his experiences with women, was he going to let an octoroon whore get the better of him? Not by a damned sight! He managed to smile at himself. If Chloe was an octoroon whore, then what was he but an octoroon whoremaster? Was he forgetting that his most vital job, a matter of life and death, was to keep the world from unmasking him as Bricktop, runaway slave? As a first step, he must forge papers that would insure his freedom. Even counterfeit papers of manumission would provide him with some protection. He went downstairs to the desk where deVeau was sitting behind the zinc counter.

Putting on his most amiable smile, Jeff asked to borrow a sheet of white foolscap, a quill, and some ink. For a tip of five cents, deVeau produced from under the counter a sheet of plain white paper, then passed Jeff an inkhorn and quill. Thanking deVeau, Jeff took these up to his room and sat down at the table, staring into space. Suddenly inspired, he dipped the quill in ink and wrote slowly in as good an imitation of Baxter Simon's hand as he could manage:

Jasper Creek, Mississippi.

Know all men by these presents:
That I, Baxter Simon of Willow Oaks Plantation, have granted complete and absolute freedom to my slave, Bricktop, who is henceforth to be known as Jefferson Carson.

BAXTER SIMON
(Signed)

Witnessed by
Ephriam Glover, Justice of the Peace
EPHRIAM GLOVER
(Signed)

It was masterfully executed, he thought, even if it was not legal. He had changed his handwriting so that Simon's letters were round and flowing, while the forged script of the imaginary Glover was cramped and crabbed. If worst came to worst, he could at least present this document to stay clear of the auction block. It was worth a try, anyway. Never again would he be a slave. He would die first.

As the horrid images of the slave cabins at Willow Oaks crossed his mind, he tried to reassure himself of his freedom by standing up and looking in the mirror over the chest of drawers. No, there was nothing in the face looking back at him that would betray his secret. It was, he felt sure, far too handsome a face to raise doubts. His skin was white and clear; his hair dark red and wavy, but not too wavy, at least not kinky. Perhaps his nostrils were just a shade too wide, but they added to his good looks by making his face more sensuous. His lips were curved and full and moist looking, but not in the least negroid. Damn it, if it were not for those telltale letters branded on his back, he would never have to be afraid. So he would not be afraid. He would put his own black heritage from his mind. He looked in the mirror and was again inspired by his own image. Men liked him and so, damnit, did women. What did he have to worry about? He smiled cockily at his reflection. Nothing at all—at least for the present. Then he realized he was clinging to that golden cross at his throat as if it were salvation itself.

He opened the door at Ramon's knock. The boy carried a large valise, which he proudly presented to his master, along with two dollars. It was a less than prepossessing piece of luggage, made of cardboard with shiny brown finish that proclaimed its cheapness. Jeff hated any sign of poverty, but he was in a hurry and couldn't be bothered with trifles. The valise would serve.

A glance at his watch showed him that it was already time for lunch, and he was hungry after the meager breakfast at Madame Hortense's. He sent Ramon running to the kitchen for whatever was on the *table d'hôte* for the day, advising him to bring his own lunch along. So for the first time in his life, Ramon sat at table and ate with a supposed white man.

After lunch they transferred the contents of the saddlebags to the valise. The saddlebags reminded Jeff of his horse, which, in the flurry of excitement, he had forgotten. He certainly wasn't going to need a horse at Barataria, so he dashed out to the stable to try to sell the beast. He was lucky to make a fairly good deal with the owner of the stable. Should he need a horse on his return to New Orleans, he could get one through the good graces of Pierre Lafitte.

Once back in his room, he sent Ramon for hot bath water, banished the boy, and scrubbed his body clean of the lingering odor of Chloe's perfume. When he had finished, he recalled Ramon and ordered him to scrub himself with the second-hand soapy water. Then, sniffing Ramon to make sure he did not smell of musk, he dressed himself in his best clothes with a change of linen.

By the time they were both dressed, an hour remained before they were to report to Lafitte. Jeff considered using the spare time to return to Madame Hortense's for another glimpse of Chloe, but he knew better. Another farewell would obliterate his sense of time. So he restlessly paced his room, stepping out on the balcony from time to time to view the traffic below. Ages later the hands on his watch finally showed a quarter past four, and he went downstairs, followed by Ramon with the valise. After settling his account, they left together for Lafitte's.

The carriage standing before Lafitte's shop looked familiar to him as he strode along the *banquette,* and as he drew nearer he recognized the black coachman. At that moment the last person in the world he wanted to see was Helen Latimer, but if he was to keep his appointment, there was no escape. He could see the frills of her lilac gown behind You's crossed legs. Well, he assured himself, he was enough of an actor to take the situation in stride. A moment later he greeted Helen more effusively than he thought possible—and realized, moreover, that it was not all acting. Helen Latimer was a most attractive woman for any age, and despite his initial aversion to her unexpected presence, he was truly glad to see her.

He threw her a kiss while darting a sidelong glance of recognition at You. He held her hand longer than the prescribed moment, remembering how eagerly this same hand had so recently explored his body.

"Mrs. Latimer!" he said, expressing the proper astonishment at seeing her. "You are the last person I expected to see here, but nothing, absolutely nothing, could have been a pleasanter surprise."

She smiled at him, her eyes traveling up to his, but lingering an overlong moment at the junction of his thighs. "It seems," she said, "that I have come just in time to see you. I arrived in New Orleans last evening, and somehow I felt compelled to see my good friend Captain You, as much for his own genial company as to find some news of you. He tells me that you are now a part of his organization and that you are leaving for Barataria this afternoon."

Jeff included You in his smile. "And now I sail with regrets, for I shall be leaving you behind."

"Yes?" Her one word was a question. "Perhaps you had better tell him, Dominique."

"As if I could tell him as charmingly as you," the old gallant simpered.

"But he is going to think it odd of me if I tell him."

"How could I?" Jeff could be as gallant as Captain You.

"Then I shall." She clicked her fan open, her eyes lingering for a moment on the painted cupids before she looked at him. "I, too, am going to Barataria. My main reason for coming to New Orleans was to find some suitable damask for new curtains in my drawing room, and Dominique has just been telling me that there is a new shipment at Barataria that has not yet been brought to Royal Street. He himself suggested that I make the trip to pick out the material, and I agreed even before I knew that you were going to be on the same boat. Alas, you will not believe me! You will think me a most conniving baggage, but it is, I assure you, only a coincidence and not prearranged."

"I would be most flattered if it had been." Jeff picked up her hand and squeezed it. "I can think of no more delightful way to enter my new profession than in your company."

"But remember," You interposed, "this is not a time for gallantry, even for a pretty lady. You have work to do at Barataria, so don't let Madame Helen distract you."

"Bah, Dominique!" She laid a reassuring hand on his arm. "I can only stay there a few days—I've many things to take care of back at the plantation—so I cannot divert him either too much or too long."

"And I, Captain You," Jeff spoke up, "have always had the happy faculty of not allowing any woman, regardless of how attractive she is (and surely nobody could be more attractive than *la belle Hélène*), to distract me from my work. I can easily divide my life into two separate worlds —the days for my work and the evenings for Mrs. Latimer during her short stay at Barataria. Yes?" He smiled at You.

"Then do just that." You nodded. "And perhaps having Helen around will take away any feeling of strangeness you might have there. She will help bridge the gap." He smiled benignly on them both. "And now, if you will excuse me, I must leave you alone. I have to talk to our good Pierre."

Helen was silent for a moment, listening to his ponderous footsteps as he crossed the *banquette* and disappeared into the darkness of the smithy. She stood facing Jeff, her hands on her hips, almost defiant.

"I hope you didn't for a moment believe all that drivel about new draperies in my drawing room. Nonsense! You don't remember, but they are practically new. I came to New Orleans for only one reason—to be with you, Jeff. I have thought about nothing else since you left me. That one night with you was only enough to make me crave more. I called on my old friend Madame Hortense last evening. She said you were to leave this afternoon, so I came over here and wangled permission from Dominique to go with you." She pointed to the carriage. "My bags are all packed. I have only to have them set down on the *banquette,* send my coachman home, and go off with you. The few days I have to spend with you, I intend to enjoy to the utmost. Dominique has offered me the guest house, and, if you stay with me, there will be no questions asked. Barataria is not New Orleans. There nobody knows or cares if you spend the nights with me."

Jeff smiled. "I can think of nothing happier than having you beside me down there."

"Nor I," she answered, "but first you must say you forgive me for being a conniving woman."

"I forgive you." He took her hand and kissed it again. "And perhaps I can prove my forgiveness to you the first night we are together." He almost believed it. She was attractive and a joy to bed down. Nevertheless he found his thoughts going back to Condé Street to linger for one nostalgic moment on his Chloe. How wonderful it all would have been if Chloe could trade places with Helen. Impossible, of course, Helen was a free woman and Chloe a slave he could possess exclusively only if he got five thousand dollars. Well, perhaps Helen could help him there. He mentally assayed the rings on her fingers. Yes, perhaps she could.

CHAPTER IX

A pale disc of rising sun struggled through mists that shrouded the delta to trace silvery patterns on the scrubbed decks of the trim river schooner. The swift boat carried Jeff and Helen Latimer down the broad sweeps of the Mississippi and through the tortuous shortcuts of creeks and bayous that led to Lafitte's settlement of Barataria, south of New Orleans. Jeff tried to stifle a yawn with his hand: he had passed a sleepless night, a fevered one, though it lacked the enchantment of his previous night with Chloe.

Both he and Helen had been received on board by a solicitous captain who had evidently been well briefed on his passengers, for he addressed Jeff as "Mr. Carson" and was obsequious toward Mrs. Latimer, whom he seemed to know. He had shown them to two diminutive cabins, and on the floor of one had provided a shake-down for Ramon.

Jeff and Helen remained on deck when they sailed, watching the ever-shifting movement of the port of New Orleans. Jeff was astounded by its magnitude. As far as he could see up and down the river, masts were silhouetted against the sky. Hundreds of ships were tied up at the levees, and as the Lafitte craft sailed down the river, he could see multicolored flags of many nations at many sterns. The levees themselves teemed with life. Long lines of black stevedores carted produce to and from the ships. They sweated under cotton bales bound for the spinning and weaving mills of old England and New England. They labored under beams of mahogany and rare hardwoods from the islands of the Caribbean, under burlap bags of coffee from Brazil, crates of porcelain from China, and machinery from the northern states. They unloaded velvets from Lyons, furniture from Paris, and all the myriad essentials and luxuries demanded by a thriving city like New Orleans and the manor houses of the inland plantations.

Jeff and Helen were content to stand, scarcely talking, hands clasped, enjoying the nearness of each other's presence. From time to time she would free her hand from his, sliding her fingers down along the tight fabric of his pantaloons until he could endure it no longer. Whispering to her that it was advisable to wait until after dark, he removed her hand. She suggested that although her tiny cabin was piled high with luggage, the narrow bunk would be plenty wide enough for both of them for such an occasion, as two would take up no more room than one.

Experiment proved her right. After a bite of supper in the captain's cramped quarters, they again stood briefly at the rail watching the rare lights on the bank reflected in the blackness of the river. When Helen's tantalizing hand and avid mouth roused Jeff's inner climate to a fever pitch, they went below.

Stopping at his cabin to shed his clothing (except his perennial shirt), Jeff found Ramon asleep on his blanket spread on the deck. Stepping around him, he opened the door a crack, made sure the coast was clear, then tiptoed down the passageway to rap lightly at Helen's cabin. The door opened instantly.

In the dark he felt the softness of her naked body. The aura of her perfume enveloped him as she pressed her breasts flat against him, kneading her body on his. His arms encircled her and he lifted her from the deck. She swung open her thighs and straddled his hips. He staggered a few steps across the cabin. His knees struck the edge of the bunk and they fell together. The narrowness of the bunk was no problem. . . .

It was nearly daylight when he stole back to his own cabin. Exhausted, he fell asleep immediately. He had scarcely closed his eyes, it seemed to him, when there was a knock on his door and a voice pierced his half-consciousness: "Wake up, mastah suh. We 'rivin' in 'bout an hour. Cap'n has coffee waitin', mastah, 'n' yo' tell that boy o' yourn he kin have coffee with the crew."

Reluctantly Jeff dressed himself, still groggy, still weak with sweet fatigue. He always marveled at how women could drain the last ounce of strength from him and still be avid for more.

He joined Helen again on deck where they watched the sun breaking through the clouds until it shone with hot tropical brilliance. The stream had widened into a body of water that was Barataria Bay. Yes, Helen admitted, she had been here several times before. In fact, she confessed, she'd once had a lover here. For all she knew, he was still here, but she was no longer interested in him. He might present a slight problem, but certainly not an insurmountable one. Whatever claim any other lover might have to her past, her present belonged to Jeff. Absolutely nobody could compare with him.

"And while I'm letting down my hair about the past, Jeff dear," she said and turned her head so that Jeff could not see her eyes, "I have another confession to make. Something you will find out sooner or later. I'd rather have you hear it from me than from someone else. I hope it will not change your feelings toward me. I realize they are not very deep, but I treasure them."

"Helen, my feelings toward you won't change, and they might not be quite as inconsequential as you think. You must realize what happened last night was not merely an act. I could not have enjoyed it as much as I did were I pretending, and, after all, why should I pretend?" He tilted her chin so that she would look at him, but she pushed his hand away and pressed her face against his chest.

"You know me only as Mrs. Latimer, the owner of a plantation and a most respectable lady, yes?"

He laughed at her unwillingness to face him. "As Mrs. Latimer, yes, but let me say one thing, my dear Helen. I would hardly call you a respectable woman, at least in bed. So-called respectable women endure contact with a man rather than enjoy it. They lie still, grit their teeth, and let a man take his pleasure, but all the while they are praying that it will soon be over. As for you—"

"I don't want to be respectable if it means lying like a

log of wood. I *like* men, and I think a woman should get as much pleasure out of sex as a man. More. I've known men before, but oh, Jeff, I've never known a man who satisfies me the way you do."

"That's gratifying. I seem to have what it takes to satisfy a woman. I've never had any complaints. But perhaps you have not had many men in your life."

"Not many? You'd be surprised. I've had all kinds and all ages—from virginal schoolboys to doddering old men—more than enough to know that nobody can compare with you."

"Then I'm unique?" He felt a glow of pride that this woman thought him so wonderful.

"Unique? Indeed you are, darling. Physically you are a phenomenon, but you are more than that. You are an ideal lover. You make love not only for your own pleasure, but also for the pleasure of the woman, and that is indeed unique. Most men don't care how a woman feels. They lunge, plunge, and gasp. Then it's all over, with no thought of the woman's feelings or needs."

"My pleasure is always heightened if the woman is enjoying herself too. And if she's driven out of her head, I go with her—all the way."

"And for that *I* am grateful. But I'm getting away from what I started to tell you—my confession, as it were. This is going to be difficult, so I might as well put it briefly and very bluntly. I was once one of the girls at Madame Hortense's house."

This time he succeeded in lifting her face to his. His forefinger gently brushed the tears from her cheek. "Is that your terrible confession, my dear? What of it? It's nothing."

"Nothing that I was a *whore,* sleeping with all kinds of men just for the money?"

"I'm sure you gave each his money's worth, from the schoolboy virgin you initiated to the old men you comforted."

She nodded silently.

"Did I ever tell you I preferred a woman who had never yet known a man?" He continued to stroke her damp cheek. "As a matter of fact, I don't like virgins and never have. Passion is a highly developed emotion, and a woman, as well as a man, must have some experience to develop it. Where, my dear, could a woman get better experience than in Madame Hortense's house where she must learn so many different ways to pleasure a man? I never mentioned it to you, but I could appreciate that you were well trained. A man can tell. So, believe me, I am all the more grateful for it. And now I, too, must make a little confession."

"What? Don't tell me that you have been a gigolo!"

"Hardly." He laughed. "But I have a confession to make nevertheless. You see, I am madly in love with one of the girls at Madame Hortense's house. . . . Does that sound strange to you?"

"It only makes me feel miserable because I love you too much. Yes, absolutely miserable, but I mustn't complain. I knew I couldn't hold you, Jeff. Far too much difference in our ages. A woman of my years can hope for only so much—so little—from a younger man. Sooner or later he is bound to drift away. That is why I have pursued you so relentlessly. I must hurry to get all you can give me while I am still attractive. My mirror tells me I won't be able to hide the rush of time much longer."

"Does it make any difference?"

"More than you could imagine. . . . But I must know who this girl is. Yes, I am jealous, more jealous of her than I can tell you, but I'll not do anything to stand in your way. Will you tell me, Jeff? I know all the girls at Madame Hortense's. You could have fallen in love with almost any of them. Which one is it, my dear? Tell me."

"But why? It will only make you more unhappy."

"I know it will. But tell me. I promise I won't do anything to spoil your romance. You see, I love you enough to want *you* to be happy too."

Jeff was silent for a moment. He stared toward the shore, watching the distant blur as it materialized into buildings. Finally he spoke. The mere mention of her name would, he knew, be gratifying. He had said "Chloe" so many times in his thoughts that it would be a relief to pronounce the name aloud.

"It's Chloe. I know she is not white, but she is supremely beautiful and I love her."

"Chloe?" She pulled away from him abruptly and stared at him, eyes dark, shadowed. "It can't be Chloe! It mustn't be!"

"But it is," he insisted.

"Have you any idea who Chloe is?" She pressed both hands on his shoulders, her nails digging into his shirt, and he could feel her fingers trembling.

"I know nothing about her. Except that I spent the night with her. I, too, am not inexperienced, Helen, and I have known many women: but Chloe, despite her black blood, is the most exquisitely satisfying woman I have ever held in my arms."

She still clung to him. Her face had grown suddenly haggard, as though she had aged ten years in ten seconds. Her voice was nearly inaudible when she said, "Why shouldn't she be satisfying to you? Chloe is my daughter."

Jeff recoiled. His mouth went dry. He swallowed several times before he could speak. "Helen, you're joking. How could Chloe be your daughter? She is black and you are white."

"Yes, I'm white. But you are overlooking one important factor: her father. He was not white. Her father was René Jiminez. He's been dead for years, but even today, if someone in New Orleans wants to make a favorable comparison of a good-looking man, he will say 'as handsome as René Jiminez.' He was a quadroon, but by far the handsomest man in New Orleans. He was not a slave; he was a free man of color from Cuba, and he was connected with Dominique You. As a man of color, he was not permitted entree to Madame Hortense's. I had seen him frequently on the streets, and the first time I saw him I was intrigued. Then I met him through Dominique You. It was love. At first sight. He loved me as much as I loved him. I looked at him, he looked at me, and we both knew it. Nothing else mattered to me—it made no difference that he was black. I was so completely wild for him that I was willing

90

to throw everything away for him. And I did."

"You left *madame's* house?" Jeff was still shaken, but when part of his numbed mind was able to think, he could see Chloe's resemblance to the woman standing beside him.

"René bought my way out. I went to live with him. He was not a poor man. We rented an apartment together. Of course, we could not marry because he was a Negro in the eyes of the law. Still, I wanted that more than anything. Then Chloe was born. Somehow having a baby seemed to come between us. He worshipped the child, and I was jealous of her. I couldn't share him, even with my own daughter. Whenever I looked at her, I couldn't help feeling that she was not my daughter but his—because she and her father were black, while I was white. I even came to hate the whiteness of my flesh.

"René and I were together for three years before I lost him. I cannot help it. I have always been grateful that he died before he could go off with another woman. He was on one of Lafitte's ships which ran into a hurricane off the Tortugas. He was swept overboard and lost at sea. I inherited quite a sum of money from him, enough for me to live comfortably, but I had Chloe on my hands. Although she was nearly white, I could not acknowledge her as my daughter. Nor did I want to. She was a constant reminder that her father whom I worshipped, was dead."

"Poor Chloe." Jeff sighed. "No wonder she needed love. She'd never had any."

"Yes, I can feel sorry for her now. Strangely enough, I don't hate her, even knowing that she has your love. But I hated her then. Passionately. Madame Hortense came to my aid. We had remained friends after I left her. She arranged for Chloe to be adopted by an octoroon woman on Rampart Street. I had to promise never to see her again. Well, you know what those octoroon women train a girl for—to pleasure a man, nothing more or less. She did not make her debut at the Octoroon Ball. Instead Madame Hortense took her into her house when she was thirteen. She had been well trained for her profession and is lovely to look at."

"The loveliest person I have ever seen. But then, Helen, I never saw you at her age."

"Thank you, Jeff." She managed a wan smile. "So that's my sordid biography—a whore, mistress of a Negro, and mother of an illegitimate child who is black. Not a pretty story. At least I've told the truth, and I feel better."

"And is that the end of it?" he asked.

She shrugged, tired. "After René's death I went to live in the American part of the city, divorcing myself entirely from the French Quarter. It was there that I met Mr. Latimer and married him. He was a wealthy man and much older than I. I tried to be a good wife to him, but I never loved him."

He placed a protective arm about her shoulders and drew her against him. "This has been a shock to me, learning that you are Chloe's mother."

"And to me that you are in love with her. But Jeff, stay in love with her. Grant me only these few days with you. Then I'll drop out of your life forever."

"How can you?" He shook his head. "If I marry Chloe, you'll be my mother-in-law."

"You can't marry Chloe." It was Helen's turn to shake her head. "She's a Negro, and you know there can be no marriage between black and white. However," she added, "there are other ways to set up housekeeping besides marriage, my dear."

The matter seemed settled for Helen, and she snuggled against Jeff's chest. But the revelation that Helen was Chloe's mother had so shocked him that he sank deep inside himself, tangled in tormenting thoughts. Automatically he kept his arm around Helen without being really aware of her presence.

The Lafitte schooner threaded its way among the small islands that dotted the expanse of Barataria Bay. Helen pointed out to Jeff the geography of his future home. Two larger islands separated the bay from the Gulf of Mexico —Grand Isle and Grand-Terre—providing Lafitte's armada of corsairs good anchorage, safe from the prying eyes of revenue cutters. Grande-Terre, which lay straight ahead, was the capital of Barataria. As they drew nearer, the settlement materialized as a small town of substantial wooden houses clustered about a three-story red-brick mansion like a brood of chicks about a mother hen. Tree-lined streets were well kept and prosperous looking. Massive warehouses lined the waterfront. A sleek three-masted sailing ship gave an impression of speed even while tied up to the pier.

"That's Jean Lafitte's house." Helen indicated the big brick house. "The smaller ones surrounding it belong to his men. Each man has his own house with a servant to take care of it, male or female, depending on his preference. Some are neat and immaculately clean, others are slovenly, just like their owner. . . . Those warehouses are for the storage of goods before they are taken to New Orleans, but there"—she pointed to an immense log stockade—"is the most important acreage in Barataria today. That is where they keep the slaves before they are sold or taken to New Orleans." Again she pointed toward the Big House. "I wonder if you will be billeted there?"

He laughed, shrugging. "Hardly. Why should M'sieur Lafitte honor a ten-dollar-a-week apprentice with accommodations in his own house?"

"Ten dollars a week? Is that all Jean offered you?"

"With a promise of more if I'm a success at learning this business."

"But you spoke of buying Chloe! Technically, she's not a slave, but Madame Hortense customarily requires payment from any man who takes a girl from her house. The usual price is five thousand. That's what René paid for me . . . I don't know how much money you have, but at ten dollars a week, it would take many years to meet Hortense's terms."

He exhaled heavily. "I have faith."

She smiled tenderly and stroked his hand. "Perhaps I can help. I might persuade *madame* to lower her price."

He laughed. "When we are talking about ten dollars a week—you'd have to be most persuasive."

"You're the one who said you have faith."

While they talked, the schooner was maneuvered up

alongside the net-strung pier. Lines were thrown out to barefooted men on the hot dock, and the boat was swiftly warped in. The docking of a packet downstream from New Orleans was hardly a sensational event in this sea vulture's rookery piled high with booty from the world's market-places, but it interrupted the sweaty monotony of back-breaking labor and silence. More than forty people, black and white, came running along the sun-struck plankings, staring, waving, and calling. When the gangplank was lowered, the captain approached them.

"May I escort you ashore, madam?" His bow was punctilious, his eyes heated, wise. "My orders say you are to be given a guest house. I'd be honored to escort you there, though I believe a carriage is awaiting you."

"It can't be for me," she replied. "M'sieur Jean did not know I was coming."

"Yet I'm sure he did." The captain took her hand to assist her to the gangplank. "We have fast messenger service between here and New Orleans. We have to have it. Undoubtedly the messenger arrived before we did."

"And that he certainly did, my dear Helen." A man strode across the gangplank and took her in his arms. "I have been waiting an hour here so that I could be the first to greet you." He kissed her and took her hand to lead her ashore, but she hesitated.

"I must introduce you to Mr. Carson, who made the trip down with me." She turned to Jeff. "Mr. Carson, may I present M'sieur René Beluche, one of Jean Lafitte's principal lieutenants."

Jeff's hand was clasped by Beluche, a stocky, swarthy man in scarlet broadcloth coat, hand-tooled Continental boots, and tight-fitting white trousers. Jeff judged Beluche to be about Helen's age: flecks of white highlighted his jet black hair.

"Yes, I heard about this young fellow. Have your bags taken ashore, lad. Then report to M'sieur Jean at the Big House. Come, Helen, we've a lot to talk about. It's been a long lonely time since I saw you." He leaned down and kissed her again. Helping her into the carriage, he swung in after her and flicked his whip.

Jeff watched them go. Helen turned and waved toward him—languidly, he thought. So René Beluche was her lover. One of Lafitte's lieutenants was his rival. He must be careful. He'd learned never to make an enemy before he had made a friend. Whistling to Ramon to follow him, he walked up the shady red-bricked street toward Lafitte's imposing house.

CHAPTER X

WITH a sweated Ramon following him, toting the heavy valise and mumbling complaints under his breath, Jeff walked toward the Big House looming grandly at the end of the street. He passed the small houses he had seen from the schooner, each flush with the beaten path that served as sidewalk. He had an occasional glimpse of gardens in the back. As Helen had said, some were carefully tended and neatly painted with flowering window boxes, others were shabby in the extreme.

A man sprawled in the doorway of one house. He was sound asleep and naked, his torso covered with golden hairs that caught the glint of the sun. He slept so soundly that the swarm of flies crawling over his body did not disturb him. His mouth was open, mucus seeped from his nostrils, and he snored raucously. He was a disgusting sight, but his indifferent nakedness brought one fact home to Jeff, this was a man's town; here men did as they wanted.

A slatternly wench, also naked, leered at him from an open window, her plump breasts hanging over the sill, her body marked with purplish bruises, her head a tangle of matted curls. She smiled a provocative greeting, and he smiled back at her, pausing for the moment to remove his hat and wipe his forehead with an already sopping handkerchief.

"*Ay qué hombre!*" She hailed him, closing one eye with a suggestive wink. "And hung likes a stud horse, I wager. You're new around here, *Verdad?* Ain't seen you before, 'cause if I had I'd remember it. A handsome young stud is hard to come by here. Mostly old bastards who've been to sea so long they don't appreciate what a woman's got between her legs."

He grinned back at her audacity, and this encouraged her. He could see poor Ramon wetting his lips with his tongue and staring at the brown, rose-tipped breasts of the girl.

"Why don't you come in? *Venga!* That goddamn Pieter, he's passed out. It's the bastard's day off, and he's been drunk since last night. Ain't no chance of his coming to, and even if he does, he's a puny varmint. Been needing me a man all night, and try as I can, I can't get him up. Like playing with a dishrag, it is. Won't take you a minute, man." She stood up, fingering herself lasciviously. "Go around to the back door so's you won't disturb the damned Dutchman."

He replaced his hat and grinned at her, shaking his head. "Thanks for the invitation, lovey, but just can't at the moment. Got to see M'sieur Lafitte at the Big House."

"Then come back when you git finished with him. Just can't wait to git my hands on you." Her finger moved faster in the dark triangle at her thighs.

"Perhaps." He doffed his hat and motioned to the bug-eyed, open-mouth Ramon to come along.

"She shore a forward wench." Ramon was wishing she had asked him in. Her fast-whirling finger had almost hypnotized him.

"Shut your mouth, boy. She's no wench. She's a white woman."

"But she's a whore, Mastah Jeff."

"But a white whore, so mind your manners down here. I don't care what you ride, but we don't want to get into trouble."

"No suh, Mastah Jeff. This yere's a funny place. Ain' never seen its like before. Nekkid men a-sleepin' practically on the street, 'n' a woman standing nekkid fingerin' herself at her window. Funny place." He picked up the valise to follow Jeff.

Jeff wondered if the whole village of Grande-Terre

would be like this. Why not? The women who came here were probably tougher than their sisters in Tchoupitoulas Street, where Ramon had taken him to visit the cribs. What other type of woman would be attracted by these rough men, gathered from the four corners of the earth, and who were actually murderers and pirates, no matter what Lafitte called them? A step down from the cribs. Still, the girl at the window had been young and might be pretty if she scoured off the grime and combed her hair. At any rate, there apparently was no dearth of women here—if you didn't care what your women were. He had been propositioned five minutes after landing.

He arrived at the wide brass-studded door of the Big House, sweating profusely and out of breath. He banged the heavy brass knocker and the door was opened for him. Sending Ramon around to the rear of the house with the valise, Jeff entered and took the chair a grave-faced old Negro indicated. It was a relief to sit down under the cooling draft of an immense ceiling fan which was operated by a nude black boy in the corner. The boy lay on his back and slowly moved one leg, activating a rope attached to his ankle and the fan. At the same time, oblivious of Jeff's presence, he vigorously manipulated an erection abnormally huge for his skinny body.

"M'sieur Jean, he a-spectin' yo', mastah." The old man bowed and turned to leave when he caught sight of the boy in the corner. "Yo', Sammy, yo' stop a-doin' that or I a-goin' to lambaste yo' proper. Yo' want hair growin' in yore palms?" He apologized to Jeff, muttering something about how shameless the younger generation was, before shuffling out of the room in his worn carpet slippers. The boy in the corner raised himself on one elbow, looked at Jeff indifferently, then lay down and began battering his rod again.

Jeff ignored him. He looked around the immense room —costly Persian carpets, carved and gilded armchairs, pendant crystal chandeliers, and a broad staircase that led to the second floor. He had never been in Europe, but he had heard about the palace of the Sun King at Versailles, which had been gutted by the Revolutionists. He imagined it must have been something like this. Certainly, it was far more elegant than either The Georgics or Willow Oaks. Yet when he examined it closely, he saw thick coatings of dust on polished tables, wine stains on the damask of upholstered chairs, and cobwebs graying the luster of the chandeliers. Again, he realized this was a man's place—this house and all of Barataria.

It was, however, astonishing to come upon so much elegance at the ass-end of nowhere. Certainly, the dark little smithy in New Orleans had not prepared him for it, nor had the squalid houses he had passed since landing. He did not have long to wait until the old colored man returned. The boy in the corner had finished his fist exercises and was dabbing at his stomach with a dirty rag. The old man did not look at the boy again. Instead he beckoned for Jeff to accompany him, and although acting as Jeff's guide, managed to stay a respectful step behind him.

They passed through tall double doors into an oriental drawing room whose elaborate *chinoiserie* must once have been cargo on some clipper en route from Canton to England. The old man, scuffling ahead of Jeff, opened a green baize door into a smaller room where, behind a broad mahogany desk, Jean Lafitte sat, his curly black hair moving in the breeze from another ceiling fan operated by another naked black boy in a corner. Lafitte did not rise to greet Jeff, but extended a cordial hand across the desk and gestured to a carved, gilded Empire chair. Jeff stared at the huge initial "N" on the back.

Lafitte's quick eyes detected Jeff's interest in the ornately carved initial. "Yes." He nodded toward the chair. "It belonged to Napoleon. A man I admire. It's no secret, to tell you that we plan to rescue Napoleon from St. Helena. We have built a house for him in New Orleans. Dominique You is going to bring him back here in the schooner *Seraphine*, which we have only recently acquired. The *Seraphine* is rated the fastest ship on the seas today. Perhaps I'll send you along with Dominique when the time comes."

Jeff was emboldened by Lafitte's smile of welcome. "First I've got to prove myself to you, M'sieur Lafitte. You know nothing about me yet, but I hope to make you soon discover that I am here to serve you in any way possible and to the best of my abilities." God, he hoped his words were not too hellishly stilted and formal; he just wanted desperately to make a good impression.

Lafitte compressed his lips and studied Jeff under veiled eyelids, appraising him. "Naturally we're going to give you a workout. That's why we brought you down here. We need men who can take responsibility. Men who are equipped to meet and deal with the public. For that, we look for educated men, businessmen, respectable looking men. Men who are the peers of the plantation owners we sell to. I've hundreds of good men here—men who'd go to hell and back for me—but I admit that most of them are riffraff, sweepings of docks from London to Tangiers. The finest men in the world aboard a ship, but no good in dealing with a stiff-necked plantation owner. I've got my brother and Dominique You in New Orleans. I've got René Beluche here. But I need more men of their caliber. Business is expanding, and we four can't handle it alone. That's why I'm hoping that you will work out." He poured two glasses of sherry from a decanter on his desk and offered one to Jeff.

"I'll do my best, M'sieur Lafitte." Somehow, sitting here in Napoleon's armchair across the desk from this purposeful man, Jeff felt more self-confident than he had ever felt before. He sipped the topaz wine, letting it travel slowly over his palate and generate a warm, comforting glow in his stomach. He felt as if he had been born for this moment, this place.

"Well, there's a lot to learn. Tell me, Carson—hell, I can't call you Carson—what's your other name? Jefferson, isn't it?"

"But most people call me Jeff."

"Jeff it is. Tell me, what do you know about niggers?"

"A little. Not too much." Jeff felt his heart quicken and wondered just how he should answer Lafitte's question. "My mother has a plantation in Mississippi. She has started to breed slaves there for the coming market, and I've had a little experience with blood lines. I've helped her pick out dams and sires who should produce good stock." It was on the tip of his tongue to tell Lafitte that he had once been a good friend of Baxter Simon's and had stayed at Willow Oaks Plantation, which Lafitte surely knew by reputation. He decided, however, to keep this fiction to himself.

"So *madame, votre mère,* has joined the ranks of those who will be competing with us in another ten or fifteen years. She isn't the only one. There's another Alabama plantation doing the same thing. Raising damned fine niggers, I'm told, but just at present *we* have the market. For every slave bred in this country, we can supply ten, even a hundred fine specimens direct from Africa.

"What I want of you, young fellow, is to learn to judge nigger flesh. That's going to be your job here. I'm not going to waste you on the folderols and the foofaraws we have for the trade in Royal Street. I can't see you measuring off yards of velvet and picking out buttons to match some society lady's frock. I want you to become an expert judge of blacks. I'm going to place you in the hands of René Beluche, who is the best judge of niggers here or anywhere else."

Beluche! Helen's former lover and a potential enemy. "I've already met him," Jeff volunteered. "He was at the pier to meet Mrs. Latimer."

"Poor René's had a hankering after that woman for a long time." Lafitte winked a knowing eye. "Strange, too, because René's never taken up with any woman here for very long."

Jeff swallowed hard. Here was the complication he had been dreading. Not that he couldn't exist without nights with Helen. The question was whether she was going to be difficult about it.

"René's a hot-tempered man. Pay no attention to him if he flies off the handle. He'll get over it and try to be a better friend to you than he was before. But don't rile him. Like all of us, he's led a hard life. He's in the habit of commanding men." Lafitte half rose from his desk and shook Jeff's hand, while pulling vigorously at a bell cord beside his desk.

"First of all, get settled in. I've allotted you a house,

but it will probably have to be cleaned out. I know you brought a servant with you, but perhaps you'll need another to keep your house and get your meals?"

"That would be fine, sir. I'm afraid Ramon has not much experience in cooking and cleaning—" He cut his sentence short when a tall mulatto man entered the room. He was immaculately dressed in the height of fashion. His long hair was oiled and fell to his shoulders. He wore a long-tailed coat of wine-colored broadcloth, and his white trousers were strapped under varnished boots. He stood at the door, his eyes on Lafitte, but Jeff was sure he had not escaped the man's peripheral vision.

"Lionel," Lafitte said, "this is Jeff Carson, whom I spoke to you about. Carson is going to stay with us here at Grande-Terre. Take him to the house you allotted him. He wants a woman to keep house for him. Get her started cleaning up for him. Issue her chits so she can lay in supplies from the store. Then take him to Beluche. He'll either be at the compound or in his own house. If he's neither place, he'll be at the guest house where Madame Latimer is staying."

The mulatto bowed, then finally looked at Jeff. "Welcome to Barataria and Grande-Terre, Mr. Carson."

Lafitte stood up, walked around the corner of the desk, and put an arm over Jeff's shoulder. "Get settled and rested up, Jeff. Get acquainted with the place. Make yourself at home."

"I shall, sir, and thank you." Jeff walked toward the door, then turned. "A favor, M'sieur Lafitte."

"If possible."

"Would you mind if I took some of this man's time to guide me around and give me the lay of the land?"

Lafitte smiled and shrugged.

"By all means. Use him as long as you want."

Jeff preceded the servant (or so he thought he was) through the rooms to the entrance hall. Out of curiosity he glanced at the boy in the corner whose leg was still waving to power the fan. His hands were still and pearly beads glistening on his black stomach testified to the successful culmination of renewed efforts. Lionel opened the big door for Jeff and they passed out into the heat and the sun.

The mulatto followed a step behind him along the sun-brazed street. Jeff saw the Dutchman still asleep in his doorway, but there was no trace of his slatternly woman. Probably she had inveigled someone else into the house and was entertaining him while the man continued to sleep off his drunken stupor.

The street ended at the waterfront. They walked along another street, which lacked the shade of the live oaks. Here houses were spaced farther apart. After only a short walk they came to a house built of wood. It was a little sprucer than the others, with the distinction of a courtesy veranda and a few blooming jasmine shrubs in front. Several tall palms grew in the rear.

Lionel signaled for Jeff to turn in, then went before him and unlocked the door. "Keep your door locked when you are away," he warned. "I don't think any of the men in the settlement would steal from you, but I'm not so sure about the women. They come and they go. Most of them are a pretty bad lot."

Something about the fellow's precise speech, especially the vowels, intrigued Jeff. Lionel spoke with a clipped English accent, far different from the slurred vowels and shortened words of the gumbo-speaking Negro. "Where do you come from, Lionel?"

"From Barbados, sir."

The snug little house was hot and stuffy. Smells of meals long since cooked and eaten dissipated when Lionel opened the casement windows and allowed a cool breeze to blow in from the bay. There was a knock on the door. Lionel opened it, and Ramon was standing there with the valise. The naked teen-ager who had guided Ramon spun on his white-bottomed feet and ran back up the street.

Jeff sat in a Windsor chair by the door, mopping his face as he took stock of his new abode. The fair-sized room had windows front and back to allow cross ventilation. A small fireplace bisected one wall, with dirty brass firedogs standing among old ashes and refuse. An elaborate but badly tarnished silver candelabrum occupied a table in the center of the floor. Small tables with silver candlesticks stood beside each chair. One large wing chair, its red damask upholstery frayed and torn, looked comfortable. The floor was of wide boards, stained and spotted with candle grease, and there was a fine although much soiled Turkey carpet covering it. Lionel led Jeff through one of the two doors of the room.

Jeff admired a huge four-poster bed hung with embroidered curtains of Chinese silk. He felt the feather mattress and found it soft and comfortable. A walnut armoire, too big for his modest wardrobe, stood against one wall. A mahogany chest of drawers against another wall, a tripod shaving mirror, and a straight-backed chair completed the furnishings. Wispy red curtains billowed inward when Lionel opened the windows to let in the wind from the sea.

Jeff called Ramon in to unpack the valise and put his clothes away, and then followed Lionel into the living room and through the other door into a kitchen where a great fieldstone fireplace yawned blackly in one wall, flanked by a hanging assortment of pots and kettles. Discovering a bunk with frowsy blankets and a soiled pillow in one corner, Jeff called Ramon from the bedroom. "You'll sleep here," he said.

"You can draw supplies from the commissary," Lionel said, "and the well is only a few steps away. Several trips a day to the well by your boy or other servant should keep you supplied. And, by the way"—he glanced quizzically at Jeff—"do you prefer a boy or a girl for housekeeper? Many of the men have been to sea for so long that they have lost their taste for women and prefer a boy both for housekeeping and for bedding, but let me warn you: the boys here are as bad as the women."

"I've never lost my taste for women," Jeff said. "I'd prefer a girl for housekeeping, and most certainly for bedding. Someone who knows how to cook and can keep a place clean. Someone to wash and starch my shirts, and, if she is not too damnably ugly, to bed with when the urge comes over me."

"Now that is going to be a difficult combination to find."

Lionel scratched his crotch. "We've got women here, but they're a worthless lot. I can get you a fine cook and housekeeper in old Mother Christmas, but you wouldn't bed her if she were the last woman on earth. And I can find you a nice bed companion in a little Spanish girl who, they say, is hotter than a charcoal brazier—but she couldn't make your breakfast coffee." He hesitated another moment, then snapped his fingers. "I've got it! The right solution for you. As long as you don't insist on a raving beauty. We've got a girl here called Gretchen—German or Dutch, I don't know which. Plain as a board wall, but she's clean, and men she has been with report she is a tolerable cook."

"Clean and neat and a good cook!"

"And like all plain girls"—Lionel winked wisely—"she appreciates a lover. She was shacked up with old man Trudeau, who died. He was too old to do anything for her."

"She's never had a real man?"

Lionel looked at him appraisingly. "Well, Trudeau was no real man, but I assure you she's had her share. She wouldn't be here if she hadn't. Far as I know, she's never lived with one permanently. Stayed longest with a Barbary Coast sailor—a little squirt who stood about five feet high —who went to sea, and then she took up with Trudeau. But I'll swear to one thing. She kept her men clean, well fed, and happy."

"Bring her around."

"I suggest, sir, that when I take you around the settlement, you stop in at the women's house and do your own picking. She'll be there, but it's best you make your own choice. Some other girl might appeal to you. Another word of warning; you'll be begged and importuned by all the girls there because everyone wants a steady man. But there's not one of the sluts I would recommend except Gretchen."

Jeff followed Lionel out of the kitchen into the living room and saw Ramon standing there. Spying a broom beside the wall, he thrust it into the boy's hand, told him to get busy, sweep out as much of the dirt as he could, and make the house as livable as possible. He and Lionel would return later with a woman who would do the cooking for them. Lionel told Ramon to go to the kitchen door of the Big House at lunchtime and he would be fed. When they left, Ramon was raising more dust with his broom than he was sweeping out.

The village proved larger than Jeff had envisaged it from the deck of the schooner that morning. Lionel informed him there were between four and five hundred men in the town, probably an equal number of women, and some fifty or so boys in their teens. Lionel had been born a slave in Barbados, he told Jeff, but had been captured by the Lafittes while on a journey to Trinidad. He did not know whether he was a slave or not. Because he had been fairly well educated in Barbados, he had become Jean Lafitte's right-hand man and enjoyed a position of prestige over the internal and domestic workings of the settlement. René Beluche, as Lafitte's lieutenant in the settlement, made executive decisions and ran the business of the place under Lafitte's supervision.

In their walk around the town Lionel showed Jeff the general store where groceries and provisions were issued on presentation of a chit; the small red-brick building that served as a calaboose where drunken and obstreperous men—and sometimes women—where confined on occasion; the promenade where the unattached women and boys strolled in the evening; the storehouses for goods en route to Royal Street; and, last of all, the barracoon. Lionel told Jeff he was not permitted to enter the slave enclosure, as this was under Beluche's supervision. They stood outside for some moments and Jeff could hear the mournful sound of the plaintive songs of the homesick Africans within, longing for the land from which they had been torn.

Finally, after an hour or so of strolling around with Lionel pointing out places of interest, Jeff found himself in front of a substantially larger house than all the rest. Unattached women stayed here until claimed by some man who wanted a change in his housekeeping arrangements or who, like Jeff, was new in the settlement. With a renewed warning about what would ensue inside, Lionel ushered Jeff through the open front door into a large living room.

No sooner had Jeff stepped over the threshold than he was the center of a mass of grasping women whose cries and screams brought others running from different parts of the house. They overwhelmed him. He was afraid they would pull his clothes off. Some were certainly trying. Avid hands sought his crotch. No sooner had one succeeded in grasping his fly than her hand was yanked away by another. Hot lips pressed against him, naked breasts dangled before him, and feminine flesh surrounded him. In the frantic milling of women he could distinguish only a few individual cries.

"I'm Elisa. Try me, man."

"Pay no attention to the bitch. It's me, Marietta, that you want."

"She's got the pox. She's a regular fireship."

"No, no, me, *señor*. I'm clean and I do things in bed no other woman can."

"Quiet! All of you!" Lionel raged. Reluctantly the female tide ebbed from Jeff and retreated to the other side of the room where the women continued to exhibit their charms. "Now line up, all you sluts. Come over here one by one so that this man can look you over and make a choice. He's looking for a housekeeper, not a two-bit whore, so behave yourselves."

Jeff had never encountered such a motley pride of women. They ranged in age from fifteen years to a couple of wrinkled old harridans in their fifties, who apparently realized that no amount of paint or powder could conceal their aging. The women were clad in everything from plain cotton shifts to the rags and tatters of finery, but lace on elaborate ball gowns was torn, embroidery unraveled, and most dresses were dirty and grease-stained. Hopefully, they passed before him one by one. Several were young and pretty enough for his consideration, but each time he hesitated, Lionel shook his head.

"She's a wanton hussy. Stabbed her last man."

"I'm your slave, honey. Don't you want to finger me?"

"You don't want her. They say she's fine in bed, but she stays there all day."

"Not that one. She's only interested in other girls."

"They say this one's poxed. Better stay away from her."

Jeff delayed until Lionel presented a girl with obvious pride.

"This is Gretchen."

Jeff looked her over. Indeed she presented a far different appearance than the others. She *was* plain, but not ugly, and her cleanliness shone out in those tawdry surroundings like a ray of sunlight on a dreary day. Her round face was scrubbed clean and radiated health. She wore no trace of the heavy *maquillage* some of the others had plastered on. Large cornflower-blue eyes, free from sooty mascara, gazed back at him over rose-pink cheeks. Her nose was short and uptilted, but her lips were full and red. When she smiled at him, her teeth were white and even. Her pale blond hair was parted in the middle and combed back tightly. By the size of the chignon at the nape of her neck, Jeff judged her hair might fall below her waist when loosened. She was a tall girl—a Teutonic Juno—with magnificent mammaries and ample hips. In contrast to the others, her cotton dress was clean. Her bare legs were milk white, her calves well rounded.

Jeff continued to study her and, in contrast to the voluptuous leers of the others, she returned his glance shyly. Despite her prim smile he somehow sensed she wanted him to choose her. He made his decision. Perhaps her decorous lips did not promise as much as the tongue-circling invitations of the others, but her full tits and ample ass promised other delights.

"Would you like to keep house for me, Gretchen?"

"If you wish, *mein Herr.*" He detected no urgency in her words, yet he saw the brightening of desire in her pale eyes.

"Do *you* wish it, Gretchen?" He wanted her to come voluntarily, not because she felt she was forced.

She hesitated another moment. "It would be nice to have a house of my own again. Here with all these females is no life for a woman."

"Granted you would like a house of your own. How about me? Do you like me?" He still wanted her to commit herself.

"Indeed, *mein Herr.* You are young and sturdy and

what woman would not like to serve you?"

"Can you cook well?"

"My mother taught me in the old country. Also I can wash and iron and keep you and your house clean. I can do anything you want me to do. I can serve you well."

"Lionel will tell you where my house is. Could you get it cleaned up a little and have supper waiting for me? My boy Ramon is there. He will help you to get water and do the heavy work for you."

"Ja." Her smile broadened. "I shall be most happy to serve you, *mein Herr*. Every woman here envies me this chance. I'll have a clean house and a meal waiting for you."

"I'll give her a chit, and she can take it to the store and draw provisions." Lionel was pleased Jeff had taken his counsel. "It's the third house around the corner on River Street," he instructed Gretchen, "and Mr. Carson will be back later in the afternoon."

Lionel turned to go and once more the girls pounced on Jeff. He managed to fight them off, but in trying to adjust his clothes, he found three buttons missing from his fly. He pulled up his trousers as best he could do to hide the loss and followed Lionel out the door. Gretchen might have been far down the list of his choices had it not been for Lionel, but even with her plainness, she was undoubtedly the best of the lot. She was clean and wholesome-looking, despite the life she had lived in Barataria, and that was saying a lot for her character. Gretchen was going to suit him well, and, he smiled to himself, that big bosom and those fantastic hips would be softer than a feather bed.

Lionel awaited him outside the house. He would take Jeff to the office of René Beluche where he would leave him.

Beluche! Helen's old lover. Jeff dreaded the encounter, but he could not let Helen interfere. Beluche was his whole career. He wasn't going to antagonize this man who was practically all-powerful here. No, sir. It wasn't worth it. He could satisfy himself with Gretchen's full breasts as much as he could with Helen's tantalizing gyrations. Women here were a dime a dozen, and if he didn't like

108

Gretchen, he could stroll out on the evening promenade and pick up anything he wished, including the clap. But, he promised himself, one thing he would not do—he would not antagonize Beluche. There was too much at stake.

CHAPTER XI

LIONEL left Jeff at the massive gates of the slave barracoon, telling him to be sure to signal him if he needed anything in the way of domestic stores or if he had complaints about Gretchen. At the gateway, Jeff's way was barred by a grizzled man gripping a musket in both hands. The fellow was scarfaced, with a black patch over one eye. Jeff explained that he was here to see Mr. Beluche on orders from Jean Lafitte. The guard scrutinized him carefully, scratched at his armpits in idiotic perplexity, then dug into his pocket and produced a soiled scrap of paper. He squinted his good eye at the writing before he asked if he might be facing Jefferson Carson. Upon Jeff's assent, the man grudgingly lowered his musket, opened a small door in the big gate, and beckoned Jeff through.

Inside Jeff saw hundreds of blacks milling in the blazing sun of the large corral. Some were aimlessly pacing like caged animals; some hunkered in the shade of the stockade wall, talking and gesticulating. Other desolated souls stretched flat on the ground, oblivious to the stench, heat, and blast of sun. In the center of the corral a tall black stood beating his chest and crying out the same unintelligible phrase over and over again. However, all was not complete despair. Jeff hesitated, watching a big buck vigorously and unashamedly sodomizing a slim youth who was hunched before him on the ground. The boy's legs were entwined around the big fellow while he screamed anguishedly sweet encouragement to his ravisher.

An acrid stink of sweat, offal, and excrement assailed Jeff's nostrils. For a moment the stench was so bad that he was afraid he would lose his meager shipboard breakfast. With difficulty, he gulped down the acrid bile in his throat and stumbled along behind the man to the small house near the stockade gate. The guard bawled Jeff's name through an open window and a moment later the door was opened and Beluche stood on the threshold smiling, his hand outstretched.

The putrid stench permeated the little house (which Jeff rightfully assumed was Beluche's office) despite the ubiquitous small boy in a corner whose rope propelled the sweep of a big ceiling fan. Although it did not dispel the terrible stench, the fan at least made it bearable. Jeff's stomach settled down, and he was able to return Beluche's greeting with a wan smile instead of the torrent of vomit he had feared. He was, however, glad to reach the safety of the chair to which Beluche had gestured. As he sank into it, he realized that he must be pale. He felt as though all the blood in his body had drained into his stomach and congealed there in a hard lump. He was happy to see Beluche lean over the desk and nod his head to indicate his understanding of the situation.

"This unholy stink get you, Carson?" His voice was kindly, solicitous. "Pretty awful when it first hits you. Enough to make a strong man puke. But, believe me, your nose soon gets accustomed to it. After a while you don't even notice it. I know because it stopped affecting me a long time ago. When we first took up slavery as a business, I thought I'd vomit every five minutes, and sometimes I did. Have a glass of wine." He poured a glass of deep ruby port for Jeff, who sipped it slowly. Jeff wondered how it would sit on his stomach what with no lunch and the glass of sherry he had drunk at Lafitte's.

"You see, Carson," Beluche poured a glass for himself and sipped it—"I was expecting you about this time so I delayed my lunch until you arrived. If the nigger stench hasn't taken away your appetite, we'll eat here at my desk. I usually do because it saves me time." He jangled a bell on his desk. A knock on the door followed and a stark-naked Negro giant entered. He deposited two linen-covered trays on Beluche's desk. With a deft movement of his wrist, he whipped off both napkins and Jeff saw delicious cold plates for two. Now that he had recovered from his nausea, he felt he could do justice to the lunch.

Beluche poured hot tea from the teapot on his tray into a delicate eggshell-thin Chinese cup and handed it to Jeff, assuring him that the hot tea would certainly settle his stomach. It did and Jeff joined Beluche in eating. He decided that although the stench had precipitated his queasy feeling, an empty stomach had caused it.

Beluche was a congenial host, attentive, courteous, and with a personality that invited intimacy. Jeff felt that while there might soon be trouble between them over Helen Latimer, he would be forced to yield to the other man's charm and good manners. Here was a man he would like to count as a friend; he would be willing to forego a few nights with Helen for this man's good will. As the brief glimpse of him that morning at the pier had hinted, Beluche was indeed a rugged, virile man, exuding masculinity from every pore. Although he was only of average height, his sturdy build and powerful shoulders made him seem taller than he actually was. His short hair, silvered at the temples, curled close to his head in tight ringlets. It seemed to have a vitality of its own, drawn from the man's vigorous body and glittering with sweat. He was clean-shaven, but blue shadow lingered along his square jaw. A diagonal scar across one cheek gave him a devil-may-care expression. His dark brown eyes, deep set under overhanging brows, were kindly and belied the otherwise dogged, almost savage face. Jeff had a feeling that the kindness in these eyes could change in a second to steely hatred. He shuddered to think of Beluche as an enemy.

Beluche wore no coat and suggested that Jeff take off his own and be comfortable. Jeff stood up to doff the broadcloth jacket and caught Beluche's eye staring at his gaping fly. Embarrassed, he apologized for the missing buttons, explaining what had happened at the women's dormitory. His recital was so dramatic that Beluche laughed, agreeing with Jeff that the women of Barataria were a carnivorous breed who would stop at nothing. Jeff sat down. He liked the man.

"We'll talk business while we eat," Beluche said. "We shall kill two birds with one stone." Beluche shoveled a forkful of food into his mouth. Slaving, he informed Jeff, was a comparatively new venture for the Lafitte organization. Previously, when vessels from Africa had been permitted to unload their black cargoes directly on the levees of New Orleans, there had been no reason for the Lafittes to traffic in ebony flesh. But now that Congress had outlawed legitimate importation of slaves from Africa, new ways had to be found to supply the plantations' insatiable demand for Negroes.

Fortunately there was still Spain. Traffic in slaves was still legal for Spanish ships. It had not been outlawed by the Spanish government because more and more slaves were required to work the cane plantations of Cuba, Santo Domingo, and Puerto Rico. A worker's life in the cane fields was a short one—eight years at the most, Beluche asserted—so there was a constant demand for new slaves on the islands. Spain—as always, hungry for gold—would not kill the goose that laid the golden egg, and cutting off the needed supply of black labor to her island plantations would mean just that. So what was the answer, Beluche asked.

Well, they had ways of solving the problem, Beluche answered his own question. First, operating under letters of marque issued by the Republic of Cartagena (at that time a small independent nation at war with Spain), they could legitimately capture a Spanish blackbirder or a slaver flying any flag, because any slaver except a Spaniard was operating illegitimately. Instead of bringing the captured slaver to Cartagena, however, they took it and its living cargo to Barataria, where the cargo was confiscated. When the slaves were sold in New Orleans, they brought a huge profit. There was, of course, another way to cash in. Did Jeff know what that was?

Jeff shook his head.

Beluche nodded portentously. If demand exceeded the supply of captured slaves, the Lafittes could always go to Havana, buy slaves, and smuggle them into the country at Barataria. A likely young buck bought for about three hundred dollars in Havana would bring about eight hundred dollars in New Orleans. Although the profit was limited to about five hundred dollars, in some ways this method paid off better than piracy. A trader buying in Havana would choose only the best, the strongest, the sturdiest of the *bozals* who had come from Africa legitimately. A captured shipload of slaves, however, might include the sickly, the unsightly, the weak, and the crippled. Some of the slaves were not worth selling and had to be disposed of.

Beluche added that it was a toss-up which method was the more profitable—consequently they used both. The market in Havana was steady, whereas they could never foresee with certainty when they might capture a blackbirder. By combining both sources, they were always sure their barracoons were full, ready to meet the demands of slave buyers.

But the source of supply, although an important factor, was not the only thing Jeff would have to learn about the slave business. Slaves had to be graded. Quality was as important as quantity. Each one of the African blacks must be examined thoroughly before he could be graded, and that in itself required training. Beluche did most of this work now, but he needed an assistant badly.

Slaves, he explained, at least male slaves—and that was about ninety percent of their business today—were graded as Fancy, First, Second, and Third Class. They received few Fancies from Africa. Today the trend in Fancies was for extremely handsome octoroons, quadroons, or even mulattos. Usually some admixture of white blood was necessary for a slave to qualify as a Fancy. However, on rare occasions, a pure black could qualify. He must be of perfect physique, tall, with excellent posture, and without blemish. These rare specimens brought unusually high prices either for plantation pets or for breeding.

The Prime Class comprised fine, strong, well-built, and good-looking African Negroes. One requisite for this class was a generous sexual endowment because slave buyers had a superstition that the larger a slave's penis and the heavier his testicles, the better breeder he would turn out to be. This, Beluche admitted—strictly *entre nous*—was a fallacy. The quality of a man's sperm did not depend on the size of his organ, but who was Beluche to disillusion purchasers? If this was what nigger buyers wanted, this was what he would sell them. Fortunately there was not much difficulty in this area because most Africans were well endowed. Those in the Prime Class were rarely sold as field hands but rather as studs to the big plantations, which anticipated the day when they could grow their own slaves.

First Class betokened good field workers, strong and healthy, but not necessarily good-looking. Second Class, of course, was a poorer grade, healthy but not as rugged physically. Third Class blacks were the bush niggers from the bottom of the barrel, but not the scrapings. The old and infirm, the sickly and the weak, were disposed of, as Beluche had previously mentioned. It cost too much to keep unsalable slaves. It was cheaper to get rid of them.

Yes, these were all things that Jeff must learn and it would take time. Once he began to make decisions on his own, an undervaluation of a slave could cost the Lafittes hundreds of dollars in profits. Conversely, if he classified a First Class as Prime, he would lose the respect and confidence of his customer.

Jeff sighed. There was more to this slave business than he had reckoned. However, he had a yardstick to go by. He remembered the black woman who reared him at Willow Oaks telling him that Ram was a Fancy. Ram certainly was an extraordinary-looking nigger. He could use his memory of Ram for judging, but he imagined there would be few who would compare with Ram, although he did not have a drop of white blood in him. At least Jeff knew something about niggers.

Carried away by his own thoughts, he had not been paying attention to Beluche, who was still talking on the same subject—slaves. He began to pay close attention. Slaves were going to be Jeff's business. The more he learned about them, the better.

So, Beluche was saying, the most important thing now was for Jeff to learn all he could about niggers. It was a big subject—one to which some men devoted their entire lives—and it wasn't easy to master because every nigger was different from every other nigger. Slaves were Beluche's business, and they were going to be Jeff's, so the more and the quicker he learned, the better. Yes? Jeff was willing to agree with him. At the back of his mind was the knowledge that he himself was a branded Negro on the run, and he wondered, if Beluche were grading him, how he would be rated. Extra Special Fancy, he assured himself.

They ate for a few moments in silence. Suddenly Beluche put down his fork with such force that it clattered against his plate. He stared across the table at Jeff. For some reason, Jeff sensed, the man was nervous. Beluche coughed, patted his mouth with his napkin, took another sip of wine, and then stared again. His mouth opened as though he wished to say something, and then he closed it. Finally he smiled oddly at Jeff and said, "You are a very good friend of Madame Latimer's, eh?"

"She introduced me to Dominique You," Jeff answered. "She has been my good friend."

"And mine, too." Beluche nodded. "The only woman I ever cared for deeply. I have known her since she was the most beautiful girl in the establishment which Madame Hortense runs in New Orleans. Did you know that she had once been there?"

"She confessed it to me. It did not alter my regard for her."

"It made her a more interesting person. Perhaps that is why she is the only woman who has ever really satisfied me." Beluche took a drink of his wine, drained the glass, and twirled the thin stem between his fingers, watching Jeff tautly.

Jeff worried over the trend of the conversation. He wanted to break the awkward silence. Unable to think of a new twist, he said nothing. Determined to give Beluche no cause to dislike him, he realized he must skirt this dangerous territory. Luckily he occupied the least involved corner of a confused emotional triangle. Helen desired him; Beluche desired Helen; but he himself didn't really care. He appreciated all that Helen had done for him, and he certainly owed her a debt of gratitude. But as long as he could not have Chloe, he was quite willing to go home and bed the plain and unfancy Gretchen.

Beluche persisted. "You have made love to Helen? Don't answer me, lad, I know you have. You're a damned attractive fellow, and I know Helen, even though I do not know you. I don't blame you. Any man would enjoy her. But . . ." He seemed at a loss as to just how to proceed.

"Set your mind at rest, Mr. Beluche." Jeff determined to be frank with this man. "I willingly relinquish any slight claim to Mrs. Latimer while she is here. Her short friendship with me is as nothing compared to the depth of your feelings. I would not in any way come between you."

For the first time Beluche smiled. "Ah, my friend, but that is exactly what I want you to do. Exactly! But I have not been able to put it into words. Now you have said it for me."

A faint glimmer of what Beluche was driving at suddenly dawned upon Jeff. He did not know whether or not he had guessed rightly. It would be better not to commit himself; let Beluche make the proposition if one were to be made.

"I mean this, Jeff." Beluche stretched his hand across the table and laid it on Jeff's wrist. "We can both enjoy Helen."

"Both of us?" Jeff was still not precisely sure what Beluche meant. He had feared incurring the man's anger and enmity, but if what he sensed were true, he wouldn't have to fight a duel (which he undoubtedly would lose) with Beluche; instead he would be cementing their friendship even more firmly.

"Yes, *un ménage à trois*. The three of us together. I can think of nothing more exciting. Absolutely nothing! Jeff, you are going to learn that this settlement at Grande-Terre is a strange place. All of us here have spent most of our lives at sea. So . . . what is the result? We enjoy our matings in different forms. We have expanded our horizons, so to speak. We have found more to enjoy than the ordinary coupling of man and woman. We appreciate variety. Why do you think we have a big selection of boys here? Because they add to our variety and enjoyment. As for me, I enjoy everything, yes, everything."

Jeff regarded Beluche's hand on his wrist. The slight pressure of Beluche's fingers did not exactly displease him: on the other hand, it did not excite him. In that simple gesture and the confession it symbolized, he saw an opportunity to ingratiate himself with this man. How better, or for that matter how more easily, could he consolidate his position here? Beluche's idea was not his first choice, but it might add a filip to his enjoyment. He remembered similar scenes back in Philadelphia, particularly the night he and his whore of the moment had invited an English sailor home with them. So why not, exactly why not?

Slowly he placed his hand over Beluche's.

"Something tells me, Mr. Beluche . . ."

"René, please."

"Something tells me, René, that you have hit upon an excellent idea. It will be a unique experience for me." Let Beluche think he had never done anything of this kind before. "Such things can be exciting *à deux,* but *à trois* . . ." He snapped his fingers. "Three together ought to be a hell of a lot more pleasure than two. So I am overjoyed at your proposition. We'll show the fair Helen something tonight that she'll never forget."

"Nor shall I." Beluche stood up and clasped Jeff's hand. "You know, Jeff, you're a handsome devil. You stir a man's blood."

"Thank you, René." Jeff grasped Beluche's hand. He drew down the corners of his mouth in a mock grimace. "First I have a weird confession to make to you. Helen already knows about it and bears with me, but I had better explain it to you. For some reason I can't accomplish a goddamned thing when I am absolutely naked. It's some strange quirk in my mind, I suppose. I just have to wear a shirt or I stay as limp as a damp rope end. Will you mind?"

"Mind?" Beluche pumped Jeff's hand. "Why should I? I once knew a fellow who could do nothing unless he wore hobnailed boots. Damned tough on the mattress, and not too easy on the girl, but that's the way it was. We all have strange quirks when it comes to the old-fashioned joys of fornication. Well, I've told you mine and you've told me yours, so we are even. We'll say no more about it and I'll pick you up at your house at eight."

"At eight it is, René, and I hope to hell that the woman I engaged today will have some hot water waiting for me so I can take a bath."

"Which floozie did you take?" Beluche relinquished Jeff's hand.

"A Dutchie by the name of Gretchen."

Beluche laughed—a loud resounding sound—and clapped Jeff on the back. "I know her. You certainly picked a good one. She'll not only have a bath ready for you, boy, but she'll scrub you clean herself. She's a good girl compared to most of the sluts we have around here." He walked toward the door. "And now, Jeff, we have settled both business and pleasure. White meat tonight. We'll have our first lesson in judging black meat tomorrow. I daresay that, even in this short time, you find the stench not as unbearable as it was at first?"

Strangely enough, the stink did not bother Jeff anymore. He congratulated himself on how well this important interview had come off. Beluche was no longer the formidable employer nor the grim rival he had feared. Instead he was a companion, and after tonight, would be even more than that. Jeff breathed in deeply.

"You know, René, I can't smell a damned thing."

Jeff was so pleased with himself that he was not even aware of the irony of the situation: Bricktop, the branded fugitive, was about to learn the fine points of the slave trade!

CHAPTER XII

JEFF sauntered slowly back to his own house, congratulating himself on the successful and most unexpected outcome of his interview with René Beluche. Lady Luck was certainly with him. How could he ever doubt it? He had been providentially delivered from the debacle of a marriage with Minnie George. True, his well-guarded secret that he was not white had been discovered, but he had neverthe-

118

less escaped the wrath of old man George, the fury of his one-time owner Baxter Simon, and the blood lust of the plantation class, who would have enthusiastically tortured him to death. Simon and Willow Oaks, Minnie George and The Georgics, were all behind him, thank God! Now he could look forward to a future that, he hoped, held both Chloe and success with the Lafittes.

Chloe! Strange to think that Helen Latimer was her mother. Well, he should have guessed it because no two women were more alike. True, Chloe had youth and a freshness that had not yet been dimmed by Madame Hortense's whorehouse, but then, Helen had a mature beauty. Good God! Helen must have been a ball-cracking beauty in her day. Thinking about Helen, he found himself anticipating the night ahead of him. Instead of dreading it, he found himself titillated.

He wondered if René wanted more than anything else to sit and watch him and Helen frolic together. René was probably a *voyeur,* but if he wanted to enter into the melee, so much the better. Jeff didn't mind. He was experienced and broad-minded. Anything new and different was worth anticipating. What was it Beluche had said? *We enjoy our matings in different forms.* Well, come to think about it, so did he. Perhaps that was why he was so attracted to both Chloe and Helen. Not only were they mother and daughter—a new experience—but they, too, enjoyed variety in lovemaking. They were both more exciting than most women, who knew and practiced only the old tiresome techniques. He should have educated Minnie, however, she would have been an apt pupil.

The sun was high and the heat had increased. Jeff stopped in the shade of a massive live oak. He removed his broadcloth coat to let the breeze dry his shirt, which was plastered to his skin. Riverlets of sweat rolled down his legs and his groin itched. As there was nobody around, he felt free to scratch himself. But what did a little heat amount to? He was going to enjoy it here at Grande-Terre. He had a house of his own, and now, for the moment, he could let the images of Helen, Chloe, and Minnie slip from his mind and concentrate on his new housekeeper, Gretchen.

She was certainly not the type of woman he would have selected had he plenty to choose from. He had never favored stout women, but somehow she seemed to fit into the picture. It would be interesting to investigate her possibilities. She might be satisfying when he had an opportunity to explore her. The more he thought about her, the more exciting the prospect became, and he experienced a moment of regret. He almost wished he was not going with Helen and René tonight. He wanted something new and novel—but hell, what was he thinking about? This evening with Helen and René would be new and novel, and afterward Gretchen would still be there. He even considered pestering Gretchen this afternoon, but decided he'd better conserve his energies to satisfy Helen and René. What the hell. He'd never failed yet.

At least he would not have to fight a losing duel with René. And he was not going to be kicked out of Barataria because René was jealous of him and Helen. He blew a kiss to Lady Luck. Here he was, free, white—well, almost white—and almost twenty-one. The whole world was his succulent oyster, just waiting to be opened, and there was a damned good chance that his oyster would have a pearl in it.

When he arrived at his own house he found it a hive of bustling activity. Gretchen, skirts looped around her plump milk-white thighs and sleeves rolled up over her arms, was directing Ramon. Ramon, who had stripped off all his clothes except his white cotton underpants, knelt on the floor in a froth of soap suds. Neither heard Jeff open the door, and he stood for a moment listening to Gretchen berate Ramon in language that would shame a sailor.

"You goddamned worthless chunk of nigger meat! You lazy, shiftless brat of Satan! Put some elbow grease into that scrubbing or I'll wallop you again, and this time it won't be with a wet rag, it'll be with the flat of my hand. I'll lay you flat on your black ass."

"Please, Gretchen," Ramon whined, the sweat running down his face.

"Don't you Gretchen me, you black son-of-a-bitch. Remember who you are, nothing but a worthless slave. Remember when you speak to me again, it's *'Miss Gretchen'*—or I'll clout you."

"I'se goin' to tell my mastah on you," Ramon's high-pitched whine continued. "He don' wan' me a-doin' work like'n this. Mastah Jeff's good 'n' kind he is, 'n' he don' mean for his body nigger to be a-scrubbin' dirty floors."

Jeff laughed. "But he does want a good clean house, Ramon." He entered the room, stepping carefully on the soapy floor. "You do as Miss Gretchen tells you. And show respect."

"Oh, Mr. Carson!" Gretchen retreated a step and made an awkward little curtsy. "Wasn't expecting you home so soon. Haven't got this pig sty cleaned out yet and never will if I can't get some work out of this shiftless nigger."

"Keep him at it, Gretchen. And you, Ramon, mind what she tells you. She's the overseer here in the house, and if you don't mind her, I'll whip you myself and send you up in the next shipment to New Orleans to be sold as a field hand."

Ramon started to bawl, tears mingling with the sweat on his cheeks. "Don' do it, Mastah Jeff. Don' sell yore Ramon. Ramon loves his mastah 'n' always will. Yo' knows I do, Mastah Jeff."

"Then get to work and prove it to me. What can I do to help, Gretchen?"

"Nothing, sir. Your bedroom is all cleaned and ready. Had a hard time scrounging fresh sheets, but I managed to steal some. The kitchen is still filthy, but I'm leaving that till last. Will you eat supper here, sir?"

Jeff nodded.

"It'll be ready for you. I don't know what it will be yet, but you will be able to eat it." She looked at him, studying his face carefully. "Mr. Carson, you look peaked."

"It's been a busy day, Gretchen. I'm tuckered out."

"You should rest. Your bed is waiting."

Suddenly he realized that he was completely exhausted. He had had little sleep the night before, and he had risen early. No wonder he was bushed.

"Think I shall, Gretchen. I'm dog-tired."

She came to him, took him by the arm, and gently guided him across the wet floor to the bedroom. She opened the door and held it for him. His bed was freshly made, the pillows plumped up and covered with white pillowcases. She ducked past him and lowered the jalousies at the window, shutting out the glare of the sun, and then turned down the bedspread.

"I'll bring you coffee, sir, and then your nigger boy and I will work quietly. Here." She came close to him, reached up, and untied his cravat. He stood still while she stripped him of his sweaty clothes, stopping her only when she started to take off his shirt. He took the few steps to the bed and sank down upon it. She came over to stand beside him, her eyes lingering to admire his half-bared torso, then gently pulled the sheet up over him. He reached up a languid hand to fondle one of her breasts. He could feel the hardness of her nipples through the thin cotton of her dress.

"Would you like I should sleep with you and clean the house later?" She smiled at him.

"No, Gretchen. Go ahead with your cleaning. I'll sleep alone. Wake me when supper is ready, and I'll take a bath and dress. I've got to be ready by eight. Mr. Beluche is going to call for me."

"No need for you to dress for dinner, Mr. Carson. I'll bring it in here on a tray and then I'll have hot water ready for your bath."

"Thank you, Gretchen. I have a feeling we are going to get along well together." Already he was so sleepy that he could scarcely keep his eyes open. She tiptoed out of the room. When she returned with his coffee, he was sleeping so soundly she didn't wake him. She put the coffee down on the table beside the bed, walked softly across the floor, and closed the bedroom door so that Ramon could not see. Then she tiptoed back to the bed and looked down at Jeff's sleeping form. She admired his face and the sturdy outlines of his chest, disclosed by the unbuttoned shirt. She slipped her hand under the sheet. Her fingers sought and found and marveled. Ach, but she was a lucky girl! Regretfully, she withdrew her hand, walked out, and closed the door behind her.

Early the next morning Jeff and René Beluche closed the door of Helen's house behind them and confronted each other for a brief moment on her doorstep. In the bright sunshine of the morning their experiences of the night before seemed fantastic. Like a couple of truant schoolboys, they winked solemnly at each other and grinned. They strolled along the dusty *banquette* toward the stockade.

It had been a night of strange and unbridled bliss. Both were thoroughly satisfied and emotionally exhausted. There were episodes which Jeff tried hard to remember and others he would as willingly forget. It was over, and he was closer to Beluche than he wanted to admit. Their steps lagged, and Jeff looked forward to the short respite they would have in René's office while they waited for their coffee to be prepared.

Neither discussed the events of the previous night, for their memories of any particular episode were vague. The writhing tangle of arms, legs, and bodies in every conceivable position was now, in the bright light of morning, difficult to separate in recollection.

When they had finished the hot coffee and the croissants, which had seemingly come from nowhere in the hands of Beluche's black servant, René yawned, stretched, and managed to get to his feet, offering a helping hand to Jeff.

"Getting too old for this sort of thing," he admitted.

"I'll never be the man you are." Jeff put an arm around his shoulders, "And now, what about my starting to learn something about our stock in trade?"

"Good idea." Beluche walked across the room and opened the door. He waited for Jeff to precede him into the courtyard with its shifting slough of black humanity.

Against one of the outer walls, not far from Beluche's office, an open lean-to with supports of barked tree trunks and roof of palm thatch provided a spot of shade. Under it were two rudely made armchairs facing a circular, raised platform about a foot high and some three feet in diameter. The same naked black buck who had served their breakfast now stood beside the chairs, awaiting their arrival.

It was a relief to get into the shade and sit down. Beluche beckoned to the black.

"Jeff, this is Mosho, and he knows quite a lot about niggers himself. He ought to, because according to his story, he's the son of some tin-pot sultan in Africa who was a big slave dealer there. He's a good boy, Mosho is, and you'll find him willing and helpful. He'll do anything you ask." He looked up at the black and gestured toward Jeff. "Mosho, this is Master Carson, who has come here to be my assistant. You'll treat him the same as you treat me, and you will help him in every way possible."

Mosho showed a smile of white teeth and knelt before Jeff. He lifted Jeff's hand and placed it on his head, then stood up, awaiting his orders.

"All right, Mosho, let's get to work. Bring us a man."

As Mosho turned to leave them, Beluche explained, "None of the men you see in the corral have been inspected or graded. You see here"—he pointed to a collection of thonged wooden discs on the ground beside the chairs— "our method of grading." He picked up a random handful and dangled them before Jeff. "After a man has been examined, we put one of these around his neck. Blue is for Fancies, red for First Class, white for Second Class, and yellow for Third. If I consider a man absolutely worthless, he gets a black disc, which means he will be disposed of. Once graded, the men are taken to separate barracoons for a course of special diets, exercise, and grooming. Naturally the Fancies and the First Class men get special attention, so their barracks are somewhat better than the others. You'll see all this later."

Jeff's eyes scanned the pile of tokens. He noticed that the red and white discs were considerably larger than the other colors. He was about to ask about this when Mosho returned, leading a black across the enclosure. The slave was little more than a boy—an adolescent of about sixteen —and it was apparent that he was rigid with fright. He walked with faltering steps, and when Mosho pushed him up onto the little platform, Jeff saw he was trembling, the muscles of his body contracting spasmodically.

"Damn you, Mosho." René was irritated. "You made a poor choice for our first man." Beluche appraised the boy with his eyes. "It's difficult to categorize these younger boys. Damned poor market for them. They're not much good as field hands, and they don't bring a very high price. Of course, they're a good investment because they'll reach their prime in a few years, but they must be fed in the meantime. Now, you watch and I'll give you an idea how to proceed. Mosho will bring a grown man next."

To overcome the boy's nervousness, Beluche walked to the platform where the boy stood and laid a gentle hand on his arm, stroking it and making reassuring, although unintelligible, sounds. In a few moments the boy had quieted down and looked at Beluche with bovine eyes wide open. Beluche continued to croon more reassurance, and although the lad did not understand the words, he could gather from Beluche's tone of voice that he had nothing to fear. With his free hand Beluche reached into his pocket for a lozenge that he tried to pop into the boy's mouth. The boy clamped his teeth tightly.

"It's nothing but a horehound drop," Beluche explained to Jeff, "but he's afraid it might be poison." He laughed, put the lozenge in his mouth, and sucked on it, then took it out and placed it in the boy's mouth. The lad sucked on it, liked the taste, and grinned his thanks at Beluche. "It's wonderful how a bit of sweet will calm them down. Usually I have lemon drops, which they like better. Trouble is that most of these fellows have been badly treated on board the slavers, and they distrust all white men."

The boy relaxed and his smile broadened. Beluche patted him on the back and watched him suck with relish on his horehound drop.

"Come nearer, Jeff." Jeff stood beside the boy, who glanced up at him, fear born anew in his eyes. "Pet him a little. Let him know you are not going to hurt him. Lacking words, the only language we have with these fellows is physical. They all understand gentleness."

Jeff let his hand glide over the boy's smooth skin and spoke to him. "What is your name, boy?" he asked.

Mosho poured out a brief, unintelligible torrent, whereupon the boy brightened and answered.

"Ibrahim," he said.

"He a Moor," Mosho explained. "That boy, he black but he a Moor."

Beluche nodded knowingly and resumed petting the boy. "Now if Mosho's right, and he probably is, I think we've got something pretty good here. Could be either Mandingo or Hausa, as they are both Muslims, like many other smaller tribes in North Africa. We don't get many of them, but they make the best house servants. So let's get to work on Ibrahim. Notice how I go about it."

His practiced hands glided over the muscles of Ibrahim's chest, assaying their depth and strength with his fingertips. "This boy'll never be big and brawny," he explained. "He'll be slender, but I'll guarantee one thing: he'll be strong. His muscles will never bulge, but they'll be of whipcord strength. It's hard to explain how I know that, but you'll get the feel of it some day."

The practiced fingers left the boy's chest and examined his arms. René nodded in confirmation of his previous estimate. When he had finished with the boy's arms and back, his thumbs prodded deeply into his abdomen. The boy flinched but did not cry out. "Best way to find out if his guts are all right. If he'd yelped from pain at my prodding, I'd know something was wrong with him."

René hitched his chair closer to the platform and carefully examined the boy's legs, picking up each foot and tweaking the toes.

"I'd say he meets all requirements. He needs some good food and more exercise, which we'll give him."

"Is that all?" Jeff was surprised that the examination had taken so little time. This was going to be easy.

"Well, that's enough for his body," René answered. "Seems to be in good condition, and remember this: for a man to be in as good condition as this after all the mental and physical hardships he has gone through betokens a good strong body and a well-balanced mentality. The only fault I have to find with him is that he's a bit thin, but as I said before, we'll condition him before we offer him for sale. What's your opinion of him so far?"

"Seems like a well set up boy. Ought to develop into something pretty good in a few years."

"Exactly. Now I'll go a little further." He ran his fingers through the boy's hair, which fell to the nape of his neck in a dark mat of curls. "Got real hair, this one has," Beluche remarked. "That shows he's got some Moorish blood in him. A full nigger's hair is either kinky or peppercorned." He lifted the boy's chin in his hands and examined the face. "Good-looking kid, too, don't you think?"

Jeff studied the boy's face. Although the skin was dark, it was not the prune black of central Africa, but rather a rich tobacco brown. He had heavily lashed, almond-shaped eyes of so dark a brown that they seemed black. His lips were well shaped and not overly full. His teeth were white and even. When Beluche opened the boy's mouth and ran his fingers over the teeth, he nodded to Jeff and motioned for him to do likewise. Jeff found the teeth all intact.

"Now, we'll proceed further." Beluche returned to his chair and motioned to the boy to stand before him. "Every slave sold today," he explained to Jeff, "must be a potential breeder. There's no way we can guarantee that a fellow is not sterile, but we can find out a few things about him."

His fingers reached up and gently squeezed the boy's testicles. "Always be sure that a boy has two balls. Occasionally you'll find only one, which means that the other has never descended. Once in a great while we find one with no balls at all. Sometimes we get eunuchs. Eunuchs are salable for house servants, but a fellow with only one testicle is graded Third Class. Chances are he won't be able to breed."

His fingers encircled the prominent penis. "This boy's been circumcised." He called Jeff's attention to the absence of a foreskin. "All the followers of Islam are circumcised, but that is no guarantee that the boy has Moorish blood because some other tribes also circumcise. Some of them do a barbaric job. However, the majority of blacks have a long foreskin, and you must always be sure that you can pull it back. Otherwise we have to snip off the end before a man is sold."

Beluche's fingers tightened and slowly caressed the boy's

penis until it rose in his hand, stiff and straight, standing out from the boy's body.

"Fairly well hung, too, for a kid of his size, and it will probably grow a little in the next couple of years. He's not unusual but passable. Most buyers today want a fellow to be enormous. It really doesn't signify a thing, and sometimes these big-cocked guys aren't as good at breeding as the smaller ones, but I say, if that's what the buyer wants, that's what we'll give him and charge him for." He continued to stroke the boy.

"Mayhap you won't particularly enjoy this part of our examination, but it's necessary." He looked across the boy's erection at Jeff. "It's the best way to judge a man's sexuality. Not quite as important on a boy of this age as on a man who's going to be bought for a breeder."

The back-and-forth motion of his fist increased, and he gripped even harder. "Normally he should spurt off in about two or three minutes, but, of course, you must realize that conditions are not normal for him, and it might take a little longer." The boy's muscles were becoming tense. He closed his eyes, his back arched, and he gasped for breath. Beluche's fist moved faster. "See, I told you so." He held up his other hand to catch the boy's ejaculation. He rubbed some between his thumb and forefinger and nodded with satisfaction. "It must have the right viscosity. Thin and watery semen is not a good sign, but notice how thick and creamy his is. It's a pretty good indication that the boy's fertile."

Jeff gingerly touched the warm fluid in Beluche's hand. He, too, tried it between his thumb and forefinger, feeling its thickness and richness. "Have to test this on myself some day." He winked at Beluche, then wiped his fingers on his handkerchief.

"No need to worry about yours, Jeff." Beluche cleaned his fingers on the boy's back. "After last night, I'd be willing to grade you in the very top bracket as a breeder."

"Must you do this to every slave you examine? Damned messy, ain't it?"

"You get used to it, just as your nose gets accustomed to the stench here. It's all in a day's work. We're almost finished with this lad now."

Beluche turned the boy around. His hand on the nape of the boy's neck bent him over. He spread the boy's buttocks and inserted a finger in his anus. "No piles," he announced, "clean as a whistle." He picked up a stick from the ground and flung it as far out into the courtyard as he could. He motioned to the boy to run and fetch it. Ibrahim loped off like a gazelle, swooped up the stick, and brought it back, handing it to Beluche.

"That's finished," Beluche nodded. "Now I've already made up my mind. I'd be interested to find out what you think, Jeff."

Jeff considered the boy before him. It was going to be difficult to grade him. Had he been an ordinary *bozal,* he would be either a First, Second or Third Class field hand, but the boy was too young to fit into these categories. He might grow up into a Fancy, and then again, he might not. He evidently had a good disposition because he had bounded off after the stick willingly, and now that he was no longer frightened, he had an appealing smile.

"It's a hard decision to make," he replied, still studying the boy.

"Granted." Beluche nodded in agreement. "Hardly fair to you that your first one had to be like this. But go ahead, give me your candid opinion. We'll see if it agrees with mine."

"He's certainly no field hand—at least not yet."

"True."

"But given a few more years, I'd put him down as First Class."

"Possibly." Beluche was evidently not going to help Jeff with his decision.

Jeff continued to study the boy who was now so much at ease that he grinned, showing his perfect white teeth.

"Well, I'll tell you what," Jeff said. "If I didn't already have a servant, I'd be willing to buy this boy. It would be fun to train him, and teach him to speak English. I'd say that he's a far better boy than the one I already have. If I were looking to purchase him, I'd start at about three hundred dollars and be willing to go up to five hundred dollars for him. That's a high price for a young lad."

"It would be," Beluche agreed.

"So in my opinion that would make him a Fancy. Right?"

Beluche negated Jeff's judgment with a shake of his head. "No, he's not quite a Fancy." Beluche rummaged through the heap of discs on the ground and picked out a red one, which he hung around the boy's neck. "Almost, I agree. But not quite. In a few years he might well be. He'll be strong, but he will never have heavy muscles. He's more suited to be a house servant than he is to be a field hand, but he's not sufficiently handsome, not sufficiently well hung to be a Fancy. Still, he's got excellent blood because these black Arabs are rare, so I'm going to grade him as First Class. And, by the way, your estimate of the price he should bring is just about correct."

"Sorry to be wrong on my first test."

"Think nothing of it. It's difficult to put these young lads in their right class—difficult even for me. But remember, you weren't far from right. Some would make a Fancy out of him, but I don't think he quite comes up to it. First Class? How's that?"

"Reckon you've got to be right."

"So we'll feed him up. We'll give him some oil for his body to make his skin shine. We'll put him through a series of exercises, and we'll purge him because he's probably constipated. If he brings five hundred dollars I'll present you with a bottle of my best Napoleon brandy for your good judgment. Now, Mosho, bring the next man."

All that morning Jeff watched Beluche as he judged man after man. Not one qualified for Fancy among the lot, although Jeff saw some First Class red discs passed out. The majority, however, were white ones with only a few yellow. The one solitary black disc went to a man whose leg had been broken on the voyage and never set. He was a pitiful sight, limping on makeshift crutches and still in great pain. Beluche took one look at him and gave him a reassuring pat on the back as Mosho led him away without even a cursory examination. No sooner had he disappeared from the corral than Jeff heard the reverberating sound of gunfire.

Beluche shook his head. "That's the end of that poor devil. Sometimes I feel like God—dispensing life and death—but it's better to put the poor bastard out of his suffering."

They quit work at noon and repaired to Beluche's office for a bite of lunch. After they had finished, Beluche yawned and stretched his arms.

"It's the custom around here to rest until midafternoon. Too hot to work in the middle of the day. Better go home, strip, and stretch out on the bed. Man, you had a hard night and a little rest will perk you up. Come back about four o'clock, and we'll work until dusk. And"—he wagged an admonitory finger at Jeff—"leave that Dutch wench alone this afternoon. You'll need a couple of hours of good sleep to recover from last night."

"One hour will do it." Jeff laughed. He had had a busy morning, but he had enjoyed it. He was beginning to learn about slave blacks. True, his judgment had not coincided with Beluche's in every case, but he had made a sufficient number of right guesses to feel confident he would soon become proficient. Damn, it was going to be a hell of a job, with a lot of money to be made. He even found it somewhat titillating to manipulate the blacks, though he would have preferred examining females to males.

"Do you ever get any women, René?" he asked as they neared the gates.

"Damned few, Jeff. The demand today is for males, and it's more difficult for the slavers to transport females. We do have a few women in another compound. Someday soon we'll go over there. But you'll find damned few virgins, if that's what you're looking for."

"I don't give a damn about virgins, especially black ones," Jeff said.

"*Au revoir.*"

Jeff was confident and extremely happy with himself. He was going to amount to something in the Lafitte organization. He and Lady Luck would see to it that he did.

He was half-tempted to take his siesta at Helen's house, but he knew that he'd get no rest there. He was sleepy—he had to admit it. But first he would wash his hands and get the smell off them. If Gretchen wanted to stretch out on the bed beside him, that would be all right, too. He could stand a little pink and white skin after all this black.

CHAPTER XIII

JEFF'S presentiment that he would be happy at Grande-Terre came true—and beyond his most fantastic dreams. He had never been happier in his whole life, not even in those few halcyon days when he lived in a roseate anticipation of bedding Minnie George. He liked his work here. What could be more interesting than working with human beings? Well, perhaps niggers weren't exactly human, but at least they had human form, and judging them made him feel entirely white. He enjoyed working with René Beluche —certainly he couldn't have found a more congenial colleague or more dedicated teacher. It was nice, too, having a home of his own, and he was increasingly thankful that he had picked Gretchen to keep his house for him. His house and his clothes were immaculate, she ruled Ramon with a rod of iron, and she was a good cook. She provided a variety of tempting menus from the rather limited stock of meats and groceries available at the company store. Also of considerable importance, she was an agreeable (if rather unimaginative) bed companion. For her, the height of passion was to lie flat on her back and passively let Jeff mount her. He decided that teaching the placid Gretchen more complex and enjoyable techniques would be too much effort.

Getchen did, however, satisfy his needs at night, and he was fully absorbed by his job with René during the day. After a few months of René's expert tutelage he had become a good—if not expert—judge of black flesh. Just when he was ready to congratulate himself that he really had nothing further to learn, something unexpected came

132

up that confounded all his experience. A tall, muscular specimen would turn out to have yaws and instead of being First Class, as Jeff would have graded him, he would be demoted to a poor Third. Well, that was something to look for in the future. Again, a short, thickset young fellow with a face like an African ape whom Jeff would have consigned to Third Class proved to be the strongest man René had ever examined, and his extraordinary musculature put him in First Class. One slender, wispy fellow with an engaging face, but with no pretensions to muscular strength, turned out to have Herculean genitalia which caused René to gasp and summon Jean Lafitte himself to see and marvel. Consequently, this black Priapus was enthusiastically graded by René as a Fancy when Jeff would have put him in Third Class. Frankly, Jeff thought, compared to his own equipment, he saw nothing unusual about the lad, certainly nothing to rate him a Fancy.

These differences in judgment proved one thing—no cursory examination could scientifically place a slave into the proper category. There were subtle ramifications which could be learned only through experience.

But Jeff was learning, and perhaps most important of all, René, his teacher, was his good friend. When he passed René's house on his way to the barracoons in the morning, Jeff would stop to pick up his friend and the two of them would walk on together in the shade of the live oaks. At René's office they would sip their chicory-flavored coffee and eat the croissants which, Jeff discovered, Mosho brought down from Jean Lafitte's own kitchen, wrapped in a napkin to keep them warm. This was a pleasant time for both of them, a time for desultory gossip and talk about the minor doings at Barataria, but rarely for business. One particular morning, however, René gestured toward the corral.

Jeff put down his coffee cup, walked to the window, and raised the jalousies to peer into the courtyard. For the first time since he had been at Barataria the big enclosure was almost quiet. Instead of the teeming mass of black humanity and the constant wailing and keening, there were

133

now only a few men pacing back and forth and conversing in small groups.

"Damnit!" Jeff let the jalousies fall with a clatter. "It sure as hell looks like we're running out of business. Can't be more than fifty or sixty men out there. Does that mean our job is finished?"

"Hardly." Beluche brushed a fly from his forehead and waited for it to light on his desk before he swatted it. "We have calls for more and more slaves, and we've got to find some way to supply them. Masfero's Exchange in New Orleans, acting as agent for one of the big plantations upriver, has placed an order for a hundred First Class blacks. Then there's to be a big auction at the Hotel St. Louis in about a month, and that's one of the best places to get rid of any Fancies we might have. We also have orders from a number of private parties for up to twenty Second Class men for work in the cane fields."

Jeff jerked his thumb toward the nearly empty barracoon. "None of which we can supply?"

"All of which we've *got* to supply or go out of business. And we haven't brought in a single slaver for over two months."

The Lafittes had been notoriously unsuccessful in taking any rich prizes of late. To be sure, another slaver could be captured tomorrow, but then again, it could be three months. Nobody could prophesy. Word by fast ship reported that several blackbirders had sailed from ports on the west coast of Africa. None had been captured yet, but, as René had said, they had business commitments. The southern states, as far north as Virginia, looked to the Lafittes for smuggled blacks.

Jeff spread his hands palms up in a gesture of helplessness and waited for the experienced René to speak.

"All of which means we've got to get over to Havana and round up some three hundred good *bozals* to tide us over. Of course, the day after we get them here, one of our own ships will come in with a goodly supply. That's always the case, but since we can't depend on it—we must get into action."

While René was talking, Jeff allowed his mind to engage

in voluptuous fantasy. Havana! All the fantastic stories he had heard about that fabulous city across the Gulf of Mexico surged through his mind. Havana—the Spanish metropolis in the New World; fabled city of adventure and excitement; home of dark-eyed *señoritas* who spoke a whole language with their painted ivory fans; city of proud *caballeros* who, because they were born in Cuba and could call themselves *cubanos,* considered themselves better than any Spaniard. *Ay, la Habana, la perla de las Indias!* He regretfully roused himself from his dream of a voluptuous Cuban beauty in silk-fringed embroidered shawl leaning over her balcony, beckoning him with a fan that echoed the invitation in her dark eyes.

"Did I hear you say *we've* got to get over to Havana?" The Cuban beauty lingered on the periphery of his thoughts.

"You may have, Jeff lad, but I didn't mean it exactly that way. I can't get away from this damned place. Much as I would like to. A couple of weeks in Havana would be much to my liking—a taste of living again after this godforsaken asshole of civilization. But I can't do it. The day after I left, a ship would probably come in. And that means rush, rush, rush to get every nigger on it graded in a matter of hours and packed off to New Orleans. No, Jeff lad, I can't go, but I'm sure as hell looking at somebody who can."

"But I haven't enough savvy about blacks." Jeff was sincere. He truly did not feel his judgment was professional enough yet.

"Well, I think you're qualified, but even more important, so does Jean Lafitte. And that means that you're sailing this afternoon. On the bark *Sainte-Claire.* Only ship we have in port at the moment. You're going to Havana and you're going to buy three hundred of the best African *bozals* you can lay hands on. If you can't get *bozals* right off the ship, see what you can get through private sales. There's a bastard of a slave dealer there called Emilio Hernandez who sometimes has good specimens, though I'd rather deal with the devil himself. Also"—he peered intently at Jeff—"we could use a couple of Fancy octoroon

135

wenches if you can find some good ones cheap in Havana. Old man Gaspard Cosette in New Orleans is pissing his breeches to slip it into something new and warm, and he's willing to pay through the nose, so we can't let him down. There used to be a queer bird named Solano who specialized in female Fancies. Try him if he's still in business."

"Now that's where you can trust me, René! If anyone can find that class of merchandise, I can. Those I pick out will be the best. Of course"—he winked at René—"I just might have to try them out first to be sure that M'sieur Cosette will be satisfied."

"I don't doubt your qualifications for judging wenches. The time will come for doing that, but now, get yourself over to your house and alert that Dutch wench Gretchen. Tell her she's got to have all your white cotton drill suits and linen shirts ready to go on board at four this afternoon. Just how in hell you're going to get three hundred slaves back here on the *Sainte-Claire,* God alone knows. A hundred would jam the vessel, but it's one of those impossible problems you'll get used to solving after you've been with Jean Lafitte a few years. He always asks the impossible and then expects to have it done day before yesterday. Presto! You'll have to be a magician to get them here, but you'll do it somehow—if you have to tow them on a line behind the ship."

"I'll put corks in their asses and float them across."

"I don't care how you do it, as long as you bring them here. Now get started. Better take your boy Ramon along. While you're getting ready, I'll have drafts prepared for our Havana bankers. Jean will be at the dock to give you instructions."

"Aye, aye, sir."

"Why so damned nautical?"

"Well, you're a captain, aren't you?"

"Once I was. Now I'm nothing but a jacker-off of niggers."

"And what am I?"

"With a little more experience, you'll work up to the same goddamn thing." Beluche smiled wanly at Jeff. "But we come in handy at times, and this is one of them."

136

Jeff was at the door, but René reached out a hand and restrained him. "Going to miss you, kid. It'll be dull eating breakfast alone."

"Same here, René. But I'll be back and we can start over."

"*Vaya con dios.* An old Spanish expression. Means 'Go with God.' Drop in here about an hour before sailing time and I'll brief you."

Jeff was excited as he made his way home. To be trusted with such an important mission after so short a time with the Lafittes meant they had confidence in him. Well, he'd show them he was worthy of their trust. He'd even cut out women while he was in Havana and stick to his work. Yes, by God, he'd do exactly that. To hell with the *señoritas* and their languid fans! They'd be like all women anyway, first making a big fuss over him, and then, after a little huffing and puffing and one final shove on his part, he'd be gasping for breath, and it would be all over, just as it had been a thousand times before. So to hell with it! He would be representing the Lafitte organization, and he'd conduct himself accordingly. By God he would!

He arrived home to find Gretchen hanging the wash on the back yard lines. His white shirts, trousers, jackets and small clothes flapped in the hot breeze. She must have had a presentiment of his leaving, for every article of clothing both he and Ramon owned (except those they were wearing) was on the clothesline.

Through the open window he called to her. "Good thing you started early. I'm going to need those clothes today, *liebchen.* Where's Ramon?"

"Gone down to the store to get flour. I need some to make dumplings to go with the beef stew I'm cooking for supper."

"Won't be needing any supper today, Gretchen. I'm sailing at four, along with Ramon. We've got to hurry to get everything ready. I'm leaving for Havana."

"Havana?" As far as Gretchen was concerned, this might be the other end of the world. The door opened and Ramon came in.

"Drop the bundle in the kitchen," Jeff yelled. "We're

137

leaving, you and I, so stir your stumps and get busy. Get the clothes in off the line as soon as they're dry so Gretchen can iron them. Get the valises down for packing."

The house suddenly rattled with activity. Gretchen stoked the fire to heat the irons and, although the clothes were damp, she said she could iron them even better. Ramon got out his shoes (he had been going barefoot since his arrival at Barataria) and his master's boots and polished them until he could see his reflection. He got out Jeff's cravats, steamed the creases out, and Gretchen pressed them. When she had finished ironing, Gretchen darned socks and mended underclothes. Jeff supervised the packing of his own valise and told Ramon what to take in his bundle. They were all so engrossed with getting ready for the trip that they completely forgot about lunch.

By two in the afternoon, all was in readiness and Jeff had Gretchen heat the iron cauldron full of water and bring in the big wooden washtub. This she filled with hot water, diluting it with cold until her finger informed her it was the right temperature. When it was ready she offered as usual to wash Jeff's back, and, as always, he refused her, although he would have liked the feel of her strong, soapy hands on his skin. When the bedroom door had closed behind her, he scrubbed his body with perfumed soap (pirated from some Spanish ship) and donned a fresh undershirt. It was only then that he called Gretchen to help him dress. The golden cross glittered against his chest.

He was surprised, when she entered, to see tears glistening on her cheeks. She closed the door and stood against it, staring at him for a moment, then began to sob.

"You're leaving, Mr. Jeff. You're leaving! You're taking Ramon with you and I'm going to be left alone here. Or must I go back to the women's house? Oh, Mr. Jeff, let me live here while you're gone. Please. I'd rather cut my wrists and bleed to death than go back with those *verdamnte* women. And . . . I don't want to serve any other master but you. Oh, Mr. Jeff, I know I shouldn't say it, but I'm in love with you. You're so beautiful, Mr. Jeff. No woman could help but be in love with you. Please, sir, please, please, don't send me back."

She stumbled across the floor to kneel before him, clasping his legs with her arms and burying her sleek blond head against him. She seemed to find comfort in the damp warmth of his body.

The pressure of her heated breath against him stirred familiar feelings, and he felt himself rising and swelling. His hands sought her head and gently turned it up so he could look at her face. With the corner of his shirtsleeve, he wiped the tears from her cheeks and smiled at her.

"Of course, *liebchen,* I'm not sending you back to the women's house. Don't worry, Gretchen, I'm not taking any chances on losing you and having to put up with one of those harridans when I get back. No indeed, Gretchen. I'll be seeing M'sieur Lafitte at the dock before I sail, and I'm sure that I can arrange for you to remain. I won't be gone very long anyway."

The warmth of her head pressed against his nakedness, and the smooth silkiness of her hair in his hand excited him even more. Now he was throbbing, breathless with desire. Her arms, entwined about his legs drew him closer to her. He felt her hand first stroking the soft inside of his thigh, then reaching up to cup his testes, her fingers gently kneading. Her other hand seized the turgidity of his maleness, grasped tightly and stroked, gently at first, and then rapidly. He sucked in his breath as he felt the wetness of her lips enclosing him and her tongue making vibrant little caresses against him. Her gesture surprised as much as it roused him. It was something she had never offered before. He suspected this was a new experience for her, that it was her ultimate expression of her love for him.

He felt the hot fluid rising within him, and he pushed her head away, but it was only for an instant. Sensing the approach of his climax, she avidly sought him out again. Her mouth closed around him. . . .

His hand plucked the hairpins from her hair, and her tresses fell to the floor in a cascade of silken gold. He ran his fingers through it. Although this was by no means a novel experience for him, it took on a whole strange newness, for he was sharing her sense of initiation. . . .

She coughed and again he moved her head away, but

she brushed aside his restraining hand and continued her ministrations with renewed vigor. Suddenly the muscles in his groin twisted into knots of exquisite pleasure. Although for the instant his whole world revolved around the continuation of her sensuous caresses, some primeval subconscious force urged him to try to resist her. His strength had left him, however, and willy-nilly he submitted to her mastery over his manhood. Yet this was what he wanted—desperately.

He arched his back, pushing himself farther into her. She felt his imminent release and clasped him tighter, her lips forming an inescapable clamp upon him. Then it happened. For one brief second, which stretched into light-years of sublime ecstasy, the glory was indescribable. He soared into an empyrean of kaleidoscopic colors until he sensed that it was no longer possible for him to stand such exquisite torture, and he floated back to earth, gasping for breath. He pushed away her mouth, which had come to seem a part of him. He leaned against her for support, then tottered to the bed and collapsed upon it.

"I shall miss you, Mr. Jeff."

"But I'll be back. I promise you that."

"Hurry back, Jeff." It was the first time she had ever used his first name without the "Mr."

With her help, he dressed. Then, while Ramon waited with the valise and bundles, he gathered her in his arms and kissed her lightly on the lips—those lips which had only a few moments ago pleasured him so.

CHAPTER XIV

THE long monotonous days at sea were a salubrious tonic for Jeff. The hot sun, the gentle salt breezes, the timelessness of being suspended between the mundane responsibilities of two ports, produced total relaxation. Gone was the tension of his daily routine of fingering and assaying blacks. Furthermore, sleeping alone and doing absolutely nothing except eat soothed his nerves, erased from his face the lines of fatigue and dissipation, and gave him a physical buoyancy he had not known in months.

There were no women aboard the *Sainte-Claire*. The first night he missed the warm, comfortable plumpness of Gretchen beside him. Frustrated by his erotic thoughts, he tossed and turned in the narrow confines of his bunk, unable to sleep. But with the dawn creeping over the sea, he finally managed his own release and dozed off.

When he awoke to the full blaze of the sun he was thankful for once in his life that there was no damp female flesh beside him. Strangely enough, this feeling continued throughout the rest of the voyage. Although he knew he could never savor it as a steady diet, he enjoyed the unfamiliar sense of freedom. It wouldn't last, but he could appreciate it for a short time. Celibacy was all right as a novelty, but not as a way of life. Not by a damned sight!

So now, reinvigorated by his abstinence and his regime of sun, sky, and rest, he stood at the prow of the ship, scanning the dim strip of land that appeared on the horizon. That blur against the clear sapphire of the sea, the captain said, was Cuba. The very thought made his pulse quicken. Cuba—where he was to represent the Lafittes, where he would have almost unlimited funds to purchase slaves for his organization and live like a lord while doing it. Cuba—where he planned to make up for his monklike continence, where a whole new world of prestige and importance was opening up for him. He had only one regret: that Chloe was not here to realize what an important personage he was becoming.

Gradually the dark blur on the horizon turned green, spotted with tiny sun-washed flecks of whiteness that he imagined were houses. Then, as they came nearer, the greenness dissolved into fields of waving cane and tall royal palms. The blue water dissolved into white spume against a rocky shore or crept in lazy laciness up sandy beaches. Nearing the shore, he saw that the white cubes were houses, red-roofed and sparkling in the sunshine. Moving dots along the dirt roads materialized as ox carts, laden high with green stalks of sugarcane. Cuba was already one of the world's greatest producers of sugar—one reason why the country had become such an avid market for slaves. The cane fields had a cruel appetite for men's lives. Slaves did not live long under the excruciatingly hard labor and smothering heat of the sugar plantations.

The ship progressed along the coast. The big farms gave way to a long row of trim, gray fortifications cresting the high hill that rose abruptly from the water. Nearby an immense fire basket stood high on wave-dashed rocks. It was obviously a beacon that burned only at night; but still-glowing coals illumined the huge iron basket. The ship, which until now had been coasting along the shore, suddenly tacked and headed for the beacon. As they came nearer, Jeff saw that the beacon marked the entrance to an anchorage. He concluded that this must be the famed Morro Castle which guarded Havana Harbor. Across from the Morro, on the other shore of the narrow harbor entrance, he discerned other forts. Havana, he could see, was well guarded. No craft could survive between the crossfire of the opposite fortifications.

The land was now so close on both sides that he felt he could almost stretch out his hands and touch the guarding forts on either shore. He could not decide at first which side of the ship afforded the best views—both were fascinating—but finally chose the starboard because it presented a panorama of the city of Havana itself—truly a metropolis, one of the great cities of the western hemisphere. For a moment he was stunned by the spectacle stretching before him—a froth of buildings in white and pastel colors, relieved by the darker gray of weathered masonry and the feathery green of palm fronds. The water on both sides of the ship was alive with small boats paddled by vociferous vendors of various tempting fruits— bananas, oranges, avocadoes, lemons, and many more Jeff did not recognize.

The *Sainte-Claire* hove to, awaiting a longboat manned by sailors who pulled vigorously on the long sweeps. When they neared the bark, one of the men caught a line thrown to him and made it fast to the stern of the longboat. Then the straining muscles of the Cubans towed the *Sainte-Claire* against a long pier extending out into the water. At the end of the wharf was a huge timber "X" used for unloading ships. This derricklike contraption, Jeff learned, gave the pier its name: "La Machina."

A chorus of curses in English and Spanish, shouted from ship to longboat and from boat to pier, accompanied the securing of the larger vessel to the pier with hawsers that would have held a ship twice its size. Then came the moment for which Jeff had been waiting: the lowering of the heavy gangplank from ship to pier. No longer were they a tiny nonentity, a speck on the boundless sea; they were now tied to the land, secure and safe. He had enjoyed the voyage, but he was glad to be on solid ground.

He wanted to run across the gangplank and plant his feet firmly on the pier, but a brisk officer, backed by two ragged-looking soldiers, barred the way. The captain, however, now that the the work of berthing the ship had been accomplished, came to the gangplank and spoke to the officer in a mixture of Spanish and English. The officer did not deign to answer him but merely pointed to a white-uniformed official sauntering along the pier, followed by an equally smartly attired mulatto carrying a small bag. The two men came aboard, greeted the captain effusively, and disappeared with him into the cabin. They reappeared a few moments later, the assistant now loaded down with bundles and packages. The boss man was introduced by the captain as the port's chief customs officer, and he bowed low while shaking Jeff's hand. In precise and stilted English he welcomed Jeff to Havana. The man's schoolboy English made Jeff aware of the difficulty he might have in trying to barter for slaves in an unfamiliar language. Somehow, somewhere, he must find a competent interpreter, one who was not only accurate but loyal.

Although not dressed to go ashore—he wore only denim trousers and an old shirt—his first foreign port intrigued him to such an extent that he bounded down the gangplank. Not only was he happy to get his feet on solid ground again, but he was also thrilled by the strangeness of this new world. The sun beat down with an incandescent brilliance and the tropical heat was even more intense than that of Barataria Bay. His shirt was already plastered to his back, his hair was damp, and his trousers clung to him like wet skin. He promised himself only a quick walk to the end of the pier, but he was so intrigued by everything he saw that his quick walk became a journey.

The long stretch of the pier was littered with crates and boxes and piles of strange-looking fruits awaiting shipment. Black stevedores, naked to the waist, their oily skins glistening with sweat, formed an endless chain, passing boxes from swaying arms to swaying arms. A continuous, low-pitched chant gave their movements a precise rhythm. Jeff passed a stall where a toothless old crone was paring oranges, the bright peel falling to her feet in an unbroken ribbon. While peeling, she, too, kept up a similar monotonous chant, doubtless a sales pitch for her wares. At another crude kiosk, shaded from the sun by a meager thatching of palm fronds, a man was squeezing fruit juice into fly-studded glass jars. Another man, sitting behind a row of small cups on a rickety table, fanned a copper charcoal brazier that supported a steaming coffeepot. The air was raucous with a pulsating din in which the quick, fluid syllables of Spanish dominated, sometimes low and sibilant, sometimes loud and bombinating.

A brazen slut, her thin blouse pulled low on one shoulder so that it barely concealed her breast, sidled up to Jeff. Her words—low, inviting, and sensual—were incomprehensible, but he had no difficulty understanding the obscene gesture of her hands. Under the heavy coating of rice powder, she was young and good-looking, no more than fourteen. Her rounded hips and heavy breasts tempted him, but he shooed her away with emphatic signs. Thereupon she erupted with a torrent of words which, although he could not understand them, seemed to be derogatory reflections on his manhood.

He came to the street and watched the continuous stream of traffic for a moment, then reluctantly retraced his steps down the long pier back to the ship. Before crossing the gangplank, he hesitated to relish the flavor of the exotic scene. Once back in familiar surroundings, he almost resented their very familiarity. Impatient to be a part of the color and vibrant activity of the city, he hurried below decks to dress. Without the cooling breeze of the ship under sail, his cabin was stifling hot, and the sweat channeled down poor Ramon's naked back as he struggled to repack the valises.

"We're here, Ramon!" Jeff picked up a boot from the floor and flung it at the perspiring black. "Come, boy, stir your stumps. Let's escape this floating hellhole and get ourselves settled. There must be a cooler place somewhere in the city. Hurry, get me a bucket of fresh water so I may get myself halfway clean before I put on other clothes. I smell like an unwashed whore, and I'm an abomination even to myself. After I finish, you scrub yourself. I can smell your stench even over my own. We both smell like niggers." He laughed at this. "Be sure to get fresh water. I don't want the stickiness of salt water mixing with my own."

"Shore glad we here, Mastah Jeff. Don' like no boats, 'n' no water neither. What yo' say this place called? Hotter'n hell in here, ain' it?"

"Then hurry!" Jeff searched through the bags that Ramon had already packed until he found a freshly laundered suit of white drill, a clean shirt, and small clothes. Then he stripped off his damp attire (all but his shirt) and stood seeking whatever stray breeze might wander in while he waited. In a few moments Ramon returned with a brimming sailcloth bucket in one hand and a large palm-leaf fan in the other. "I fans yo', Mastah Jeff, whilst yo' gits cleaned up." He looked at his master as if half expecting a reciprocal offer.

"If you think I'm going to stand around fanning you, you black son-of-a-bitch, you're wrong. Now heist your ass out on deck while I wash." When Ramon had closed the door, he soaped a washcloth to a good lather and scrubbed himself all over. He rinsed himself off and diligently applied the towel, but he felt as wet as ever when he finished.

Ramon returned and bathed while Jeff dressed. As Jeff's fresh clothes seemed nearly as wet as those he had taken off, he tried a liberal application of eau de cologne to overcome any residual body stench. However, he was sure

145

nothing could cloak Ramon's; the exertion of fanning his master while he was dressing had made the boy as sweaty and musky as before.

"Mayhap after we get out in the air we'll cool off a little." Jeff spoke more to himself than to Ramon. While Ramon strapped the valises, Jeff reached under the bunk for an oversize leather wallet which he opened to choose two envelopes. Then he closed the case. From one addressed envelope he removed a quantity of Spanish gold and silver coins, which he pocketed. The other envelope was addressed but unsealed. Jeff studied it for a moment. The address intrigued him.

Señor don Cipriano Olivarez
San Felipe 128,
La Habana, Cuba

This gentleman, Lafitte had informed him, was his confidential agent in Havana, a powerful man with fingers in many pies, especially those backed by the corrupt Spanish government of Cuba. Jeff had only to present this letter and anything he needed would be immediately forthcoming. Never before had he possessed such an open-sesame to authority. He did not forget that it all started with the letter of introduction to the Lafittes from Helen. He touched the cross at his throat.

Without Helen's letter he would probably have ended up as a pimp or a paid stud in some New Orleans whorehouse, getting a percentage from the men he brought in, and earning small handouts of cash from women whose husbands were neglecting them. Helen's letter had saved him from that. Perhaps this letter would be equally effective. He certainly hoped so because he still had to prove himself *to* the Lafittes. And to get full use out of this new letter, he had to prove himself *for* them. Both tasks were equally important to his future. Olivarez? What would the man be like? Well, he'd hope for the best. Surely with the Lafittes behind him, he was halfway home.

Two other letters still in the wallet he knew to be addressed to two banks in Havana, giving him almost unlimited credit for the purchase of the blacks he had been sent to acquire. There was also a third letter addressed to

Señor Hernandez, the leading slave dealer in the city. He would not yet need these letters, as he was going first to Olivarez. Perhaps through him he would be able to meet some companionable people in Havana. He hoped so. He had no desire to lead a solitary existence in a city bubbling with life and luxury.

With Ramon struggling with the valises and complaining under his breath about their weight, they stepped ashore. The pier was still bustling with activity. As they made their slow progress down it, dodging stevedores and itinerant merchants, Jeff felt a tugging at his coattails. The tugger was a lad whose dark curls and spontaneous smile encouraged him to slow his footsteps.

The boy, who looked to be around nine or ten, might have been presentable under the accumulated grime covering his eager face. His ragged shirt scarcely covered his shoulders, and his pants, equally ragged and full of holes, left no doubt as to his sex. But his smile was engaging and his manner ingratiating. Jeff stopped, grinning down at him.

"You American?" the boy asked.

Jeff nodded.

"I Vincente." The boy grinned impishly up at him. "I speak American. See, *señor,* I clean your shoes." He pointed to Jeff's dusty shoes and then to the box slung over his shoulder by a leather strap. "They need it. Important *caballero* like you don't want no dust on his shoes. For just one centavo I make them look like new."

Jeff stared first at his shoes and then at the boy's upturned face. Indeed, his shoes were a bit dusty, and he would talk to Ramon about that later. Meanwhile it would certainly do no harm to have them shined.

"I've no copper centavo with me, boy. Only silver."

"I get change for you. I not run away, *señor.* I am honest. They call me Honest Vincente, that's what. I'm a good boy, *verdad?*"

"You look like an imp of Satan to me. But get to work. Can we find a shady place?"

"I wipe off your man's shoes, too." Vincente pointed to Ramon's boots. "Maybe not make so much shine as yours, for he is nothing but a nigger, but serving fine master like you, he must look good, too. I think he very lazy to let fine *caballero* go out with dusty shoes." He scanned the pier and pointed to a spot of shade in the lee of a pile of packing cases. The three of them walked over to it.

Jeff rested his foot on the box while the boy produced black liquid and a brush and set to work. He applied the polish, brushed heartily, then spit copiously on Jeff's shoes and polished again. "Spit makes good shine," he said.

Jeff drew the letter from his pocket. "You speak English well, boy. Where did you learn it?"

"From American sailors."

"Then perhaps you can tell me where is a street called San Felipe?"

"*Sí, señor,* but *muy lejos*—long distance from here. Too far for walk. When I finish your shoes and wipe off your man's, I fetch *volanta* so you can ride there. That will be another copper centavo, señor, for my services."

He gave a final flip of the rag to Jeff's shoes. Never before, Jeff had to admit, had they looked so brilliantly clean. When he had finished with Jeff's, Vincente perfunctorily wiped the dust from Ramon's shoes. After Jeff had passed him the piece of silver, he darted among the crowd to the man who was vending coffee and returned quickly with the change, which he carefully counted into Jeff's hand. Then, shaking his head wisely, he pointed to Ramon and the valises.

"Tell him go back to ship with valises and wait for you. A *volanta* will not hold us and valises too. You come back for him later. I go with you so driver don't cheat you. I also bring you back. I better go to speak Spanish for you." Jeff agreed, sent Ramon back to the ship, and followed his new guide to the end of the pier. Here they waited until a conveyance such as Jeff had never seen before came along. It was a mule-drawn vehicle with two unusually high wheels and a hood of battered canvas.

"What number on San Felipe do you go to, *señor?*"

Jeff told him.

"The house of Don Cipriano Olivarez, yes?"

"Yes."

"Muy importante, este caballero." The name of Olivarez impressed the boy. *"Muy importante.* But, *señor, un momento, por favor."* Vincente beckoned with a grimy finger to Jeff. "I say something to you in *confianza."*

Jeff leaned over, the better to hear the boy's words.

"You like to fucky-fuck, sucky-suck, *señor?"* Vincente made an obscene gesture, closing the fingers of his left hand around the forefinger of his right and moving them suggestively while his tongue made slurping sounds against his lips.

Jeff laughed at the boy's earnest impertinence. "Who doesn't, Vincente?"

"Then, *señor,* you are lucky man. I have for you my sister. She is young, *señor,* only eleven, and most beautiful. Ay, so beautiful! *Qué linda!* Clean, too, *señor."* He inserted his finger in his mouth and sucked on it avidly, his eyes rolling in ecstasy. *"Sí,* what she won't do for you, *señor,* my sister Perla. She can do everything and she is the best. She's a nice girl, not fully a *puta* yet." He smiled up at Jeff. "You want? What is an hour?"

Jeff shook his head. Yes, he did want—God knows how much he wanted—but he had promised himself (and even now he regretted the promise) that this time business would come before pleasure. He remembered the long nights at sea with his feet braced against the bottom of the bunk. An hour! No, for once he would discipline himself. "Perhaps later, Vincente."

"Then, *señor,* I go with you and wait while you are in the house of don Cipriano. Without me, who knows how much this son-of-a-bitch driver of broken-down mules will charge? I protect you, *señor,* because you do not speak the Spanish. I wait for you outside Don Cipriano's, then I will help you find a hotel. Indeed, *señor,* in all Havana you are safest in Vincente's hands."

"But . . ."

"No but, *señor.* These damned *cubanos,* they skin your eyes and sell the hide if I do not watch over you. You need me, *señor.* I sit beside driver and point out the beautiful sights of Havana."

CHAPTER XV

ONCE he managed to clamber over the high wheels and settle himself inside on the worn cushions, Jeff found the well-sprung *volanta* quite comfortable. The hood sheltered him from the sun, but left Vincente, who had climbed up beside the driver, quite exposed. Vicente, however, born to the heat of the tropical sun, did not seem to mind. Thanks to his voluble guide, Jeff's first journey through Havana was an education. He was surprised by the industrious bustle of the town; it seemed as though every inhabitant—at least every male, from ragged urchin to well-dressed businessman—was out in the narrow streets, crowding the minuscule sidewalks, dashing to avoid the heavy traffic, or stopping to embrace each other with Latin effusion. Each man or boy seemed to have the determined air of one who knows just where he is going, but is in no hurry to get there, instinctively respectful of the tropical heat.

Most conspicuous, however, was the almost complete absence of women on the streets. Always on the lookout for a pretty face, well-outlined breasts, or shapely ankles, Jeff noticed—subconsciously at first—that there seemed to be none in Havana. The occasional few he did see were always in pairs. These pairs consisted invariably of a younger, well-dressed woman accompanied by an elderly female, usually clad in rusty black, in contrast to the brilliance of her younger companion's costume. How strange! And yet, there must be as many women as men in Havana. Where were they?

His curiosity, compounded by his desire to see a pretty face, prompted him to ask Vincente. Were all the women in Havana hidden behind the iron-grilled balconies, and if so, why?

Vincente appeared surprised by the query. What was so unusual about that? Condescendingly, as though the answer should be self-evident, Vincente informed him that no woman ever appeared alone on the streets of Havana except for some emergency, but always in the company of a *dueña,* an older woman whose presence would frighten off any male daring to accost her. A respectable lady seldom left her home, except to visit her friends. If she needed new shoes, jewels, or material for a dress, a note sent to a merchant would bring a representative of the shop to her home—usually an elderly woman. If she did go without her *dueña,* her social position would be jeopardized.

Of course, there were women who appeared on the streets alone, usually in the evening, but these were the *putas*—the whores—and they were far from the best class of prostitute. Every self-respecting whore (and it was a profession considered respectable by its practitioners) either had an *alcahuete*—a pimp who drummed up business and brought it home to her—or else worked in a respectable whorehouse.

For instance, Vincente explained, there was his sister. She was a respectable whore who depended on Vincente for her clients, and the only time she ever went out on the street was for a short trip to the *especiería* on the corner to get black beans, rice, or other groceries for their supper.

Once started on the subject of his sister Perla, Vincente began to expatiate to his captive audience on her charms and the many ways she had of pleasing a man. Yes, she was well-versed in the *manera francesa*—he again put a grimy thumb in his mouth to demonstrate. She was, Vincente averred, a *puta* without a rival. Why shouldn't she be? He had taught her all she knew, and young as he was, there was no better teacher in all Havana. She was not old enough—only eleven—to have a professional pimp, but he considered himself far better than a professional. He also allowed her to keep most of her money for herself, so he was cheaper for her in the end.

Eventually, in a couple of years, Perla hoped to go to La Casa de Josefina, which, Vincente told Jeff, was the best whorehouse in all Havana. But it was difficult for a girl to get in there. If by chance, the *señor americano* did not care for his sister Perla, Vincente would willingly take him to La Casa de Josefina. There was a blond Spanish girl there whom every man in Havana wanted, but in Vincente's opinion, she did not compare with his sister. *Ay*, what beautiful hair, what soft skin, what dazzling eyes, and what accomplishments! Let *el señor americano* just try her, and if he was not entirely satisfied, there would be no charge. And, of course—Vincente turned to stare at Jeff—if by chance the *señor* did not care for women, there was always Vincente. Yes, he himself was most certainly available.

Jeff laughed in his face and assured him that he was not in the least interested in young boys. However, he would consider his sister and, most probably, La Casa de Josefina, but later, much later. Just now, he was interested in business. He knew as he spoke that he was lying. Just now, more than anything else, he wanted either Vincente's sister or the blonde at the House of Josefina. Damn! After those nights at sea with nothing but his hand for company, he would have settled for the old woman selling oranges on the pier. If he could only find release, he felt he could concentrate better while talking with Don Cipriano. But no! He had promised himself that business would come first on this trip, and Vincente's Perla would still be there when he got through. At least, with Vincente acting as Jeff's guide, he would not be able to drum up business for her.

They left the narrow crowded streets and swung onto a wide boulevard of trees and stately homes. This avenue, according to Vincente, was called El Prado, and led straight to the sea from the small park in front of the Tacon Opera House. According to Vincente, Don Cipriano's house was in this new and prosperous part of the city. Vincente knew the house, and there would be no difficulty in finding it. As Vincente turned to speak to the driver, Jeff found himself staring at the way the black hair curled around the boy's neck. Good God! Was he so hard up he was even looking at a boy with desire? Nonsense! But he sincerely hoped Vincente's sister was equally attractive.

Following Vincente's gesturing arm, the driver turned

into a narrow side street, peering intently at the numbers on the houses.

"No need to stare like a starving sparrow looking for a horse turd," the boy said in Spanish. "It's Don Cipriano's house he wants, and I know where it is. Even you should know that."

"*Sí, sí,* but I had only the number. Why didn't you tell me it was Don Cipriano's house?"

"Because I did not know you were so stupid," the boy replied. "Had I known it, I would not have engaged your broken-down dung cart for the *Americano illustre.*" Vincente pointed down the street to an imposing house of brilliant white stone. "There it is."

The house before which they had stopped was an ornate, fanciful structure of white masonry and red-tiled roofing. Bronze gates opened upon immense double doors of carved mahogany. Had it not been for Vincente, who clambered down before him, Jeff would not have known how to gain entrance, but Vincente had spotted the bell pull. He yanked at it and waited beside Jeff for the doors to open.

"I tell driver to wait, *señor,* and I wait with him because without me you can't get another *volanta* here. Even if you can, can you tell driver to return to La Machina wharf for your man and your bags? And when Don Cipriano does not offer you hospitality because Cubans do not take strangers into their homes, I am glad to take you to a good hotel, *señor,* and see that you are comfortably settled."

Jeff nodded in agreement. The big mahogany doors opened and a black servant whose immaculately white clothes made him seem even blacker came down the steps to open the gates.

"Mr. Jefferson Carson," Jeff announced to the black, "to see Mr. Olivarez."

"*El ilustre señor Don Jefferson Carson, quiere ver al Don Cipriano,*" Vincente translated as the black stared dumbly at Jeff. "Let him in and don't keep him waiting out here in the hot sun, you ignorant black *hijo de puta.* Otherwise, your master will send you to the public whips and you'll not sit on your ass for a week."

The black answered sharply in Spanish to Vincente, and

motioned Jeff to enter. He turned for a moment to reassure himself with Vincente's white-toothed grin and then ascended the steps. Somehow, he was reluctant to leave the boy who had providentially befriended him. Although he had no doubt that Don Cipriano could speak English, he was grateful for this ragged street boy's service. Had Vincente been cleaner and better dressed, Jeff might have insisted that he come in with him. He felt helpless without an interpreter.

"Wait for me," he called out as he stepped inside the closing doors.

"Seguramente, señor, if I have to wait all night."

The dim coolness of the house was a relief after the humidity of the sun-struck street. Jeff noted the high ceilings, the cool, uncarpeted tile floors, and the stiff formality of the rooms without draperies and upholstered furniture. He followed the servant into an immense front room, where many cane-seated rocking chairs were aligned in four rigid rows, facing the center of the room. There stood the life-sized figure of a nearly nude female, obviously intended to attract the eyes of all those sitting in the chairs. The servant indicated a chair for Jeff and mumbled something in Spanish as he left the room. Almost at once a tiny black boy dressed in white glided into the room on bare feet, took his seat in a corner, and started pulling on a long cord. A big fan suspended from the ceiling swung into slow motion. Jeff detected a slight stirring of air.

Alone in this stately house, except for the black boy who stared at him, Jeff had a curious feeling of alienation. He was tempted to go to the window and call for Vincente. There was something eerie in this oddly dim interior. The ghostly white figure of the marble woman stared him in the face. The sensuous curve of her full breasts under the thin marble veil made him think of the promise of Vincente's sister. It was something to anticipate. But only eleven! Still, women were older sooner in hot climates. What was this mysterious kinship he felt for an unknown little girl and for the brother who pimped for her? How strangely and precipitously people came into his life.

154

The silence was broken by the crack of leather heels on the marble stairs in the hall. Good! He would no longer be alone in this mausoleum with its funereal statue. He stood up as a man entered the room, an elderly man with snow-white hair whose eyes were brightly alert and whose step was light and springy as he advanced across the floor, hand extended.

"Señor Carson. El que viene de mi buen amigo, Jean Lafitte! Hemos recibido su carta. Que lástima que mi hermano no está aquí. El habla inglés, pero yo . . ." He spread his open hands, palms up, in a gesture of helplessness. *"Pero, quisáz usted habla español, señor?"*

"Not a word." Jeff had caught the word *inglés* and shook his head in helpless negation as he grasped the other man's hand. Aware that he would not be understood, he withdrew the letter from his pocket and handed it to Don Cipriano. He did not know if it was written in Spanish or English.

The old man bowed graciously as he accepted it and then after opening it and scanning the page he handed it back to Jeff. It was written in English.

"Es en inglés," Don Cipriano said.

Jeff smiled impotently at the man. They were at an impasse. He could say nothing and neither could Don Cipriano. They were unable to communicate. Then Jeff thought of a possible solution—young Vincente. But Vincente with all his filth? Did he dare suggest to the immaculate Don Cipriano that he allow this street arab with his torn clothes, unwashed body, and tousled curls to step across the threshold of his house? Impossible! And yet, it was the only available solution. Although he realized that the words would be unintelligible, Jeff murmured a "With your permission" and walked over to the tall windows whose *persianas* were tightly closed to keep out the light. He examined them for a moment, conscious that Don Cipriano was watching him, then turned and faced the older man and, after pointing to the blinds, put his palms together slowly, then spread his hands.

Don Cipriano gave him a searching look, probably wondering if this agent of the powerful Lafittes were in his right mind. Comprehending that Jeff desired the blinds open, he crossed the room and pulled a cord at one side of the window. The blinds opened, admitting barred streaks of sunshine into the room. Jeff peered out. The horse and carriage were waiting in the street and, seated on the curb nearby, was Vincente.

Jeff pointed out the window to the boy. "He," he spoke loudly and slowly, as if speaking to a deaf person. "He speak English. English." He frantically searched the small dictionary Lafitte had given him. *"Hablar inglés y español."* He had to look up every word and pronounce it haltingly. "But he is *sucio, muy, muy sucio. Desear el"*—again he searched the pages for the right words—*"entrar su casa?"*

Don Cipriano had evidently understood, because he smiled at Jeff and let forth a spate of Spanish that terminated in his crossing the room to pull a bell cord. Jeff could hear the distant jangling of a bell, and in a few seconds the manservant entered the room to be greeted by another spate of Spanish. He then strode to the front door and called out, *"Tu, muchacho, ven aquí."*

The bronze gates opened and closed and then Jeff heard the voice of Vincente in the vestibule. There were steps in the hall and the servant entered, prodding Vincente ahead of him. Vincente advanced, first cast an appraising glance at the statue, then made a courtly bow, the effect of which was somewhat marred by the shoeshine box hanging from his shoulder. "Don Cipriano."

The old man looked aghast at the boy. "Vincente!" He stared at him for a moment, then loosed another flood of Spanish. At the conclusion he turned toward Jeff, shrugged his shoulders, pointed to Vincente and then to Jeff. It was a signal for Vincente to speak.

"Don Cipriano," Vincente bowed slightly toward that august personage, "wishes me to say to you that although I have been a frequent visitor to this house, this is the first time I have ever been permitted to come in the front door. You see, I have known Don Cipriano all my life. He has given me permission to say to you that he is my father, although I am a bastard. So, I am allowed to come here once a month to the back door and this Juan, Don Cipriano's servant, hands me an envelope which contains four silver pesos. It is for my sister and myself, for although my sister Perla is not Don Cipriano's daughter, he nevertheless helps her, too, because she is the daughter of my mother, whom Don Cipriano knew at one time."

"Un de mis bastardos." Don Cipriano smiled paternally at Vincente.

The word was close enough to its English equivalent for Jeff to need no translation. Already he knew two Spanish words. *Sucio* meant dirty and *bastardo* meant bastard. Rather a good combination, he thought: *sucio bastardo,* dirty bastard. Now he had a firm foundation in the language.

Don Cipriano spoke again to Vincente, who translated facilely.

"Don Cipriano says that I am a rascal, which is not true. He also says that my sister is a whore, which is indeed true. "But"—Vincente flashed his most engaging smile at both Jeff and his father—"he also says I have enough of his blood in my veins to make me sufficiently trustworthy to be a good interpreter for both of you."

"Then first read this letter to him." Jeff handed him the sheet of neat copperplate writing.

"Alas, *señor,* I do not read."

"Then I shall read it for you in English and you shall translate it for your father." He unfolded the letter and read it slowly, stopping at the end of each sentence so that Vincente could translate it into Spanish. Don Cipriano listened attentively.

Esteemed friend Don Cipriano:

I hope this letter will find you and your brother Don Eugenio in good health, as indeed I am through the grace of God.

This will serve to introduce Mr. Jefferson Carson, who is to act as our agent in Havana, with your kind help and assistance. We are in urgent need of some 300 fine strong male slaves, which Mr. Carson will purchase, with possibly a dozen extra-Fancy female slaves, if such are on the market.

We have arranged letters of credit for Mr. Carson at both the Banco Real de España and the Bank of Barcelona.

Anything you can do to help Mr. Carson will be sincerely appreciated.

Your indebted friend,
JEAN LAFITTE

Through Vincente, Don Cipriano remarked that it would indeed be a pleasure to serve Señor Jefferson Carson, and anything he could do to expedite matters would most certainly be his pleasure. As a matter of fact, a ship had arrived in Havana only yesterday—a Portuguese ship—with, he understood, about a hundred good males. It had previously stopped in Port-au-Prince, and possibly the best had been unloaded there, but he would send messengers and arrange for Don Jefferson to see them at the barracoons of Emilio Hernandez, across the bay in Regla. And there were other sources. As to the Fancies Señor Lafitte had mentioned, these would be at Solano's. Policarpo Solano was the leading slave merchant in Havana for that type of chattel. He would dispatch another messenger at once. Furthermore, if Don Jefferson wished him to handle the letters of credit with the banks, he would be happy to do so.

Jeff thanked him.

Don Cipriano regretted, so Vincente said (and had foretold), that he could not offer him the hospitality of his home while he was in Havana, as he and his brother were both bachelors and lived very simply. And, speaking of his brother, Don Angel would be back in Havana tomorrow and he spoke excellent English.

Jeff thanked him again and asked if he would recommend a hotel.

Indeed he could. The Hotel de Paris was conveniently located on the Prado and was new enough to be comfortable. Also, they had a prize-winning master chef there and the cuisine was highly recommended. He would dispatch a messenger to reserve a room.

"Make it a suite of two rooms," Jeff said. "I have a servant with me, and although I have not quite made up my mind, I believe, if you agree, *señor,* that I shall retain young Vincente as my interpreter, after cleaning him up a bit. Without an interpreter, I find I am helpless in Havana."

Vincente grinned as he translated.

"Don Cipriano says I must first clean myself up." Vincente shrugged. "And he will provide me money to buy new clothes, which I must promise to keep clean. But that will not be difficult if I do not shine shoes anymore."

The interview was over. With a low bow to Don Cipriano, Jeff turned to leave. Vincente followed him. Don Cipriano put a retaining hand on his son. He jingled some coins in his pocket and gave them to Vincente. Then, with more formal adieus, they left, escorted to the door not by the manservant but by Don Cipriano himself. Once out in the sunshine, they entered the *volanta.*

"To La Machina, Don Jeff, to collect your man and your baggage, and then to the Hotel de Paris."

"Hell no, boy." Jeff slapped him on the back. "I looked at the tits on that marble statue so long, I got such a hard-on I had to keep my hand in my pocket to hide it. Let's stop at your house and see if your sister is busy."

"You'll not be disappointed, Don Jeff." The boy stared admiringly at Jeff's crotch. "My sister, too, will be very happy."

CHAPTER XVI

THE hut in which Vincente lived was deep in a maze of crooked old streets which had not changed since Havana was a walled city. Although these alleys grudgingly allowed the passage of a slow-moving ox cart or a mule-drawn dray, they were little more thans paths, so narrow that a pedestrian meeting traffic had either to duck into a doorway or flatten himself against a wall. Their very narrowness almost blotted out the sun. As they penetrated farther into this rabbit warren, Jeff became increasingly apprehensive.

He was totally dependent upon this small boy, whom he had met only by chance. He could make himself understood only through Vincente. And now he was being led deep into slums where any of the drinkers in the tiny *bodegas* and coffee shops, any of the men lounging at street corners and in open doorways, might be assassins. They were mostly young, debonair in an oily way, and came in all flesh tones from white through *café-au-lait,* to brown and ebony. There seemed to be little color distinction in Cuba. Blacks and whites mixed much more freely than in New Orleans. A few *hombres* skulking in the shadows looked as though they would gladly slit his gullet for a tenth of the gold he carried in his pocket.

Yet, when he looked at Vincente sitting up beside the driver and the boy turned to grin at him, he lost some of his apprehension. Vincente made another obscene gesture with his fingers and said *"pronto."* Jeff hoped the word meant "soon."

A few blocks farther Vincente ordered the driver to stop before what Jeff was sure was the most disreputable hovel on the most odious of all the by-ways they had traversed. Moreover, they had stopped in the center of the most raffish crowd he had yet seen—young bravos, gaunt scarecrows of old beggar women, ancient men with evil etched in their faces, and a screaming swarm of urchins. With Vincente's help, he alighted before a large arch opening in a gray and mildewed wall surmounted by rusty iron-railed balconies. Men lounging in the doorway cast sidelong glances at the pair as they entered; one called Vincente by name. Once inside the inner patio they dodged naked children playing among heaps of debris, ribs of old furniture, and a conglomeration of dirty papers, broken boxes, and the litter of hundreds of families who had lived there before. One of the children ran up and chattered at Vincente, reeling off Spanish sentences.

This inside courtyard was lined with iron railings on all

four sides on each of its three stories. A bedlam of shouts and curses reverberated off the walls as slatterns, hanging over the railings, called to children below and yelled at each other. Vincente beckoned Jeff to follow him and mounted a flight of worn stone steps inside the arched opening.

They ascended two flights of broken, cracked, and filthy steps to the accompaniment of jeers, catcalls, and female invitations. Jeff distinguished the words *Americano, puta,* and *Perla,* as well as an occasional *Vincente.* He reasoned his errand to the house was not a secret.

On the third floor, Vincente beckoned Jeff to follow him along the gallery. They ran a gauntlet of women of all ages, several of whom offered themselves brazenly to Jeff. One reached with her sweaty hand for the bulge at his crotch, and another loosened her bodice to reveal her plump breasts. Although he could not understand their words, their gestures and catcalls plainly expressed the opinion that the unknown Perla was about to draw a prize. Probably few well-dressed *Americanos* ever entered this den of thieves and prostitutes.

Vincente pushed through the brawling crowd of women, opening a way for Jeff to follow. He scanned the women crowded about them for his sister. When he failed to see her, he urged Jeff ahead and knocked on a battered door.

"Are you busy?" he asked in Spanish.

"No," came the answer through the door. At least here was one Spanish word Jeff could understand. Vincente opened the door; they stepped inside and Vincente closed the door and shoved home a thick bolt to secure it. Jeff exhaled a deep breath.

It was not an overly large room. Jeff was glad to see the aging tiles, cracked plaster, and unpainted wood were clean. A double bed covered with a clean white sheet stood in one corner. A smoke-blackened hole in the masonry counter which ran along one wall apparently served as a charcoal stove. The only other furniture besides the bed was a plain deal table with one leg mended, a straight-backed chair, and a box that also served as a chair. A big window with unglazed French doors faced the street, and beyond this Jeff saw the scaling iron of a balcony. One corner of the room was curtained off with a tattered piece of flowered cotton, now an overall gray from many washings. That was all except for a meager collection of feminine garments that hung from nails over the bed. Perla was not visible.

"Where's this sister you have been talking so much about?"

Vincente's thumb jerked in the direction of the screened-off corner. *"Un momento,"* he said, anticipatory pride brightening his face.

And it was only a moment before the curtain was lifted and a girl emerged. She was unabashedly naked. Jeff was cognizant of the fact that Vincente may have been a handsome child under his grime, but he was quite unprepared for the beauty and delicacy of the girl who stood before him. She looked, as Vincente had said, under twelve. Her short life as a prostitute had not robbed her of a virginal look. The innocent appearance of childhood, the youthful bloom of springtime and chastity, lingered. She was a trifle taller than Vincente, with a heart-shaped face framed by long dark curls. Her eyes were a disturbing gray-green, which seemed unusual with her tea-rose skin and black hair. These eyes stared at him from under long sooty lashes with childlike anticipation. Her breasts, not yet fully formed, were beautiful in their youthful plumpness. The rosy points of her nipples were hard and upstanding. Her waist was slender—he felt he could almost encompass it with both hands—but her hips swelled in provocative curves. A dainty patch of black hair punctuated the rose-and-white complexion of her body, and Jeff guessed from the beads of moisture on it and the freshly toweled glow of her skin that she had just finished bathing. She wore no makeup. She needed no heavy *maquillage*. She was still a child. Yet, she had never been a child. . . .

"My sister Perla," Vincente whispered. Then, in Spanish, he spoke to her. "A rich American. See that you treat him right. He is a friend of Don Cipriano's."

Her small bare feet made no noise as she moved close to Jeff. Smiling up at him, she raised her arms and clasped her hands like a garland behind the nape of his neck. For a long moment her eyes appraised his rugged handsomeness. Jeff smiled down at her, torn between consideration of her age and his desperate need, and felt a tightening at his crotch. She was aware of it and moved away from him so she could see what she felt. Then she pressed her body against his, slowly undulating her hips. Her lips, moist, pink, and rose-petal soft, touched his mouth, gentle as a baby's, knowing as a *puta's.* He returned her kiss, responding to the soft, warm, wet, and tender tip of her tongue between his teeth.

"Ay, tan joven y tan guapo!" She turned and smiled her appreciation to Vincente who stood stolidly looking on.

"Will you get the hell out of here, Vincente?" Jeff said.

"I'll not leave you, Señor Jeff, but neither will I be any trouble." He lifted the curtain to disclose a pallet on the floor alongside a washbasin and damp towels. "I shall clean myself up and take a little nap perhaps. It's better that I stay, because if you need anything I'll be here to tell her in Spanish what you want."

"A *dueña,* huh?"

"But a blind one, Señor Jeff."

"But not deaf?"

"What can you say to my sister that she will understand?"

"Nothing." Jeff shook his head. "But at times when his blood runs hot, a man speaks out and a girl understands. So be it." Jeff dismissed Vincente from his thoughts and turned his attention to Perla.

She stood before him, smiling, completely unself-conscious about her nudity. He drew in a long breath and expelled it through half-pursed lips. Good God! She was so damned young and so damned beautiful! Child though she was, her body held great promise. Her skin was a shade lighter in color than her brother's. Her youthful rosiness shone through the faint tinge of olive. True, her breasts were immature, but perfectly rounded with an aureole of sepia surrounding the taut pink nipples. His eyes strayed to the patch of dark hair between her legs and his fingers itched to touch that triangle of sable.

Her tiny hands busied themselves with his cravat. She loosened it and draped it over the back of the chair. His white coat followed. She spread his damp shirt over the box. She tried to pull the knitted silk undershirt over his head but he stopped her by shaking his head and moving her hands to his groin where his pulsating tensity was all too apparent. Her fingers stroked and caressed him through the cloth, then rose to work impatiently with the brass buckle of his belt. His fingers stopped fondling her breasts long enough to help her. She unbuttoned his straining fly, stripped down his trousers and his underpants, and stared in delight when his rigid maleness, freed from its prison of cloth, popped out in all its magnificence.

"Ay, qué magnífico! Pero tengo miedo que está demasiado grande para mí."

"She says she's afraid you are too big for her," Vincente called from behind the curtains. "But you are not to worry, she'll manage."

Her hands left him reluctantly while she pulled off his boots and stripped off his socks, waiting while he stepped out of his trousers and underpants. Then she knelt before him, her hands caressing him while he teetered on his feet, holding her head between his trembling hands as her wet mouth and darting tongue conspired to tantalize him beyond endurance. Marvelous as she was, he stopped her, determined to delay the *dénouement* as long as possible.

He pulled her up to him, his mouth seeking hers, and then curtailing this pleasure too, he picked her up in his arms—she was light and fragile—and carried her to the bed where he lowered her to her back. He let his eyes gaze over her before he lay beside her. Now it was his turn to seek out the secret parts of her body, letting his mouth taste her moist freshness. Although she was a professional, he was convinced her squirming and gasping for breath were entirely unfeigned. He had had too much experience with women not to recognize the real thing.

For long moments they played with each other—that little game in which strangers in love explore each other's bodies—seeking and discovering unknown treasures. Their fingers and lips heightened their passion until she extricated herself from under him and turned him gently onto his back. Mounting him, she raised and lowered herself rhythmically upon his rigidity.

He felt the hot liquid building up within him. Unable to take more of her exquisite torment, he overturned her and spread-eagled her on the bed, holding her shoulders with both hands while he mounted her in turn. The golden cross swung swiftly—a metronome gone wild.

Her legs clasped him. Forgetting everything but the desperate urgency to fulfill his own great need, he plunged into her and although she cried out, her nails clawing his back assured him his brutality was more satisfying to her than gentleness. Then in a cataclysm that started in his toes and rushed like red-hot lava through his loins, he exploded within her. Panting for breath, he fell inert on the mattress beside her.

Her hand reached down to fondle his increasing limpness, trying to resuscitate him, until he pushed her away. He turned his head slightly. Vincente, the curtain raised with one hand while the other pumped himself vigorously, reached a climax and the curtain fell again. Finally there was no sound in the room but all of their breathing, mingled with the daytime noises of the street below. Jeff rested beside the girl, listening to the splashing of water in the curtained-off alcove. His eyes closed heavily in a sleep of exhaustion. He heard activity in the curtained alcove, and out walked Vincente—a changed boy.

It was Vincente, but he was *clean*—so clean he seemed to glow all over. He wore a fresh shirt, and although the white pantaloons were darned and patched, they also were neat. He sported a pair of rope-soled *alpargatas* on his feet. He was indeed a different child, as handsome in his way as his sister Perla was beautiful.

"So you have enjoyed Perla? Didn't I promise you? You would not have believed me if I had told you she was the best fuck in all Havana, but now! *Ay,* Vincente never lies, never."

He spoke to his sister in rapid Spanish and she nodded and said something.

"And she agrees, too, that it was the best she ever had,

although she says you did hurt her a little. She says, judging from you, Americans are better than Cubans. Cubans —wham! They push a girl down on the bed, spread her legs, stick it in, and it's all over. They have no patience. Get it in and get it out. That's all they ever think about."

Jeff sat up on the bed and grinned at Vincente over Perla's body, glistening with sweat. "And you enjoyed it, too, didn't you? I saw you banging away like a stallion on a mare."

Vincente grinned, a nine-year-old satyr. "That's how I get my pleasures, watching Perla perform when there is nothing else to do. *Sí señor.* She takes a man to her room. I watch. Sometimes when the man is gone, she lets me get in bed with her. She says these damned *Cubanos* never give her time to get satisfied herself, so I have to help her along. I teach her, too. All she knows is what I've taught her, and I've been a good master, no?"

"You seem to be pretty good at everything."

"Ah, *señor,* but you did not try me. You would have had a much better time had I been in the bed with you, too. But *Americanos* think only a woman can please . . . what about a girl and a boy together?" He rolled his eyes. "Ah, *señor,* that is real *extasís!*" He shook his head vehemently to give accent to the spoken words. Then, turning on Perla, he cursed her in Spanish for not getting up to wash Jeff and help him to dress.

She climbed out of bed, poured water from a pitcher onto a clean rag, and went over Jeff's body with it, washing him carefully. Then she poured a few drops of eau de cologne onto the palm of her hand and wiped his face.

"It is almost time for our *almuerzo,* and you must be hungry, Señor Jeff." Vincente was impatient. "You've been working hard. Come, you and I will eat at El Paraiso—such *langosta,* such Morro crabs, such shrimps." Vincente waited while Perla helped Jeff with his clothes. They were dry now, and although he would have preferred a bath, the only water in the apartment was that in which both Perla and Vincente had already bathed. He would have to be satisfied with Perla's cat-licking.

When they were ready to leave, Jeff took out one of the

smallest gold pieces from his pocket and gave it to Perla.

"And now I am going to work for you for four silver pesos a week, with my food and a bed in your hotel extra," Vincente announced.

Jeff laughed. "So you have already made up your mind, have you? You've even settled on your salary. But if you work for me, who's going to pimp for Perla?"

"I'll ask Jorge, a friend. A damned mean bastard. He'd slit his grandmother's throat for a copper. A real *ladrón*, that Jorge. But he'll keep Perla flat on her back and get his own for free." Vincente hesitated. "Remember, he spoke to us on the street?"

Jeff vaguely remembered one of the toughs in the doorway speaking to Vincente as he eyed him. He sat down so Perla could ease his boots on. She had not dressed and her small breasts quivered with her movements, giving him a renewed urge, but he stifled it.

"The one with long pointed *patillas* on his cheeks. Because he's so handsome and so well hung he thinks he shouldn't pay a whore but she should pay him." He leaned over Perla. "Don't give him too much, Perla, even if he is pimping for you."

"I'll not," she answered, "but you keep in touch with me. It's going to be strange around here without my *hermanito*."

"I'll see you often because I'm sure my boss will want to come here often."

Jeff was surprised at the crowd collected around Vincente's door when they went out. He heard the murmurs of both men and women.

"*Ay qué guapo!* How fancy looking he is."

"*Americano.*"

"And rich. They say he's worth millions."

"So young! I'd share my bed with him."

"And what a man! Look at that crotch."

"Ay, poor Perla will walk spraddle-legged for the next week."

All this chatter went on as they pushed past the excited Cubans collected around Vincente's door. Vincente signaled to the suavely handsome fellow who had spoken to him previously, and took him aside. Their conversation concluded with a nodding of heads. He returned to Jeff and escorted him down the stairs. In the street Vincente suggested they walk, as it was only a short distance to the restaurant at the head of La Machina wharf.

"Are you hungry, *amigo mio*?" Vincente asked. It was *amigo* now and not *señor*, Jeff noticed. Wasn't there a fable about a camel with his nose in the tent?

"Starving, *amigo mio*," Jeff answered.

"Then, *señor*, if we are friends, will you tell me something? Why is it when you took your clothes off to go to bed with Perla, you did not remove your undershirt? It is strange a man in this weather should even wear an undershirt. Stranger still that he should not take it off when he is fucking."

"There's only one word that will answer your question and that's a word you won't understand. It's an idiosyncrasy of mine, that's all."

Vincente pondered a moment. "Ah, we have the same word in Spanish. *Idiosincrasia*. Now I think I know what you mean. You don't enjoy unless you wear your shirt. Just like a friend of mine has to look at a woman's shoe —*cuando re goza*—when he plays with himself. Right?"

Jeff wondered briefly why he clung to his secret in this country where there seemed to be no color line. There was no explanation—except that he still awoke at night in a cold sweat, remembering his narrow escape in Mississippi. No, whether in Cuba or New Orleans or Barataria it was safer that Bricktop remain buried.

CHAPTER XVII

THE rooms reserved for Jeff at the Hotel de Paris were far more luxurious and comfortable than he had anticipated. The bedroom was large, high-ceilinged, with two tall French windows opening on balconies facing the

Prado. There were plenty of cane-seated mahogany rocking chairs and a ponderous mahogany wardrobe with immense mirrored double doors. The enormous double bed was shrouded with white mosquito netting that gave it the appearance of a full-rigged ship under sail. Off the bedroom was a dressing room where he had a cot placed for Vincente. He had another cot for Ramon placed in the bathroom, with its big high-backed tin tub.

On another floor there was a servants' dining room where Ramon could eat with other black servants. Vincente, being accepted as white, would either eat from trays sent up to the room or occasionally with Jeff in the elaborate hotel dining room whose big windows opened wide on the street. Food at the hotel was good— Cuban cuisine prepared by a French chef—which made every meal a delightful experience.

The first morning at the hotel a messenger arrived from Don Cipriano to say that his brother had returned and would call at eleven to pay his respects to Señor Carson. Fortunately Vincente was there to interpret. Jeff wondered what he would do without Vincente. He was amazed that igorance of a language could be such a handicap.

Promptly at eleven Don Cipriano's brother arrived, a pompous version of the older Olivarez. Through Vincente again, the brother informed Jeff that his name was Don Angel and that he was ready to serve Jeff in any way possible. Don Angel spoke halting English but scarcely enough to carry on a conversation, which made Jeff all the more grateful for Vincente.

In his slow and stilted English Don Angel informed Jeff that if convenient, he would return after lunch and, even though it would be siesta time in Havana, he would go with Jeff to the barracoons of one Señor Hernandez across the harbor in Regla. A new shipment of slaves from Africa had just arrived a day or so earlier. Hernandez was about to auction the men off singly, but if he had a chance to sell a large parcel at once, he might dispense with the auction. Moreover, Don Angel informed Jeff, they would probably cost less if bought by the hundred. Fortunately for Jeff, Don Angel said, slave prices were down a bit, as several slavers had arrived within the past month and more were expected soon.

So, Don Angel continued, he would return home for lunch; no, it was gracious of Jeff to invite him for *almuerzo* at the hotel but he had business to attend to at home. He would be back at two o'clock *al punto.* Would this be satisfactory? Jeff assured him it would be, and that he would be waiting. To kill time, Jeff had Vincente take him to the Mercado, that vast sprawling jungle of a marketplace where everything from a freshly killed chicken to a vest of Lyons velvet could be bought. The clothes on Vincente's back were evidently the only ones he possessed other than the disreputable rags he wore as a shoeshine boy, and Jeff wanted him to look respectable when accompanying him on business missions. He preferred bilingual Vincente to Ramon. He knew Ramon resented this. Rivalry between the two had already developed after only one day. Arguments as to who should wait on him were usually won by Vincente, who was far more aggressive than the lazy Ramon. It had been Vincente who had helped him dress that morning; Vincente who had first used his bath water after he had finished; Vincente who had buttered his hot croissants for breakfast; and Vincente who would have chewed them for him had that been possible.

It was Vincente, too, who led Jeff to an obscure stall in the Mercado where there were Cuban shirts for sale —something called *guyaberas*, really more jacket than shirt—embellished with a multitude of fancy tucks and four capacious pockets. Jeff had noticed many men wearing them in lieu of a jacket, and they certainly appeared cooler and more comfortable. While buying several for Vincente, he laid in a stock for himself and a few for Ramon. Then there were new white-drill trousers to buy for Vincente as well as a pair of shoes. Shoes for Vincente! He had shined so many pairs for so many other people and now at last he had a pair for himself. They were, he confessed to Jeff, among the luxuries in life he had most wanted.

By the time they had returned to the hotel and Jeff had changed his shirt and Vincente had donned his new clothes, marveling again that he should own a pair of shoes, it was time for lunch. The two of them ate in the lower dining room to allow Vincente an opportunity to show off his new finery. Jeff marveled at the boy's impeccable table manners—until he discovered that Vincente was watching him to copy his every movement. Smart lad! Nobody would ever guess that only yesterday he was shining shoes on the pier.

Don Angel arrived while they were still eating and drank a cup of coffee with them. He invited them to share his carriage to ride to the harbor. Again Vincente occupied the seat beside the driver and Don Angel, having run out of his meager stock of English, sat silently with Jeff. Once at the waterfront, Don Angel dickered with a boatman to take them to the little town of Regla across the harbor. The trip took only a few minutes.

Regla was a sleepy little Cuban settlement that seemed centuries removed from Havana's cosmopolitanism. There were no carriages waiting here, so Don Angel hired a lumbering ox cart with seats of the hardest planks Jeff ever sat on. The cart bumped them through the cobbled streets of the town to the outskirts where a palisade of logs marked the barracoons.

Once inside the guarded gateway, Don Angel introduced Jeff to Señor Hernandez. Hernandez was one of the least likely persons Jeff would have envisaged in charge of a slave barracoon. He was a man of indeterminate age with sparse white hair and steely blue eyes that squinted through a pair of square brass-rimmed spectacles. His high-pitched voice matched his body— weak and quavering. He walked, with some difficulty, with the aid of a thick mahogany cane. After their introduction he invited Jeff and the others into his office, which was almost a duplicate of Jeff's own office in Barataria. Even the rank all-pervading odor of barracoons was the same, making Jeff feel queasy in the belly, and quite at home.

Yes, Hernandez agreed to Jeff's question as translated by Vincente, he had just received a shipment of slaves from Africa—a whole shipload. They were of good quality, he assured Jeff, mostly Fantis from the Gold Coast, plus some Kromantis and others, but all good men. Unfortunately he had not had time to condition them but they were all fine specimens, quite the best he had received in a long time. He again apologized to Jeff for their present poor condition after the long sea voyage, but said they would present a much different appearance in a few days, with rest and good food. He had, he explained through Vincente, intended to have an auction when the men had been reconditioned, but, of course, if Señor Carson wished to see them in their present state, he would be happy to show them. As to how many he had, there were about two hundred fifty in this shipment, but he had another fifty or so from local sources for sale. Señor Carson was welcome to look at them also. Would he like to see them now or wait until early the next morning? The next morning, Hernandez said, would be far more satisfactory as he could get things lined up and the men would be more presentable after a hearty breakfast and a liberal rubbing with palm oil.

Jeff agreed to wait. He had to make himself known to the banks before he could enter into any negotiations, but he did ask Hernandez if he might take a casual look at the men before he left. Hernandez was willing, and after a glass of sherry, they went out into the hot sunlight to see the slaves.

A wide thatched roof surmounted the four walls of the interior compound within the palisades, and most of the men were sitting on the ground in its shade or lolling on the plank beds that rose in three tiers under the shelter. Jeff quickly saw that most of the men were thin and emaciated, listless, and apparently mentally depressed. There were no smiling faces and few of them even bothered to look up as he passed. They had survived the long cramped voyage from Africa, and now they did not know what ordeals lay ahead. However, he noted

172

that most of them, despite their dispirited appearance, had strong, muscular frames. When they were rested and fattened up a little, they would be first class specimens. He spotted several who might be more than first class, almost Fancies. He could probably fill his whole quota right here, with the exception of those few female Fancies Lafitte wanted and for whom he would have to go to— Solano's, was it?

Also, he reminded himself, he must stock his own ship with food and water for these men, and again he wondered just how he was going to accommodate them all on his small craft. But it was a short voyage and they would have to put up with a few hardships. Once in Barataria, they could be fattened up, exercised, and fully conditioned.

He took his leave of Hernandez, promising to return early next morning. When they returned to Havana, he told the younger Olivarez brother that there was no need to rouse himself so early to accompany them, as he had Vincente to act as interpreter. Don Angel seemed most grateful but assured Jeff that he would be at his service any time.

When they returned to the hotel Vincente informed him that the hour of the siesta was over, and the banks would be open. As neither of Jeff's banks was far from the hotel, they could walk to them easily, giving Jeff his first real taste of walking the streets of Havana.

He found the city increasingly fascinating, despite the absence of women. He loitered in several shops, buying a high tortoise-shell comb for Gretchen, and an elaborately embroidered and intricately fringed Spanish shawl as a present for Perla, whom he planned to visit again that evening. When he informed Vincente of his desire to see Perla again, Vincente begged his leave to run home after they had made contact with the banks. He promised Jeff it would take less than an hour for him to make sure that Jorge would leave Perla's time open. When they had finished their business at the banks, where the La-fitte name earned Jeff a most cordial reception, Vincente left. Jeff remembered the turnings they had made and found his way back to the hotel easily. He stopped at the same shop where he had bought the comb and the shawl to purchase a pair of long jet earrings he had seen, which he would add to the gift of the shawl to Perla. Then, remembering Chloe—had she ever been far from his thoughts?—he bought another pair of earrings, these set with pearls and tiny diamonds. The thought of Chloe brought Helen to mind, and he purchased a heavy gold bracelet engraved with *"Recuerdo de la Habana"*.

But although he remembered Chloe with love and Helen with affection and gratitude, his immediate thoughts were with Perla and his anticipated visit this night. Chloe was far away, Perla was near. He hoped that Jorge had not been overly assiduous in bringing her customers. She must not be too tired to entertain him as excitingly as the night before. She was a hot little bitch. Damn! He wished he had gone with Vincente now. It would be a long wait until tonight. True, the longer he waited, the better it would be, but he wished to hell it could be *now*.

When he returned to the hotel the jalousies had been drawn and it was dimly cool inside. Not having eaten anything since his early breakfast, he was hungry. It was now long past lunchtime and the dining room was closed, but he sent Ramon downstairs to see if he could get a sandwich and a cup of coffee. Ramon had already eaten and sped off on Jeff's errand. When he returned with the food, he stood before Jeff while he was eating, shifting his weight from one foot to another, obviously wanting to speak and yet not daring. Finally he could stand it no longer.

"Kin I ask yo' somethin', Mastah Jeff?" He twisted his hands and spoke haltingly.

"Now what's bothering you?" Jeff was tired and a bit irritable. The siesta hour, he had decided, was a good idea and the white sheets of the bed were most inviting. Now that he had satisfied his hunger, he wanted only to strip off his sweaty clothes and stretch out for a long nap.

"Ain' nothin a-botherin' me, Mastah Jeff, but why cain' I go out with yo' no more? Yo' takes that Vinthentay everywhere yo' goes 'n' I stays here. Ain' nothin' to do, ain' no work to do, ain' nobody to talk with. It a-gittin' mighty lonesomelike a-settin' here all day a-waitin' for yo' to come home."

Jeff looked at Ramon, actually seeing him for the first time in days. His own irritability disappeared and he tried to picture himself in Ramon's place. He had forbidden the lad to leave the hotel for fear he might get lost and, knowing no Spanish, be unable to find his way back. Now Jeff was going out again this evening with Vincente and Ramon would again be abandoned. Jeff was suddenly in a mood to be generous. After all, Ramon was a man like himself and, black or not, he had the same needs.

Still chewing on the last mouthful of his sandwich, he smiled. He had no complaints against this boy: Ramon had always served him with loyalty, even affection. Since they had landed in Havana Jeff had been so busy he had quite forgotten about him. It was Vincente he depended upon now. He felt sorry for Ramon.

"Tell me something, boy. How long since you've been laid?"

"Good Lord, Mastah Jeff, it bin so long I plumb forgotten. Musta bin that little yellow wench what lives in the house of M'sieur Delacroix out near the barracoons. It all of a month ago, Mastah Jeff. She mighty pretty but . . ."

"A month, huh? That's a mighty long time, Ramon."

"Shore is. Like'n yo' knows, Mastah Jeff, my pecker, it ain' such a big one, but it shore git lonely. Reckon as to how it make no neverminds how big it is, needs wenchin' jes' the same. Shore a-wishin' I like yo', Mastah Jeff. Then I don' find it such a hard time to git me a wench. If'n I like yo', onct she has it, she wants it again."

"Ain't many like me, Ramon. Sure was born lucky. Don't know just where a black boy like you is going to get himself a piece of tail down here, but I'll wager Vincente knows. Tell you what. You can go out with us tonight, and while I'm getting mine from Vincente's

175

sister, I'll see to it that he takes you somewhere and lets you get rid of your load. How's that? Better than sitting around here all alone, huh?"

Ramon fell on his knees before his master and took his hand, covering it with kisses. "Yo're jes' the best mastah in all the world, Mastah Jeff. How yo' know that's what I bin wantin' most of all? Yo're good, Mastah Jeff, —'n' I promise yo' I'll always be good. Loves yo', Mastah Jeff, 'deed I do. Loves yo' 'nuff to die for yo'."

Jeff patted his head. "Nobody's dying, Ramon, but I sure know that a boy like you gets horny and needs a piece once in a while. Now that that's settled, relax. I'm going to lie down for a while. When I wake up, you scuttle around and see if you can find me some hot water for a bath. Then we'll dress up—you can use one of your new shirts—and Vincente will be back and take us wherever we're going. How's that?"

With Ramon's help, Jeff peeled off his clothes and sought the comfort of his bed. He was asleep almost as soon as he hit the mattress and slept soundly for hours, awakened only by Vincente's return just as the sunlit strips on the floor were fading out and the dusk descending. He would willingly have slept all night had he not been itching for Perla. Vincente informed him that he had arranged for Perla to be free after eight o'clock, although he had quite an argument with Jorge, who had scheduled several patrons for her. Cancel them, Vincente had ordered. Perla was *his* sister and Jeff was a rich American, able to pay more than all the paltry silver pieces the Cubans could cough up among them. Yes, Vincente had winked at Jeff, he had told Jorge how very rich and important Jeff was and that had ended the argument.

Vincente promised that while Jeff was with Perla he would take Ramon to a girl he knew. Of course, Ramon could not expect anything very luxurious, and he might have to wait in line behind two or three who would be ahead of him, but although the girl was black, she was young and not too bad-looking and she charged only fifty centavos. Cheap, yes, but he had heard she was good; that's why she always had so many customers. He would wait until Ramon finished, which never took very long with this girl. Then they would come back and collect Jeff. But, he assured Jeff, he was not to hurry. They would wait for him.

Once everything was settled, Jeff bathed and dressed in one of his new Cuban shirts. He then had a meal for himself and Vincente sent up to his room; Ramon ate in the servants' quarters. After dining, he sat out on the balcony watching the life of Havana flow past until it was time to go. Vincente negated the use of any conveyance, saying that he knew shortcuts that would get them to Perla's house in no time and it was foolish to spend money on a carriage for so short a distance. It was cool now, the sun had gone down, and they would not mind walking.

Although it was not far, Jeff felt uneasy walking through the almost deserted streets. He wished that he had left some of his money at the hotel. The alleyways that Vincente led them through were dark and scabrous, with shadows within deeper shadows. Almost before he knew it, however, he recognized the crumbling facade of Vincente's house and then once again he was in the room with Perla. This time he was alone, for Vincente and Ramon had departed on their errand.

Perla was delighted to see him again and even more entranced with her gifts. She draped the shawl around her nude body, looking at herself in the small mirror. Her gestures indicated it was something she had long wanted. She hung the earrings in her ears to show Jeff their lustrous effect. She kissed him and swiftly stripped off his clothes.

Her gratitude extended to her lovemaking, which was even more ardent than it was the night before. This time he insisted that she blow out the candles, and in the all-enveloping darkness he shed his shirt. The voluptuous satisfaction of a woman's body against his own without intervening fabric was an unusual and ecstatic experience for him. Perla was not satisfied with one exhausting climax but resuscitated him with her fiery little tongue until he became rampant again. She was passionately essaying to revive him a third time when there was a discreet knock on the door and Vincente's voice asked if he were ready. He was not to hurry, Vincente assured him; he and Ramon would wait out on the balcony. Jeff was fully satiated for one evening, however, and he submitted to Perla's efforts to clean him and help him dress. When he opened the door Vincente and Ramon were waiting for him, Ramon with a shit-eating grin stretching his face.

"Jes' wonderful, Mastah Jeff! Wonderful! That Cuban gal, she much better'n any N'Orleans whore. Thank yo', Mastah Jeff. Cain' never forget that little girl, cain' never."

Once again Vincente insisted it would be easier to walk than ride, so they trudged off through the maze of narrow streets. They had scarcely left the house when Jorge, who Jeff recognized by his long, pointed sideburns, accosted them. Jeff and Ramon waited against a wall while Vincente carried on a long and heated conversation with Jorge. Both were angry. This was evident by the tone of their conversation and their belligerent gestures. Vincente's eyes blazed, but he was no angrier than the powerful Jorge who would have struck Vincente had not Jeff walked between them. Jorge heeled to curse Jeff. Jeff could not understand him so he about-faced and pushed Vincente ahead of him, leaving Jorge shouting at their backs until they turned the corner.

Vincente informed him, when his anger had cooled enough for him to speak coherently, that Jorge was damned mad. He had lined up two customers for Perla when Vincente came back with Jeff. Canceling the arrangements had not only put him in a bad light with his clients, but had also lost him money. However, Vincente insisted, he was not afraid of the bastard. Jorge might be bigger and stronger but his knife was no longer than Vincente's and his skill at using it no greater. Just let him start something; Vincente would carve his initials deep on Jorge's belly. He'd be damned if he'd give him any money for Jeff's visit to Perla. Perla was his sister, and if Jeff wanted her, to hell with Jorge and the bastards he had lined up for her! He didn't need Jorge's help. Perla was acquiring an enviable reputation and soon she wouldn't need anyone to pimp for her, not even Vincente. So, he promised Jeff, as long as he was in Havana, he could have her whenever he wanted and to hell with Jorge—*hijo de puta* that he was.

They turned off the narrow street into an even narrower alley where they had to walk single file, Vincente first, then Jeff, with Ramon at the rear. It was so dark in the alley that Jeff could barely see the blur of Vincente's white shirt ahead of him. There was no moon, not even one of the typical Havana lamp posts with its guttering candle to dissipate the darkness of the deserted lane.

They were well into the alley when Jeff heard a noise behind him. He turned quickly, in time to see the dark figure of a man briefly silhouetted against the stars. The man leaped from the roof to a high wall and then plummeted to the ground and charged toward him. Jeff ducked. The man slipped and fell, but was up like a cat and lunged again at Jeff. Vincente came running, but Jeff had already tangled with his assailant.

The muscular thug seemed charged with superhuman strength. For a few moments the two men struggled in the darkness. There was no sound but the scuffling of feet and hoarse panting as they gasped for air.

Suddenly the thug got one hand on Jeff's throat and tightened his grasp. Jeff tried to pry away the fingers—and couldn't. He choked. The grip tightened. Jeff remembered the tricks of street fighting he had learned while pimping in Pittsburgh. He thrust a knuckle into his antagonist's eye. The man grunted but hung on. Jeff's windpipe was burning. He tried to suck in an ounce of air. He was growing faint.

Abruptly the grip slackened. Jeff dimly saw Ramon grab his attacker from the flank, pulling desperately on one arm while banging the man on the side of the head. Simultaneously Vincente grabbed the man from behind.

The thug disposed of Vincente with a backward mule kick. Then he squirmed in Jeff's bearlike grasp until he faced Ramon. There was a gasping sob of agony—then an eerie silence. Ramon slid slowly to the pavement. The assailant fled, with Vincente in pursuit.

Vincente caught the toe of one boot as the man reached the top of an adjoining wall. The other boot swung out to strike Vincente in the face. He fell backward as the unknown one vanished.

Jeff sank to his knees beside Ramon. He tried to lift the boy. His hands felt the warm stickiness of blood.

"He's hurt, Vincente. He's bleeding." Jeff could scarcely speak.

"We'll carry him to the corner."

Vincente lifted Ramon's feet while Jeff picked up his shoulders. They carried him to the end of the alley and stretched him out on the narrow sidewalk in a patch of candle light flickering through a window of the corner *bodega.*

Jeff knelt beside Ramon. He winced at the sight of the bright red blood against the darkness of Ramon's skin. Ramon's throat had been gashed open. He was no longer breathing.

In a matter of seconds a small crowd had gathered around them and Jeff heard Vincente presumably explaining to the men what had happened. A man fetched a candle from the *bodega* and knelt beside Jeff. The blood was barely oozing from the gaping wound in Ramon's throat. The man placed his hand over Ramon's heart, and shook his head. Ramon was dead.

Jeff shuddered deep in his guts. Ramon had given up his life to help him. The boy had carried out the promise he had made to Jeff at the hotel—he had died for him.

Vincente was still explaining what had happened when a uniformed policeman arrived. Vincente began his story anew. He and the American *señor,* and the *señor*'s black man, were on their way to the Hotel de Paris when they were set upon in the alley by an unknown man. No, Vincente did not know who it was, but the American carried money on him. Where had they been? To visit Vincente's sister. They were returning to the hotel. There were more questions in excitedly high-pitched Spanish and Jeff stood in stunned silence, listening to the ebb and flow of the strange language. He walked heavily into the *bodega,* pointed to a bottle, and made the motions of drinking. The proprietor poured him a glass of fiery brandy and Jeff downed it in one gulp. The warmth of the brandy in his stomach steadied him. At least he could think a little straighter.

They waited for an hour until a horse-drawn dray came to pick up Ramon's body. Jeff inquired of Vincente where they would be taking Ramon and Vincente replied that there was a public cemetery for slaves. All he would have to pay was for digging the grave. Nothing more? No, Vincente assured him, that was all. Slaves were not buried in a box nor did they have any funeral service. A hole was dug, the body put in the ground, and that was that.

Jeff shook his head. No. Ramon had saved his life. He could not bear to think of his poor body unprotected in the earth. Could he not have a decent burial? This, Vincente told him, after arguing with the policeman, would be impossible. Slaves could not be interred in hallowed ground. However, he could arrange for a wooden box for Ramon. Would that be satisfactory? Jeff nodded. He supposed so. It could be arranged for two gold pieces, Vincente said.

Jeff paid the policeman, waited while he signed a receipt with the stub of a pencil, then watched while Ramon's body was carried to the dray. Because Jeff had paid for special treatment, the men from potter's field laid the black boy gently in the bottom of the dray, folded his hands across his chest, and drove off. The soles of his boots as the dray passed from the circle of candle-light into darkness was the last Jeff saw of Ramon.

From somewhere in the night a *volanta* appeared and Vincente hailed it. They rode in silence to the hotel as Jeff examined his thoughts about his dead servant. Too bad Ramon had to die, but at least he had not died in vain. Had it not been for Ramon, Jeff himself might have been at the bottom of the dray. At least Ramon's last night on earth had been one of the high points of his short life. Jeff had given him something he had wanted badly, and obviously he had enjoyed it.

He had been fond of Ramon and would miss him. He

could replace him when he returned to Barataria—if he wanted to. But he really didn't need a servant with Gretchen to take care of him. And he certainly didn't need a servant to heighten his prestige in Cuba as long as the Lafittes were his sponsors.

No, he must not mourn Ramon. He had to look forward, not back. He had to go on forgetting the people who had played a part in his life, even those who had helped him. Minnie was no more than a name to him now, and he supposed he had loved her once. He must have; he had almost married her. And he never thought of Veronica whose bed he had shared and rented out. . . .

They pulled in before the hotel, paid the driver, and climbed the stairs to their room before either spoke.

"Do not feel bad, Señor Jeff," Vincente was consoling. "I will take care of you while you are in Havana and I'll do it even better than Ramon."

Jeff nodded.

"You know, Señor Jeff, I'm sure it was that damned Jorge." Vincente took the key from Jeff and opened the door. They went inside. "Jorge knew that you had money with you. *Ladrón!*"

"But we can't prove it, Vincente."

"No, we can't prove it, but take my advice, Señor Jeff. Don't go back to see Perla at my house again. I'll take you to Josefina's if you need a woman. It's safe there. It's too dangerous for you to go to my house. The next time Jorge will get some of his friends. It just shows how stupid he is to go after you alone. So, Señor Jeff, promise me that you will forget Perla."

"I've already forgotten a lot of women in my young life. But I really liked your sister."

"*Si señor,* I know you did."

"And a man has to have a woman."

"Yes." Vincente nodded in agreement.

"But there is always Josefina's house," Jeff added. He walked to the tall window and stood staring down into the candlelit street.

CHAPTER XVIII

WHEN Vincente roused him early next morning, the last thing in the world Jeff wanted to do was cross the bay to see Hernandez about buying slaves. In fact, he was physically and mentally incapable of any such effort. Tomorrow perhaps, but certainly not this morning. The shock and aftermath of poor Ramon's death had upset him so, he had spent a sleepless night. He did not close his eyes until dawn, and he had no desire to open them now despite Vincente's persistent nudgings.

Vincente was not to be denied, however. He had gone down for coffee, and after propping up Jeff with pillows, insisted on his drinking it. The strong brew made life seem slightly more worth living. Jeff felt better able to face the problems of the day. He slid out of bed and automatically bawled for someone to haul his lazy ass around to help him dress.

When only Vincente responded to his call, the ugly reality of the night before rushed back. Never again would Ramon help him dress. Damn! He did miss that dawdling black boy. His life was a pattern of using people and walking away from them. Soon he'd leave this place. He'd miss Vincente, too. And Perla. Particularly Perla. Just thinking about her could make him horny. But he had a day's work ahead of him. He had to stop thinking about Perla. He'd stop thinking about all women. No women could be permitted to interfere with his job for the Lafittes. To hell with women! At least until tonight. Tonight he'd go to the House of Josefina and see if these Cuban whores were as professional as they were touted to be.

His resolution stayed with him all the way to the waterfront and across the harbor. Landing in Regla, however, he saw a girl whose dark eyes and mobile hips intrigued him. Beyond turning to stare at her and receiving a ghost of a smile in return, nothing happened. So, on to the barracoons! When he arrived there, Hernandez had a cup of hot coffee waiting for him. It nearly scalded Jeff's throat but it served to wake him further and dispel the awful gloom of loss and the colorful fantasies of women that plagued him.

Hernandez escorted them out into the vast quadrangle with its floor of hard-packed earth. A table had been set up under a kiosk of thatch which provided a comfortable oasis of shade in the sun-drenched arena. Noting that there were only two chairs, Jeff asked Hernandez if another might be brought for Vincente. The boy, he told Hernandez, would play an important part in today's negotiations, and he wanted him to be as comfortable as possible. Hernandez gave instructions to his two black helpers and the chair was brought. Jeff grinned. He could almost see Vincente grow in stature as he sat down.

After a babble of shouting, halooing, and pushing, the Hernandez men finally got the despondent slaves lined up in a long straggling black file, awaiting Jeff's inspection. Peering out from under the shade of the palm-leaf shelter, Jeff was pleased to see that the men appeared far better-looking this morning than they had the night before. Their skins glistened with rubbed-in oil. They had eaten a substantial breakfast and the anticipation that something important was about to happen had somewhat revived their sagging spirits. They were talking among themselves. Some of them were even looking around curiously while they lined up in the blast of sun. The heat did not seem to bother them as much as did the swarms of buzzing flat-bellied flies which they constantly brushed away.

Jeff had Vincente explain his system to Hernandez. Those slaves he would consider buying he would dispatch to the left of the compound where they could rest on the plank beds. Those he would not consider he would send to the right. Herandez agreed to this, and after writing materials had been brought, Jeff launched into his new job. This was what it was all about. This was what Beluche's long training course had led to, the test of his value to the Lafitte's—his chance to share their fortune.

He beckoned to the man at the head of the line. As the man faced him, Jeff appraised him carefully. He was a formidable brute in his late teens or early twenties. He stood well over six feet, and had broad, muscular shoulders, thick, smooth neck, a muscle-ribbed belly that narrowed into slender hips, strong legs and feet planted firmly on the ground. He was not the shiny prune-black of Africa but rather a mellow chocolate brown. Africa produced brawn but rarely beauty. This man had both. His lips were thick and raisin-colored but not blubbery. His nose was wide and straight—not flattened against his face. One ear supported an earring of crude carved gold. The eyes, black, limpid cornea in nacreous white, gazed directly at Jeff. The fellow needed only a period of good feeding to replace the weight he'd lost.

Jeff motioned to him to walk around the table and kneel at his feet. His fingers ascertained that the man had all his teeth—strong, white, and glistening. Jeff ran his hands over the matted cap of short, crinkly hair, then down to examine the pillar of the thick, muscular neck and the broad shoulders. Finally the inspection continued along the arms to the hands, with their thick, spatulate fingers. The pressure of Jeff's hands under the man's arms caused him to stand.

The slave was circumcised and Jeff nodded to himself in self-corroboration. He had suspected he came from one of the northern Muslim tribes. His color, his bearing, and his lack of a foreskin all attested to it. Good! Muslims brought the highest prices. He hoped there were more. Jeff clasped the long smooth penis in one hand and manipulated it slowly. He noted the signs of an incipient erection—the heavy purple glans was beginning to swell. He'd be a good breeder, Jeff thought as he cupped the black's testicles, weighing them in his hand. He next slowly appraised the muscular legs, lifted each foot and examined the toes. He turned the man around, made him bend over, and spread his buttocks. No visible hemorrhoids. As far as he could see, this man was in perfect condition and he wondered if Hernandez had placed him first because he was such a prime specimen. But no; the next man in line appeared to be equally fine.

Jeff pointed to the left and Hernandez's man led the buck away, first stopping at a big basket for a joint of sugarcane which he gave to the slave to chew on. Suddenly Jeff remembered he had forgotten to check one thing—the black's coordination. Although he was quite sure the man was a splendid athlete, he spoke to Vincente, who relayed his demands in Spanish to Hernandez. The ensuing shouted command caused the Negro to run the length of the compound with an easy, loping stride and return. Jeff nodded his satisfaction. At least he had one fine specimen to take back to Barataria.

And so with the next and the next and the next after him. Jeff congratulated himself with every black he passed. These were Fancies, and although they would be capable of even the most taxing work in the fields, they were far too valuable to waste their sweat cutting sugarcane or chopping cotton. These men were studs, destined to sweat in the creaking rope beds of slave cabins, their nights passionately devoted to propagating another generation of handsome, strong-backed slaves for their masters. Jeff was willing to accept Hernandez's observation, passed on by Vincente, that this was one of the best shipments he had received in years. Evidently some petty Arab princeling had raided his neighbors' slave corrals.

Through Vincente Jeff questioned Hernandez. Yes, they were all, or practically all, from the caravans of a certain tin-pot Sultan of Sa'aqs who had a reputation along the whole west coast of Africa of having the finest slaves to be obtained on the continent. Sa'aqs had for a long time supported his own slave market in Trinidad. Since the English had outlawed slavery, and Haiti, now independent of France, no longer imported slaves, the big Sa'aqs monopoly in Africa was sending human cargos to Havana, one of the few remaining slave markets in the world.

Jeff continued his tedious job. There were some sad exceptions; there had to be in such a large number of men. He found one man with suppurating skin sores which Jeff diagnosed as yaws. Another man's testicles were swollen to the size of apples. Another had been born with hammertoes. He rejected yet another whose milky eyes marked him as nearly blind.

Along the way he came upon a most remarkable specimen—a young lad in his teens with ivory skin and dark hair coiling in ringlets to his shoulders. He was as slender as a reed but well formed, with a glistening skin highlighting well-rounded muscles. His mincing walk and the languid movement of his hands and arms set him apart from the rest. He was the only one in the whole courtyard who sported any sort of personal decoration apart from earrings. He wore a string of red coral beads, of which he seemed inordinately proud as he kept twirling them in his fingers. Jeff studied him and pondered. Here was no burly stud to knock up a plantation's wenches; no field hand to chop cotton all day; no cane cutter, no swashbuckling male to pit against the fighters from other plantations. However—and Jeff nodded to himself—here was the ideal butler or house servant who would delight the owner's wife and daughters, and possibly even the plantation owner himself. . . .

The boy was unquestionably a Fancy, far removed from the ordinary run of slaves. Hell, they were all Fancies, but this was an extra-fancy Fancy. Jeff's examination showed the youth to be well endowed sexually, which added to his value in a weird and roundabout sort of way. At least he would bring a whopping price in New Orleans. He immediately passed him to the left without having him run. This boy didn't need athletic ability. His good looks were sufficient. If he could stagger from bed to bed, he had it made.

Jeff felt a vague tightening in his groin as he probed the boy and was immediately alarmed. What could be happening to him? He felt better when he saw Vincente staring with mouth open and eyes slightly glazed. If the boy could have this effect on the two of them here, in this filthy hole, what would he be like when cleaned up and dressed? Jeff visualized black velvet trousers and a white shirt. He pushed the boy toward the left and watched Vincente's eyes follow him to the shade of the sheltered wall, where he was immediately embraced by several of the black huskies who had already run the gauntlet.

The morning wore on and Hernandez called a halt for lunch. He would drive them to a café in Regla which was noted even in Havana for its excellent food. After Jeff had scrubbed himself to get the oil and slave musk off his hands, they departed in Hernandez's carriage to a cool and breezy restaurant where they leisurely ate a delicious meal of *arroz con pollo* washed down with a dry Spanish wine. Hernandez suggested that they skip the usual siesta because he knew that Jeff was anxious to get on with his work.

Vincente, who had been engrossed in the morning's proceedings, begged Jeff to allow him to judge one slave. Well fed, Jeff was ready to humor the boy. On their return to the barracoons he let him examine the first man in line, a handsome buck. Seldom had any slave had a more thorough examination. Vincente had closely observed Jeff all the morning and now went about his task like a professional. He did everything he had seen Jeff do, although, Jeff saw, Vincente paid considerable more attention to the man's genitals than was necessary. As a result the man passed over to the left-hand side preceded by a monumental erection, which was pointed at by his taunting companions. Vincente grinned. "Damn good man, I say. *Verdad*? He make many fine pups." Jeff had to agree.

By four in the afternoon they had finished their assignment, including inspection of local slaves who were also for sale, although only a few of them satisfied Jeff's requirements. He had Hernandez's man total his choices and found that in all he had two hundred fifteen good specimens ready to be transported to Barataria. So far no price had been discussed. The three of them retired to Hernandez's little office where they again sat down at a table covered with foolscap, quills, and ink. Jeff was anxious to close the deal.

"Very well, *Señor*, I have examined your blacks, and now if we can arrive at a price that is mutually satisfactory, we can conclude our business."

Vincente was busy translating.

"You must agree, Señor Carson, the blacks you selected this morning are all of superior quality."

"Good, yes, but superior, no." Although Jeff was pleased with the quality, he wasn't going to admit it to Hernandez. "Shall we speak in dollars, sir? It is easier for me than getting embroiled with gold duros or pesetas or whatever."

Vincente's head bobbed from one to the other as he tried to keep the conversation flowing.

"Then I would say a hundred and fifty dollars a head."

Hernandez waited a long moment. "I would lose money at that price, *señor*. Make it two hundred a head and I will furnish their food for the voyage to Louisiana."

Jeff's heart pounded. He was well aware that slaves of this caliber would fetch from eight hundred to one thousand dollars and more in New Orleans. Even though two hundred dollars was an extremely fair price and would allow a handsome profit, he wanted a better deal. It would do no harm to try. After all, the Lafittes *stole* most of their merchandise, and it was the Lafittes he had to impress.

"I'll pay you two hundred dollars a head, Señor Hernandez, but on one condition." He held up his finger.

"Que quiere mas, señor?"

"I need three hundred blacks. I've got two hundred and fifteen now. I'm after a few female Fancies, but they don't count. So if you can get me fifty or sixty more slaves equal in quality to these, I'll take the whole lot off your hands at two hundred dollars a head and your agreement to provision my ship for Barataria."

When Vincente had finished, Hernandez sat for several minutes, doodling with his quill. He'd make money on his own slaves, and he'd make more on the fifty or so men he'd have to purchase. Victualing the ship for the slaves would not cost too much. He decided to accept Jeff's offer.

"A gentleman's agreement," he said, shaking Jeff's hand.

Jeff smiled tautly as he grasped Hernandez's hand. A gentleman? If Hernandez only knew who he really was—Bricktop, a white-skinned nigger with brand scars —would he still be willing to shake hands with him?

"Agreed, Señor Hernandez. As soon as you are able to find the additional blacks, my bank here in Havana will pay you for everything."

At this moment Jeff was anxious to return to the Hotel de Paris. It had been a taxing day and the idea of cool white sheets was most inviting. With formal leave-takings and expressions of lofty sentiments, Hernandez offered his carriage for the short drive to the Regla pier.

Once back at the hotel, Vincente begged permission to go to his house to see how Perla was. Jeff readily granted it, wanting nothing more than his bed. After the hearty luncheon they had eaten in Regla, he had no desire for dinner.

When Vincente returned to the hotel at eight Jeff suggested that he send down for a plate of cold meat, but Vincente informed him that he had shared black beans and white rice with Perla and was not hungry. But Señor Jeff? No, he wasn't hungry either and had decided that he would not go out tonight. Vincente said that if Jeff wished, he could send a carriage later that evening to bring Perla to the hotel, but for once in his life Jeff was too fatigued for a woman. He thanked Vincente, and also negated Vincente's counterproposition that he go to Josefina's. He would be content to stay at home for one night.

The dull boom of a cannon startled Jeff. Vincente informed him that it was the nine o'clock curfew. The cannon was fired from El Morro every night.

"We've got to start early tomorrow," Jeff said. "Tomorrow we visit Solano."

"That bastard!" Vincente answered. Didn't Jeff know Solano was the most despised man in all Havana? The rottenest rumors about him were all true. He was a bad man, *un maricón*, and any slave committed to his house to be sold had the pity of all Havana, particularly if

that slave happened to be a young man or boy. Yes—
Vincente stuck out his middle finger and curled two
others in an obscene gesture—*qué maricón!* He was an
old man now but he was still *that way!* If Jeff knew what
he meant. Jeff did, but nevertheless, he informed Vincente,
they were going to get up early, dress, and be ready to
leave the hotel at eight. He had important business with
Solano, regardless of his sexual habits.

"Then you will sail away?" Vincente's black eyes
brimmed with tears—he *looked* nine years old.

"I must. There's a time for everything and my time
for buying slaves is nearly over."

"And I go back to shining shoes and pimping for
Perla." Vincente's eyes glistened. He stood beside the
bed where Jeff lay, propped up by two pillows.

"Oh, Señor Jeff!" Vincente was so choked up he could
hardly speak. "I can't go shining shoes again. I like clean,
decent clothes. I hate rats like Jorge. What happens to
me here?"

"Nothing, I guess." Jeff shook his head and picked
at an imaginary hangnail. "Nothing at all, Vincente, but
on the other hand if I took you with me, what would you
do?"

"I would be with you."

"What about Perla?"

"Perla big enough now to look out for Perla. She
maybe go in Josefina's, or set up her own house. Alone,
she can save her money and get some other girls and she
won't worry. Girls have it easy, *señor*. Girls got something men want and they sell it. But not me. Oh, *señor*,
can't I go with you and learn how to pick out slaves?
You saw me today. I learn fast, Señor Jeff."

Jeff motioned to the boy to sit beside the bed. He
honestly desired to help him. He had grown fond of the
street urchin and he trusted him. Despite the child's
capabilities, he hesitated to take him back to the Lafittes'.
He did not want the responsibility. Besides, Vincente
could never be a servant like Ramon. Yet Jeff hated to
see him return to shining shoes.

Vincente started to speak but Jeff's lifted hand checked

him. He needed to think. He had made his own way in this life through lies and subterfuges, and he was still living a lie. But his own lie was a matter of life and death to him. To live honestly would mean death or a return to slavery. Vincente faced no such handicap. The boy was accepted by society and would never be confronted with Jeff's problem. He was Don Cipriano's son, even if he had been born on the wrong side of the blanket. Evidenly Don Cipriano liked him or he would not be contributing to his support. Perhaps if Jeff suggested to Don Cipriano, he would help Vincente.

Jeff slid over to the edge of the bed and stuck both feet out in front of him. "Help me off with my boots, Vincente, and then we'll talk."

Vincente grabbed Jeff's boot with both hands and bent over. Jeff placed his other boot on the child's backside and pushed while Vincente pulled. The first boot slipped off, but Vincente had to tug harder on the other one. Finally he stood with both boots side by side at the foot of the bed. Jeff loosened his belt and undid his fly. He raised himself on both elbows while Vincente pulled off the tight white trousers. He removed his shirt and underpants. Then, clad only in his silk singlet, he stretched out on the bed. He felt the boy's eyes appraising him and for a fleeting moment felt the fluttering in his groin. He reflected that Vincente's were not the only male eyes that had scrutinized him more with envy and curiosity than with unholy desire.

"You said a while back, Vincente"—Jeff reached down and pulled the sheet up over him—"you'd like to go into the slave business, you'd like to learn how to assay blacks."

Vincente nodded.

"Well, it's a good business, boy, a damned good business, and it's going to be an even better one. The cane plantations here and in Louisiana, and the cotton plantations all over the American South, are going to need more and more slaves every year. I'd like to see you get some profit out of it."

"With you in *los Estados Unidos*?" Vincente sat down on the bed beside Jeff.

Jeff shook his head. "No, boy, with you right here in Cuba. Listen Vincente, think for a minute of Hernandez. He's an old man. He needs someone he can trust to do much of his work for him. I'll speak to him, and if Don Cipriano's influence is added to my own, perhaps he will take you on. You'll learn and soon you will be one of the best judges of nigger flesh in Havana."

Vincente listened with attention, but when Jeff had finished, he said, "I rather go with you, *señor*."

"You wouldn't see much of me in Barataria. I'll be busy in one place or another. Besides, you'll want to be here to look after Perla."

Vincente bowed his head.

"Yes, Señor Jeff. If you say so. You really think you can get me in with Hernandez?"

"I'll try, son. I'll speak to Don Cipriano, too." He looked up at the boy. "Now all you've got to do is to learn your end of it."

"I'll learn, Señor Jeff." With a quick motion he grabbed the sheet that covered Jeff and snatched it away. He picked up one of Jeff's feet, examining it in detail. Jeff laughed and pulled his foot away.

"What in hell do you think you're doing?"

"Just starting my first lesson, Señor Jeff. You got good feet—you got all your toes and no hammertoes, neither. Of course I not examine rest of you very good but I say you sure First Class."

"What?" Jeff laughed. "Only First Class? You mean I'm not a Fancy?"

Vincente's eyes swept Jeff's body. "Yes, maybe call you super Fancy. Anyhow you make one fine breeder, hung like you are."

Jeff laughed aloud and reached over to cuff him but the child was already halfway across the room.

"You want to know all about black niggers, ask Vincente," he boasted "That fellow gonna be *numero uno* about slaves in Havana."

CHAPTER XIX

JEFF and Vincente stood in the brassy sunlight and waited for a carriage outside the Hotel de Paris next morning. Jeff, well fed and rested, was grateful that he had spent the night in his room instead of seeking whatever bizarre amorous connections Josefina's house might offer. His head was clear, his eyes bright, and his confidence in his own judgment unlimited, yet despite his self-congratulations on abstinence, he was already making plans for this very evening.

This evening he'd take Vincente along to Josefina's and give the lad a treat. The boy's previous sex experiences had almost certainly been confined to his sister and the five-centavo whores of the waterfront, so a visit to what was reputed to be the most elegant brothel in Havana would be indeed an education. It was high time the boy learned what screwing was like in clean beds with white sheets. He would probably amuse Josefina's wenches, too. Nothing like a young boy to bring out inventiveness and the mother instinct in a sex-hardened tart. Jeff had seen it work when he was pimping in Pittsburgh and Louisville. Yes, he'd get a lot of fun out of his project, and the thought gave him a fillip of excitement that lasted all through the ride from the hotel to the Solano barracoons.

Barracoon was hardly the word, Jeff decided after ringing the bell and entering the littered courtyard through the heavy iron gate. The place looked more like a prison. The courtyard walls were lined with empty iron-barred cages whose sagging doors testified to long disuse. As Solano had grown older, he had let his slave business decline. Now he was specializing only in Fancies, and they were evidently kept elsewhere. None was in sight.

Echoes of the bell were still reverberating inside the building when Jeff and Vincente stepped into the courtyard. A boy, apparently no older than Vincente, crossed the weed-grown patio, his mincing steps carefully avoiding the rubbish scattered in the knee-high vegetation. Jeff hesitated, revolted by the boy's languid arm movements, the affected gestures of his hands, and traces of mascara around his eyes. He spoke a soft, sibilant Spanish with the lisping accents of Castile.

"You wish to see Don Policarpo Solano, *señor*?"

He addressed Jeff, who gestured with a thumb over his shoulder to Vincente. A quick appraisal of Vincente apparently convinced the affected one that the lad was equally worthy of special interest and he quickly switched his attention.

"Don Policarpo Solano is now finishing his breakfast, but he will see you." The boy smiled at Vincente. "If you will just follow me, please." Crossing the littered courtyard, Jeff stumbled over broken pieces of furniture that seemed to have been lying there for at least half a century.

It was pleasanter in the little room at the rear of the patio where Solano was having breakfast. Meager strips of sunlight managed to penetrate the cobwebby slats of the blinds to settle in a luminous pattern on the still-handsome mahogany table where Solano sat. Jeff's first impression was that this was by far the most enormous man he had ever seen. Gross welts of fat padded his body, and were it not for the polished bald pate and the small black eyes staring out like raisins in a bun, Jeff would have had trouble orienting himself as to where the slave dealer's anatomy began and ended.

Don Solano made no effort to rise but greeted his visitors with outstretched arms and curious little beckoning movements of pudgy fingers, gestures Jeff interpreted as part welcome and part apology for not getting to his feet, a maneuver which probably could not be accomplished without outside help.

"I am very pleased to meet you, Señor Solano," Jeff said, not quite truthfully. He felt he already understood the man's unsavory reputation in Havana.

Solano's reply to the words of greeting were delivered in a piping breath-robbed voice that seemed incongruous coming from such a mountain of a man. Vincente translated.

Solano was delighted and honored to greet the distinguished *Americano* under his own roof and was consumed with *vergüenza*—great shame—because his physical condition did not allow him to leave his chair for a proper welcome. However, Solano hoped that their relationship would not be encumbered with formalities. Instead of calling him Señor Solano, could not *el Americano* address him by his given name—Policarpo? Because Señor Carson—could he call him Jeff?—was a person *muy simpático*. Would he be seated and share a mouthful of his humble breakfast?

"Thank you, Señor Solano—I mean Policarpo—but we have already breakfasted."

Vincente's translation was interrupted by a shrill protest. Jeff would at least have a cup of fragrant Cuban coffee? And some delicious Cuban fruits? Had Jeff ever tasted *anona*? Then he must . . .

Jeff found himself being forced into an easy chair while the child-servant with mascaraed eyelashes sliced a small green nobby round fruit and an orange-colored ovoid the size of a goose egg. The fruit was presented on a sèvres porcelain plate while the coffee was being drawn from a large silver urn. The green nobby fruit, Vincente explained, was a custard apple; the other was a mango. Inside the thick green rind, Jeff found, the fruit indeed had the consistency of custard, but he almost swallowed the big black seeds. The mango puzzled him. The flame-colored juicy meat tasted like turpentine at first bite, but was sweet and pleasant at further venture. The single big lozenge-shaped hairy seed, however, was a source of frustration. As he was struggling to suck the juice and the last bit of sweet pulp from the hairs of the oval seed, Don Solano emitted a high-pitched giggle and said something in Spanish to Vincente.

"Señor Solano asks," Vincente translated, "if the hairs on this *gran cuesco peludo* remind you of something?"

"Tell Policarpo that I have never set teeth in anything like this before," Jeff replied, wiping his face and fingers with the hot damp towel that the precious boy provided him. "Tell him also that I am anxious to get on with our business. Does he know that Jean Lafitte has commissioned me to purchase a dozen Fancy female bright-skins?"

Vincente's translation brought Solano's answer. Of course he knew of the mission of the eminent Jeff. All Havana knew what Jean Lafitte's agent was seeking. But unfortunately the Solano stock of *mestiza* beauties were no longer kept here in Havana. There had been too much vandalism and plain thievery—sometimes romantic, more often crass kidnapping for resale and profit. Don Solano was now forced to keep his girls on a sequestered farm outside of town. Guadelupe was not far from Havana, but it would be necessary to take back roads to elude possible pursuers. The location of Don Solano's treasure house of female beauty must be kept secret at all costs. Why didn't Jeff and his friend stay the night here so they could all get an early start for Guadelupe in the morning? He would do his best to make them comfortable . . .

Even before he heard the translation, Jeff had a queasy feeling about Solano's invitation. The wheedling, cajoling tone conveyed unpleasant associations. He was quick, therefore, to plead important business in town that prevented him from accepting Policarpo's kind invitation. If it was not possible to make the round trip to Guadelupe today, perhaps Jeff could return tomorrow?

Solano heaved a great sigh that involved the entire mass of his huge body. He spread his hands in a drooping gesture of sadness. *Qué lástima*! He would have enjoyed so much being host to the distinguished and handsome agent of the eminent Jean Lafitte. But, of course, if it is not possible . . . they would go to Guadelupe today.

Solano ordered the horses hitched to his *calesa*, and when the four-wheeled carriage was brought to the front of the house, it took two servants to hoist him into it. He occupied all of the rear seat under the accordion hood, so Jeff took the one facing him. He was glad he was not required to squeeze into the little space adjacent to

197

the fat man, although he was not happy to have Solano's tiny eyes constantly fixed upon his fly with that prurient glitter. Vincente sat beside him.

The ride through the steamy countryside was a revelation to the young man from the States. The road ran at first between tall hibiscus hedges ablaze with yellow-tongued scarlet flowers. Behind the hedges Jeff caught an occasional glimpse of an opulent-looking villa. When the *calesa* had passed the immediate suburbs and began rattling down side roads, the graceful coconut palms became fewer, and patches of steaming jungle alternated with cane fields. Brilliant birds swooped, perched, and disappeared amid tropical foliage.

Solano didn't stop talking for a minute. Jeff made no effort to understand him. He was fascinated by the lush and ever-changing scenery. Whenever he did look at the man opposite him, he found Solano staring at his crotch. He finally crossed his legs.

Suddenly the *calesa* stopped. The pretty child-servant (whose name was Tobalito) jumped down from his seat beside the coachman and searched both directions along the road. When he was sure there was no other vehicle in sight, he climbed back and the horses turned in the direction they had come. When they had retraced their steps for a hundred yards, they turned sharply right into a narrow lane, at the end of which was a great wrought-iron gate. Behind the gate loomed an astonishing edifice of black and white stone, with a forest of columns supporting Moorish arches, surmounted by a bulbous Saracenic dome.

"*Mi casa*," said Don Solano proudly. He chatted immediately in Spanish, which Vincente translated, while the gates were being opened and the slave dealer hoisted from the carriage.

He had built this house when he first arrived in this tropical paradise from his native Spain. It was something to remind him of his home town, Granada, in Andalusia. It was an imitation of one small corner of the Alhambra. Didn't Jeff admire the Alhambra? Or perhaps he didn't like Moorish architecture?

198

Not only did Jeff not know where the Alhambra was, but he could not tell Moorish architecture from a hole in the ground.

Via Vincente, Solano apologized that he had never learned English. Oh, he had picked up a few words when he was in New Orleans ten or twelve years ago. He had gone over with a shipload of slaves to try his luck at the Hotel St. Louis auctions. This was before he began to specialize in Fancies, and some planter from Mississippi had bought most of the lot. Solano couldn't remember the slaver's name.

They paused under the arches of the colonnade. Solano handed a huge ring of heavy keys to his mincing assistant. While pondering the name of the man who had purchased his slaves in New Orleans, he seemed to be staring at Jeff's bright red hair for a change.

". . . Willow Oaks . . ."

The words stood out from the stream of Solano's incomprehensible Spanish.

An icy hand traced its way down Jeff's spine. He waited tautly for the translation.

Don Solano had completely forgotten the name of the planter, but he remembered the name of the plantation. Apparently it was quite famous. Had Jeff heard of it?

"Willow Oaks? Indeed I have. Everyone knows that Willow Oaks blacks are the finest in my country. Bred right on the plantation." Jeff decided it was safe enough to boast a little about his association with such a famous source of slaves. "In fact," he said, "my mother owns a plantation not far from Willow Oaks. We were always friends with the owners." No one would pursue a fugitive slave to Cuba. Or would they . . . ?

Jeff was relieved when the ironbound door swung open and the subject of Willow Oaks was dropped. He had never seen anything to match the luxurious Moorish interior of what amounted to a salesroom for female flesh instead of a rental agency like La Casa de Josefina or Madame Hortense's Riding Academy in New Orleans.

Two black giants guarded the inner portals, one armed with a Toledo blade, the other with an obsolete-looking weapon that Vincente called a *trabuco* but which Jeff, had he been familiar with ancient weapons, would have called a blunderbuss. Jeff asked, "Isn't it risky having these big bucks loose in a house with all these fancy females?"

When the question was translated, Solano guffawed. No danger, he said, the black giants had been emasculated. "Cut and nutted," was the way Vincente rendered the phrase.

Just beyond the guards was a room with no windows, lighted by two tall ten-branch candelabra. The fragrance of incense hung on the warm air. The inevitable small boy in the corner hauled on a rope to activate the ceiling sweeps, feebly stirring up tepid drafts. Directly in front of him was a spectacle that stopped Jeff in his tracks. He stared bug-eyed at two naked women squatting on a handsome oriental rug, bent over a layout of Tarot cards.

"A game," said Vincente, "called *buenaventura*."

Solano stopped panting and said, "Yes, *buenaventura*. You call it fortune-telling." The effort of speaking English seemed to have exhausted the fat man, and he lapsed immediately into Spanish. Vincente translated: "You don't like these Fancies? Maybe too black?"

"They're not bad-looking wenches," Jeff said, "even if they are a little dark." The two women continued to study the Tarot cards as they were turned up.

Faint mists of perspiration shimmered on their shoulders and breasts. "I'd like a closer look at the big one," he added, "the big-titted brown gal."

"Ah, *la princesa*," said Solano.

A princess?

Well yes, she was reputed to be a Songhai princess. Everybody called her Koko. The Songhais used to be the royal family of Timbuctoo, but the Fulahs and other tribes had been battling them for centuries, it seemed, and she had got herself captured by slave traders. One of Solano's guards was part Mandingo and he had got her history. She spoke a sort of Mandingo; they all did, the tribes of the western Sudan—the Tschis, the Krus, the Yorubas.

Jeff was impressed with Solano's knowledge of the African tribes. It was certainly not what he would have expected from a man of such gross appearance and curious sex practices.

But Jeff was even more impressed by the physique of the Songhai princess. Solano motioned him to a low settee covered with purple silk, and with the aid of his servants, lowered himself to adjoining cushions. When he had caught his breath again he piped, "Koko, *ven acá*."

The Songhai girl did not look up.

Solano giggled briefly, bowed in mocking deference, and said, "*Alteza, por favor!*"

"He says, 'Please, Your Highness,' " Vincente translated. The second nude gathered up the cards and disappeared.

Koko unwound her long legs and stood up. She was tall and statuesque, her straight black hair (not at all kinky) braided and coiled about her proud head. Her shoulders curved backward, holding her large breasts firm and high. As she walked toward Jeff with long, slow strides, his mouth parted in astonishment. He gasped. Never in his life had he seen such an extensive and luxuriant thicket of pubic hair.

Midnight black against the warm tan of her skin, the curly carpet extended from her navel beyond the pudendum and down the inside of both thighs halfway to her knees. For all its unusually large area, the patch over the heart of the matter stood out as distinctly as if it had been neatly parted with a comb, like a forked beard. And glowing at the very center was a spot of pink like a rose petal. No, Jeff decided as the girl approached, the floral term was wrong. More like the lips of a pink sweetpea.

Jeff had previously never thought of the female genitalia as having an existence of their own. Of the dozens he had serviced during his short life, he had never considered one as anything but an adjunct to the male, a convenient receptacle for an erect penis in search of pleasure and satisfaction—and, of course, the proper place to deposit a man's seed if he is breeding for profit. But a vagina with a personality of its own? Unheard of in Jeff's experience. Whatever was conveyed through the act which was known on the plantations of the American South as "pestering" was a reflection of the personality of the whole woman, her capacity for deriving pleasure from the male equipment. Yet here was a magnificent furry component of love mechanism that certainly had individuality. He continued to stare in fascination as the big brown girl approached. Her labia majora stirred slightly with each step like the wings of a roseate butterfly caught in tangles of moss.

When Koko stopped before him Jeff yearned to reach out and touch the object of his enthrallment. He tried quickly to recall if he had ever heard a set of standards for judging female Fancies. He had his own scale of values, of course, based on personal sampling, but he remembered no instructions from René Beluche on choosing marketable brightskins. He had watched his former owner Baxter Simon buy black women for Willow Oaks, but Simon was looking for solid breeders who could produce a sucker every year, women who were comely rather than beautiful, good healthy brood mares with big tits and broad pelvises. But Jeff was sure that M'sieur Gaspard Cosette of New Orleans, the Lafittes' prime customer for *mestiza* flesh, was looking for something entirely different.

"The princess is a little dark," Jeff said, "but I may be able to get rid of an article like her if she's not too expensive. I'll have to finger her first, though, even if she does look sound."

Solano grunted approval.

Jeff motioned the girl to kneel before him. He ran his hands over the back of her shoulders and down the outside of her upper arms; good solid well-muscled flesh, no doubt about it, but not the flesh he was most interested in. He would try to hold off a little longer. He slipped a hand under each moist armpit and as he moved his fingers downward to feel her pectoral muscles he let his thumbs brush her breasts. He started the

202

routine oral examination and withdrew his fingers just as her jaws snapped shut. She continued to gaze at him impassively with just the hint of a sneer on her lips.

So the wench was going to bite him, was she? Well, she'd have to be taught. He was no longer hesitant. Without further ado he thrust a forefinger through the woolly thicket toward the gleaming jewel that had held him hypnotized for the past five minutes.

Instantly something exploded against the left side of his head. His ear rang. Stunned, he still had the presence of mind to grab the brawny right arm of the Songhai girl as she drew it back for a second swing.

"*Ramera!*" Solano's bloated face was scarlet as he screamed imprecations at the girl. The princess screamed back at him. So she spoke Spanish.

Jeff held up one hand, still clinging to the girl's arm with the other. "Shut up, everybody! What's going on here?"

Vincente translated. "Señor Solano is furious. He is taking the bitch to the public whipping yard when we return to the city, a place where slaves are punished for their misdeeds by being chained to a post and lashed by a professional flagellator until the master decides they have learned to behave."

"No, no." Jeff shook his head. He had seen slaves strung up by the heels at Willow Oaks until their backs were cut to a mass of bloody pulp by blacksnake whips. The wounds healed in time but left ugly welts. Nobody would pay top prices for a slave with a welted back and legs. "Vincente, tell Solano I don't want her whipped."

"He says she must be punished, *señor*. She hit you."

"Tell him I can't sell a nigger wench if she's all scarred up. I won't buy damaged goods. What's the matter with Koko anyhow? She acts like a virgin but she's just a slave."

"She says you can't fool around with her snatch until you buy her," Vincente explained.

"Tell Her Highness I won't buy unless I know she's good and healthy. Tell her I don't lay girls in public, and that I must make sure she's not all poxed up. I can't take her to New Orleans to start an epidemic of clap. Tell her I'm going to finish my examination."

At last he got down to the business of exorcising the obsession that possessed him. His approach was gentle this time, and instead of a prodding forefinger he used the second and third fingers, first to part the hirsute decor, then to separate the glistening pink labia. He felt a quiver run through the girl's body, and her reaction was contagious. Despite his professed strictly business attitude, Jeff couldn't help being horny in the presence of such a stimulating wench. He stood with his back to Solano in the hope that his instinctive response would not be visible in profile to the fat man's leacherous eyes.

Yes, the princess with the bearded underbelly possessed not only sensual but marketable possibilities. He was glad he had been able to restrain his natural urge to retaliate when she had struck him. Now he could probably buy her cheap and sell her for a pretty penny in Louisiana.

"Señor Solano asks how can you punish her if you don't whip her?" Vincente asked.

Jeff answered without turning around. "We will humiliate her," he said. "Her Highness is a proud wench and she's worth two or three hundred gold dollars at least. If you sell her for thirty, forty dollars like a cheap whore, she'll feel like dirt."

Solano protested (through Vincente) that he had paid more than fifty dollars for her in the first place.

"I'll give you sixty," said Jeff. "That's as much as you'd get after having her whipped and marked up."

Solano wailed a little, but finally agreed. After all, a disobedient wench must go. Slaves obeyed only because they were taught terror.

"Mark it down, Vincente," said Jeff, knowing full well that the boy could not write, "and tell our fat friend that I'm ready to look at some mustees for a change. No more princesses."

Solano waved Koko out of the room and piped instructions.

In a few seconds an old crone in a rusty black dress

led two light-skinned *mestizas* into the room.

While Solano was shrilly describing their backgrounds and proclaiming their fine points, Jeff was making his own assessment. They were attractive wenches, both of them, although quite different in everything except the light shade of their tan complexions. They were certainly quadroons, perhaps even octoroons. One girl was petite, small-boned, and minxlike. She had eyes too big for her animated pixy face. Her long eyelashes curled. She wore nothing but a scarlet lace mantilla draped over her jet-black hair and brought forward over her shoulders to fall across her bosom. A lively piece in bed, Jeff speculated.

Her companion was a head taller and considerably thicker. Or maybe she looked fatter than she really was. She was wearing what looked like a trailing, short-waisted nightgown with short puffed sleeves and long flowing flounces. Jeff considered the costume tawdry—he could not know that it was a soiled and shopworn copy of an Empire gown, now the latest thing from stylish Paris—and he had to see what sort of wench was concealed beneath it. He was not discouraged, for there was a languid air about the woman, a sultry expression around her eyes and a sense of restrained power in her movements, that promised a smouldering nature ready to burst into flame at a flick of the tongue.

Solano had finished his harangue in Spanish and Vincente was struggling with the translation.

These two trollops were the last in the Solano stable who claimed titled lineage. The little vixen—Panchita—liked to call herself Countess because she was once mistress of Conde de Lunablanca, the Vice-Governor of Cuba. The Count had her condemned to the public whips to be beaten to death because, in a fit of rage at finding him with another woman, she had bitten off one of his balls. However, Panchita had screwed her way out of the death sentence, leaving two of the Count's bodyguards to bear the brunt of his wrath. Panchita was a hot number in more ways than one, and Solano would be relieved to get rid of her. But if his friend Jeff found her to his taste, he must be warned to take the utmost precautions in smuggling her aboard ship; otherwise he would never get her out of Cuba.

"Have no fear," Jeff said. "I'll sneak her aboard if we have to hide her among the Princess's twat hair."

Solano was already launched on his selling talk about the Duquesa, showing an extensive knowledge of contemporary Caribbean politics and history in addition to his ethnic knowledge of African tribes. The hussy in the fancy nightgown was an octoroon from Haiti, which Jeff assumed was somewhere in Africa. The human blood in her was French. She called herself Antoinette, the Duchess of Limbé, a daughter of His Serene Highness Prince Jules de Limbé, one of the courtiers of King Henri Christophe of Haiti, by the King's *lingère,* the mistress of the palace linens. After Napoleon sent General Leclerc to Haiti to reestablish slavery and Christophe was overthrown, the Duchess was forced to flee for her life. Some French officer sold her to a Spaniard, who brought her to Cuba with a coffle of niggers from Haiti and Santo Domingo.

"Tell the Duchess to shuck down," Jeff ordered. "Let's see how she's built."

"Deshabilles-toi, Antoinette!"

Solano spoke to the Duchess in what Jeff supposed was French; it sounded like the language he often heard in New Orleans. Did the surprising fat man have any more unexpected learning up his ample sleeve?

Antoinette complied with the order, although she displayed the modest gestures appropriate to a former aristocrat. Her efforts to conceal her most intimate features while undressing did not fool Jeff, however. She betrayed herself—deliberately, he was sure—by the slight smirk that hovered on her full lips, the faintly suggestive movements of her hands, and especially the expression of her eyes as they focused on the growing evidence of Jeff's reaction to his exploration of her contours. Her tongue flickered briefly between her lips as that evidence increased. Well, some things were beyond his control. . . .

Jeff was flattered that the Duchess seemed to like what she saw. Showed she appreciated the best things in life, and if he were any judge, she was also a wench of considerable talents. Yes, he was going to bring back a fine variety of mouth-watering goodies for the pleasure of M'sieur Gaspard Cosette and his likes. And he was also getting to be a more expert judge of what he thought the Lafittes were looking for. As Solano's doxies passed in review, Jeff devised a formula for counting up a point score in the rating of female slaves for the love market.

Solano displayed the choicest flowers from his Garden of Venus one by one, and Jeff gave each his close personal attention. Since the Princess Koko had made him aware of the forceful individuality of what he had previously thought of only as a twat or a cunt, he now carefully noted the different types. Their variety amused and amazed him, and once he had a chance to compare them with actual performance, he would have a standard for evaluation. There was the rounded, plump, friendly vagina like Rosita's, for instance. How would that compare in action with Isabel's long, lean, hungry-looking organ? Or a neutral childlike vagina like Adelita's? Or a fiercely bewhiskered paraphernalia like Carmen's or Juanita's that from its appearance might well have teeth? Did the nearly bald or scantily feathered genitalia of Beatriz and Maria merely illustrate the saying that grass never grows on a busy street? He certainly did not trust the relaxed appearance of Magdalena's baited trap, which to him seemed ready to spring shut on the first unwary penis.

Well, all this would require research, which Jeff planned to do on the sea voyage to Barataria. He would also have to decide how to award points according to breast shapes. Did pear-shaped tits offer greater passion than the apple models? And what about the conical numbers with long dugs like Adelita's?

He would also have to make his own standards for judging hips. Hips would mean something different to Lafitte customers than they did to Baxter Simon, who was looking for the width that indicated good breeders.

Buyers like Gaspard Cosette would be more interested in plump, well-rounded buttocks. Shapely legs were always exciting, of course, but what about feet? Well, Jeff would award pretty feet extra points, particularly if they were equipped with nicely-cushioned heels that would arouse a man ten degrees higher when they dug into his back.

Man! Was Jefferson Carson, née Bricktop, learning to look at women and sex in a new light! René Beluche was still by far the much better judge of black bucks, but Jeff was proud of the skill he had developed in the last few hours in rating lightskinned and lighthearted wenches. He hoped that Jean Lafitte would appreciate the selection of bright-skins he was bringing back. And the one African wench he was getting for a bargain would turn a nice profit in New Orleans.

After a break for lunch—a huge bowl of spicy shredded beef that Jeff found delicious despite its unappetizing name of *ropa vieja* (old clothes)—they finished the inventory of Solano's stock by early afternoon. Jeff picked eleven *mestizas* and the tan *princesa*. He rejected only three: one was too thin, a second had suspicious-looking warts on her thighs, and the third, Tía Mía, was too old; she must have been thirty-five at least. Solano argued that she was a first-rate cook and would bring a good price, but neither Lafitte nor Beluche had asked him to buy cooks. Jeff wasn't even sure Beluche would approve of the *princesa,* in which case he was sure he could dispose of her himself. After all, what was sixty dollars?

"Shall we now get down to business?" Jeff suggested.

By all means, said Solano through Vincente. We will adjourn to the *parlatorio* and bargain in a friendly way. He clapped his pudgy hands and the coachman and secretary appeared to hoist him to his feet and help him waddle into the next room. The Louis Quinze furniture had been reduced to a state of dinginess by the heat and damp of the tropical climate, but it seemed elegant to Jeff. The slave dealer was installed behind an elaborate escritoire and he waved Jeff to a spindly-legged gilt chair with mildewed tapestry upholstery.

"I propose," Jeff began, "to make an offer for the lot of wenches as a whole, rather than bid on them separately. Except for Koko, of course. We agreed on a price for her."

Solano grunted agreement. He suggested a lump sum of eighty-five thousand reales.

"No reales," Jeff countered. "I can't figure in this foreign money. Let's talk dollars. Gold dollars."

Solano giggled. He didn't see what was so difficult about counting in Spanish reales, which were worth eight to the dollar. Surely the Lafittes must have explained to him about pieces of eight . . .

Jeff made a mental calculation. At that rate eighty-five thousand reales would make each wench cost almost one thousand dollars. "Ridiculous," he said. "I'll give you two thousand dollars for the whole shebang."

Solano threw up his hands and emitted a little treble scream of horror. Only sixteen thousand reales? Had his friend Jeff forgotten that Solano had been in New Orleans and was familiar with U.S. prices? He was no ignorant *peon*.

"You must consider my expenses in getting these wenches into the States," Jeff said. "There is the cost of refitting the ship to take care of my slaves, the wages of the crew, the cost of feeding them aboard and in Barataria, to say nothing of the bribes I will have to pay in case we are intercepted by a revenue cutter. I might even have to go to jail."

As the bargaining proceeded, Solano ordered cold drinks brought—a mixture of fruit juices a liquor called *ron,* a spirit of the sugarcane.

"Rum," Vincente translated.

Jeff, who had taken nothing stronger than brandy since his disastrous experience with corn-whiskey toddies at the George plantation, found the drink pleasant indeed. He sipped it while they argued over who would pay to feed the wenches until Jeff took delivery, the cost of local transport and security guards on the way to the dock, and other incidentals.

"Tell you what," Jeff said, putting down his empty

glass. "I'll give you two hundred fifty dollars apiece for the eleven Fancies, plus the sixty dollars we agreed on for the princess. That's my best offer."

Solano pondered a moment, shook his head sadly, heaved a mountainous sigh, then nodded, and extended his fat hand across the desk.

"*Convenido*," he said.

When Vincente confirmed that an accord had been reached, Jeff grasped the hand. Solano immediately ordered fresh drinks and fussed in his desk for writing materials. He interrupted himself when Rosita arrived bearing the tall glasses.

"*Salud!*" he said, raising his glass to touch rims with Jeff's.

Vincente struggled with a translation of what he said next. The gist of his ceremonial speech upon the conclusion of their agreement was that it was a pleasure to do business with his friend Jeff, and that next time he had especially fine Fancies he thought Jeff would like, he would write him in care of Señor Jean Lafitte. There was one more thing that Solano must insist upon. There must be a clause in the formal agreement to the effect that once the wenches left his house, Jeff would assume full responsibility for their past and future, as well as their present behavior. This was to protect Solano in case the police or Count Lunablanca's henchmen should intercept the carnivorous Panchita on her way to the docks.

"My bank will send you the money in the morning," Jeff said. "But you'll have to keep the wenches here until I have made the *Sainte-Claire* ready to receive them." Jeff was beginning to feel the effect of the rum. Warmth crept from his belly to his arms and now reached his cheeks. This heat was superfluous in the normal tropical temperature of Cuba, but Jeff did not find it at all disagreeable. In fact, as he took another long pull at the drink Solano called *leche de tigre*—tiger's milk, according to Vincente—he found his tongue strangely loosened. His formal education was limited to the time he spent in old man Carson's school in Philadelphia.

He had never proved particularly brilliant academically, despite a keen native intelligence. Yet here he was, holding forth glibly on the stupidity of the United States Congress in prohibiting the import of slaves, on the importance of slavery to the American economy, on the essential kindness and paternalism of American plantation owners despite their occasional cruelties.

Solano could not know, of course, that Jeff's discourse was the second-hand philosophy of Jean Lafitte, René Beluche, and even Baxter Simon. But he nodded agreement frequently, and occasionally added a few words of approval.

Suddenly Solano clapped his hands for more drinks, got up with great effort, waddled around the desk, and plopped down at Jeff's feet. He had not stopped talking.

"What's he saying?" Jeff asked Vincente.

The boy made a face as though he had bitten into something sour. "He says you are smart as well as beautiful. He wants you to stay the night here. The guest room is clean and very nice. He says you should try some of the wenches you have bought. He thinks you want to fuck the *princesa*."

"Well, he's right there." Jeff took a gulp of his third *leche de tigre*. After all, he had spent most of the day poking, stroking, and fingering some pretty exciting specimens of female flesh and he had been in a continuous state of rigidity. He was due—long overdue, in fact—for relief, and either Princess Koko or the carnivorous Panchita would do very well. Maybe both.

"Please don't stay here, *señor*," Vincente pleaded. "Please tell me to say no."

"Boy, don't start telling me what to do!"

"But Señor Jeff, this big fat fag wants to bugger you."

Jeff set down his glass. The lad was right, of course. The rum must be getting the better of him. Solano was totally repulsive physically, and the thought of contact of any sort with him sent a shudder through Jeff. He became sober instantly.

"Tell Don Policarpo Solano," he said to Vincente,

"that I am sorry I cannot accept his hospitality. Tell him that important business calls me back to Havana and I must be there by sundown."

While Vincente was translating, a curious change came over Solano. His round red face seemed to decompose. His mouth opened but no sound came. Tears welled up in his eyes and rolled down his cheeks. A silent sob shook his huge body, which then appeared deflated as his shoulders sagged in disappointment. At last he spoke in a tight child's voice.

Solano was desolate, he said. His friend Jeff was so beautiful. Could he not spare another hour? Was his business in Havana so important?

Indeed it was, Jeff thought. Since he was not able to meet his physical needs here, he must get to La Casa de Josefina as promptly as possible.

"Yes, I must see my bankers," he said, "so you will get your money tomorrow. I will see you in a day or two to arrange details of delivery. Now, if you can call your carriage, Don Policarpo . . ."

At the mention of money Solano brightened somewhat.

CHAPTER XX

JEFF'S night at La Casa da Josefina was not exactly the carnal adventure he had anticipated. It was fun, of course—what big-city bawdy house is not?—and the lovelies there who indulged him in his favorite pastime were exotically charming and more than proficient at catering to his pressing physical needs. Josefina herself had a certain charm. She was not a Madame Hortense with a Spanish accent, an elaborately embroidered shawl, and an enormous ornate comb gleaming in the crown of her raven hair. She was younger than Hortense, and although both were daughters of the Caribbean, Josefina's manner was much warmer than Hortense's hardnosed professionalism.

Josefina entered into the spirit of Jeff's desire to initiate Vincente into the niceties of sex among those who charge in gold coin instead of small change—a real pleasure for a counterfeit white man who in a short time had graduated from the slatterns of Pittsburgh and Louisville and the bed wenches of the Mississippi plantations to self-styled southern belles and the gilded New Orleans parlor houses of the rich.

"Señora Josefina," said Jeff, pushing Vincente into the presence of the Mother Mackerel, "have you got anything especially nice that will fit this youngster? I'd like to treat him to something really high class—if it comes in boy sizes."

"How old is this little eel?"

"Let's say he's twelve."

"If you insist."

"I say it merely to allay your concern, *Señor*. Chronological age is meaningless. But a horn is a horn."

Josefina's laughter tinkled as brightly as the little marble fountain that spurted and sparkled into a fern-filled basin in the middle of her reception room. "Our girls do not deal in boy sizes, *señor*," she said. "But they have—how do you call it?—*habilidad*?"

"Skill," Vincente volunteered.

"Right. Eskeel. They have the eskeel to make small things grow beeg." She clapped her hands and raised her voice. *"Pedro! Llama a las chiquitas!"* she called.

Music from unseen stringed instruments sounded nearby and half a dozen olive-skinned girls strolled leisurely into the reception room, fanning themselves languidly with one hand as the other toyed in mock modesty with the ends of their multicolored mantillas—they were exactly what Jeff, while still in Barataria, had imagined romantic Havana *señoritas* to be. His spontaneous reaction did not escape Josefina. Her eyes widened as she saw his breeches change shape.

"The *señor también* has problems of size," she said, "even more serious maybe than the *mozuelo* here."

She spoke in Spanish to the girls who had seated themselves on a semicircular red velvet divan that was set against the wall of bright ceramic tiles. The invisible musicians stopped playing. From her gestures she was calling attention to the dimensions Jeff's distorted fly had assumed. She was apparently offering them a chance to withdraw from a possible ordeal. They all smiled and shook their heads. Josefina also smiled.

"Please choose, *señor,* the one who pleases you," she said, "and also one for the *muchacho.*"

"The *muchacho*," said Jeff, "can take his pick of any but the one with the green fan and the breasts like melons."

"Ah, you like my Lolita? *Bueno,* she is yours for the night if you wish. She is veree beauteous, no? *Muy hermosa!*"

"Look, Señor Jeff, can I take—?"

"Vincente, take your time and take your pick." Jeff pressed two gold pieces into Josefina's hand. "But Lolita and I have urgent business upstairs." He imprisoned the girl's waist. "And Josefina, please send some wine. Lead the way, Lolita."

Jeff was in such a rush to mount—the day's excitement had built up a head of steam beyond even his usual high pressure—that he forgot all about his plan to watch Vincente's first performance in luxurious surroundings.

Lolita was indeed beautiful, Jeff mused as she lay naked beside him, smiling as his rapid breathing returned to normal. She was almost as lovely as Chloe, with the same tearose skin and luminous eyes. She was proficient, too, in the arts of love. His own hunger, combined with her manifest ardor, had brought him quickly to a dizzy, towering climax, much more quickly than was his habit. He noted with satisfaction, nevertheless, that she had fully shared the pleasure of their coupling, so his record of never leaving a woman ungratified was still intact.

The ecstasy that Chloe had given him, however, was missing. Nobody ever lifted him to such heights as Chloe. Nobody ever would. Chloe was unique. There could be no doubt. He truly loved her. Sleeping with other women

214

was fun. Making love was the greatest pleasure in life, but making love to Chloe was more than pleasure; it was enchantment. It was what fucking must have been in Eden.

Lolita was talking to him in Spanish. He understood not a word, but her voice was caressing and the language was musical. And he could guess what she was saying. She was probably asking him if he always wore a shirt while screwing, why he did not take off all his clothes like everyone else. Luckily he didn't understand so he didn't have to go through the tiresome business of explaining about idiosyncrasies. Suddenly he thought he caught a familiar word as she pointed at his chest and said, *"Tú es clérigo? Tú es Católico?"*

Jeff realized that in his haste to get into Lolita he had left Helen's lucky diamond-studded golden cross hanging around his neck. She probably thought he was a priest or something. He wondered if padres ever came to Josefina's for a little missionary work among the girls. Maybe she had a secret door for them.

"Sure I'm a *Católico,*" he joked. "My father was a bishop."

He laughed but Lolita merely looked puzzled. She kissed him and tried gently to arouse him again. She reached under the hem of his shirt and stroked his belly. Her fingers were softly tantalizing as they fondled him. Apparently he was not yet spent, for he rose to the occasion. She opened her thighs to him again. As he rolled her over, mounted her, and drove deep, he felt her heels press into the small of his back. . . .

Strange, but through his mind flashed thoughts of the afternoon, his plan for setting up standards for correlating a woman's lovemaking potential with her physical characteristics. Never before had he let extraneous thoughts intrude at moments like this. He was becoming a real slave trader at heart. Or perhaps not . . . he was now finding it difficult to concentrate on the afternoon's ideas. She really had something, this Lolita. She knew how to drain a man's strength so sweetly, so sweetly . . . so goddamn completely.

Jeff raised himself on his elbows, and gave a startled gasp.

Perched on the headboard of the bed was some sort of minianimal—maybe a small lizard?—staring at him with big eyes in which the elliptical pupils ran north–south instead of east–west. As it stared at him, the little beast made small derisive noises in its throat that sounded like *gecko-gecko*, over and over again.

Jeff raised a hand to swat the insect or whatever it was, but Lolita grabbed his arm.

"No matas al tarentolita!" she exclaimed excitedly. The torrent of Spanish that followed ended in two English words, probably her entire vocabulary: "Bad luck."

Jeff rolled over and swung his legs off the bed. What the hell kind of whorehouse was this where they had lizards sitting at the head of the bed to stare at you during the high point of the evening? He dressed quickly and went downstairs to pay for the wine (which he had not touched) and to collect Vincente.

On the way back to the hotel he interrupted the boy's glowing account of his first sexual adventure in paradise, a description in detail of how it felt to go to bed with an angel.

"Glad you liked it, Vincente," Jeff said, "but did you have any animals in your bed?"

"Animals?"

"Some little reptile with big eyes kept staring at me from the head of the bed. Damned near spoiled my repeat performance. When I went to swat it, Lolita almost killed me. 'Bad luck,' she said. The damn thing was talking to me. What does *gecko* mean in Spanish?"

"Gecko?" Vincente laughed. "That's the bedroom lizard we call *tarentola*. American sailors call it English-speaking lizard because it say 'fuck you,' not *gecko*."

"Fuck you? I guess that does sound a little like *gecko*. But what's a lizard doing in a bedroom anyhow?"

"It good luck, *señor*," the lad replied. *"Tarentola* eat mosquito and other biting bugs. You got one at Hotel de Paris."

"I have? You sure? I never saw or heard it."

"I see him yesterday. He live topside your *guardarropa* —your clothespress, eat all your mosquito," Vincente said.

"Not all," said Jeff. "Anyhow, I'll listen for him tonight and talk back to him."

Jeff did not hear the gecko that night, though he lay awake for hours. Which was curious, for he should have fallen asleep immediately. He had had a hard day with Solano and his slave girls—if you liked puns—and Lolita had taken care of his pressing physical needs satisfactorily. He had concluded his commissions for the Lafittes. He should have enjoyed the rip-roaring carefree evening that he had been looking forward to when he had finished his purchase of the three hundred black bucks and the dozen fancy floozies that René Beluche had ordered. It must be that he was just realizing the magnitude of the task that still lay before him.

He had joked with René about the problem of getting his human cargo across the Gulf from Havana in such a small barque—"I'll put cork in their asses and float them across," he had said—but now he had to think about it seriously. First thing in the morning, after he'd given instructions to the banks, he'd have to go down to the wharf, look the *Sainte-Claire* over, and have a talk with the captain.

He finally fell asleep trying to remember the captain's name—was it Dundee? Or MacTavish? Something Scottish. Not a particularly pleasant man, as he remembered from his outward journey—a dour seagoing character with a fringe of gray whiskers that fitted under his chin and jowls like a bib. MacFarland, that was his name, Jeff remembered just as he was drifting off. . . .

He awoke next morning with a vague feeling of dread at the responsibilities that lay immediately before him. There was not only the confrontation with Captain MacFarland, and the technical problems of making room for his slaves aboard the *Sainte-Claire,* but the business of transport and security. When the skipper moved the *Sainte-Claire* to the pier in Regla, he could probably march the coffle of three hundred blacks aboard right from

Hernandez's barracoon without even spanceling them. He'd have to keep them spanceled aboard ship, however. If they ever ran riot, the three hundred of them could easily overpower the crew. He'd have to take that up with the captain.

Then there was the business of the Fancy females—not only getting them aboard, but also quartering them there. There was the extra problem of Panchita, the carnivorous Countess, who was wanted by the Vice-Governor's police. Maybe he had made a mistake in including her in his purchase. He had joked with Solano about smuggling her aboard hidden in Princess Koko's luxuriant pubic hairs, but if the Havana police ever grabbed her while Jeff was in the process of exporting her, he'd be in deep trouble. Perhaps he should try to get Solano to keep her, although the fat man was in less than a conciliatory mood when Jeff had left him. Hernandez had offered to furnish provisions for his *bozals*. Jeff wondered what they ate. Probably the female Fancies would not eat the same thing. He'd forgotten to ask Solano. No way to avoid it—he'd have to see the fat sodomist again.

CHAPTER XXI

IMMEDIATELY after breakfast Jeff sent Vincente in search of a carriage and set out for La Machina where the *Sainte-Claire* was moored. He considered leaving the lad behind, as he had no need of an interpreter to communicate with her officers, polyglot gang though they were. However, on second thought he took him along; he would need him later in the day for other negotiations.

The steamy morning was already suffocatingly hot when the *volanta* neared the end of the long wharf. Jeff had not seen the *Sainte-Claire* for several days and she looked lifeless tied up to the dock. He realized now that she had been a living thing under sail—her canvas bellied with the wind, the sea purling under her bows, and the deck lifting gently with the long swells. Motionless in the burning sun, she was a dead object. There was no sign of life aboard. A few crewmen sprawled on the foredeck in the shade of furled sails, probably sleeping off a binge.

The sight of a gaudily uniformed customs officer lounging at the foot of the gangplank reminded Jeff again of one hazard that lay ahead of him: getting the Vice-Governor's ex-mistress to the waterfront undetected and then smuggling her aboard. However, the *aduanero* seemed friendly enough. Although he made a desultory search of Vincente's clothing, he let both of them aboard without difficulty.

Jeff found Captain MacFarland in his stifling cabin, stripped to the waist, sweat pearling the gray hair on his chest. The worn uniform cap perched jauntily over one ear bore grimy, almost invisible insignia that Jeff had noted on the outward voyage but had been unable to identify. He wondered if the skipper had once been an officer in the Royal British Navy, and if so, what had made him desert King George's ships of the line for Jean Lafitte's freebooting fleet. Had he murdered a fellow officer? Or made off with the wardroom mess fund? Or maybe knocked up his commander's daughter?

The skipper was in earnest conversation with his first mate and bo's'n. Talk ceased when Jeff appeared.

"What's the snot-nose doing here?" demanded the bo's'n, a lean, dark, bettle-browed brigand whose black hair grew down to the middle of his forehead. His name was Cugino, and he was reputed to be a cousin of Vincente Gambi, a tough pirate and an off-and-on lieutenant of Jean Lafitte's. Cugino had also sailed with another hard-boiled Lafitte aide named Nez-Coupé-Chighizola.

"Now, now Coojie, don't be nasty to the big boss's pet," said the first mate. Jeff always marveled that the mate's face, beard, and bald head were all the same color—brick red. Not surprisingly, his fellow officers called him Red.

"Come in," the captain said. "What might be ailin' yer spirit, lad?"

Jeff sidled in to sit on the edge of the skipper's bunk. Vincente waited outside the bulkhead.

"When will you be ready to head back for Barataria, captain?" Jeff asked.

"I'll need three, four days to finish loadin' victuals, soberin' up the crew, and fillin' the water casks," MacFarland answered. "When can we take yer cargo aboard?"

"Whenever you're ready, skipper," Jeff said. "I can button up the odds and ends while you're finishing up here. Then we must move across the harbor to Regla to embark the slaves."

"Regla?" Captain MacFarland tore the cap from his head and banged it down on the table before him. "*Must* move to Regla? First of all, nobody says 'must' to MacFarland, especially when yer speakin' o' an asshole port like Regla. I doubt there's enough draft at Regla pier to float a bark the size of the *Sainte-Claire*, even at high water and wi' no cargo. And wi' a full load—how many niggers are we takin' on?"

"Three hundred bucks," Jeff replied, "and a dozen—"

"Good God Almighty and the Twelve Apostles!" The captain sprang up raising his arms to heaven. "Three hundred niggers in the *Sainte-Claire*, which ne'er carried more than fifty and has no room fer more. Good God Almighty!"

"We'll make room," Jeff said.

"Fifty niggers stunk us out of 'tween-decks," said the first mate. "Three hundred will suffocate us to death."

"Three hundred will sink us," said the bo's'n.

"Talk sense, lad." The captain sat down and tried to speak calmly. "The *Sainte-Claire* was built for cargo. Ye canna just stack three hundred blacks in the hold in layers like kippers."

"Beluche told you what our cargo would be," Jeff said. "We'll have to build shelves along the walls of the hold and—"

"Ye'll not be borin' holes in my hull to anchor bunks fer no black bucks!" the captain said. "What's more, in heavy weather when we batten the hatches, they'd be pukin' and crappin' all o'er one another. I'll not have

220

it. Wi' fifty, we could bring 'em up on a leash now and again to shit to leeward and not foul their own nest. But three hundred . . . ! I'm shorthanded as 'tis. I've no third mate. My crew won't have the time to help ye control the bastards. They could take o'er the craft. They'd outnumber us ten to one."

"There'll be no problem of control," Jeff said. "I'll spancel the lot."

"Ye'll what?"

"Spancel them. I'm sure a ship chandler will be able to furnish the necessary ironwork before we sail."

"So ye'd fetter the blacks?" The captain shook his head.

"Exactly. And fasten the shackles to the side of the vessel."

"There ye go again, makin' holes in my hull. I'll not have it, I tell ye. The whole thing's daft and I'll have none o' it."

"My orders, and yours, are from M'sieur Jean Lafitte, captain. We are to buy and bring back three hundred healthy Negro slaves."

The gray fringe of the captain's beard seemed to bristle. "I'm commander o' the *Sainte-Claire,* lad, and what I say goes."

Jeff suddenly knew he had to assert his authority. After all, he was Lafitte's agent, with all the power and financial backing that commission represented. He saw this was a Lafitte test as surely as fingering any black. He stood up, kept his voice casual.

"That's true to a certain extent, captain. You're the boss. As long as we're at sea. But with the *Sainte-Claire* tied to the dock, as *your* boss's representative, *I* have the authority to carry out M'sieur Lafitte's orders. Order your carpenter into the hold to see if he agrees my idea is practical for putting up my blacks for the short sail home. We can march three hundred slaves to the leeward to shit, but we're moving them out of here—at the soonest, sir."

"The carpenter's ashore." The captain shrugged. "And who said it was a short sail home?"

"It took us only three days coming down."

"Lad, ye know naught o' the Trade Winds or the currents in the Gulf," said the captain, "so I counsel ye to lay in eno' victuals for your slaves to last at least a week."

"Very well. I'll put the supplies aboard when you come alongside the pier at Regla."

"*If* I berth at Regla."

"I'll be back tomorrow with a ship chandler. You'll have your carpenter aboard and sober."

"He'll be sober eno' to hinder ye from makin' a sieve of my strakes."

"And another thing, captain. Since you don't have a third mate, I'll need the third mate's cabin. Furthermore, I'll need the second mate's cabin, too. Your two mates will have to double up for the homeward voyage."

The first mate roared obscenities.

Captain MacFarland clasped and unclasped his fists. "And what," he asked sarcastically, "might be the reason fer such nonsense?"

"I've bought a dozen Fancy bright-skinned wenches," Jeff said. "And while I can take two or three in my cabin, I'll need someplace for the others to sleep."

Again MacFarland jumped up.

"Holy Willie and St. Elmo's fire!" he bawled. "Wenches! And in my own bottom! I've sailed from Zanzibar to the North Cape and from Cormorin to Cape Town, but ne'er in my life have I carried a woman or a priest. Ye want bad luck guaranteed? Ship a skirt or a cassock. But not me. Never!"

"You'll start with my wenches then," Jeff said. "Exactly as M'sieur Lafitte ordered you. I'll leave you now, captain, but I'll be back in the morning. Vincente!"

The Cuban lad's head popped out of a companionway. "Right here, Señor Jeff."

"We're going ashore," Jeff said. "We're heading for the bank. Need any money, captain?"

Jeff felt taller as he climbed into the *volanta* at the end of the dock. Never—he was echoing the captain's last word—never, he was willing to wager his own life's blood, had a fugitive slave masquerading as a white man stood up so boldly to a white sea captain (and a buccaneering captain at that) and got away with it. Of course, MacFarland was right in being tough; he knew his business. But so did Jeff. And Jeff's orders had to be precisely the captain's orders, for they were both working for the same man: Jean Lafitte. Consequently their business was the same: to get these black bucks back to Barataria. Captain MacFarland had been identically instructed. So Jeff was bound to win out in the end. But he had a right to feel satisfied with this morning's triumph. The captain had thrown his weight around. And Jeff had stopped him. He was still congratulating himself when the carriage drew up in front of the Banco Real de España.

The bank official—a tall, thin, distinguished gentleman wearing two commas under his long nose in the guise of a moustache—escorted Jeff and his interpreter into his private office. It was cool in the interior of the bank because small boys stood outside and splashed pails of water on coconutfiber mats hanging outside the barred open windows. The manager waved to big chairs. Vincente remained standing. As Jeff sat down, he noted two geckos scurrying across the bright ceramic frieze at the top of the inside wall. They were everywhere, these little English-speaking lizards.

The bank manager spoke English, too, so Vincente was actually superfluous.

"How can we serve you today, Señor Carson?" he asked.

Jeff explained that he had engaged himself to pay sixty thousand dollars to Don Emilio Hernandez of Regla, and he assumed that Lafitte credit was good for that amount.

The manager smiled tolerantly. Indeed it was, many times over. Had Señor Carson found the number of good healthy slaves he was seeking?

Yes, he had, thank you. There would also be a few thousand dollars—two thousand eight hundred ten dollars to be exact—to be charged against the Lafitte credit for payment to another slave dealer, a specialist named Solano. Perhaps the manager knew him.

"Indeed I do." The bank manager's smile became a smirk as he pronounced the name. "Policarpo Solano. We will pay his bill."

"I will have a few other bills," Jeff said, "although I do not yet know how much they will be. I must first find a ship chandler."

"Ship chandler?" The manager turned to Vincente with a puzzled frown.

"*Un cabuyero*," said Vincente, who had done his homework since he had heard Jeff talking about his needs. He explained in Spanish what his employer had in mind.

"Ah, yes." The manager nodded. "You may have to go to an ironmonger to get everything you want."

"Good. Fine." Here was a chance to make contact with tradesmen and artisans independently of Captain MacFarland. He didn't fancy dealing with people who might be getting kickbacks from the skipper. "Could you give me the names of a few men who could do a good, honest job for me?"

The bank manager could, indeed. He wrote down several addresses and handed them to Vincente. Jeff intercepted the paper. He pretended to seek the manager's help in pronouncing the Spanish names and numbers, which he read aloud. No use exposing the fact that Vincente could not read. The boy had a good memory.

After signing the appropriate papers and shaking hands with the *banquero,* Jeff was again out in the blazing morning.

"Where first?" asked Vincente, as the *volanta* started rolling again. "The *cabuyero* or the *ferretería?*"

"Don't make fun of my Spanish," Jeff said.

"Oh, no, señor. Not me. You have very spry tongue for Spanish words. You can learn Spanish easy."

"Maybe on my next trip to Cuba. Meanwhile, which is the ironmonger?"

"The *ferretería.*"

"Let's go there. He may have some ideas. We can see the chandler tomorrow when the carpenter's back aboard."

Jeff leaned back in his seat, closed his eyes, and relived the intoxicating moments of his first experience in high finance. He had not been the least bit self-conscious in the presence of the *banquero*, had he? He couldn't have been more nonchalant when he tossed off figures like sixty thousand dollars. Sixty thousand! Quite a difference from his first business venture in Pittsburgh, where his stock in trade was a string of two-dollar whores. And yet sixty thousand was small change compared to what the slaves would bring on the New Orleans market. Those three hundred blacks should sell for at least two hundred fifty thousand dollars and probably as much as three hundred thousand—a 300 or 400 percent profit. Jean Lafitte should be properly appreciative of the shrewd dealings of his ten-dollar-a-week apprentice. A quarter of a million dollars! Jeff hoped he would be appreciative enough to pay a fat bonus. Would five thousand be too much to look for? With five thousand he could go directly to Madame Hortense's Riding Academy and buy Chloe's freedom. Dear, dear Chloe! Well, at least he could dream. . . .

The *volanta* stopped. The sign over the door read: PEDRO LOPEZ, Ferretero, and the door was like a dark cave mouth in a mossy cliff of gray stone. Once he had passed through the open door and advanced beyond the glare of the noonday sun, Jeff found the interior cool and damp. Also deserted.

"*Hay alguno?*" Vincente challenged.

After a moment a short, bow-legged, white-haired specter materialized from the gloom and introduced himself as Pedro Lopez. He led his visitors to a table in a corner surrounded by garlands of chains, kegs of nails, and tools of various kinds.

"*Sientase, señor.*" He waved to chairs adjoining the table, clapped his hands for a servant, and would not allow commerce to be discussed until cool glasses of cocoanut milk had been brought.

Lopez had been half expecting his American visitor,

he said. He had been sent by Don Hernandez, no?

"No," Jeff said when Vincente had translated. "You were recommended by the manager of the Banco Real de España."

"*Verdad*?" Lopez was surprised that they had not come on Hernandez's recommendation, for Hernandez warned him that an American named Carson had made an important purchase and would need three hundred *cadenas*. Lopez had just received a shipment of one thousand *cadenas* directly from Spain. Luckily.

When he came to the word *cadenas* in translating, Vincente seemed stumped.

"He must mean spancels," Jeff said. "Iron bracelets or leg irons." He thought, people are all the same, everywhere. Anything to turn a dollar. Hernandez had tipped off his ironmonger friend in the hopes of getting a rake-off on whatever Jeff bought. Three hundred spancels ought to bring him a nice percentage.

Meanwhile Lopez was singing the praises of his fine Spanish fetters, security guaranteed, keys for each set provided at no extra charge.

"Tell the man our real problem, Vincente," Jeff broke in. "Tell him we have to find some way to fasten the spancels to the bulkheads of the ship, because we've got so many blacks we're going to have to have several layers, and the captain is raising hell because he thinks we're going to make holes in his hull."

Lopez grinned and nodded his white head as Vincente interpreted.

"The *señor ferretero* says no problem," the lad announced. The Lopez solution involved stretching chains the length of the hold. No bolts or other fasteners need be set into the skin of the ship. Chains could be fastened to the deck at each end, and to the deck or the beams at intervals. Chain loops would attach the spancels to the long chains.

Lopez promised to go aboard the *Sainte-Claire* and take measurements of the hold. He was prepared to install the chains, furnish the loops, and deliver the *cadenas* to wherever Señor Carson wished. Because of the size of the order, Lopez could give an attractive price to Señor Carson.

Lopez also had ideas for accommodating the slaves in layers in the hold without damaging the ship's hull. He would simply build scaffolding that would hold three or four tiers of planking. Now, he just happened to know a *maderista* who would furnish the planks at reasonable prices . . .

"Yes, I'm sure you do," said Jeff. It was the damnedest thing how tradespeople everywhere tried to cut all their friends in on every pot of gold. Just the slightest smell of money set them off in pursuit like a pack of hounds after a bitch in heat. "But our ship's carpenter has his own . . . ah . . . his own—"

"*Maderista*," said Vincente quickly.

The chef at the Hotel de Paris had made such ambrosia from lobster meat sautéed à la Catalana that Jeff ate himself into a state of somnolence that required the customary Cuban two-hour siesta to correct. He awoke sweaty and calling for Vincente to bring bath water.

"Better rinse yourself off when I'm through with it," he said while Vincente was filling the tin tub. "You're beginning to smell like Hernandez's barracoon."

"We go again to La Casa de Josefina?" the boy's eyes brightened.

"We do not." Jeff tested the water with one toe. "I'm afraid we'll have to go and see that Solano again."

Vincente frowned. "No, señor. Please. Why must you see again that fat *maricón*?"

"I'm going to try to call off my deal for that little bitch who calls herself a countess. I've decided she's too dangerous. Hand me the soap."

"If we get caught, yes. Dangerous. But I think Solano will not take her back. He too happy selling her."

"You think if I tried to cancel the deal, he'd pawn her off anyhow and tip the police?"

"No," the boy said. "He no like you because you don't let him bugger you. But he like American gold."

"We'll have to think of some way to get her aboard

227

then," Jeff said. "Give me that towel."

"I think of some *juego de manos*—how you say? Trick?"

"It'd better be a good trick," Jeff said, "because I hear your Cuban jails are god-awful."

"Oh, it will be very good, *señor*, I promise. You will see, I know very good trick."

Vincente opened the *guardarropa* and fumbled for the fresh linen. He helped Jeff thrust his arms into the sleeves, and watched in silence as Jeff tucked Helen's diamond-studded gold cross into his undergarment before he buttoned the shirt. He frowned thoughtfully.

"You are *Católico*, Señor Jeff?" he asked at last.

"No," was the reply. "Why? The wench at Josefina's asked me the same question last night."

"In Cuba everybody is *Católico*, and you have this golden cross around your neck like a padre . . ."

"The cross happens to be a good-luck piece."

"You can maybe play you are *Católico* for one day or two?" The boy smiled broadly.

"What for?" Jeff sat down on the bed and stretched out his legs for Vincente to help him on with his boots.

"For trick to fool *policía* of Conde de Lunablanca when you put that wench Panchita on ship," the boy explained.

"For that," Jeff said, "I would be a *Católico* for a week." He stretched out the other leg. "How would it work?"

"In the Calle Lejana is a little church," Vincente said. "I know the padre. He is good man. He will help, I think."

"I see." Jeff laughed. "How much will it cost?"

"Not much. A few reales for the *cepillo de pobres*— money for his poor people."

"I'll give him the money," Jeff said, "if you'll show me what I have to do to be a *Católico*."

"Oh, yes, I teach you to kneel, to make cross with fingers, and dip in *agua benedita* when we go inside church."

"Tell me how it's going to work." Jeff stood up and flexed his toes in his boots.

Vincente paced the floor as he recited details of his scheme. His excitement over his planned intrigue lighted his already expressive face. Failure to recall an English phrase did not interrupt his animated flow of words.

The little street arab began telling about his friend Padre Diego, the priest whose church was the Iglesia de la Virgen Triste. No, Vincente had no idea who the Sad Virgin was or what miracle caused the little church to be named after her, but she was probably black. Padre Diego had very modern ideas about Negroes. He believed they had souls just like white people, and he was always trying to save them. Vincente first met Padre Diego as a boy when his mother was still alive. His mother had been a pious Catholic—*muy Católica*—and went to Padre Diego for confession. She had taken his sister Perla to Padre Diego's church for her First Communion. That was before Perla had become an apprentice *puta*, of course . . .

"What the hell has all this got to do with sneaking that little bitch Panchita aboard the *Sainte-Claire?*"

"Much," said Vincente. *"Casi todo.* You see, Padre Diego also likes saving souls of whores. We tell him you are taking these *mestizas muy claras* to New Orleans to learn sewing or English, or maybe go to school. You will say you want the padre to come to dock to bless the wenches for a *buen viaje.* You will give him money for his *pobres* and he will come. You see."

Jeff shook his head. "I don't see how that is going to get Panchita aboard."

Vincente stopped pacing. "Easy," he said. "We dress her like a *monja.*"

"Like a what?"

"A *monja.* How you say? A lady monk?"

"A nun?"

"Sí. A nun."

Jeff sat down on the edge of the bed, then collapsed across it in convulsions of laughter. The idea of that sensuous little minx of a Panchita with her pixy face and wicked eyes, her every curve proclaiming lechery awaiting release—the image of that phony fugitive countess posing as a nun was the highest farce. He laughed until he was gasping for breath. Then he laughed again until he almost choked.

"How," he begged, tears dampening his cheeks, "how do you expect to make even a temporary nun out of a red-hot wench like Panchita?"

"Those black dresses and big white nun hats hide everything," Vincente said. "And she can wear *anteojos*." Vincente made circles with the thumb and forefinger of each hand and raised them to his eyes. "Like so."

Jeff was no longer laughing. He stared at the street child admiringly. "Tell me more," he said.

"Police not stop girls who have nun for *dueña* and padre to pray for safe sailing, I think. *Aduaneros* also not searching *dueña*, I think."

Jeff considered the scheme as carefully as he could. The boy's plan seemed logical. The religious touch was ideal for sailing on a ship named after a lady saint, even if he didn't know who Sainte Claire was. Still there were many angles that needed study. Everything had to be worked out in advance and in detail so that nothing could go wrong. He could not risk disaster—but he did want that Panchita wench aboard. The way she wiggled her little ass would be worth an extra three or four hundred dollars in New Orleans. Besides he had personal reasons: she could do a lot to make the sea voyage less monotonous.

"Where are we going to get a nun's habit?" he asked at last. "From your friend the priest?"

"No, *Señor*. For Padre Diego she will be *sordomuda*" —Vincente pinched his lips together and stuck his fingers in his ears—"going to your country to see big professor *médico* to learn to speak."

"Where do we get nun's togs, then? I don't want you to steal them."

"No, you can buy. If I say where, can I go with you to get them? Please, Señor Jeff?"

Jeff hesitated. What else did this precocious kid have

up his sleeve? "If you'll behave yourself, you can come along. Where do we go?"

"La Casa de Josefina."

"Balls! Don't tell me Josefina has sisters working for her as whores."

"No, *señor*. But she has good customer with a funny thing—like you *idiosincrasia*—about fucking. You have to keep shirt on. This fellow, Don Antonio, this big rich *hacendado*—owns much plantations—he can't do nothing except with *monja*. So Josefina have nun dresses and nun hats for girls when he come. She sell you one, I think. You got money and she like you."

CHAPTER XXII

THE little Church of the Sad Virgin on the Calle Lejana was a masonry structure in the midst of palm-thatched hovels built on stilts to raise them above the swampy ground of Havana's outskirts. Jeff's *volanta* stopped in front of a canopy of purple bougainvillea growing over the entrance. Jeff remained outside, sweating profusely, while Vincente went in alone to pave the way. After all, Vincente and his sister Perla had been communicants at Father Diego's church before they had embarked on their joint venture in the oldest profession.

"Well, you young *bribón*, it is months since I have seen you," the padre greeted the lad. "I hope you have not come to confess, for I can spare you only half an hour and I am sure your confession would take many hours. Pimping. Bribery. Theft. Fornication—"

"No, Father, I have no need to confess, for you have told me that God knows everything that goes on and therefore He does not need me to remind Him of my sins. As for you, I'm sure my sister Perla keeps you up to date on my evil when she comes to confess during Lent."

"What brings you here then, my son?"

"There is waiting outside a very rich American who

231

wishes to put money in your poor box."

"I see." The little priest ran his fingers through his gray hair and shook his head in anticipation of some impossible request. "And what unholy favor am I supposed to do in return?"

Vincente told how Señor Jefferson Carson was taking a dozen wayward Cuban girls to New Orleans to teach them English and give them a chance for a better life. He wanted Padre Diego only to bless the start of the voyage and thus make it easier for them to mend their ways in the new land.

The old priest continued to shake his head. He laughed sadly. "I don't believe you, my son," he said. "And you don't believe this rich American, either."

"I know only what he tells me, Father. He is a very nice gentleman and very generous. Will you see him, Father?"

Still shaking his head, the priest sighed. "Very well, bring him in. I will wait in the sacristy."

Jeff performed all the well-rehearsed gestures Vincente had taught him. He genuflected, dipped his fingertips in the holy-water font, crossed himself. In fact, in a reversal of roles, he now imitated Vincente. He followed the boy down the narrow aisle in the gloomy interior. He had never been in a church in his life, Protestant or Catholic, even though Veronica, his former mistress had been married to an itinerant preacher. When his eyes became accustomed to the half-light he saw nothing unusual in the fact that the rudely carved Christ hanging on the cross above the altar was dark enough to be of mixed blood; no doubt most of the padre's parishioners were also dark.

Just before they entered the sacristy Vincente made sure that Jeff's heavily jeweled golden cross now gleamed prominently outside his shirt.

Padre Diego rose to his full five feet as Jeff and his interpreter came into the room. As Vincente started his introduction, the priest interrupted him by raising one hand.

"I speak English, Señor Carson," he said, extending

the other hand. "I was chaplain for the last Spanish troops to leave New Orleans not so many years ago, and I studied—"

He stopped abruptly in mid-sentence, staring at Helen Latimer's cross suspended around Jeff's neck. His lips remained parted and his eyes seemed reluctantly fixed in focus, like someone fascinated by a snake coiled to strike.

"That is a very handsome piece of ecclesiastical jewelry you are wearing," he said at last. "Do you have some official connection with the church in Louisiana?"

"Not official, no," Jeff replied nervously.

"Where did you get this cross?"

"From a very dear friend. It was a gift—a talisman. It is supposed to brink me luck—and it has."

"Would you allow me to look at it more closely, Señor Carson?" The little priest shifted his fascinated gaze to Jeff's eyes, as though seeking some secret there. He smiled slightly.

"Please do, father." Jeff met his full-face challenge without flinching. What had he to flinch about?

With a hand on his shoulder Padre Diego gently turned Jeff so that he faced the light from the single window. He lifted the cross in his fingers and examined it intently. His lips moved silently. Was he counting the diamonds? There was a sunstruck golden glitter as he turned it over and studied the back for a long moment.

"I thought I had seen this cross before," he said at last, "but I may be mistaken. The cross I saw had three words engraved on its back. Of course, this cross may be a copy. Or the engraving could have been effaced. I seem to see faint marks—the traces of some tool . . ."

"Where did you last see it, father?"

"In New Orleans. I held it in my hands. If it is the same one, it may indeed bring you luck. The man who asked me to hold it was a very pious Catholic who did not want to wear the sacred emblem of universal love while trying to kill another human being in cold blood. He had been challenged to a duel, and before he

233

accepted the pistol from his second, he took the cross from around his neck and handed it to me. A moment later I gave him last rites, for it was he who died in the duel. Had he continued to wear the cross on what he called the field of honor, perhaps—" The little priest sighed, sat down, and seemed to stare at a lizard scampering along the top of the frame of a bad copy of El Greco's "Pietà." "I don't suppose you want to part with that cross?"

"I sure don't," Jeff said. "What's the name of the man killed in the duel?"

"I can't tell you. I am sworn to secrecy."

"Whom did you give it to when the man was killed?"

"His widow, of course. She was left penniless. I suppose it ended up in a *casa de empeños*." The priest looked for help to Vincente who shook his head. "Ah. Pawnshop." The padre forced a smile and clapped his hands as if to say he was now ready to talk business.

"We digress, Señor Carson," he said. "You must forgive me. But you come with a request, no?"

Jeff nodded, still fingering the gold cross. He liked this little man in brown bathrobe. He felt relaxed in his presence. He glanced around for a place to sit down. There was no other chair, but there were several bamboo baskets of vegetables, no doubt contributions from parishioners in lieu of cash tithes. Jeff sat on a sack of potatoes and told his well-rehearsed story of the girls he was taking to North America to find a new life and who wanted the benediction of the Church on their departure.

The padre listened without interrupting. He sat in silence for a moment, then fumbled in his desk to find a long, thin, crudely rolled cigar. He held it out to Jeff.

"Have a *claro*?" he offered.

"Thank you, no," said Jeff.

"*Qué lástima*," said Father Diego. "It calms the nerves." He produced a block of friction matches, split off one thick match, and brushed its tip against the stone wall behind him until it sputtered and bristled into flame.

Fumes of sulphur stung Jeff's nostrils before the fragrant cigar flared.

"I'm considering your request," the priest resumed. "It is highly unusual. In the first place, I don't believe these girls are going voluntarily to New Orleans in search of the finer things in life. They are undoubtedly slaves and prostitutes that you have bought and expect to sell at a profit. Second, I don't believe they have asked for my benediction on their departure. I have no idea why you have chosen to surround their sailing with the odor of sanctity, and I can only hope it is legitimate and will not involve me in the trouble I always anticipate when I deal with my little friend the pimp here."

The padre paused to contemplate the bluish smoke coiling from the end of his cigar. Vincente watched him anxiously.

"I am also convinced that you are a rogue," the priest resumed. "However, you are a rogue not entirely without compassion. There is something in your face which speaks of decency, no matter how deeply buried. And suffering—older than both of us. If it were not for the color of your skin, I would say you know from experience what it means to be a slave. A Negro chattel to whites. So I think these girls may have a chance for a happier life with you in your country than they have here. And since you say they are of mixed blood, they are bound to better themselves. I know an octoroon can do quite well in New Orleans. If only one of them succeeds in escaping from her bondage, my blessing will be justified."

"Thank you, father," said Jeff. Vincente beamed.

"Just a moment," said Father Diego. "I believe there is a matter of an offering for the poor. That will be payable in advance. And in my hand. I don't mind the more desperate of my flock occasionally filching coppers from the poor box, but since this is not a matter of coppers, I will take it personally."

"No indeed, father. I promise you gold coin. I had in mind one hundred dollars."

"Two hundred," said the priest. "You have twelve

wenches. That comes to less than twenty dollars a benediction." He smiled broadly, put out his cigar, and extended his hand.

Jeff counted out the gold coins. "I will send a carriage for you on the day we sail," he said. "Vincente will come the day before to tell you at what time."

The sun had been shining brightly when they entered the church. When they left, a tropical rain was coming down in torrents. It was only a few steps from the church entrance to the carriage but Jeff was drenched before they reached the shelter of the hood over the back seat of the *volanta*. Vincente apologized for the whimsical behavior of the Havana weather.

He had reason to apologize. They had not ridden more than five minutes when the horse stopped suddenly and tried to back up, neighing wildly. Frenzied use of the whip by the *cochero* only produced louder equine protests. The driver got out to investigate and found that they had stopped at the edge of a swirling freshet. What had been a muddy dip in the road an hour before had become a gurgling brown torrent. And the rain was still drumming and splashing on the hood of the *volanta*. The driver got out and walked to the foaming brim of the new water course. Gingerly he took soundings with his whip. He was shaking his head as he came back.

"No se puede traversar," he said.

"Can't cross," Vincente translated. "But rain can stop in five minutes. Rain play funny tricks in Cuba."

"Suppose it doesn't stop for an hour. And then it takes another hour for the water to go down. Do we have to sit here all afternoon and evening in the rain?"

"No, *señor*. There is bridge across the *arroyo* not far from this place."

"Let's go," Jeff said.

A moment later, as if on cue, the downpour tapered off to a drizzle, then stopped altogther. The sun erupted through the clouds and a rainbow appeared above the glistening leaves of a nearby banana *finca*. The hot ground steamed with the lush, damp redolence of growing things.

Vincente gave directions to the *cochero*. Water still dripped from the hair plastered close to Vincente's skull, but he launched into the campaign of self-promotion he had obviously been rehearsing since they left the church.

"I told you Padre Diego would help us," he said. "I think Vincente smart boy, no?"

"If the rest of your scheme works out, I'll think you're hellishly clever, yes."

"So smart you must take me to New Orleans, yes?"

Jeff laughed aloud at the arab's brashness. The *volanta* crossed a wooden bridge and rolled into a cobbled street. Jeff had to raise his voice to be heard above the clatter of the wheels on the stones.

"I thought that was settled," he said. "Don Cipriano is going to arrange for you to learn the slave trade from Hernandez."

"So you don't think I'm smart, *señor*."

Jeff made an appeasing gesture. "Of course you're a smart boy, Vincente. You're nine years old, going on forty. But you'd be of no use to me in Louisiana because you can't read or write. Matter of fact, you'd be of more use to me right *here* if you *could* read and write. I think I'll ask your father to send you to school, if I have to pay half myself."

Vincente sulked. "You don't like Vincente, Señor Jeff."

"That's just not true. You'll learn quickly. Next time I come back I want you to know more than just how to pick slaves. I'll try to persuade the Lafittes to put you on their payroll as soon as you learn your lessons."

Vincente's disappointment was expressed by his sullen silence.

"Come on, boy, buck up," Jeff said. He clapped an arm about Vincente's shoulder. "Or I won't take you to Josefina's tonight."

Vincente forced a smile.

Josefina was amused but puzzled at Jeff's inquiries about a nun's habit.

"She think you want it for yourself," Vincente translated. "She surprised you have funny need like Don Antonio because Lolita tell everybody you *muy macho* —don't need no fancy tricks. But I explain."

Vincente's explanation took liberties with the truth. Jeff had decided that if the Conde de Lunablanca was really determined to arrest and punish the fugitive Panchita, he must have spies everywhere; certainly someone at La Casa de Josefina was in his pay. And the walls had ears. So the yarn Jeff and Vincente had cooked up was that Jeff had taken a shine to the young wife of a rich but impotent old man from some backwoods village and wanted to smuggle her out of the country. However, with a suspicious husband on the alert . . . surely Josefina would understand . . . ?

Josefina not only understood but was delighted at the idea of outwitting a jealous husband in an affair of the heart. Anything she could do to insure success of the intrigue, Jeff had only to ask. She had religious costumes for several orders and in several sizes because she was never sure which of her girls would be free when Don Antonio arrived in search of his sacrilegious erotic thrills. How big was Jeff's adulterous enamorata?

"She comes up to about here on me." Jeff raised a hand to his chin. "She's about as big as that Lolita wench I had last night. Is Lolita busy tonight? No? Then dress her up like a good sister for me, will you, Josefina?"

Josefina clapped her hands and gave orders to Pedro. A few minutes later, while Jeff was sipping a glass of sweet ebony-colored Malaga the madame had offered him, Lolita appeared. She was dressed as a Carmelite sister—a long white mantle over the rough drugget robe, with a long black veil covering her head and falling below her shoulders.

"Perfect!" Jeff was amazed, not only by the demure appearance the habit gave to a wench he had last seen in naked abandon, but by the aphrodisiacal effect this saintly garb was having on him. He stood up to give slack to his tight-fitting trousers, then reached into his pocket for gold pieces.

"See that Vincente is taken care of." He handed the coins to Josefina. "Lolita and I are going upstairs to find out how I compare with Don Antonio."

CHAPTER XXIII

IT was soon clear to Jeff that the *Sainte-Claire* was not going to sail for Barataria in the three or four days Captain MacFarland had predicted. The delay was largely because of the skipper's own stubbornness. Jeff had followed through on all his preliminary chores. The Carmelite disguise for the wench Panchita, with the addition of a pair of rectangular iron-rimmed spectacles, was carefully packed away in his room at the Hotel de Paris. Padre Diego's cooperation had been confirmed. The banks had settled with the slave dealers, Hernandez and Solano. Carriages had been arranged to transport the dozen female Fancies. The lumber for building the scaffolding to accommodate three hundred buck Negroes had been delivered to La Machina dock. Pedro Lopez, the *ferretero,* had sent three hundred sets of spancels to the Hernandez barracoon as ordered, and had tried to install the chains aboard the *Sainte-Claire*—unsuccessfully. The whole trouble lay there: Captain MacFarland would not let Cuban workmen aboard the *Sainte-Claire* to install the chains or build the framework for the slaves' bunks.

The skipper's natural disdain for all landlubbers—particularly an unknown newcomer as young as Jeff—was reinforced by the open hostility of his officers, particularly the first mate and the bo's'n. The second mate—a bowlegged Spaniard named Palo—was apparently neutral. He had been absorbed into Havana and was seen by his shipmates only twice since they had been in port—when he came aboard to badger the captain for an advance on his pay. The ship's carpenter, a white-mustachioed old seadog named Joe, was perfectly amenable to building Jeff's bunks or anything else—as long as he got his tot of rum at regular intervals.

There was nothing for Jeff to do but force the issue. In the end the skipper would have to agree to a compromise of some sort. They both worked for Lafitte. If Jean Lafitte wanted three hundred slaves brought from Havana, no ship's master in the fleet could dare refuse to take them aboard. MacFarland prepared a channel of escape for himself when it became apparent that he could resist no longer: he told Jeff that he positively could not consider any of his plans—until the *Sainte-Claire* was provisioned, minor repairs completed, and fresh water taken on.

Old man Carson had once said something that Jeff had forgotten until now. Jeff had been trying to achieve some goal by threats and bluster when the teacher had intervened to say, "Be a diplomat, Jeff. Tact will get you further than violence. Honey catches more flies than vinegar." All right, he would spread honey for Captain MacFarland as far as he could. On the pretext of getting the captain to look at the dock in Regla, a perfectly logical request, he invited him to lunch at the little seaside restaurant where he and Hernandez had lunched so well a few days before. When the skipper was full of good food and drink, the two of them would certainly come to some reasonable conclusion.

When MacFarland grudgingly agreed, Jeff said, "I'll be on the wharf with my carriage at ten tomorrow morning to pick you up, captain."

"What fer?" MacFarland asked.

"Why, to drive to where we can get a ferry to Regla."

"You'll do naught o' the sort. We'll go all the way by water, as befits a seafarin' man. I'll take the *Sainte-Claire*'s longboat. These clumsy louts that call themselves *balseros*—I wouldn't even let them handle a dory of mine. I don't trust these foreigners wi' an oar."

"Then we'll do it your way, captain."

At ten the next morning Jeff and Vincente sat with

Captain MacFarland in the stern sheets of the longboat while four piratical-looking stalwarts rowed them away from the harbor entrance and across to Regla.

MacFarland ordered the boat to drift along the Regla waterfront while he compared the few ships moored there with the draft of his command. He had his crew put him ashore at one landing stage so that he could examine the pilings, then the cleats and bollards on a vacant dock to which the *Sainte-Claire* might be moored. Jeff held his breath during the whole tour of inspection. When the skipper had finally agreed that it would be feasible for the *Sainte-Claire* to dock here, he nodded— and Jeff breathed with relief. One obstacle out of the way.

Jeff suddenly decided to postpone his planned visit to Hernandez—and for good reason. He was going to make his lunch with the captain a convivial affair, a sort of peace conference. The food at the little restaurant was excellent, and there was no sense in spoiling the skipper's appetite, which would inevitably happen once they got within smelling distance of the Hernandez barracoons. The monumental stink arising from three hundred sweating Negroes could turn off a starving dog. They would eat first.

Jeff asked MacFarland to have his crew row south toward a little cay marking the entrance to the inlet that Hernandez had told him was called Guasabacoa Bay. When he spotted the red-tiled roof and blinding white veranda of the Cantina de los Dos Tecolotes, he signaled the skipper. Captain MacFarland barked orders and the longboat slid through the mangrove thicket that lined the shore and made fast to a landing stage below the restaurant.

Jeff took Vincente along as far as the veranda to interpret his menu wishes to the proprietor, then sent him back to help the crew of the longboat forage for lunch. The host greeted Jeff effusively; apparently he remembered him from his previous visit with Hernandez, who was a good customer. At any rate he elaborated on the instructions that Vincente had transmitted from Jeff.

They were first served *cangrejo moro*—succulent crabs with deliciously spiced rice. For the *arroz con pollo*, which Jeff had ordered, the *patrón* took the liberty of making a substitution. He brought to the table an English-speaking waiter to explain. Since the *cangrejo moro* was accompanied by rice, he would not recommend more rice, particularly as today was the day that the Cantina de los Dos Tecolotes regularly barbecued a suckling pig. Therefore if the *caballeros americanos* did not mind, he would suggest the *lechón*.

The *caballeros* did not mind at all. In fact, they were in high good humor from the mood-elevating properties of the straw-colored manzanilla wine that accompanied the crab. Jeff was developing a taste for wine. He had first tasted it in Louisiana. His previous drinking had been confined to the rot-gut of waterfront dives and the corn whisky toddies of Mississippi plantations. And more manzanilla accompanied the *lechón*.

The dessert—a compote of tropical fruits drenched with an anise-flavored liqueur from Catalonia—was washed down with Vidonia, a sweetish wine from the Canary Islands. The *patrón* proudly recited the pedigree of the wine.

"Aye, Canary wine, the tipple o' the poets," said Captain MacFarland, whose Scottish burr thickened with each glass. "The poet laureate o' England is paid off wit' I dinna ken how many pipes of Canary."

"Who's the poet laureate?" asked Jeff.

"Last I heerd it was Robert Southey," said the skipper. "Pity Sir Walter Scott would have none o' it. Dinna care fer Canary, no doubt. An inferior talent, Southey. But he did write two lines I well remember. 'Thou hast been called, O sleep! the friend of woe. But 'tis the happy who have called thee so.' A most inferior talent. Now Bobbie Burrrns—"

"Who's Bobby Burns?" interrupted Jeff, who had been listening in incomprehension.

"No matter," said MacFarland, draining his glass.

"We're not here concerned wit' mice nor men, now are we, laddie? We're here to put our heads together an' come up with an answer to the impossible problems of transportin' I've forgotten how many black assholes home to that French pirate in Barataria. Aye, lad?"

"Aye," Jeff echoed dutifully. Looked like he was going to have to learn still another language on this job, though he couldn't tell whether it was Scotch or sailor jargon.

What a lot there was to learn in the world besides judging slaves, he mused. Especially about people. It was not surprising that an old queer of a slave dealer like the fat and odious Solano should know all about tribal distinctions in Africa, but that he also knew the history and politics of the neighboring islands amazed Jeff. And now this buccaneering sea captain with his talk of poets and poetry. . . .

"I take it," said Jeff, "that we may now go ahead and build those plank bunks in the hold."

"No," said the skipper. "No 'we.' That deceesion is mine alone. I'm still givin' it thought."

MacFarland was getting redder and redder in the face but the stone wall of his command mentality was intact. He was at least getting more approachable, however. His iron-gray fringe of beard no longer seemed to bristle.

"Would you like to take a look at the coffle that's going to be our cargo, captain? The barracoon's just a mile or so from here. Just to give you an idea—"

"I've no need o' black ideas," said the skipper. "As ye may have infurred, I've no love fer niggers, neither their sight nor their smell. I'll see an' smell more than a suffeeciency before we get them ashore in Barataria."

"But you wouldn't mind bedding a well-washed light-skinned wench, would you now, skipper?"

"A clean, lively, and comely lass has sometimes come favorably to my attention, if she's not too dark. And a bit of hooghmagandie never did anyone harm. What's on yer mind, lad?" The skipper was more congenial. His heavy eyebrows lifted and he almost smiled.

"I thought it might help solve our space problem on the *Sainte-Claire*," Jeff suggested, "if one or two of those octoroons that Lafitte ordered were to sleep in your cabin. They might give you a little fun when you're off watch . . ."

"Aye, off watch." MacFarland chuckled mirthlessly. "Yer an innocent, lad. These Carib seas can keep a man on watch for days on end, an' if a *vendaval* blows far eno' east, he may have to lash himself to the binnacle to keep from goin' overside. However, I thank ye fer the thought, an' if we have a calm passage . . ."

"Oh, I'm sure we will," Jeff said. He was about to say they were bound to have good luck because the voyage was to have the special benediction of a Cuban Catholic priest, but caught himself just in time. He remembered Captain MacFarland's superstition that nothing brought misfortune like a priest or a woman aboard ship.

He was on the point of explaining to the skipper that the nun who would be coming aboard with the octoroon Fancies was not really a nun but a high-class whore and was not to be considered an evil omen, but changed his mind about this, too. The fewer people who knew that he was smuggling the former mistress of the Vice-Governor aboard the *Sainte-Claire,* the better.

No, Jeff was not going to jeopardize his project by getting MacFarland's back up. Not only was Panchita going to bring a good price in New Orleans, but Jeff also looked forward to sampling her talents. In fact, just thinking about the hot little wench made him as horny as a schoolboy in a harem, even in the anaphrodisiac presence of Captain MacFarland.

"How about another touch of that Canary wine, captain?" Jeff said.

"A far more attractive proposal than a visit to yer nigger vendor's salesrooms," said MacFarland. "Just a wee drop."

Jeff signaled the waiter. Keeping the skipper in a good mood was more important to his project than visiting the barracoons today.

Next morning found Jeff aboard the *Sainte-Claire*—

at the skipper's suggestion. He sent Vincente with messages to Lopez the *ferretero* and the *maderista* to get their hardware and planks aboard the bark before the captain changed his mind. He also bought a demijohn of rum for the white-haired ship's carpenter, who would supervise the installation.

The captain's change of heart did not cause an outbreak of brotherly love among his officers, however. They watched in glum silence as Cuban workmen carried planks, kegs of nails, and the other impedimenta across the gangplank. All but Cugino, the beetle-browed bo's'n, were glum and silent. He was furious and voluble.

"Gardammit, skipper, how can you let this snot-nose bastard turn this vessel into a stinking nigger pig sty!" he shouted. "He oughta be keelhauled."

"Save yer breath, Coogie," said the skipper. "He's just carryin' out Lafitte's orders." He laughed. "Just like I am."

"Why in hell can't Lafitte let us snatch our niggers on the high seas like we always done? Why all this damn foolishness about letters of marque if we gotta act like frigging merchantmen? Next thing he'll have us carrying passengers."

"Big boss's orders, Coogie," the skipper said. "If ye don't like 'em, ye'd better jump ship before we sail."

"Big boss, big shit." The bo's'n spat in Jeff's direction. Then he turned around, bent over slightly, aimed his lean buttocks at Jeff, and emitted a resounding fart.

Jeff's first reaction was to launch a swift kick at the offending posterior, but he was able to restrain himself. With the skipper on his side, however halfheartedly, and the Lafittes' authority behind him, he opted for the better part of valor. He would not make the captain's task more difficult, even if it meant ignoring an insult. He would not, however, ignore the hostility expressed by the bo's'n's gesture. Cugino would be his enemy until they reached Barataria, and might well not hesitate to express his enmity in more violent ways than breaking wind. Jeff would have to protect himself.

The incident caused Jeff to delay his visit to the

Hernandez barracoon. He would make sure construction of the bunks got off to a good start and that there was no malicious interference with the stringing of those first chains. He persuaded the captain to accompany him into the hold on several tours of inspection in the hope that the skipper's presence would discourage any acts of disruption. There were none.

The work progressed without interference next morning. Jeff completed final arrangements ashore, returning to the dock only to make an act of presence and to satisfy himself that all was normal.

He made his twice-postponed trip to Regla to confer with Hernandez. Captain MacFarland convinced him that feeding three hundred men in addition to the crew would be too much for the ship's cook to handle, so in the interests of peace aboard ship Jeff had Vincente explain the situation to Hernandez. He was to persuade the slave dealer that in addition to providing food for the coffle, he should put aboard at least two or three overseers familiar with the care and feeding of blacks to handle their problems at sea. Jeff would pay these men and see that they were repatriated by the next Lafitte ship leaving Barataria for Cuba.

Hernandez received Jeff with his customary formal politeness and the ritual glass of sherry. The wine did little to dispel the barracoon stench, which had been absent from Jeff's nostrils for the past few days. While Vincente interpreted, the slave dealer's cold eyes peered at Jeff through rectangular spectacles; his hands were clasped on the head of his mahogany cane.

Yes, Hernandez replied in Spanish, he quite understood the situation, and was prepared to let Señor Carson have two expert slave handlers. They were good men. One spoke Ashanti, which was more or less understood by most Gold Coast blacks, and they were both well versed in African customs.

Of course, Hernandez continued, Señor Carson must understand that he would have to replace these men during their absence and men of their caliber and experience commanded good pay. He must count on being deprived of their services for at least a month, probably more. Would Señor Carson be prepared to pay two hundred dollars for the use of these experts?

Jeff nodded when Vincente had translated. "I am prepared to guarantee payment up to two hundred dollars. However, I will pay you now only one hundred dollars. If for any reason the men are not back inside one month, my bank will pay you another hundred. Agreed?"

Hernandez ran his fingers through his thinning white hair during the translation. Then he smiled.

"*Convenido*," he said, extending his hand. When Jeff shook it, he added, "*Tomaremos una copita mas*." And he poured more sherry.

His usual squeaky voice became grave as he continued speaking in Spanish. His face fell as though he had just learned that his best friend had died.

"He got bad news," Vincente announced.

The bad news turned out to concern one of the Fancies Jeff had chosen, the young boy with ivory skin and long dark ringlets. The lad was ill and would have to be withdrawn from the shipment.

"That's bad news indeed." Jeff remembered the youngster well—a slender boy with mincing walk and a necklace of red coral. "How sick is he?"

Too sick to travel, was the answer. Hernandez hoped he did not have *la plaga*, but he had separated the lad from the other slaves just in case. *La plaga* was *muy* contagious, but he was sure he had taken precautions in time.

"Damn!" Jeff said. "That boy is valuable property. He's worth at least a thousand dollars as a butler or houseboy. Vincente, do you think this old bird got a better offer for him and is holding out on us?"

After a brief exchange in Spanish Vincente reported that Hernandez would be glad to show Señor Carson the place where the boy lay sick, but would not go himself, because after all it just *might* be *la plaga*. . . .

"We better trust him, I think," Vincente added.

Hernandez understood that Señor Carson was particularly taken by the boy with the red beads and he would replace him with a specimen of equal quality. He would offer several for Jeff's choice whenever he desired.

"Tell him to have the replacement here when the *Sainte-Claire* docks in Regla," Jeff said.

Before tying up any more loose ends, Jeff took some anti-Cugino defensive measures. Vincente accompanied him to an *armería*—the best gunsmith shop in all Cuba, the lad boasted—to buy sidearms. He came out with a brand-new type of flintlock—a pistol said to have been invented by an American living in England—which fired a number of shots separately and consecutively. Bullets were contained in a cylinder that was rotated by hand after each shot was fired and the pistol cocked again. It was an ingenious weapon and quite expensive. As the shop also specialized in Toledo steel blades, Jeff bought (on Vincente's suggestion) a short dagger which was easily concealed and would be more readily available should he be jumped from behind, than his complicated pistol.

A more pleasant last-minute errand was a courtesy visit to Don Cipriano to thank him for his many favors and to discuss the future of his illegitimate son. There was more ceremonial sherry, more toasts to the loyal friendship with Jean Lafitte, and pledges of further aid on Señor Carson's next trip to Cuba—all faithfully translated by Vincente, whose new clothes looked less out of place in the mausoleumlike grandeur of the Olivarez mansion than had his rags on his first visit.

When the time came to discuss Vincente's future, the boy seemed not at all embarrassed to translate Jeff's words of highest praise.

"I have been most pleased with his services as interpreter and general guide," Jeff said. "In fact, he has been indispensable to me. He is a very bright lad. Clever far beyond his years . . . good blood line certainly."

The dignified old Cuban made a slight bow as though the praise was for himself. He was not surprised, he said

248

through Vincente. After all, the boy was of his own loins.

"I would appreciate your help in developing his extraordinary intelligence," Jeff went on. "If you will get him accepted in a good school, I will pay the tuition. He must learn to read and write, at least in Spanish. Otherwise half his intelligence is wasted. Will you attend to the education of your bastard son, Don Cipriano?"

Indeed he would. He would give him a letter. Don Cipriano pleaded guilty to negligence, but excused himself on the grounds that it was the custom of his class and his country to show little concern for the offspring of casual matings. He was pleased that Vincente showed such promise.

He would arrange for Vincente's apprenticeship at the barracoons of the aging Hernandez. What a great thing if this boy, born on the wrong side of the blanket, could in time earn a place in the important Lafitte organization.

When he had finished translating, Vincente engaged Don Cipriano in a long and spirited dialogue, obviously on his own behalf.

"What is this?" Jeff cut in. "What's going on?"

Vincente looked sullenly at his shoes.

"I tell Don Cipriano I rather go with you on ship, Señor Jeff," he said. "He say no."

"Of course he says no, just as I do," Jeff replied. "You first must learn to read and write. I predict it won't take long. Now, will you tell your father how much I appreciate his help and courtesies, and that I look forward to seeing him and his brother on my next trip to Cuba?"

Vincente obliged.

Don Cipriano bowed and shook hands. *"Vaya usted con Dios,"* he said.

Once begun in earnest, the refitting of the *Sainte-Claire*'s hold for human cargo proceeded rapidly. Jeff spaced his visits of inspection to no more than one or two a day in order not to inflame the bo's'n and his fellow potential mutineers unduly, though he found it hard to believe these thugs were stupid enough to go against Lafitte. It made no sense. But he stayed on guard. On the fourth day he found the ship's carpenter directing the sweeping up of sawdust, shavings, and metal filings.

"We sail in the mornin'," Captain MacFarland announced. "We'll cross to Regla an' pick up your niggers an' supplies at the second change o' watch. I'll want yer wenches aboard by ten o'clock."

Despite Jeff's impatience to get underway, the captain's announcement came as something of a shock. His experience of exotic Havana was ending almost before it had begun. There had been nothing romantic about slave barracoons or the curious negotiations with the pederast Solano. Vincente's sister Perla was a sweet piece of ass and his couplings with her had been exciting despite her sordid surroundings, and the tragic murder of poor Ramon. The only really exotic episodes of his brief tropical stay were his nights at Josefina's, and they were too much like familiar routine once the outer trappings were stripped from the wenches. Of course, he had to admit that he had never before engaged in erotic gymnastics with an English-speaking lizard looking on.

He bestirred himself and made final visits to both banks to confirm that the slave dealers and the various merchants and artisans had been paid. He also drew enough money to pay his hotel bill and take care of eleventh-hour expenses.

He bought more gifts to take back with him—brilliantly-embroidered mantillas for his beloved Chloe and for her mother Helen, a bottle of French scent for Madame Hortense. On second thought he bought a bottle of scent for Perla. He even toyed with the idea of spending his last night in Havana with the girl, but vetoed the idea when he recalled her squalid lodgings. He'd have Vincente take the gift to her, and then go to Josefina's for a final fling. To leave Havana without making some woman happy would be a crime against nature—his own. And he was horny enough to be in need of emergency treatment tonight.

When he charged Vincente with the mission, however, the lad made a counterproposition. Señor Jeff would present the scent to Perla himself. No, not at their home. Right here in the hotel.

"She desires much to wear that fine shawl you gave her," Vincente said, "and I bought her a new dress to go with it—you can repay me if you like. So she will not disgrace you if she comes here. *Le gusta a usted*? You like?"

Jeff hesitated. He had visions of that murdering pimp Jorge following Perla and raising unholy hell—if not bloody murder—in the Hotel de Paris. Still, he needed a woman and Perla was very much to his taste. Having Perla for a farewell romp between clean sheets would be a fitting windup.

"You sure that bastard Jorge won't make trouble?"

"No chance," Vincente replied. "Outside our own *vecindario* Jorge is small mouse."

Perla arrived after dinner with her new shawl over her new dress, a simple dimity sheath. She slipped them off while Jeff was giving instructions to her brother.

"I don't want to see hide nor hair of you for at least an hour," Jeff said. "In an hour you can bring a tub of warm water. When you knock on the door I'll tell you if I need anything else. Now disappear."

When he locked the door and turned around, Perla stood naked before him. Her dark eyes burned with a desire he would have thought impossible in a girl for whom passion was an article of trade. Her virginal pink nipples were hard and distended as she pressed herself against him. She threw her arms around his neck and kissed him. As she felt his rigidity growing against her bare abdomen, she reached down to undo the buttons of his fly. Instantly his swollen phallus sprang out at her. He disengaged his lips.

"Not so fast. Let me get some clothes off."

For reply she prodded him a few steps toward the bed, clasped both hands behind his neck, stood on tiptoe, gave a little leap, swung her legs apart, and planted her heels against his buttocks. Almost without realizing it he slid into her. He was her prisoner.

He was scarcely aware of her subtle undulating movements. He was aware only that his whole being was flowing toward his loins, concentrating in a brimming reservoir of sweetness. He tried to hold off the climax but he was helpless against the tenderly relentless demands of her hips. She was the eternal and inevitable female, not to be denied. The strength flowed from his body into the girl in ecstatic surges. His knees buckled and he staggered backward against the bed. He toppled over on his back, gasping for breath. He lay motionless.

Still astride his hips, the girl moved her body in tiny, gentle circles to drain the last drop of his manhood. Then she extricated her feet to kneel beside him. She nuzzled the hollow under his chin.

"Perla, Perla, Perla!" he murmured when he got his breath.

She laid a finger across his lips and started to undress him. She had a little difficulty getting his boots off, but succeeded when he regained sufficient energy to flex his instep. The trousers, tight as they were, posed no problem. Neither did his shirt. When she tried to remove his undershirt, however, he sat up to resist.

Wasn't he being silly? After all, he'd probably never see this girl again, and who in Cuba cared whether he had Negro blood in his veins? Still, he must cling to his habit of secrecy for his own protection. Carelessness had almost cost him his life in Mississippi. He must never be careless again. When Perla pulled up on the hem of his undershirt, he seized her wrists. He smiled, shook his head, kissed her. She smiled back. Obviously her brother had explained his idiosyncrasy.

She stretched out beside him on the bed, speaking softly in his ear. He didn't understand a word she said, but he enjoyed the sound of her voice, the intonations, the lilting syllables. Spanish was indeed a most musical language, he decided, especially when spoken by a sexy young girl. Just listening to her mellifluous phrases made him randy all over again. And when she started sketching circles around his navel with the gentle forefingers of both hands, he was erect again. When the expanding circles began running through his pubic hair, he was rigid. He rolled her on her back and instantly was into her again.

This time he was in command—or so he thought. This was routine copulation, the response to a physical need, his partner was of no importance personally. The rhythm was to be his, the usual long strokes to excite the girl under him, the tempo to increase as she reacted. However, he had scarcely reached his deepest intromission when he became aware of something strange happening. Each time he plunged and was about to draw back, the tip of his penis was caught in a gentle squeeze. The girl must have muscles far inside her genitalia that she could contract at will. It was driving him mad. Impossible to hold back. He increased his speed involuntarily. At the end of each stroke there was still this exquisite little nip. Then he lost all control. Pounding away madly, he had no thought but to achieve the ultimate ecstasy and release as quickly as possible. . . .

The girl's gentle moans reached a crescendo just as an involuntary cry escaped his own throat. Perla dug her heels into his back. They had achieved climax simultaneously.

This time she had exhausted him. There could be no repeat performance. Even when he caught his breath it was long minutes before he could move. This girl was something. She was no Chloe, true, but then, he was in love with Chloe. Perla's techniques—they seemed really too instinctive to be called by the self-conscious formalized term "technique"—were more exciting even than those of an old pro like Helen. Perla would be a sensation in New Orleans. For a moment he toyed with the idea of taking her with him, but knew better. She was not a slave, even though in a way she was in bondage to Vincente, so she could not be put up for sale like the dozen wenches he was bringing back. He couldn't very well sell her to Madame Hortense, even though she would surely soon get star billing at the Riding Academy.

Maybe Hortense would give him a bonus—or at least credit toward the release of Chloe—if he could smuggle Perla in as his personal import. No, there were too many complications. He had better forget the whole business. . . .

"My God! What are you doing to me, Perla?"

While Jeff lay prone, musing upon Perla's impressive talents and wondering how he could turn them to his own profit, the girl had been busy with a project of her own. He had scarcely noticed when she turned him gently on his back. He was vaguely aware of the feathery touch of her tongue caressing his scrotum. He thought: she's an optimist; she'll never get a dead horse to jump the fence. When her fingers danced lightly over the limpness that had very recently been his pride and joy, he felt definite stirrings. And when her tiny pink tongue flickered along the growing length of it, he knew she had won again.

Jeff tried to sit up but she pushed him back almost before his shoulders had left the bed. She bent over for a final encircling kiss, then she was quickly astride his loins and he was into her again. Or rather she had absorbed him with her hot, quivering lubricity.

By shifting her weight from one knee to the other she rotated her body in half-circles, slowly at first, then faster and faster, her torso erect, her hands clasped behind her head. As the tempo increased, she added another dimension to her frenzied movements. She bent forward and back, raising her buttocks with each half-turn, lowering them with the next.

The fierce paroxysm was upon Jeff with pulsating, almost agonizing suddenness. He cried out, clasped Perla to him, rolled from side to side, lay still, panting.

There was a knock at the door. Perla squirmed off the bed.

The knock was repeated. "Señor Jeff, it's me, Vincente."

Jeff placed his feet unsteadily on the floor. "Get the bath water," he said.

"I got the buckets here."

"Then get me clean towels."

"But Señor Jeff—"

"Go get the towels. I'll let you in when you come back."

Jeff waited a few seconds, then unlocked the door and yanked it open. He half expected to find a peeping Vincente lingering at the keyhole, but the boy was gone. He quickly closed the door, went to his clothes and drew out a gold coin. He placed it in Perla's palm.

"Keep this for yourself," he said. "Don't share it with Jorge. Not even Vincente." He pointed and gestured, shaking his head as he indicated the door through which her brother would enter, and nodding vehemently when he pointed at her. "Can you hide it?"

She apparently understood. She smiled impishly and said something in Spanish as she took the money. Then she turned her back and squatted. When she stood up and faced Jeff the coin had disappeared.

At this point Vincente returned. While he was pouring water into the tin tub, he queried Jeff.

"Perla do good this time? Good enough for New Orleans, you think?"

Jeff hesitated before sitting in the water. Curious and diabolical that Vincente and he should share the same idea. He wondered if the boy had coached his sister to put on a special performance—a sort of sample of goods suitable for export? If so, he had been a good tutor or Perla had been an apt pupil or both. No matter. He still was convinced her intuitive feelings, an instinct that could pass for sincerity, would alone make her very popular in a house like Madame Hortense's.

"What did you have in mind, Vincente?" Jeff asked. He sat. Perla ministered to him with a cake of Castile soap.

"You know Perla too good for *ladrones* like this pimp Jorge, no?" Vincente said. "Then why you don't take her with you tomorrow, Señor Jeff?"

"Impossible, Vincente. Perla's not a slave. I couldn't sell her as we will be selling Solano's wenches."

"She could make believe she is *mestiza*, no?"

255

Jeff laughed briefly, bitterly. Or perhaps it was Bricktop, the Negro slave, who laughed ironically at the idea of a white girl's posing as a mulatto. He said, "You don't know what you're trying to do to your sister, Vincente. In Louisiana, all over the American South really, a *mestiza* is a Negro and a Negro is not even human. Here she is free and white."

"Why can't she be a free white *puta* in New Orleans? I go along and be her *alcahuete*. Padre Diego say many Spanish remain in New Orleans. And for Americans who want Cuban whore, I translate. She need be black only at sea."

Jeff stepped out of the tub and let Perla towel him. She listened intently, trying to understand.

Jeff said, "It's not as simple as that. I might be able to get her into a good house through Captain Dominique You. But I must have permission from Lafitte to take her aboard, something I don't have for this trip. I'll speak to Captain You, and if he says yes, I'll take her next trip."

"And Vincente, too?"

"Only if you learn your lessons, boy. You'll stay in Havana until my next trip. That's settled."

"*Qué lástima!*" Vincente shook his head sadly, made a drooping gesture, and turned a mournful face to Perla. "Too bad! Because I think Perla loves you."

Jeff took his trousers from Perla's outstretched hands and fumbled in his pocket.

"This is your commission," he told Vincente, "and carriage fare to take Perla home. I don't want her molested by Jorge."

The girl put her arms around Jeff's neck and kissed him. Then she turned to her brother and said something in Spanish.

"She say," Vincente translated, "you don't give her that French scent you promise."

Jeff laughed. He opened the armoire and produced the bottle of perfume. Perla kissed him again.

CHAPTER XXIV

MORNING was just exhaling its first warm and humid contribution to the tropical day when Jeff's caravan arrived to pick up the flower of the Solano Fancies. They were three closed *carrozas,* which would hold four wenches each, and a *volanta.* Jeff did not dare reveal the Carmelite nun disguise until they had left Don Policarpo Solano behind. He did not trust Solano. The erudite pederast was the sort of bird who might tip off the police to intercept the iniquitous Panchita before they reached La Machina wharf in order to cement his official relations. On the other hand, if Solano betrayed Lafitte, he would destroy himself.

Solano had transferred the dozen wenches from his spurious country Alhambra to his dilapidated premises in Havana. He waddled out to greet the caravan with a fawning welcome. He crossed the courtyard, supported on one side by Tobalito and on the other by his part-Mandingo boy. As Jeff stepped from the *volanta,* he saw Solano struggling to free his arms from his servitors and he hurried to shake one hand in order to forestall a more intimate embrace.

Solano made an effusive speech of farewell with appropriate gestures. He had enjoyed their relationship and hoped next time Jeff came to Cuba they would get to know each other better—much better.

After Vincente had translated, Jeff made a businesslike reply, as courteous as he thought necessary, and said they must start immediately as they were behind schedule. Solano's huge face contorted into a desolate *moue,* and he clapped his puffy hands. The sound was almost inaudible, but his effeminate cry brought out the wenches in a colorful procession.

The women were dressed in their Sunday best—a variety of costumes that spanned the Caribbean and reached across the Atlantic. There were brilliant mantillas, Haitian imitations of Parisian styles, the latest from Madrid in copies by Havana *modistas*. There were bangles, earrings, a few necklaces. The trollops all carried clothwrapped bundles, except Antoinette who had a scuffed leather bag.

Leading the group was Koko, the Songhai Princess whose proud bearing and stately stride gave no hint of the magnificent bearded underbelly beneath the bright African scarves with which she was draped. Close behind her were the other pseudo peeresses—Antoinette, the so-called Duchesse de Limbé, with her full lips and suggestive walk, very French in her imitation Empire gown; and Countess Panchita, the big-eyed little minx who did not yet know that she was on the verge of taking the veil.

Jeff tried to remember how he had rated the other girls when he had examined them intimately a week ago. As they stepped into the carriages at his indication, he reviewed the names that stuck in his mind and made an effort to match the bodily attributes that went with each. There was Rosita, who had the plump, friendly vagina, and Magdalena, whose genitalia reminded him of a baited trap. There were Carmen, Juanita, Beatriz— which one had the pearshaped tits?—Maria, Adelita —who had the apples, who the melons? Well, there would be time on the way to Barataria to refresh his memory. . . .

Jeff climbed into the waiting *volanta*, turned and waved to Solano.

"*Vaya con Dios!*" Solano's voice squeaked.

"*Hasta luego,*" Jeff called.

The caravan rolled down the avenue of ceiba trees for half a kilometer until the Solano house was out of sight, then turned off into a side road and stopped. While Vincente kept watch at the junction, Jeff opened the door of the first *carroza*. He shooed out three of the girls, then stepped inside with the bundle of Carmelite apparel.

Panchita's shrill staccato protests when Jeff began to undress her became squeals of laughter when she saw the drugget robe, the white mantle, the long black veil, and realized what they were for. She fumbled in her effects for a fragment of mirror to adjust the veil and to fit the squareframed eyeglasses on her nose. She giggled as Jeff rolled her lay clothes into a wad and stuffed it into a sugar sack he had taken from the galley of the *Sainte-Claire*. He then got out and shooed the three wenches back in.

"*Adelante!*" he cried proudly. In another week or so he would be speaking Spanish fluently.

The lavender bougainvillea growing across the facade of the little Church of the Sad Virgin was resplendent in the hot, dazzling sunlight as Jeff's caravan of female Fancies braked to a halt. Vincente jumped down, ran up the few steps, and entered the church. Jeff followed, but more sedately. When he reached the top step he stopped. He felt something was wrong—he had no idea what it was but a curious feeling had come over him. Perhaps it was some subtly unrecognizable smell or a barely perceptible sound he could not identify. Vincente had disappeared from view, so Jeff advanced a few paces more, past the holy-water font, into the gloom of the nave. Two candles burned in the half-light at the end of the nave. As his eyes became used to the dimness, he made out a bier and several elderly women with shawls over their heads kneeling before the altar. The drone of prayers, punctuated by sobs, came clearly to his ears. He stopped short, a cold spot forming at the nape of his neck.

The cold spot trickled down his spine. He felt an urge to turn and run but his feet were frozen to the floor. He was not afraid of death, but he had a superstitious fear of the dead. He hated death because it was a cessation of life, which he loved, but he was awed by the mystery of death. He felt he must do something to show his respect for the unknown corpse, so he awkwardly made the sign of the cross as Vincente had showed him when they were plotting to involve Father Diego in their fraud. Then he back-pedaled into the little vestibule, turned, and ran down the steps into the sunlight. He breathed deeply, listening to the stupid beating of his heart.

"Bad news," said Vincente when he emerged from the church. "Padre Diego can't come with us. You want he give back your money, Señor Jeff?"

"Why can't he come?"

"One of his *parroquianos* is dead. He must say the mass and bury him."

"Why can't he just duck down to the wharf with us now, like we planned? He could come right back and bury his pal," Jeff pleaded.

"No, *señor*. The padre is very busy and very sad. One more *parroquiano* is dying, he think, and two *parroquianas* also very sick. The padre must pray for them, pray very hard because he think there is *epidemia*. Is *la plaga, I* think."

"*La plaga?*" That was what Hernandez had said was the matter with the young slave with the red coral beads. Very contagious, Hernandez had said. Three long strides and Jeff was in the *volanta*. "Let's get the hell out of here." He sprung up into the cart, yelling, "*Adelante!*"

Vincente jumped in. The coachman cracked his whip.

Damn, thought Jeff as the horses clop-clopped their way into downtown Havana, everything was going wrong! Now this disease they called *la plaga*. It must be like "the fever" in New Orleans—a good thing to keep away from. *La plaga* had smeared hell out of their carefully drawn plan for smuggling Panchita aboard. What the hell was the matter with that stupid priest that he couldn't take an hour or so off for two hundred gold dollars? His pious corpse would not be any deader when he got back, and his burial would be just as holy an hour later. His prayers weren't going to help any sick people, either. Without the ecclesiastical blessing of Padre Diego on the whole group of wenches, would Panchita's seraphic disguise pass muster with the police, or customs, or whatever uniformed service might want to stop her? As the wheels of the *volanta* rattled noisily over the cobbled streets leading to the Havana waterfront, Jeff leaned forward and slapped Vincente on the rump.

"Hey, big thinker," he said, "what do we do now that your smart scheme collapsed?"

"I have your money back next time you come to Havana," Vincente said without turning around.

"It's not the money. Can we pass Panchita without the padre?"

"Sure, *señor*, sure. Don't worry." Vincente turned and grinned. "Vincente always got more tricks, no?"

Jeff shook his head and grunted. At the end of the street he could see the thicket of masts and spars that marked the dock area. He would soon know if Vincente's nonchalance was justified. If the padre were along, Jeff would have asked him to start praying right now. Damn the padre! Damn *la plaga*!

The horse slowed. Jeff leaned out on one side to peer ahead. A tangle of stalled vehicles of all sorts blocked the entrance to the wharf. A score of nondescript soldiers was making some sort of inspection. One barefooted soldier reached up and grabbed the bridle of the *volanta* horse.

The coachman shouted at the soldier and raised his whip. Vincente grabbed the coachman's arm and joined in the shouting match. Two other ragged soldiers loped up and started pulling open the doors of the carriages in which the dozen wenches were riding. A fourth soldier, a noncom of some kind, ordered the women to get out and line up. At this point Vincente jumped down from his seat beside the driver, running.

"Vincente!" Jeff shouted after him. "Where the hell—?" But the lad had disappeared in the crowd.

All four soldiers were now engaged in searching the wenches. Jeff gesticulated and protested loudly. They ignored him. The noncom showed especial interest in Panchita, not in the least impressed by her religious garb. She was screaming at him.

"See here," Jeff shouted. "You've got to show respect for this nun."

No reaction.

Jeff swore impotently. Served him right for being so

goddamn stubborn about getting this little bitch aboard. He was going to have to start thinking with his head instead of with his balls.

The noncom parted the white mantle with his dirty hands and pawed the drugget robe. Panchita swung and landed a resounding smack on the side of his head. He drew back one foot to kick her when an officer in a smart white uniform approached, a letter in his hand. The noncom came to attention and saluted.

One pace behind the officer's dangling sword came Vincente.

"*Mi capitán,*" said Vincente, "*quiero presentar el caballero americano,* Don Jefferson Carson."

"*Muy alegre,*" said the captain, handing the letter back to Vincente. He gave an order and the search was abandoned. The angry wenches got back into their carriages, Jeff and Vincente resumed their places, and the officer waved the caravan through the barricade.

"Jesus. That was a close one." Jeff mopped his brow. The carts rattled down the long wharf. "What the hell was going on? Was there a tipoff about Panchita?"

"No, *señor.* They did not want Panchita." Vincente looked very smug. "Some *puta* stole the archbishop's gold chalice, so they search all women on every dock. They don't want she take it from Cuba."

"And what was that letter the officer gave to you?" Jeff couldn't help admiring this enterprising little boy.

"That was from my father, Don Cipriano." Vincente made a nonchalant gesture. "He give it to me when you ask him to help me to school. It say, 'Show my son Vincente every courtesy and give him all help he needs and oblige Cipriano Olivarez.' Capitán is impressed, no? Cipriano Olivarez very important name."

"But why didn't you show the letter to the soldiers, Vincente, instead of running off like a bat out of hell and leaving me here alone and scared pissless?"

"Because, Señor Jeff"— Vincente was pontificating— "I must find officer. These soldiers can't read."

"Neither can you, Vincente."

"True," was the reply. "But I know what letter says. I tell my father what to write."

As the trollop caravan drew alongside the *Sainte-Claire*, a kaleidoscope of bright hats and head cloths appeared in the carriage windows. Two were pushed unceremoniously aside to make way for the fanciful headdress of Princess Koko. The Songhai woman twisted her head and craned her neck to look up at the masts and rigging of the bark moored to the wharf. Jeff marveled at the intricate way her thousand little black braids were interwoven to form what resembled a birdcage. Probably took her all day to fix it. He wondered what happened when she washed her hair—then decided she probably never did. The warm breeze brought the smell of cocoanut oil to his nostrils. . . .

Captain MacFarland stood at the rail shouting at him through cupped hands.

"Good God Almighty and the Twelve Apostles!" he yelled. "I said the second watch, an' we're still waitin' for ye an' Lafitte's goddamn constellation of cunts. You get those waggletails aboard pronto because in three minutes there'll be no gangplank, an' those that can't fly will be left behind."

There was a cackle of approval from the officers at the rail and a few obscenities from the bo's'n. Jeff tried to ignore the chorus and organize his Fancies. Vincente interrupted to say, "I'll take your bags aboard, Señor Jeff. Then I'll go. I won't say goodbye, because I might cry, *señor*. I don't like to get all choked in my throat. Little boys cry. So I'll just say *hasta luego, amigo*. Come back soon."

"*Hasta luego,* Vincente. Take care of Perla."

Vincente grabbed Jeff's two bags and scurried up the gangplank. Jeff forced him out of mind once the boy disappeared with the bags. He busied himself herding his Solano Fancies up the gangplank, trying to ignore the obscenities bellowed from the rail. As the wenches ascended the incline, ignorant of the meaning of the crew's raucous cheers, Jeff became aware of shouts from above. For the first time he noted that there were men in the rigging and astride the yards. The square sails were reefed on the foremast and mainmast, but the fore-and-aft triangle was flapping at the mizzen for reasons beyond him. He supposed it had something to do with the fact that the *Sainte-Claire* was being towed across the harbor to Regla and would not really get underway until the three hundred blacks were aboard.

A roar from the skipper brought him back to reality. Jeff was climbing the gangplank with the last of the wenches, one hand firmly gripping the arm of the pseudo-Carmelite.

"Hell's bells an' Paul's balls!" the captain bellowed. "What are ye doin' to me, laddie? I'm stretchin' a point fer yer quail tail, but ye know full well I canna take an ecclesiastic aboard." He stretched a hairy arm across the head of the gangway.

"Captain, I know your rules," Jeff shouted back. "But this trollop is not really a nun. She's not even a virgin, as I'm sure you'll find out before we get back to Barataria. Skipper, I was planning to put her in your cabin, remember?"

"But why in holy hell—?"

"The masquerade? Simple, captain. She's a runaway. She's running away from a bastard who beats her."

"You mean she's a runner?" The captain's expressive eyebrows went up.

"No, no, no, skipper. The bastard who beat her was not her legal owner. He lured her away with lying promises he never kept. He never even had a bill of sale—"

"All right but strip those sanctimonious duds off her before I have a mutiny on my hands. Lock her up with the rest of the cunts an' let's get underway." MacFarland tossed Jeff four heavy iron keys. To one of them was attached a damascene plaque inlaid with a gilt thistle; this one he held back an instant. "Ye'll returrrn this one to me before we cast off from Regla," he said.

The key with the plaque attached fitted the captain's

own cabin door. The others locked the doors to the cabins of the first and third mates and Jeff's own.

Jeff led the wenches to their allotted sleeping spaces. He heard the loud thump of the gangplank being dropped to the dock. Immediately afterward he heard the skipper shout, "Cast off aft." A pause. Then, "Cast off forward."

After turning a key in the fourth lock, Jeff made his way to the helmsman's station to return his own key to the captain and remained on deck to watch the sweating, straining backs of the Negroes bending to the oars of the two longboats towing the *Sainte-Claire* across the harbor.

Docking at Regla was accomplished quickly and routinely. Jeff was mildly surprised to see the white-haired Hernandez standing on the pier, his hands clasped on the head of his mahogany stick. Next to him stood a handsome young Negro, more than a head taller than the slave dealer.

Jeff shouted a *"Buenos dias"* to Hernandez—and suddenly felt dumb without Vincente at his side. How dependent he had been on that nine-year-old boy as interpreter. He was wondering how he could carry on last-minute negotiations with Hernandez when the Negro shouted up at him. His voice had a marked British accent.

"Mr. Carson, Señor Hernandez regrets to inform you that the young slave you liked so much died yesterday. He is offering me to take his place. My name is Trafalgar."

"All right, Trafalgar, but you understand I'll have to finger you first and decide if you pass muster," Jeff answered. "Ask Señor Hernandez to come aboard with you for a glass of sherry."

"No sherry," said Captain MacFarland, who had listened with interest to the exchange. "Give him a tot of rum."

Hernandez climbed the gangplank with the help of the muscular black. He refused the proffered drink but took a seat in the captain's mess, speaking constantly in Spanish during Jeff's examination. That Trafalgar was a perfect physical specimen was evident to the eye, but

Jeff went through the routine of poking, feeling, hefting the testicles, and peeling back the foreskin. Without being prompted, the Negro bent over for Jeff to part his buttocks to check for hemorrhoids. After straightening up, he took Jeff's silence for approval and asked permission to resume his only garment, a pair of duck trousers. Any other garments, Jeff supposed, were in the goatskin sack on the deck beside him. He nodded permission.

"You a Fanti?" Jeff asked.

"Yes, Mr. Carson, sir."

"Where'd you learn to speak English?"

"As a boy I was body servant to an officer of the Royal British Navy, sir. He was killed in the battle of Trafalgar and I was captured by a Spanish naval officer."

"Who consequently changed your name to Trafalgar?"

"Yes, Mr. Carson, sir. And he brought me here to Cuba where he sold me at auction. That was some years ago—long enough for me to learn Spanish."

"Hernandez has been speaking Spanish for the last fifteen minutes without stop. What did he say?"

"He wanted you to know, Mr. Carson, that he had been obliged to pay considerably more for me than the average price of the slaves he sold you. However, he does not regret the extra expense because he knows your heart was set on the unfortunate youngster who died. He hopes you will be pleased."

"Tell him you'll do nicely." He would indeed. This was not a plantation hand or a breeder of field hands. Trafalgar would bring a handsome price. He'd like to own him himself. "You still speak Fanti?"

"Yes, sir."

"Then I'm not going to spancel you. You can help manage the coffle coming aboard. I hope you've got no ideas about running?"

"None, sir. I'm looking forward to this voyage. I've never been in the American colonies before."

"They're not colonies any more—haven't been for over thirty years, in case you haven't heard, Trafalgar.

266

Anyhow I'm going to test you. Help Old Man Hernandez ashore. Take him to the end of the pier. I'll be watching you, and I warn you I'm a pretty good shot."

Trafalgar grinned, showing a wide white octave of teeth. "You don't have to prove your marksmanship, Mr. Carson, sir."

Jeff liked this big Fanti. He was ingratiating, he was intelligent, and best of all, he was respectful. He made Jeff feel he really was a white man, just as the bullying of the ship's officers had begun to make him feel he was fated always to be Bricktop, the white-skinned Negro slave.

CHAPTER XXV

JEFF stood in the bow of the *Sainte-Claire*, relishing the wind in his face and watching the sun sink into the sea. He breathed deeply—for the first time in days, it seemed. The hurdle of language and the obstacles of doing business in a foreign land had been cleared, his self-created problem of smuggling a fugitive from the country had been successfully solved, and the cargo of blacks and Fancy trollops was safely aboard and bound for delivery to Barataria. He hoped the Lafittes would be properly appreciative of his efforts.

The afternoon was well advanced before the *Sainte-Claire* was able to sail. Loading three hundred slaves and their provender had taken longer than Jeff had calculated, and was more trying. Sacks of beans, maize, lemons, and pork were carried aboard on the sweating backs of the shackled blacks themselves. After surveying the throng of Africans as they plodded out from the barracoons, Captain MacFarland decided to load extra casks of fresh water—a time-consuming operation, as it turned out.

The actual embarkment of the Negroes had given Jeff a queer uneasy feeling. As they trudged aboard in clanking groups of ten he could detect an undercurrent of potential rebellion in their mood, their bearing, and their incomprehensible talk among themselves. This would be his first prolonged contact with *bozals* just off a boat from Africa, and he found the contrast with American-born and domesticated blacks startling. Plantation hands, even when they chafed under the yoke, were good-humored in their resignation. These blacks were surly, resentful, desolated by their recent loss of freedom. Their unfamiliar lingo seemed menacing compared to the friendly if highly idiomatic talk of the tame slaves of Mississippi.

Jeff sensed the melancholy hostility of his charges when, as each group came to the foot of the gangplank, the captain bellowed from the deck, "Carson, have yer niggers pee off the end o' the dock before they come aboard. Make them crap, too, if they can. That will delay the stink in the hold fer a day or so."

Jeff transmitted the order to Trafalgar, who passed it on to the two overseers Hernandez had sent along. That the message came thirdhand did nothing to soften the cold resentment of the slaves.

He made trips to the hold with the first few groups to oversee the assignment of sleeping space and the attachment of spancels to side chains. Keys to the spancels were held by Cugino, the flatulent bo's'n, whom the captain had charged with discipline and security. The hold was hot and stifling, and as Jeff watched the sweat dripping from the black bodies, he said to Trafalgar, "Tell them it won't be so hot when we get to sea."

Trafalgar rendered Jeff's reassurance into Fanti in an expressionless tone. The faces of the blacks remained expressionless.

The birds of the Solano paradise were angry about being locked in airless ovenlike cabins during the long process of getting to Regla, loading the blacks, and preparing for sea. They were not bashful about expressing their displeasure, plaintively at first, then forcefully, and finally with violence. Timid knocks and polite requests through the locked doors were followed by pounding and loud demands. Then came kicking, banging, and raging protests that included profanity in several languages, including English. Jeff wondered which one of his bright-skins was threatening, among other things, to "esheet onda ceiling" if she wasn't let out instantly—and where she had learned her English.

While the sails were being set and the *Sainte-Claire* was being towed out to the entrance of the harbor to catch the wind, Jeff began taking the wenches for a walk around the deck, two by two. Perhaps he was being overcautious, because the crew was occupied with the business of seamanship, but he felt he might be overextending himself if he exposed more than a pair at a time.

The *Sainte-Claire* had cleared the Morro Castle and was headed in a westerly direction on a starboard tack by the time Jeff had got all the females back under lock and key and given them a sketchy meal. In his own cabin he had billeted the three supposed peeresses. He did not know if he could service all three of them this night, but he'd try. At least he wanted to give "Countess" Panchita a good hump before passing her on to Captain MacFarland as promised. After all the trouble and risks he'd taken to get her out of danger, and out of Cuba, he felt he was entitled to the first crack. Then, of course, he'd have to exorcise himself of his obsession with Princess Koko, she of the splendid pubic shrubbery. Duchess Antoinette might have to wait until morning if the first two exhausted him. They'd have to take turns sharing his bunk. He'd spread a blanket on the floor for the odd peeress.

When he'd finally got his dozen doxies settled, he made his way forward to stand in the bow and relax. The beauty of the sunset and the quiet of the evening soothed his taut nerves. Clouds that had been banking along the horizon as the sun went down seemed to catch fire. He had never seen such flaming colors—scarlet, crimson, and bloodred streamers filled the western sky and were reflected in the long green swells of the Gulf of Mexico. Gulls that had been following them since they left Havana grew golden wings as they swooped and dove after flotsam dumped from the galley.

A raucous voice rose above the muted swish of the sea cleft by the prow. Jeff turned. At first he saw only the bellied canvas of the fore sails, now dyed pink by the sunset. Then he made out the figure of the first mate, shouting orders at crewmen in the rigging. The mate's beard and polished pate appeared redder than ever in the sunset glow. When the maneuver aloft had been accomplished, the mate came a few steps forward to stand beside Jeff, peering ahead.

"I was admiring the sunset," Jeff said. "Beautiful, isn't it?"

"Not to me it ain't." The mate did not turn his head.

"Oh? What's wrong?" Jeff hadn't anticipated an argument.

"Everything. Too damn red, to start with. And I don't like the way them clouds are piling up."

"Bad sign?" Jeff wished he hadn't started this dialogue.

"Maybe." The mate shrugged. "Can't tell. But I don't like it."

And then he was gone. Without a word he disappeared in the gathering dusk.

The sunset had been fading for the past few minutes, but now the colors seemed to wink out with a suddenness characteristic of the tropics. Thunderheads billowing above the horizon turned to lead. The first stars pricked through the pale afterglow above. Jeff walked aft.

As he passed an open hatch he paused to listen to the desolate chant in minor key that drifted up from the hold. It was a mournful sound that somehow tightened the strings in his gut. There was nothing in the future that held promise for those poor bastards. He shivered. There but for the grace of God . . .

"Hold on, Countess, wait a minute. Stop that, Panchita, don't pull on that. Wait till I get some clothes off."

As soon as Jeff entered his cabin he was set upon by the naked little minx he had saved from being whipped to death. Panchita began undressing him with more enthusiasm than method, pulling and unbuttoning at random. When she managed to get his trousers down as far as his knees, Jeff took over. Now fully aroused, he pushed her against the edge of the bunk and parted her thighs.

The fact that the bunk was already occupied made no difference. Princess Koko lay there naked, stretched full length, and she languidly raised herself on one elbow to watch. The Duchess from Haiti was curled up on the deck in a corner of the cabin. She opened one eye sleepily, but apparently found little of interest, for she closed it again.

Panchita devoted herself wholeheartedly to her task with great zeal and considerable talent. Though Jeff was enjoying her, he could not help being aware of the teeth that had got her into her near-fatal difficulties. Maybe knowing her history kept him from finding her quite the frenzied piece that he had expected. Perhaps she was merely showing her gratitude—combined of course with natural homage to his superior endowment. Despite his preoccupation with prosaic thoughts, her antics brought him quickly to the agonized heights of sensation. He cried out as his vitality peaked and surged into Panchita.

An instant later he cried out again—in pain.

Princess Koko had bitten him on the left buttock!

"Hey!" Jeff had been too engrossed to notice Koko maneuvering herself into a position where she could attack his bare buttocks. She bit him again—on the right buttock. Damn! Did all these wenches have cannibalistic tendencies?

Jeff remembered how she had tried to bite his hand while he was fingering her at Solano's. There was no controlling her now. Inflamed by watching Jeff copulate with Panchita, the Songhai girl moved quickly. She pulled Jeff off of Panchita even before he had lost his rigidity. Holding him securely, she brushed Panchita rudely off the bunk with her elbow. The fugitive Countess yelped as her bottom thumped on the deck, but the Princess was regally unconcerned.

Koko's eyes were bright with admiration as she clasped

Jeff's generous equipment in both hands. She hefted the heavy scrotum like a slave dealer judging the procreative powers of a purchase. Her long fingers tested the rigidity of his erection, then added a few deft strokes to insure its firmness.

During all this Jeff stood immobilized beside the bunk. His pants still half-masted at his knees hobbled him.

With a little moan Koko fell back on the bunk, clasping Jeff to her full firm breasts, dragging him down on top of her. She swung her legs around his bare hips. Jeff felt himself absorbed—that was the only word to describe it—into the copious thicket he had so admired. It was like plunging deep into the heat and humidity of a mysterious tropical jungle. He drove deeper and deeper. . . .

The next minutes were indescribable. To Jeff they were more like a wrestling match than any copulation he had indulged in before. The Princess rolled her hips and shoulders like a soul in pain. She reared and bucked like a wild mare being broken to the saddle, but her arms and legs tightened around Jeff to keep him close. Her quickening breath came in harmonic gasps, tonal syllables that seemed to form a plaintive chant. Jeff wondered if this was some sort of ritual liturgy when the tempo increased and the notes ran together in a thin keening wail that increased in volume until it became an animal howl. Her body trembled violently like someone in the throes of a high fever. Jeff's whole system vibrated in tempo until he achieved a biological response—and an involuntary yell burst across his lips.

He lay inert and exhausted, he didn't know how long, before he was aroused by a timid knock on the door. Only when the knock was repeated did he summon the energy to reply, "Who's there?"

"Petty officer of the watch, sir," came the answer. "Need any help, Mr. Carson?"

"No, no, no help, thank you," said Jeff. He really could use help, but it wasn't the sort the petty officer of the watch could provide.

"You're sure you're all right, Mr. Carson?"

"You're sure you're all right, Mr. Carson? You're not in any trouble, sir? I thought I heard—"

"Oh, that." Jeff tried to sound reassuring. "We were having a heated argument in here. Sorry we disturbed you. Everything's fine."

"Good night, Mr. Carson."

Jeff fell into overwhelming sleep, regretting he had not been able to service the Frenchified wench from Haiti . . . must apologize . . . must take care of her . . . morning. . . .

The banging on the door would have wakened someone three days dead. Jeff sat up, every nerve aquiver from being roused from a profound slumber.

The banging—it was not the timid knock of the petty officer of the watch—was repeated noisily.

"Who is it?" Jeff asked. It was pitch dark. The lighted candle had gone out.

"Never mind who," said a grating voice. Jeff recognized Cugino, the bo's'n. "Skipper wants to see you. Better haul ass up to the wheelhouse, and pronto."

When Jeff tried to swing his legs off the bunk he realized he was still hobbled. His legs were still entangled in his trousers. He managed to hoist the pants waist high and, fumbling in the dark, found the buttons. He could not find his shirt but he had his under shirt on. He opened the door slowly. A lantern burned dimly in the empty passageway. He staggered forward toward the wheelhouse.

Only Captain MacFarland's face was visible in the glow from the binnacle lamp as Jeff entered. "As ye probably know, Carson, we've got ourselves a stowaway aboard. Aye. Cook caught him stealin' vittles in the galley."

"But why should I know anything about it?"

"Ye sneaked him aboard. He's yer lad. Stand up, scum!"

Jeff made out a tiny figure cowering in a corner, untangling his legs to stand up. "Vincente! Oh Jesus . . ."

273

"Just couldn't stand your going away without me, Señor Jeff."

"Oh, goddamnit," Jeff said. "You promised to take care of Perla, and here you are miles from Havana. You promised to learn to read, and—"

The skipper interrupted. "Carson, I'm goin' to assume this brat did not come aboard wi' yer connivance."

Jeff shook his head.

"Then he's a downright stowaway," the captain declared. "I could put him in the brig, but I'll put him to work instead. He can earn his passage in the hold, helpin' tend the niggers. See if he can stand the stink." He cupped his hand and shouted, "Bo's'n!"

"Señor Jeff, help me!"

"He can't help you. I'm master of this bark. Bo's'n!"

"Señor Jeff, don't send me back to Cuba. Please! Vincente help you fool police with that Panchita wench, no? Please don't send me back, Señor Jeff." Vincente was on his knees, sobbing.

"Once we dock, what happens to him is up to Jean Lafitte," the captain said. "Bo's'n! . . . ah, yer here at last. Take this stowaway an' lock him up till mornin'. Then set him to emptyin' slop buckets an' moppin' the hold. And between times he can holystone the afterdeck."

"Aye, sir." Cugino grabbed Vincente's arm and yanked him to his feet. "Come along, spick." He pushed him from the wheelhouse with a raised knee.

Captain MacFarland was silent for a long moment. Only the upper part of his body was illuminated by the binnacle lantern, making him look like the sculptured bust of some Roman emperor. The light emphasized the biblike fringe of his gray beard transforming it into a jawbone of pewter. He was staring straight ahead as he announced, "That's all, Mr. Carson. Ye can now go back to yer friggin'."

CHAPTER XXVI

JEFF was never afterwards sure what awakened him. At first he thought it was the motion of the ship, which during the night had developed a side-to-side roll in addition to her slow rise and fall as she slid through the long swells. Then he became aware of a pleasurable sensation in the vicinity of his groin. He opened his eyes.

Lying prone at the foot of the bunk was the Duchess from Haiti, her full bosom bulging against his knees as she watched the growing effect of her busy hands. Her eyes were wide with admiration as the dimensions expanded. Her head dove forward, mouth open.

Jeff sat up, torn between desire and alarm. A man had to be wary of these tropical wenches. Impossible to tell whether they were going to kiss or devour. Damn cannibals. He'd take no chances. Reaching out he seized the Haitian girl under the arms and turned her on her back. Then he crawled over to begin the orthodox papa-mama routine, always a pleasant, if unimaginative, way to start the day. He was warming up to his task and approaching climax when there was a knock on the door.

In full crescendo Jeff couldn't possibly stop what he was doing. His breath was coming in short gasps, so he couldn't even ask who was there.

The knock was repeated. Jeff was not only breathless and speechless but was floating somewhere in space.

"*Quién es?*" It was Panchita who awoke to challenge the intruder.

"Mr. Carson there?"

Panchita looked around the cabin. "*El señor esta muy ocupado,*" she said. "Veree beezy."

"I gotta see Mr. Carson," the voice insisted.

Jeff returned to earth. He managed to collect his

faculties and summon enough strength to call out, "Who is it?"

"It's me—Pops." Pops was the ship's cook, a venerable Greek from Malta whose full name was Something-populos. "Got coffee for you."

Jeff disengaged himself from the Haitian duchess and got off the bunk. He opened the door just wide enough to take the steaming mug.

"Gotta talk to you, Mr. Carson." The cook tried to open the door wider but Jeff pushed it shut.

"Later," Jeff said. "I'll be in for breakfast in ten or fifteen minutes." Or sometime today. . . .

When he sat down at the bare table used by the ship's officers, he was clad in seagoing togs—faded denim pants and a torn shirt. He was alone in the mess; the officers had breakfasted much earlier. The cook came in with more coffee.

"Morning," said Pops. The ends of his long white handlebar mustache turned down, giving his rugged face a mournful expression. "You want me to cook some of your eggs now?"

"My eggs?" Jeff stared up at him.

"Yoh, must be yours. I didn't believe him when he said he brought 'em, but—"

"Who didn't you believe?"

"That Cuban kid been hanging around you all week. I catch him in galley with sack of eggs. He say he bring eggs for you, but I think he stole 'em, so I take him to skipper. Guess I done him a wrong, because this morning when I count eggs I find fifteen extra. I go to skipper again and say my mistake, but skipper say no difference, he stowaway. You want now eggs? How you want I fry? Upside down?"

"Upside down is fine," Jeff replied absently. Vincente! What a tricky little bastard! He had doubtless remembered hearing Jeff complain of the lack of eggs on the menu during the outward voyage of the *Sainte-Claire*. He had probably planned to make his first official appearance this morning, serving Jeff a plate of eggs. Maybe he would talk to the captain about him after all, Jeff thought.

But he was disturbed about Perla being left alone in Havana. He knew she could get along without Vincente, but he hated to see her youth and talents wasted when they might have brought profit to the three of them. . . .

After breakfast Jeff walked out on deck for a breath of air. The weather had deteriorated overnight. The wind had risen, so there was an eerie humming in the rigging. Land birds were no longer following the ship. Scraps of low cloud scudded beneath the high dome of the dark overcast. The motion of the ship had changed again. Instead of the stately waltz time to which she had glided through the swells, she now danced to a quicker, more nervous tempo. Jeff had a queasy feeling in his stomach. He walked to the rail. He had never known seasickness and had no intention of learning about it now. He had every intention of keeping possession of his breakfast eggs. He looked over the side and noticed for the first time that the surface of the sea seemed strewn with some sort of orange vegetation; it looked like a field of marigolds. He reeled toward the wheelhouse.

The first mate stood outside, legs apart, his red beard parted by the wind as he lifted his head to study the set of sails.

"Morning," Jeff said. "Strong breeze blowing."

"Yes," said the mate.

"Think it will help speed our trip home?"

"No."

Red was not in a talkative mood. Jeff decided not to inquire about good or bad signs.

"What's all that orange stuff floating out there?"

"Gulfweed." The mate shook his head. "Don't know why they call it gulfweed. Don't grow mostly in the Gulf. Books call it sargassum 'cause it grows in the Sargasso Sea." He frowned. "Never seen this much of it this far west at this time of year."

Jeff didn't ask for an explanation. He was sure it would not be favorable. He asked, "Captain MacFarland in the wheelhouse?"

The mate shook his head. "Skipper's gone below to get some sleep in advance," he said. "Expects to be on watch all or most of the next twenty-four or forty-eight hours. Glass is way down and still dropping."

Jeff didn't understand what glass was down or what it could possibly have to do with the captain's sleep. He'd rather not know. From the expression on the mate's ruddy face, he judged the news was bad.

"You ain't asked my advice," said the mate, staring coldly out to sea, "but if I was you I'd start bringing your niggers up out of that hold in tens or twenties, so they can empty their guts and pee to leeward. My guess is that we'll have to batten down the hatches afore nightfall."

"I appreciate the tip." Jeff felt a twinge of guilt. Until every one of the three hundred was delivered to Barataria, his job was not done. "I'll see the bo's'n at once."

"You still ain't asked my advice," the mate said, staring up at the bulging foresail, "but if I was you I'd look to those niggers yourself." And he walked away.

Jeff climbed down the ladder into the hold, clinging tightly to each rung to avoid being swung off by the motion of the ship. He realized he hadn't seen Trafalgar since the previous evening. He had purposely left the big buck unfettered so that he could make periodic reports on the state of the human cargo. What with the excitement of Vincente's unexpected appearance and his own eagerness to sample his merchandise from Solano, he had been neglecting the business at hand. Still, he could not understand why Trafalgar had failed to report, and thus remind him he was still working for the Lafittes.

The further Jeff descended into the hold, the more fetid and oppressive the atmosphere became. The hatches were open, but the warm effluvia from three hundred sweating Negro bodies was overpowering. Even in the open air of the barracoons black flesh in the mass was redolent with a special funkiness. Within the confines of a ship's hold in the tropics the stench was an active threat to the stability of a man's stomach. Jeff swallowed hard as he stepped off the bottom rung and walked into the half-light. He heard a strange dissonance, the chorus of a hundred alien tongues blending in an ugly savage buzzing.

"Trafalgar!" Jeff shouted. He peered into the gloom. The angry buzz ceased abruptly. The silence raised hackles on his neck. He had to shift his feet to keep his balance on the slanting deck. The changed angle from the deep roll of the ship allowed a broad beam of sunlight to flash across the hold, striking sparks from the chains that stretched alongside the rude bunks.

"Trafalgar!" Jeff called again. "Trafalgar, where are you?"

A weak, halting voice came through the heavy silence. "I'm here, sir."

Quick strides brought Jeff to where the voice had originated. Trafalgar lay on a mid-tier bunk completely naked, shackled hand and foot, the foot shackles attached to the running chain. Dark stains spattered his rumpled white duck trousers, which lay on the deck nearby. He did not look at Jeff.

"Trafalgar, what's going on? I gave instructions you were not be be spanceled. Why are you shackled like this?"

"Because I resisted," said the big Fanti, eyes still averted.

"Resisted who?"

"The man with no forehead. A white man whose black hair grows down to meet his eyebrows."

Damn! The description fitted Cugino. What right had the bo's'n to chain up this man?

"I'll get the keys and unlock you right away," he said.

"Mr. Carson, sir, am I *your* slave?" Trafalgar turned his head so that he looked squarely at Jeff with anguished eyes. "Do I belong to you?"

"In a way, yes. Temporarily."

Trafalgar sighed. "Mr. Carson," he said, "I quite understand. As a slave I have no rights. I am a piece of property. You, as my master, can do with me as you will. But my previous masters have always respected my rights to my own person. I mean, except for being lent occasionally to impregnate a female slave, my body is at the sole disposition of my master. Mr. Carson, sir, have you authorized anyone—? I mean, sir, am I expected to submit to—?"

"Good God!" Jeff said. "Did that son-of-a-bitch of a bo's'n chain you up so he could—?"

Trafalgar nodded. "A painful experience, Mr. Carson, sir," he said, "and believe it or not, my first—in spite of my years in His Majesty's Navy."

"Goddamnit." Jeff was outraged, not as much by the painful violation of Trafalgar's person as by the bo's'n's consummate gall in chaining up a slave that he had ordered left free.

He was suddenly conscious of dozens of eyes in addition to Trafalgar's staring at him. Every slave within earshot seemed to be trying to understand their conversation. Some listened propped up on an elbow, others were sitting up as best they could in their spancels. One man was kneeling in his bunk to see better. The clank and rattle of chains sounded loud in the silence.

"I'll be back soon," Jeff said, patting the Fanti on the shoulder.

One of Hernandez's men spoke and Trafalgar translated. "Mr. Carson, could you tarry a moment, sir?" Hernandez's men were engaged in the morning feeding. They were only four or five bunks away now. Each carried two buckets and a gourd dipper. The first man set the buckets down in front of the tier and ladled out a dipperful of some viscous pottage. Each slave would hold up two cupped hands close to his face while the slumgullion was poured into them. When some of the sticky stuff dripped through his fingers, the slave would carefully lick his hands front and back after he had swallowed the double handful. Then the second guard would pass a gourdful of water.

Jeff turned his head away. His gorge rose. His queasy stomach wouldn't let him watch any longer. He swallowed repeatedly. "What . . . what's in that stuff?" he asked.

"God only knows, Mr. Carson. Beans, I suppose. Stale bread possibly. Scraps of meat. Wormy maize probably. Rather nasty, Mr. Carson. Last night it ran out before we reached the end of the aisle. These ain't the rations Señor Hernandez provided."

Jeff swallowed harder. The stench, and the sight of the feeding system which reminded him of the way they slopped the pigs at Willow Oaks, were turning his stomach.

Jeff's hand-over-hand ascent up the ladder was so rapid that he was not even aware of the roll of the ship. He lunged up the last two rungs and sprawled out on the deck. He lay for a moment breathing raggedly. When he stumbled to his feet he had trouble keeping his balance. Lashes of salt spray stung his face.

He found the skipper standing outside the wheelhouse, scanning the horizon through a spyglass. The first mate stood beside him, facing in the opposite direction, head bent back, shouting orders to crewmen aloft.

"Captain MacFarland," Jeff said, "I'm lodging a complaint against your bo's'n. He's spanceled a man I ordered free. What's more, he took advantage of his helplessness to sodomize the poor bastard. I demand that Cugino turn over to me the keys to the spancels."

The captain did not answer at once. He was still peering through his spyglass. When he lowered the long glass, he said, "Ye come at a bad moment, Carson. Just now, sir, I've no time to supervise the sexual behavior of my officers or men. The slaves are yer responsibility, entirely. Ye want the keys, find the bo's'n an' take them. Meanwhile, look yonder."

Against the darkness of the lowering clouds Jeff saw the darker outlines of two monstrous funnel-shaped specters. The broad mouths of the funnels reached up into the thunderheads, while the tapering stems twisted downward to meet the sea.

"Jesus! What's that?" he said.

"Water spouts," the captain told him. "Seagoin' tornados."

CHAPTER XXVII

THE hatches had been battened down for two days now. The nightmare began an hour after the captain pointed out the water spouts. The wind rose to gale force before the afternoon was well advanced. Before nightfall the seas were running high and the waves had assumed mountainous proportions. Driving rain swept the decks. The *Sainte-Claire* would lift sickeningly as it climbed the near side of a wave, then plunge dizzily into the trough of the next. Green water poured over the bow and ran along the deck in a boiling white torrent. Cries of anguish arose from the hold as the flood streamed into the open hatches.

Sailors appeared from nowhere to drag the hatch covers into place and haul tarpaulins over them. Jeff protested to the captain.

"They'll smother to death in there, skipper."

"Canna be helped, Carson. Ye can see for yerself the sea pourin' in. They'll not only all be drowned, but the *Sainte-Claire* will founder wi' the rest o' us."

"You'll destroy a valuable cargo, skipper."

"Maybe some will survive." MacFarland shrugged. He had to shout to be heard above the howl of the wind and the rush of water in the scuppers. "If'n they don't all suffocate in their own stink."

The captain walked away to bellow at half a dozen sailors inching their way up the shrouds, clinging to the ratlines for dear life. The skipper was reducing sail. The bark was barely answering her helm.

That night had been harrowing. The captain's last words had been "fer Godsake, Carson, stay inside. If ye have to come on deck, keep to leeward if ye can find the lee, and hang on like a leech to whatever ye can find that's tied down." Jeff managed to reach his cabin after nearly knocking himself out banging his head against the bulkheads on the way, trying to keep his balance. There was complete silence when he entered. The cook had left a tray of bread and dried beef, but it was untouched. The three wenches sat stiffly side by side on the edge of the bunk, obviously terrified. When he had opened the door the candle flickered and went out.

There was plenty to be frightened about, Jeff admitted as he shed enough of his spray-dampened clothing to be comfortable. The creaking of timbers as the ship soared on the crest of a wave, and the shuddering crash as she plowed into the trough; the rush of water along the deck, and the gurgling in the scuppers; the shriek of the wind in the shrouds, and the thunderclap of canvas as the sails caught a change of helm or sudden shift in the erratic blasts. No wonder the trollops were cowed.

He pushed his way between two wenches to stretch out full length on the bunk behind them. He lay with his eyes open, listening to the ominous ship noises. He had no thought of sleep or lovemaking. The wenches were equally uninterested in sex; they were too sure that this night would be their last. Jeff could feel them trembling as they inched backward against him.

Suddenly a crash more violent than anything that had come before shook the ship. The *Sainte-Claire* shuddered and stood on her beam ends. Jeff and the trio of Fancies were thrown off the bunk and dumped to the deck. There was one scream, then all lay in a silent heap.

What seemed like minutes passed, and the deck remained slanted precariously, keeping Jeff and the three women, now a tangle of arms and legs, pressed tightly against the bulkhead. Pots and pans clanked to the galley deck and they heard the crash and clatter of breaking crockery. Would the ship never right itself?

At last by a series of spasmodic lurches the craft gradually gained an even keel, only to heel over the other way. One of the wenches whimpered. Someone reached out and touched him; he thought it was Panchita. The warmth of her fingers aroused him, and he lifted an arm to clasp her to him. Still not sure who she was, he quietly, almost imperceptibly, entered her.

It was an embrace without passion—a gesture of fear seeking security, of near-panic finding calm reassurance. Another hand reached out to hold his. He felt a cheek pressing against the cheeks of his buttocks. He fell asleep.

There was no abatement of the storm by morning. The *Sainte-Claire* proved seaworthy, though, through all the violent battering. The galley was a mess, however. There was no hot breakfast. One particularly huge wave cascading the length of the craft extinguished the fire in the cook stove and ruined half the comestibles in the food locker. Jeff hoped his live cargo was not deteriorating too horribly. He didn't know what in hell he could do for them. But he had to do something.

Making his precarious way along the careening, slippery deck, he was drenched before he reached the wheelhouse. He envied the captain his yellow oilskins, but not his worried frown or his bloodshot eyes. The man had obviously not slept.

"Captain MacFarland," Jeff said, "we've got to do something about those slaves."

"They're yer niggers," the captain said. "Ye bought 'em. Yer responsibility. Clean. Entire."

"Since you battened the hatches, they've been without food and water."

"They can go without victuals fer a few days. They'd only puke 'em up anyhow in this storm. An' there's a dozen barrels o' drinkin' water in the hold."

"They can't get to it, captain. They're spanceled."

MacFarland turned away from Jeff to shout orders to the helmsman. The wheel had spun violently from his grasp.

"What the hell happened to those two nigger tamers we shipped at Regla?" MacFarland asked at last.

"They were caught up here on deck when the hatch covers went on, skipper. I can't let Lafitte's niggers rot down there."

"All right, lad. Then go below yourself. There's a small ventilatin' hatch aft big eno' to accommodate a man yer size. I'll have it opened an' lower ye down wi' a rope."

Jeff's stomach turned over. The very thought of that foulsmelling, revolting mess that must be in the hold by now—the stink of urine, feces, and vomit—brought him to the verge of vomiting himself.

"Turn my boy Vincente loose and we'll lower him into the hold with me. Where has the bo's'n got him locked up? Where is that bastard of a bo's'n?"

"Leave the bo's'n be, Carson." The captain shouted to be heard above the wind. The *Sainte-Claire* sloped sharply to starboard. "For once he's earnin' his screw. He's aloft wi' the men, reefin' sail. We're about to heave to. In another hour our canvas'll be whipped to shreds."

"But the boy, captain."

"If I know the bo's'n, ye'll find the boy locked in Cugino's cabin. Here's a master key. Now busy yourself wi' landlubbers' business an' let the rest o' us deal wi' the sea."

As the captain predicted, Jeff found Vincente locked in Cugino's cabin. The lad lay prone on the deck when the door swung open. He sprang up, cringing, until he recognized Jeff. Then he dropped to his knees, clasping Jeff's legs.

"Oh Señor Jeff! Thank God. Thank the Mother of God!" He wept. "Get me out of here."

"Where the hell are your pants?"

"I do not know, *señor*. That bo's'n hid them. *Qué animal, señor. Qué bruto.* He hung heavy, almost like you. I hurt when I sit down. Please, Señor Jeff."

"All right, Vincente. You asked for whatever you're getting. I don't know what will happen when we get to Barataria, but I'm going to let you out of here on one condition. You'll go down into the hold and do what you can for those niggers I bought. See that they get water and whatever food you can find."

"If you say so, Señor Jeff."

Vincente was lowered by rope through the ventilation hatch—alone. Jeff found Hernandez's men so seasick they were useless. At nightfall the lad was hauled up, pale and shaken. He staggered to the rail and threw up until he could manage only dry heaves.

"*Qué zahurda!*" A pigsty would be like the Hotel de Paris in comparison. He had given water to the slaves. They were miserable. Those who weren't violently seasick were insane with fear and rage. The big Fanti fellow was doubly furious. "No food, no water, and he got sore asshole, too," Vincente said. "Then that fella in next bunk gonna die. He got *la plaga,* I think."

"Just seasick," Jeff tried to convince himself. Anything else was too dreadful to contemplate.

"I think no." Vincente shook his head. "He don't crap crap. He crap like bath water. He puke water, too. *La plaga,* I think. When you gonna unlock the spancels, Señor Jeff?"

"When the storm's over, Vincente."

"Do I have to go back in that filthy stinking place again, Señor Jeff? Please no. I'll die, Señor Jeff, I swear."

"You'll go back tomorrow morning. That's part of your punishment. You can sleep on the deck of my cabin tonight. But when the hatches are opened, you'll help clean up the mess." Jeff himself gagged at the thought of the process. "The captain says we'll have to get the slaves on deck and pump water into the hold to sluice the shit into the bilges."

Vincente stumbled to the leeward rail and threw up again.

During the third night after the hatches were closed, the wind dropped to moderate gale force and by morning the sea began to flatten out. When Jeff came on deck the crew was at work repairing the damage. The staysails had been blown away. The fore topsail had been ripped to shreds before it could be reefed, and the yard split. The tarpaulin covering one of the hatches was torn to tatters. But at last MacFarland ordered the hatches opened.

Jeff stood by while the tarpaulins were dragged away, the battens knocked off, and the covers lifted. He imagined he could actually see the effluvia rising like a miasma; he could certainly smell it, even upwind. He waited five minutes before he sent Vincente and the two Hernandez men down to test the noxious fumes like canaries in a coal mine. After they had gone down the ladder he listened for cries or other sounds indicating trouble. There were none. At last he summoned the courage to go down the ladder into the nauseous atmosphere himself. The stench was incredible. He retched three times before he felt strong enough to push his way to the bunk occupied by Trafalgar.

"Trafalgar!" The big Fanti was lying with his back to Jeff. He did not turn around.

"You all right, Trafalgar?"

"By the grace of God," said Trafalgar. He still didn't turn around. "You were in no hurry to come back to see us, Mr. Carson, sir."

"Jesus, Trafalgar! There was some slight trouble with the weather. As you may have guessed."

"We guessed." Trafalgar gestured over his shoulder with his two manacled hands. "If it's of any interest to you, Mr. Carson, sir, the man in the next bunk is dead."

"Dead? What . . .? How . . .?"

"Cholera," said Trafalgar.

"Then it's not what the Cubans call *la plaga*?"

"It's one of the maladies the Cubans call *la plaga*," Trafalgar replied. "But in India where I served a year with my master, Lieutenant-Commander Smith, they call it cholera. I've seen much of it. Symptons are unmistakable. The pains, the high fever, the vomiting and diarrhea like skimmed milk—"

With scarcely a glance at the dead man in the next bunk, Jeff fled. He clambered up the ladder to the open deck.

Captain MacFarland was less than overjoyed by his news. He located the bo's'n on a yardarm and ordered him to go below and release the dead man for tossing overside.

Ten minutes later Cugino was in the hold with his keys. He prodded the corpse with the toes of his boot and asked Trafalgar, "When did he die?"

"Last night." Trafalgar turned around at last. He tried to sit up. "Cholera."

"Nobody ast you what it was." The bo's'n drew out a set of keys, unlocked the dead man's manacles, and yanked the corpse to the deck.

At that moment Trafalgar sat erect, raised his arms high above his head, and brought them down with all his strength. The steel fetters crashed against the back of Cugino's skull. The bo's'n collapsed against Trafalgar.

Trafalgar raised his arms and swung the manacles again and again until the bo's'n's head was a bloody pulp. Blood ran from Cugino's eyes, gushed from his nose and mouth, dripping off Trafalgar's knees to form an expanding puddle on the deck.

When Trafalgar was convinced he was dead, he pushed him off to slide to the deck. He took the keys from Cugino's dead fingers and unlocked his own fetters. Then with a savage cry he whirled the manacles about his head and brought them down again to slash the dead man's face.

"You bastard, you bastard, you dirty bastard!" he howled. Then, to make sure the spirit of the late bo's'n understood, he repeated the devil's benediction in half a dozen other languages. *"Puerco 'maldito! Suwar-ka-bacha! Sale con!"*

His voice rose in tone and in volume. The suave British veneer of speech evaporated. His savage scream came from deep in the jungles of Africa. The elemental values of his ancestors came shrieking back through the centuries, with all their naked barbarism. He stopped to pluck a knife from the belt of the dead bo's'n. Brandishing the blade above his head, he leapt along the tiers of bunks, howling in Fanti or some dialect of Ashanti, stopping before each black who had the strength to raise himself, and unlocking the fetters. His animal screams were echoed as more and more Negroes jumped up, released from their irons, swinging their manacles as weapons in imitation of Trafalgar.

Vincente, who had been tempted to follow Jeff up

288

the ladder when he left to report the death of the cholera victim, was shocked into immobility by the brutal murder of Cugino. As much as he hated the bo's'n, he was stunned by the emergence of stark savagery from the previously urban Trafalgar. When the significance of Trafalgar's release of the slaves dawned on him and he ran toward the ladder to warn Jeff, he was caught in the beginning of the stampede. Yelling blacks, swinging their unlocked fetters above them, were already blocking the approach to the ladder.

Vincente reversed his course. As he raced aft, he bucked the stream of released slaves and was knocked down twice by blindly rushing black giants. He staggered to his feet, heading for a patch of daylight he spotted toward the last tier of bunks.

CHAPTER XXVIII

"WHAT the bloody hell is *la plaga*?" demanded Captain MacFarland.

"I'm not sure, skipper," Jeff replied, still shaken. "But that big Fanti, the ex-flunky to a British naval officer, says it's what in India they call cholera."

"Cholera!" The captain's eyebrows lifted.

"Hell's bells an' Paul's balls! If we got cholera aboard, we're sunk. We'll be lucky we don't lose all yer niggers an' half my crew. Get the hell below an' make sure the bo's'n jettisons the dead nigger overside first thing."

Jeff nodded.

"Another thing, Carson." The captain caught Jeff's arm. "Find Joe the carpenter. If he's sober eno' tell him I want him to go wi' ye an' see if he recognizes any more cholera amongst yer niggers. If he finds any symptoms, we got to get rid o' the poor bastards before we all get it."

"Right away, skipper."

Jeff walked out of the wheelhouse and stopped as if poled. The first of the Negroes were swarming up out of the hold. What the hell had got into that bastard of a bo's'n that he had unshackled the slaves and let them come on deck in such numbers without any escort? There were thirty or forty and they were still coming. It was only when a chorus of yells arose from the blacks and they began to move away from the hatch, the pallid sun flashing on the manacles they twirled above their heads, that Jeff's puzzlement gave way to terror. At that instant he heard a voice behind him shouting, "Señor Jeff! Your keys! Quick, your keys!"

Jeff wheeled around "What's up, Vincente?" he demanded. "Where's the bo's'n?"

"That *maricón* is dead. Killed. Your keys, Señor Jeff. Quick. I must get your pistol. I know where it's packed!"

"We don't want gun play, Vincente. Why—?"

"You must have pistol, *señor*. We have *motín*, I think. There is riot."

Jeff took one more look at the screaming savages and produced the key to his cabin. Vincente ran.

The naked blacks, nearly a hundred strong, were now advancing toward the wheelhouse. At their head Jeff saw Trafalgar, knife in hand. Jeff walked to meet him.

Behind him he heard the captain bawling for the first mate. The significance of what was happening was immediately clear to MacFarland. "Muster the starboard watch immediately, Mr. Reddy!" he ordered.

Jeff planted himself in the path of the big Fanti slave. "Hold it, Trafalgar." He tried to sound calm. "Where do you think you're going with those men?"

"Out of the way, Mr. Carson. We are going to confront the captain."

"Ye'll do naught o' the sort," bellowed the captain. "Take yer bloody blackamoors below where they belong."

"Stand aside, Carson." "Mr." had been dropped along with the "sir." The bo's'n's knife flashed in Trafalgar's hand.

A dozen sailors of the starboard watch came trotting around the wheelhouse carrying capstan bars and brandishing rope ends. Trafalgar shouted something in Fanti,

290

and the Negroes yelled in unison. They advanced slowly, swinging their fetters in overhead circles.

"Order yer men to charge, Mr. Reddy!" said the captain.

Before the sailors could move, twenty Negroes released their spinning shackles like missiles. Metal flew, glittering through the air. Two sailors went down. The line of capstan bars and thrashing rope ends moved forward.

"Here, Señor Jeff." Vincente breathlessly handed Jeff his new-fangled gun. "Bullets already in."

A length of chain struck Jeff on the cheekbone. He staggered backward, one hand raised to his bleeding face. Trafalgar stooped and snatched the pistol from his fingers. Vincente tried to grab it back. The Fanti kicked him in the groin. Vincente howled, released the gun, and clasped his lower abdomen, sinking to his knees.

The swinging fetters were giving way before the longer capstan bars. The battle was still joined, however, and there were bloodied heads on both sides.

While Trafalgar fumbled with the unfamiliar mechanism of Jeff's pistol, Captain MacFarland bawled new orders.

"Mr. Reddy," he shouted, "I want these bloody niggers back in the hold immediately!"

"One moment, captain." Trafalgar had resumed some of his former dignity. He threw back his shoulders. "We are slaves, sir, but we are also men, not animals. Before we will return to the filth and muck—"

"Ye'll go at once!" the captain roared. "I'm still master here!"

"No longer." Trafalgar raised his right arm. Jeff's pistol in his hand was aimed at MacFarland. The first mate shouted. A shriek rose from a hundred black throats. Trafalgar pulled the trigger. The hammer clicked down. The charge did not ignite.

Captain MacFarland calmly drew a dueling pistol from his waistband, pointed the long barrel at Trafalgar, and fired.

The big Fanti's torso jerked backward, then straightened up. He seemed to be making an effort to keep his arm outstretched, but inch by inch it went down. The gun dropped from his fingers, and his knees buckled. He collapsed to the deck in slow motion. Blood oozed from his head in a crimson halo. The Trafalgar mutiny was over.

The whirling spancels stopped and sagged limply. The rebellious chorus fell silent. The black phalanx retreated, step by step.

Vincente retrieved the pistol that had failed Trafalgar. Then he put his arm around Jeff and lifted him to a sitting position on the deck. He tore strips from the tail of his long Cuban shirt and tried to wipe the blood off Jeff's face. The wound was merely seeping blood now.

"Mr. Reddy," the captain called to his first mate. He calmly put away the dueling pistol. "Please select whatever men ye'll need from the starboard watch to carry out the following duties. One, I'll want a guard to insure that them nigger mutineers remain in their present position on deck. Two, ye'll immediately dispose o' the corpse o' the mutinous nigger I had to kill to maintain discipline. Three, ye'll take a detail to the hold to reclaim the bodies o' Bo's'n Cugino and the slave that died of cholera. Ye'll be takin' precautions, naturally, to protect yerselves against infection. Four, ye'll dispose o' the nigger cholera victim as quickly as possible. If we can find anyone who can read the prayers for a Christian funeral, we'll give Cugino a proper burial at sea, though I doubt he was e'er a Christian. Five, ye'll take over the disciplinary an' security duties o' our late bo's'n. Organize the able-bodied slaves into work details to help flush the shit an' corruption out o' the hold. That dead nigger may have had a point."

The captain paused and looked wistfully at the body of Trafalgar lying on deck.

"Six, after the carpenter has bandaged up our friend Carson, I want him to make sure we have no more cholera aboard. And last, ye'll resume yer regular duties an' get us the hell under full canvas again. We've been blown at least forty miles off our course, an' we're behind schedule. Got that all clear, Mr. Reddy?"

"Aye, sir," the first mate replied.

"Good. Fine, Red." The skipper grinned and relaxed his formal command manner. "When ye have somethin' to report, come an' tell me about it." The skipper disappeared into the wheelhouse.

The carpenter was smearing Jeff's battered face with nards and ointments prior to putting on the bandage. Two sailors dragged the body of Trafalgar to the side of the ship. He was a heavy corpse, and they had trouble lifting him high enough to clear the rail. Jeff closed his eyes to shut out the sight of the honorable Fanti being consigned to the deep. He could not, however, shut his ears to the dread sound that spelled the end. He opened his eyes and stood up to see the turbulent spot of foam that marked the slave's disappearance in the clean vastness of the sea. He tried to ignore the sinister sleek black sharks that streaked the surface of the water and began to circle the spot before it was lost to sight.

Jeff remained on deck while the macabre proceedings continued. He had expected to feel no regret when the body of the bo's'n was hoisted from the hold, but when he saw the pitiful bloody mass of what had once been Cugino's sneering face, he could not suppress a few qualms of compassion. Nobody could be found to read a prayer for the hard-boiled shipmate of Nez-Coupé-Chizighola, but because he was a part of the complement of the *Sainte-Claire,* his body was lashed in sailcloth before it was slid into the sea.

No such niceties were accorded the body of the nameless slave dead of cholera. Not only was he swung into the sea with the same rope that had hoisted him from the hold, but the rope itself was jettisoned. The sailors who had touched the cadaver decontaminated themselves by scrubbing their hands with crushed tobacco, potato peelings, and rum.

Jeff forced himself to go below with Joe the carpenter

on his medical inspection of those two hundred slaves still spanceled in their bunks. To his dismay, they found another dead man, and two more slaves who were, according to Joe, dying of cholera.

"Gotta get 'em outa here right away," said Joe.

"All three?"

"All three."

"What will you do with the two who aren't dead?"

"Overboard," said Joe.

"What?" Why was Jeff shocked? Was his one-eighth Negro blood showing through? Was the fellow-feeling of a runaway slave fighting the white man's mentality he had tried so hard to develop? Hell, no. He deplored the waste, that's all. He had already lost three of his human cargo. "How can you toss a nigger overboard while he's still alive?" he demanded.

"They sick." Joe twisted one end of his long white mustachios. "Captain's orders."

"But they might get well, Joe. You can't just dump a thousand dollars in the sea. Let's give them a chance to get well."

"Captain's orders," said the carpenter, attacking the other end of his moustache. "They got the cholera. Captain don't want nobody else catching the cholera."

"I can't believe the skipper is so anxious to throw away Lafitte money," Jeff said. "I'm going to speak to him." And he climbed the ladder.

But Captain MacFarland was deaf to argument.

"Can't risk it," he said. "They'll probably die anyhow. An' I'll not have a cholera epidemic in my fo'c's'le."

"The Lafittes'll be mad as hornets at all that money gone to the bottom."

"Come, come, lad." The captain smiled paternally. "The Lafittes are rich men because they like to squeeze a dollar, but they're businessmen. They expect normal losses. What's yer debit count so far?"

"Five," said Jeff, "including the one you shot."

"A piddlin' pittance. Less than two percent of three hundred," said the captain with a gesture that could have been intended to wave away an imaginary gnat. "In this trade, Carson, a ten percent loss is always expected. Remember, yer dealin' in a perishable commodity, an' a twenty percent shrinkage is acceptable. Yer doin' fine, lad. Why not go aft and diddle one o' yer Fancy wenches. Just leave it to MacFarland to get the rest o' yer cargo safe to port."

Despite the captain's half-facetious disposal of the matter, Jeff agonized over how his maiden performance as a slave trader would look in the eyes of men like Jean Lafitte and René Beluche. If he lost many more of his blacks he could say goodby to his expectations of a fat bonus, fat enough to ransom Chloe. He did not "go aft and diddle." He steeled himself to the ordeal of watching the execution of the captain's sanitary measures. He was not alone—a fact that added to the solemnity of the occasion. The hundred rebel Negroes who had been disarmed—if manacles could be called arms—and herded together under armed guard near the forward hatch stared in desolated silence.

The casual watery discard of the mortal remains of the second anonymous cholera victim was witnessed in despairing silence by both Jeff and the slaves. The second burial—that of a living patient—was also accomplished without much emotion because the victim was comatose and so far gone he did not struggle when he went over the rail. The third, however, was something else again.

He was a sinewy black Ashanti from the Gold Coast. He knew very well what was happening to him, and although he was so dehydrated and debilitated from diarrhea and vomiting that he was unable to put up an effective resistance, he was determined to cling to life. He fought with the seamen who hauled him out of the hold. His lack of strength was almost compensated for by the reluctance of his executioners to come into physical contact with a sufferer from a contagious and deadly disease. Even though he was overpowered, he could not be silenced. Although his shrill screams were incomprehensible to Jeff, their meaning was clear: he did not want to die. His screams became howls and his howls swelled to shrieks as his captors overcame his feeble struggles and dragged him across the deck. Jeff was sure that as long as he lived he would never forget that final wail as the black was hurled into the sea.

He turned his back so he would not have to watch the sinister black fins streaking toward the spot for the *coup de grace*. . . .

It was not until the quarreling sharks had been left far behind the *Sainte-Claire* that Jeff realized he had missed a chance for target practice with his new-fangled multiple-shot pistol. He certainly needed to learn how to use it if it were not to fail him in an emergency the way it had failed Trafalgar. And what better targets to practice on than cruising sharks?

Jeff retrieved the gun from Vincente, who, he found, had been put to work in the hold. Vincente had hidden the pistol in one of the many pockets in the voluminous folds of his Cuban shirt. He had already discovered why the pistol had not fired for Trafalgar. He explained to Jeff that Trafalgar had not released the safety catch— "See. Right here"—which locked the trigger and prevented the gun from going off.

Back on deck Jeff practiced shooting at brightly colored jellyfish that floated past. He quickly mastered the mechanism that allowed him to fire consecutive shots in fairly rapid succession. Rotating the cylinder by hand to bring fresh bullets to the barrel was awkward at first, but it was certainly faster and more convenient than reloading separately after each shot. . . .

Jeff intercepted Captain MacFarland on his way back to the wheelhouse after taking a much-needed half-hour nap. He had noticed Vincente in action during the trouble, the skipper said, and agreed that the boy should be rewarded. After he had finished helping out with the sanitizing of the hold, he would allow him his freedom to serve as body servant to Jeff.

"Bright lad," said the skipper. "Incidentally, Carson, I have a message fer ye from one of the wenches ye drydocked in my cabin. Remember a sprightly trollop named Rosita?"

"Indeed I do." Jeff certainly did remember Rosita—

she with the plump, friendly vagina.

"Well, Rosita sends word that she'd like to see ye at yer earliest convenience. I gather it's a private matter." The captain winked broadly. "By the bye, Carson, do I recall correctly that ye mentioned smugglin' aboard that counterfeit nun fer my personal inspection an' possible approval?"

"Aye, that I did." Jeff was beginning to talk like MacFarland.

"Then lad, now that the sea has calmed somewhat an' we are on course again," the skipper said, "I think the time may not be far off when I might give serious consideration to yer offer."

CHAPTER XXIX

THE first shore birds had appeared that morning and were now riding a following wind as they hovered hopefully over the *Sainte-Claire*. The breeze carried new smells —the scent of damp foliage with just a hint of wood smoke.

"We'll make landfall by sunset," said Captain MacFarland. "If the wind holds, we'll be in Grande-Terre before the sun's o'er the yardarm tomorrow."

Jeff heard the announcement with mixed feelings. He was happy to return to Barataria because he would be close to New Orleans and his beloved Chloe. Still, he felt trepidation now that the Lafitte judgment on his mission was imminent.

The last days of the voyage from Havana were comparatively uneventful. He had lost two more slaves— an insignificant figure, according to MacFarland. He supposed he should consider himself lucky that the captain's draconian measures had prevented the cholera outbreak from assuming epidemic proportions.

First mate Reddy had taken command of the slaves and their quarters and proved himself an efficient manager. He had brought the whole coffle up out of the hold and made them live on deck for twenty-four hours of cold tropical night, warm tropical rain, and burning tropical sun while he had the hold flushed out. He then fumigated the space by burning brimstone and tobacco leaves.

The tobacco leaves were the mate's idea. Personally, he said, he found the stink of brimstone as bad as the stink of niggers, but since that foul odor could kill rats and roaches it ought to be foul enough to exterminate whatever evil humors brought on the cholera. But he bought the tobacco leaves in Cuba because he thought the pleasant smell when they burned would tame the brimstone. He didn't share the popular idea that tobacco leaves alone were a cure-all.

They were certainly a failure as far as counteracting the odor of brimstone. The *Sainte-Claire* reeked of sulphur for days and still smelled faintly sulphurous as they approached Barataria. The smell, of course, offended the three putative peeresses. The other nine female Fancies also wrinkled their noses prettily at the pervading reek, but their strongest protests were against the quality and quantity of the food. Since the storm had played havoc with the galley and the galley stores, everybody had been on short rations.

The wenches also complained that Jeff had been rationing himself too closely. Since his responsibility for the final transport and welfare of the slaves had been impressed upon him by the violent events of the first days of the homeward voyage, he had neglected his planned classification of his female purchases according to their physical characteristics. He had been spending a good deal of his time practicing with his patented rotary-feed pistol. He also spent considerable time in the hold, making sure that his live cargo would arrive in the best of shape. Consequently, some of the wenches had been deprived of his favors. He had by no means spent a monastic ten days, but he had not functioned as he had anticipated.

All grousing among the trollops stopped, however, as soon as word was passed that landing was imminent.

Priming and prettification became their full-time occupation.

At daybreak the *Sainte-Claire* had passed the long fingers of muddy water that marked the protrusion of the Mississippi delta into the Gulf. By midmorning they approached the islands guarding the entrance to Barataria Bay, but Captain MacFarland cautiously kept his course more than three miles offshore, outside the territorial limits of the United States. A lookout in the crow's-nest kept his spyglass on a constant 360-degree watch around the horizon. When he shouted the word that there were no U.S. revenue cutters in sight, Captain MacFarland came about sharply, and the *Sainte-Claire,* with the colors of the Republic of Cartagena (whose letters of marque she carried) flying from her main mast, headed for Grand Pass. Jeff had to admire the captain's seamanship as the bark slid neatly between Grand Isle and Grande-Terre and shortened sail. Shortly before noon the last of the torn and patched canvas fluttered down and the lines were made fast to the dock at Grande-Terre.

The *Sainte-Claire* had been spotted by a land-based lookout before she came through the pass. There was a small crowd waiting on the dock. As Jeff stood on deck waiting for the gangplank to be raised, he spotted the figure of a husky man in a scarlet coat and skintight white trousers. So René Beluche had come personally to greet them.

René was the first man aboard. After shaking hands with Captain MacFarland, he threw his arms around Jeff's shoulders as though welcoming a long-lost friend.

"Good to see you, Jeff boy," he said. "We were half expecting you last week. From the looks of your ragged canvas and the cockeyed yardarm you must have hit some dirty weather."

"On the contrary," Captain MacFarland interposed. "The dirty weather hit us."

"I've got one hell of a lot to tell you, René, as soon as we wind up our business at hand," Jeff said.

Beluche stared at Vincente who stood by the gangplank with Jeff's bags. "I see you got yourself a new boy," he said. "What happened to that black youngster you had? What was his name? Ramon?"

"He got himself killed in Havana," Jeff answered. "Stabbed to death. This kid here is really a stowaway. Sneaked aboard without my leave. What happens to him here is up to M'sieur Lafitte."

"Jean is in New Orleans this week," Beluche said. "I'll make the decision for him. Do you want to keep him?"

"Yes, I do. Vincente has been very useful to me, both in Havana and aboard ship."

"Far as I'm concerned he's earned his passage," the captain said.

"Keep him then," Beluche said. "Take him up to your house and introduce him to Gretchen. She's waiting for you. Impatiently. I'll take a quick look at your *bozals* while you're gone."

As he stepped off the gangplank, Jeff felt like kissing the solid ground. Grande-Terre was no garden of Eden, but after the long nightmare of the return voyage any corner of terra firma would have resembled paradise. Hurrying home, he found that even the shabby huts he passed on his way to the third house from the corner on River Street had a pleasant homey look.

Vincente straggled behind, setting down the heavy bags now and then to pant and look around him. He was obviously puzzled by the mixture of neat cottages and neglected hovels, and impressed by the big brick Lafitte mansion at the end of the tree-lined street.

The news of the *Sainte-Claire*'s arrival had preceded Jeff, for the Junoesque Gretchen was standing outside the front door waiting. Her plain blond wholesomeness looked good to Jeff, although he certainly could not complain of lack of feminine companionship since he had left her. She opened her arms and clasped him to her pneumatic bosom.

"Welcome, welcome, Mr. Jeff," she gushed. "*Ich bin so glücklich*! I was lonely here."

"Glad to be back, Gretchen. I missed you, too," he

lied. "I brought you a little present from Cuba. But first meet Vincente. He's going to work here a while."

"So?" Gretchen stared at the curly-haired boy with surprise tinged with hostility. She wasn't sure she was going to like the idea of a stranger in the house. "Where's Ramon?"

"Ramon is dead. Got himself killed down there in Havana."

"*Ach, schade!* What a shame!" Gretchen was genuinely grieved by the news of Ramon's death, although she had certainly yelled at him and browbeat him unmercifully when he was alive. "Did you buy this fellow in Havana?"

Jeff worked himself free of Gretchen's embrace.

"Vincente's not my property, Gretchen," he said, "but he'll be my servant for the time being and help out around the house. M'sieur Lafitte will say what he wants done with him when he gets back from New Orleans." He looked sternly at Vincente. "We may send him back to Havana."

"Oh no, please no, Señor Jeff, I want to stay with you." The lad seemed about to burst into tears.

"I told you we'd have to wait and see," Jeff said. "But right now you can unpack my bags. Gretchen will show you where to put my stuff. And you do whatever she tells you, you hear, Vincente?"

"I hear, Señor Jeff."

"And no Señor Jeff while you're in the United States. It's Mr. Jeff here." He turned to Gretchen. "I'll see you for dinner."

He started for the docks at a trot, but soon slowed to a walk. Funny he should forget so quickly that in the humid bayous of Louisiana, too, perspiration lies close beneath the skin.

Jeff found René Beluche in the captain's cabin, having a drink with MacFarland and the first mate.

"Nice work, Jeff," was Beluche's greeting. "You picked a fairly good assortment of bucks. You've developed a pretty shrewd eye on your first buying trip."

"You think M'sieur Lafitte will be pleased?" Jeff asked eagerly. "He won't be too unhappy about our losing seven niggers on the way up?"

"He always expects to lose a few." Beluche drained the glass before him. "And the survivors ain't in what you'd call the peak of condition after the trip. Fact is, some of 'em are downright seedy. But we'll fatten 'em up some and have 'em rested and oiled and in good shape by the time Jean gets back."

"Did you get a look at the wenches I bought from Solano?" Jeff was still thirsty for praise.

"I got a quick look." Beluche put down his glass. "On the whole you brought back a good marketable product. Some of 'em are real elegant—ought to make Old Man Cosette piss his britches, wanting to get into all of 'em at once. There's one, though, that's a little on the dark side. Her with the bird-cage hair."

"That's the Princess," Jeff explained. "I got her cheap —only sixty dollars. Solano was glad to get rid of her. Wanted to have her whipped for acting sassy. If you don't want her, I'll buy her back. I think I can make a good deal for her. She's damned good in the hay. And you never saw such twat hair. Reaches from her belly button nearly to her knees."

Beluche reached over to poke Jeff playfully in the stomach. "Guess you can guarantee 'em all personally, hey Jeff?" he said. "Tested and found up to sample, yes?"

Jeff laughed with mock bashfulness. "They've all got what it takes," he said. "I picked the best the old fart had on hand. What happens to them next?"

"Jean wants to put 'em up in one of the guest houses till he gets back. We got a couple of fat black mamas to feed 'em and get 'em back in shape." Beluche winked broadly. "And keep the doors locked against horny trespassers looking for a free piece."

"These wenches can protect themselves," Jeff said. "They bite. One cute little bitch bit off one of the balls of the Vice-Governor of Cuba. I had to smuggle her past the Havana police to get her aboard."

"But she didn't make a soprano out of *you*, apparently." Beluche laughed. "Or doesn't she like white meat?"

"I kept my chastity belt on," Jeff said. "By the way,

if you're going to keep the wenches locked up, do I get a passkey?"

"You?" Beluche's laughter swelled to a guffaw. "Jeff boy, you won't need a passkey. If I'm any judge of what you've been shoving into these wenches—and don't forget I've seen you at work—as soon as they find out where you live, they'll be jumping out the windows and racing each other to get to your place."

"The lad's probably hung like the bells of St. Swithin's," Captain MacFarland volunteered. "His seagoin' wenches speak highly o' him." He seemed to notice for the first time that Jeff was still standing. "If yer goin' to yarn much longer with this blackbirder here, ye'd better sit down, lad. Ye might even drip yerself a drap o' the elixir here."

The captain's burr indicated that he personally had been dripping the elixir for some time.

Jeff sat down but did not avail himself of the elixir. "Seriously, René," he said, "what's my next step in seeing this Cuban deal of mine through to a conclusion?"

"Your part?" Beluche poured himself another drink. "Just sit tight, Jeff. If you want the honor of escorting your wenches to the guest house, fine. But the business of the *bozals* is all a matter of routine. Mosho and his strong-arms will be down this afternoon to get them up to the stockade. From then on, it's all in the hands of Jean Lafitte."

Jeff squirmed uneasily in his chair. "You think maybe he might want me to take the coffle up to New Orleans to auction off on the vendue table—at the Hotel St. Louis, maybe?"

"Maybe." Beluche shrugged. "But sometimes he holds his auctions down here. Planters like to come to Barataria because they have a real carnival here. All they can eat and drink, and real choice bed wenches. Jean gets better prices here, too."

"I sure would like to take at least a hundred to New Orleans, René. I really would."

Beluche frowned. "What's so special about—? I forgot. You got a special itch for Helen's daughter up there in Hortense's parlor house."

Jeff said seriously, "It's more than an itch. I'm in love with her. I want her all to myself. I'd like to ransom her from the Riding Academy. Do you think M'sieur Lafitte will give me a bonus for my Havana job—at least enough to make a down payment on Chloe?"

Beluche shrugged. "How much does Hortense want to release the gal?"

"Five thousand dollars."

Beluche whistled. "That's quite a hunk of dough."

"I know," Jeff said. "But he'll make at least a quarter of a million dollars out of my trip to Havana. Surely that's worth more to him than the ten dollars a week he's paying me."

"True," said Beluche. "Quite true. And Jean is usually generous with his men. He may come through. In the meantime, why don't you relax? Have a little fun until Jean gets back. Go home and make love to Gretchen and pretend all is right with the world. Yes?"

"I'll try," said Jeff.

And he did. He didn't realize how tired he was until he got home. He was so nearly exhausted that he didn't really appreciate the homecoming dinner Gretchen had prepared. She had *Kasseler ripchen*—she had no idea how the commissary came to have pork chops, smoked German style; one of Lafitte's corsairs had undoubtedly captured a German ship, because there was good Bavarian beer, too—and sauerkraut cooked with caraway seeds. He told her how delicious everything was and went immediately to bed. When Gretchen came to bed after overseeing the cleaning up of the kitchen, he woke up and made love to her perfunctorily. Then he went to sleep again and dreamed of Chloe.

CHAPTER XXX

MADAME Hortense, madame of the Riding Academy, had nearly finished her morning chocolate and brioche.

Although she wore a frilly pink negligee as she reclined in her gilded chaise lounge, she was already heavily made up. Every hair of her brassy dyed coiffure was in place, and her fabulous jewels flashed at her ears and on her wrinkled hands. There was a knock at her door.

"Yes, what is it, Lancer?" she called.

"That gentleman from Willow Oaks still here, *madame*," came the reply through the closed door.

"Then show him up in five minutes."

Madame Hortense spent the interval verifying the cosmetics of her face in a small gold-rimmed pocket mirror and making sure the feathery lace at the throat of her negligee fitted snugly enough to conceal the wrinkles on her neck. She was proud of the innate charm which had survived both her years and the brazen professionalism of her calling.

Lancer ushered in a well-built dark-skinned man who carried himself with the confidence of success despite the social awkwardness that marked him as an up-country planter. Madame Hortense extended her bejeweled fingers, and the man clumsily kissed them.

"Mayhap yo' don' 'member me, ma'am," he said, "but I'm Baxter Simon o' Willow Oaks Plantation."

"Indeed I do remember you, M'sieur Simon," Madame Hortense said. "I even recall the first time you came here as a boy." She motioned to a spindly gilt chair and Baxter sat down. "What was it you came to see me about?"

"Two things, ma'am. First off, guess yo' kin figger I come to N'Orleans to sell a herd of niggers. I cain' decide whether to auction 'em or sell 'em at private sale. 'Course Willow Oaks niggers git high prices either way, but since that damn fool law makin' it criminal to ship in *bozals,* nigger market's way up." Simon leaned forward in his chair. "I bin thinkin', ma'am, that since all the riches' planters get to Madame Hortense's sooner or later, mayhap yo' know some big visitin' plantation owner jes' desprit to buy some high-class Willow Oaks bucks at private sale. Mayhap—"

"No, M'sieur Simon." Madame Hortense held up her hand to stop him. "I'm surprised no one has ever told you that any man from out of town is anonymous at the Riding Academy. All the local aristocracy, even the local *haute bourgeoisie*, come here as to their club. I know only their first names—officially. But a planter from New Iberia or Alabama or Mississippi—for me he has *no* name. I don't want to know it. I'm sure if you go to the St. George Hotel, or one of the big vendue houses, they will give you names galore. But that's not really why you came to see me, is it? Confess."

Baxter colored slightly. "That right smart thinkin', Miz Hortense," he said. "Papa always says yo' right smart. He the one say yo' shore to have news 'bout who in town with pockets stuffed with cotton money lookin' to buy Willow Oaks niggers."

"And the other thing you came to see me about, M'sieur Simon? Let me guess." Madame Hortense placed two jeweled fingers against her temples and closed her eyes as if in deep thought. *"Ah, j'y suis!"* The eyelids popped open and she smiled. "It's about Chloe."

Simon's jaw dropped. "Yo' shore a mindreader, Miz Hortense. How—?"

Madame Hortense picked up her fan and snapped it open. "No trick at all. Every young man falls in love with Chloe at first sight. She's the most beautiful of my girls, perhaps the most talented. And you spent a whole night with her."

"Never had nary one like her," said Simon, shaking his head as though he still didn't believe his experience had been real. "Like to take her home with me."

"I'm afraid that's impossible," Madame Hortense said.

"Ain't nothin' impossible," said Simon, "if'n yo' got the money. 'N' the Simons has." The Simons certainly had. A conservative estimate would be more than half a million. "How much it take to git title to Chloe?"

"M'sieur Simon—or may I address you as Baxter?"

"Call me Bax. Ever'body do."

"Bien. Bax it is. Bax, this is not entirely a matter of money. I have promised Chloe to someone else."

306

"Oh?" Simon made a gesture which seemed to say, *So what?* He actually asked, "How much this lucky gent gonna pay yo'?"

"Five thousand dollars." Hortense closed her fan with a snap.

"Five thousand?" The figure shocked even Baxter Simon. Despite the hundreds of thousands of dollars coming out of Willow Oaks, the Simons were not accustomed to handing out that kind of money, even for a prime stud with other talents to boot. And for a wench, *never*. Papa Simon would die of heart failure at the very thought. Still, there were ways of presenting accounts —a thousand here, a thousand there—when the total take was added up after the blacks were sold. "Ain' that a penny high for a unproductive wench?"

Hortense snapped her fan open again. "That's the going rate for an octoroon much less beautiful than Chloe," she said. "There's no use trying to bargain, because Chloe is not available. I can offer other girls of almost equal beauty."

"Nobody like Chloe," Simon said. "Nobody. Who this rich bastard who think he kin take what I want?"

"Why do you ask, Bax?" Hortense was suddenly cautious. She didn't like the note of arrogance that hardened his voice. She put down her fan and sat up straight. "What do you intend to do?"

"Buy him off," said Baxter Simon. "Lik'n offerin' yo' six thousand 'stead o' five, then a-temptin' this rich cocksman with another thousand . . . who is he?"

"I don't think you'd interest him." Hortense shook her head. "He has an important job with Jean Lafitte. Chloe is more than a matter of money to him."

"Where kin I find him?"

"You can't." Hortense was being just as stubborn. "He's somewhere in Cuba on vital business."

"When he comin' back?"

"I don't know."

"I kin fin' out," Bax said, " 'n' I kin wait till he come back. I shore hanker for that Chloe, so I'll be comin' back here ever' day 'n' ever' night till I sell all my niggers.

Thank yo' kindly, Miz Hortense. Goodbye."

He stalked out, one arm moving in quick short arcs as though he were brandishing a blacksnake whip.

Hortense did not see him again for two days. She did not miss him, but she was uneasy about the way he had left. As it turned out, she had reason to be. When he burst into her ground-floor office in midafternoon, his face was flushed, his eyes blazing, and his lower jaw thrust out.

"I bin askin' aroun'," he announced angrily, " 'n' from what I hear, yo' promised to sell that Chloe to a nigger."

"Don't be ridiculous, M'sieur Simon," Hortense said. "Please sit down and calm yourself, or I'll have Lancer put you out. The man to whom I've promised Chloe is as white as you are."

"White?" Bax laughed bitterly. "He fool yo,' too. He preten' his name Jefferson Carson?"

Hortense's uneasiness increased sharply. "What difference would a name make?" she demanded. Why quote Shakespeare to this lout?

"Plenny," Bax declared. "Ain' he got firelike red hair?"

Hortense opened her mouth to reply but said nothing. She was stunned. She could not deny the bright red hair.

"That nigger, he purentee polecat," Bax pursued without giving her a chance to reply. "Yo' ain' believin' he mustee, yo' jes' take off his shirt. That stinker got my nigger brand down his spine from neck to asshole."

Madame Hortense bristled. Gentlemen didn't use coarse language in the Riding Academy. It was the oldest cliche in the world—you treated a whore like a lady.

"Suppose he should be a mustee," she said. "He's a very handsome one and he certainly deserves a beautiful mate like Chloe. You forget that Chloe, too, is an octoroon. There's nothing to stop their getting married, in fact."

"Ain' there?" Bax Simon said. "Since when kin a runaway nigger slave git married?"

"What is all this nonsense? Are you trying to tell me that Jeff Carson is an escaped slave?"

"Yes, ma'am. I bin tellin' yo' that this mustee call hisself Jeff Carson ain' Jeff Carson 'tall. This polecat callin' hisself Jeff Carson ain' got no real last name. His ma call him Bricktop on account of that purentee red hair. Next time he come here, ma'am, yo' je' look at his back. You'll find my brand."

Madame Hortense took up her fan and worked it furiously to hide her confusion. She didn't want to believe him, because she was fond of Jeff and detested this lout. Yet he seemed sure of his facts.

"I still don't believe you," she said at last.

"Then I bes' tell yo' the whole story," Baxter said.

"Please sit down, M'sieur Simon." The fan still fluttered nervously. Simon sat down.

"Reason I know," he said, " is that goddamn Bricktop what call hisself Jeff Carson onct belong to me. He my nigger. He been my nigger since he born. I paid Mary a good dollar for him the night he war born . . . Mary was a virgin till—"

Hortense laughed. "Surely, m'sieur, you jest."

He stared at her. He saw no humor in the situation. "Why?"

"A virgin . . . Mary."

His eyes glittered with rage. "She war a virgin. I was savin' her aside to be my bed wench . . . I like 'em musky. Cain't no way abide flesh white like a slug-belly. Mary war a mustee. Beautiful. Like a new-minted gold piece. But the bastard she drap war white. Whiter than me! He war purentee polecat, but he war white! Even he old man war a skunk, first class. What you 'spect of a sucker a skunk plant?"

She laughed. "Somebody beat you to her."

"Tha's right. This hyah redhead salesman come through. Spent the night at Willow Oaks. Took advantage of mah hospitality. Don't reckon now what he war selling, but I never fo'get what he war planting! Somehow he sneak 'round and get to Mary. Her war jes' comin' ripe and bustin' fo' a man. Next thing you know she draps this sucker what grow up white—an' mean—an' arrogant. Should of batted in his skull first time he crossed me. Never in his life took no order from me without no backsass from him. I laid the whip to his bare ass. An' it done no good—"

"You couldn't break him." She whispered it in a kind of keening triumph.

"Not yit, ma'am. But ah will. He a uppity nigger from the day he born."

"You truly hate Jeff, don't you?"

"I truly do, ma'am. I hate him 'cause he look like a white man but he a nigger. I hate him 'cause he pretend he white. But he a nigger. Cain't fool me, ma'am. I know niggers. They fingernails. And the roots of they hair. They nigger—no matter how white they skin." Simon leaned forward, grinding his teeth as he relived what he considered a monumental wrong. "Las' year this runaway Bricktop mustee have the livin' gall to come back South. When I meet up with him in Memphis, that lyin' bastard tell me he Jeff Carson, thinkin' I fool enough to believe him. 'N' he talkin' that highfalutin' nawthern talk 'stead of plantation lingo like the rest of the niggers. Never did learn to talk like us southern folks, he say, 'cause he went to school in the no'th where they teach nawthern talk."

Simon clenched his fist and his voice sank to a hoarse whisper. "I livin' cain't stand no mustee shammin' to be white. I knowed he my nigger slave with my brand on his back. When he was a boy growin' up, he was always pesterin' ever'thing female at Willow Oaks—chicken, sheep, or sluts. I whup him until his ass in shreds. And he runaway.

"But I cotched him, ma'am. With dogs. That when I lay my brand on him. Big W and O—showin' he a runner, a runaway nigger that belonged to Willow Oaks. But even when gittin' branded, he fit. Like a wildcat. He grabbed that hot brand. Tried to wrench out'n my hand —he still carry that scar on he palm."

Simon's indignation at his former slave's perfidy was so violent that his face slowly went bloodless, his cheeks grew pallid and rigid, his eyes showing whites.

"Well, when I sell his ma, he howl so loud, I decided to sell him, too. But he run away from the coffle to Natchez. Musta broke both his foot and the spancel. I nevah laid eyes on him again till I war invited to the wedding of Miss Minnie George to one Mr. Jefferson Carson of Philadelphia."

He drew the back of his hand across his mouth. "When that dirty nigger bastard had the goddamn nerve to try to marry up with Miss Minnie George of The Georgics Plantation, that too much. She mighty pretty for a white lady, an' when I tell her she almost marry up with a nigger, she almos' die. . . . I don't know wheah he met Miss Minnie. On that steamboat south from St. Louis, likely. But I know he had her talked into marryin' him 'fore they got to Cairo—"

"I can believe that," Madame Hortense said with a faint smile.

"Her paw, Mr. George, he went to flog Bricktop to death. Would of, too, if'n that Bricktop ever had got his dirty mustee pecker into Miss Minnie. We decided to hang him—and use his body for target practice."

Her gaze met his levelly. "Why didn't you?"

"Reckon we drank too much corn. I did. Passed out cold," Simon said. "We drug that nigger out to the barn and spanceled him, on the night afore he think he gonna marry a white lady. Miz George—Miss Minnie's ma— she stop us from stringin' him up on the spot."

Madame Hortense smiled secretively. The double conquest—of mother and daughter—sounded like the Jeff Carson she knew and loved.

Simon swore with cold savagery. "But durin' the night that bastard stole a horse and run. Don't know yit how he got out'n them spancels. I sho' glad to know where he is. When you reckon he comin' back from Cuba?"

"I told you I didn't know, M'sieur Simon. I know nothing of the lives of my clientele away from here." Hortense's lips scarcely moved when she spoke, and the icy stare with which she dismissed him should have frozen Simon's smug smile.

"I'll fin' him. Don't you fret none." He stood up and put on his wide-brimmed hat. "I warnin' you, ma'am.

You keep that dirty mustee away from Chloe. I buyin' her. 'N' when I fin' that Bricktop, I gonna whop him to shreds afore I spancel him and takes him back to Willow Oaks where he belong. I'm warning you ma'am. Jes' don't no way tangle yo' pretty self up with the law for harborin' no runaway slave." He walked out without a formal farewell.

Madame Hortense sat motionless for several minutes after he had gone. The big Spencer clock ticked loudly in the silence. At last she reached for the bell pull.

"Lancer," she said when the lithe, muscular young professional stud appeared, "I want you to send a boy to the Lafitte blacksmith shop on St. Philip Street and tell Captain Dominique You that he must come here as soon as possible. Say it is urgent."

Twenty minutes later the corpulent white-haired Captain You was sitting in the office of Madame Hortense's Riding Academy mopping his round florid face.

"And what, *ma chère amie*, can possibly be of such urgence in the heat of the day?" he asked.

"Dominique, I think you may be in trouble," Hortense announced.

"Trouble? At my age? You must be mistaken, *chérie*."

"Not you personally, perhaps. But your organization. When does that young rascal Jefferson Carson get back from Havana?"

"I got word just today," said Captain You, "that the *Sainte-Claire* reached Barataria Wednesday noon. Jean is quite pleased with the lad's work. You should be seeing him in a few days, I hear."

"He must not come here," Hortense said.

"Ah?" Captain You held his breath. "Why not? He's still in love with Chloe, I understand."

"That's just the point. The young man's in trouble."

"What kind of trouble?"

"First of all, his name is not Jefferson Carson. He's really an octoroon, a runaway slave called Bricktop. That's why he might mean trouble for the organization."

"Why should that mean trouble?"

"Does Jean want to be charged with giving shelter to an escaped slave?"

"*Mon Dieu, mon Dieu!*" Captain You's bulging belly shook with laughter. "My poor Hortense, have you forgotten that Barataria today gives shelter to murderers, thieves, rapists, and fugitive brigands of every shape and color? What do we care if Carson is a mustee and a runaway slave as long as he does his work well?"

"*Tout de même,*" said Hortense, trying to hide her pique, "don't you think you should get a word of warning to Jeff? He should be told that a man named Simon from Willow Oaks Plantation, formerly his owner and more recently his deadly enemy, is looking for him with blood in his eye. He should know that Simon has identified him as a slave called Bricktop. Furthermore he should be alerted to the fact that I have told Simon that I had promised Chloe to Jeff as soon as he can raise five thousand dollars. I have told Simon that I will not go back on my word, despite the fact that Simon would pay more. Jeff—and Jean Lafitte and René Beluche, too—should know that this Simon will kill Jeff without hesitation, not only to have Chloe, but also to punish Jeff for being a mustee who pretends to be white. *Tu es d'accord, n'est-ce pas?*"

"*Écoute, ma petite,*" said Captain You. How many times have I told you, *maintes fois,* that Jean Lafitte takes care of his people, black or white, French or English or American or Spanish—felons and pirates and cutthroats and garotters—as long as they are loyal to him. Isn't that enough?"

"No." Hortense's jaw was set. "You haven't said that you will get warning to Jeff before he leaves Barataria."

"*Enfin!*" Captain You flopped his arms like wings. "All I can do is send word. It must go overland and by canoe through the bayous to get ahead of river communication. Jeff may have left already. I know he is anxious to see Chloe. I can hope. I cannot pray because I have forgotten how. That's the best I can do. I want to help that boy. Will that be enough, *mon amie?*"

"Yes, if you say so, *mon vieux pote.* As for the prayers, I will ask the Abbé Bontemps to act for us. He comes every Friday."

CHAPTER XXXI

JEAN LAFITTE returned to Barataria from New Orleans by the most direct route—overland by horse, through the creeks and bayous by canoe, and the last lap across Barataria Bay by sloop. It cut off the long, roundabout journey by sailing ship which entailed traveling the final length of the Mississippi to the outmost tongue of the delta and heading back northwest to his island base. He arrived at Grande-Terre during the night while Jeff Carson was ensconced in the comfortable embrace of his placid Gretchen.

After the bizarre exciting amours of the Caribbean wenches and the harrowing emotional experience of the *Sainte-Claire*'s homeward journey, Jeff welcomed the homey, *gemütlich* caresses of his blond housekeeper. They aroused him without overstimulating him, satisfied him without exhausting his vitality, and actually left him soothed and relaxed. He was able to sleep long and soundly, for René Beluche decreed that until Jean Lafitte returned, their usual routine would be slackened somewhat. Consequently, Jeff had been sleeping late and not joining Beluche at the baracoons until midmorning. He had just awakened to the aroma of fresh coffee which Gretchen was bringing him in bed when Vincente burst into the room with the excited announcement: "Wake up, Señor Jeff—I mean Mr. Jeff —the *jefe* is back!"

Jeff sat up in bed so suddenly he almost upset the coffee. "You mean M'sieur Lafitte?"

"Right," said Vincente. "M'seur Beluche's black man Mosho just now came to our door. Say you must come to Big House in half-hour to meet with M'sieur Lafitte and M'sieur Beluche. You want I get your clothes ready, Mr. Jeff?"

Jeff nodded, scalding his lips with the hot coffee. "Pronto." He got up. Vincente lingered in the doorway. "I told Mosho you be right on time," he said. He hesitated. Then, "Mr. Jeff, can I ask you something?"

"What is it you want?"

"When you see the *jefe*," the lad said, "promise me you'll ask him if I can stay here with you. Tell him you need me, Mr. Jeff. Don't let him send me back to Havana."

"I'll do my best, Vincente."

As soon as he reached the door of the red-brick mansion, Jeff was ushered into the big boss's presence by Lionel, the mulatto with the wine-colored jacket. Jean Lafitte got up from behind his desk, came around, and greeted Jeff warmly with a friendly clap on the shoulder.

"Congratulations," he said. "René here tells me your maiden voyage was quite a success." He nodded to Beluche, sitting beside his desk. "I've already made the rounds this morning to check up on your work, and I agree with René. You've made a good beginning— for an amateur. Of course, you must realize you've still got a lot to learn."

"Thank you, sir." Jeff was glad that at least Lafitte didn't seem too upset about the slaves he had lost en route. "What did I do wrong, sir?"

Lafitte sat down again and riffled through some papers on his desk. "Of course, I can't blame you for the bad weather and the damage to the *Sainte-Claire*," he said, "but I wonder—" He paused.

"You're not blaming me for the cholera aboard, are you, sir?"

"Not exactly. But I was wondering if there were any cases among Hernandez's blacks before you shipped them? Did Hernandez try to hide anything from you?"

"No, sir. There was one case of sickness—a fine specimen, a real Fancy—that ended in his death. I had no idea it might have been cholera. Hernandez was quite open about it, and assured me the sick man had been isolated from the rest."

Lafitte ran his fingers through his curly black hair. "In a case like that," he said, "I think I would have taken better precautions. You've always got to watch out for disease in the tropics. After learning of one man's illness and death, I would have delayed loading of the coffle for four or five days to see if an epidemic was in the making."

"Captain MacFarland was very anxious to get underway, sir."

"You'll have to learn to deal with sea captains, boy."

"You can hardly blame me for the bo's'n getting murdered, can you, M'sieur Lafitte?" Jeff was hoping for a little praise at this point.

"No, certainly not. Cugino was a mean, scurrilous bastard, but he was a good fighter and a first-rate sailor. He'll be hard to replace." Lafitte brought the flat of his hand down hard on the pile of papers. "There's one criticism I must make about your mission, though, Jeff. I think you spent too much money refitting the *Sainte-Claire* to accommodate the slaves."

Jeff flushed. "I didn't build those tiers of bunks because I thought the niggers had to be treated like humans," he protested. "The spancels and the chains prove that. I only wanted to deliver your cargo in the best possible shape. The *Sainte-Claire* is such a small ship that if I had tried to pack the niggers in a single layer, I could have lost—"

"Yes, yes, I understand that, and I certainly approve of your intentions," Lafitte interrupted. "But by making a capital investment of that size you condemn the *Sainte-Claire* to the slave trade exclusively."

"You told me, sir, that the slave traffic had become the most important part of the Lafitte enterprises." Jeff was surprised to find himself arguing with his boss.

"True," said Lafitte. "But Captain MacFarland and his crew resent being restricted to blackbirding. The *Sainte-Claire* carries letters of marque from the government of Cartagena, and the skipper likes to be free to seize any Spanish cargo he finds. So we may have to charge off the cost of refitting to this single voyage, and that would make a dent in the profits."

"Which will still be considerable, you will admit," said Jeff. Thinking of those profits in the hundreds of thousands of dollars always made him bold.

"True again." Lafitte smiled and nodded agreement. "But if you are going to grow in importance to the Lafitte organization, I want you to be cost conscious. People in New Orleans like to speak of me as 'Lafitte the Pirate,' but it would be more accurate to call me 'Lafitte the Trader.' I am really a merchant at heart."

Jeff smiled to himself. Merchant indeed! With a sales staff of cutthroats and ruffians! "Speaking of costs," he said, "I have a personal problem, sir. René may have told you that my black boy Ramon was killed by a hoodlum in Havana, and I employed a Cuban lad as body servant and interpreter. His name is Vincente and I found him very useful. He boarded the *Sainte-Claire* without my permission and Captain MacFarland considered him a stowaway. However, he did work his passage, and René has authorized him to stay on Grande-Terre. Do you agree?"

"You say he's a bright lad?"

"Very. He's a woods colt of your good friend and agent in Havana, Don Cipriano."

"Well, well! Don Cipriano!" Lafitte leaned back in his chair and smiled wistfully, obviously remembering some common experience. "He's got good blood in him, then. Of course he can stay."

"Only thing is," Jeff pursued, "I'm paying him two dollars a week and found, until he can make a place for himself in the organization. That takes quite a chunk out of my salary of ten dollars a week."

Lafitte and Beluche threw back their heads and guffawed in unison.

"Carson, you have a delicate way of asking for a raise," said Lafitte when he had stopped laughing. "First of all, we'll take care of Vincente and depend on you to work him into a job he can handle. Then we'll obviously have to make new financial arrangements with you."

"Thank you, sir." Jeff grinned.

"From now on," said Lafitte with an expansive gesture of both hands, "we'll pay you one hundred dollars a month and found."

Jeff's grin disappeared. A hundred a month was only a little more than double ten a week. His heart sank. Goodbye to his dream of a bonus big enough to ransom Chloe. "I sort of hoped," he said, "that you'd be pleased enough with my purchases to offer me a little lagniappe . . ."

"Lagniappe?" Again Lafitte and Beluche guffawed in unison. "Do you expect lagniappe," Lafitte demanded, "in addition to your shares?"

"Shares?" Jeff's heart started to pound again but he didn't dare feel elated. Not yet. "What shares?"

"All members of the *Sainte-Claire*'s crew share in the profits of the voyage," Lafitte said. "And while I don't think you should have a captain's share on your first trip, we might let you have a first mate's shares."

Jeff felt weak with relief. Nobody had told him about shares. He asked, "About how much do you think that will be?"

"Can't tell," Beluche answered, "till after we sell the cargo. Then Dominique You figures out the costs and the net profits. Finally we get together with Captain MacFarland and I allot the shares."

"Think it might come to as much as five thousand?" Jeff held his breath.

"Might," said Lafitte. "What do you need the five thousand for?"

"He wants to buy himself a wench in New Orleans," Beluche volunteered. "He picks out a dozen beautiful Fancies from Havana, but no, they're not good enough for him. He's got to have Chloe, Helen Latimer's daughter, who's one of Madame Hortense's prettiest. And Hortense has to have her drop of blood."

"I'm in love with Chloe," Jeff said. "I want to see her soon. When can I take the coffle to New Orleans, M'sieur Lafitte?"

"You can't," was the reply. "The niggers aren't yet

in shape to be sold. Besides I'm not sure I want to put them all on the vendue table. I let the word get around in New Orleans that a big shipment of *bozals* had just arrived from Havana and I'm sure that by now a good many tongues are hanging out. I think I can load up the brigantine *Jena*, now lying in the curve of the river at New Orleans, with about twenty rich planters. They love to come to Barataria because we have good Cuban rum and Spanish wines here *à volonté*. And they eat well here, an *à l'oeuil*. What's more, they have money and they know black flesh. Any blacks left over I can auction off in New Orleans. *D'accord,* René?"

"*Qui, tout à fait,*" said Beluche. "Sorry, Jeff. But love springs eternal. Or is it hope?"

"Whatever it is, I have to see Chloe or I'll go crazy." Jeff pointed his two fingers at his temples as though about to blow his brains out twice. "What about the Fancies, M'sieur Lafitte? Are they fit to be shown? Can't I take them to New Orleans soon?"

"Ah, yes. M'sieur Cosette's order. I think they are in condition for the market. They seem to have been well taken care of." Lafitte winked broadly at Beluche. "René, do we have that ketch ready to move up the river to-morrow or the next day? The *Jerome*? She'll accommodate the dainty dozen, yes? Good. We'll ship them on the *Jerome*."

"And me?" Jeff perched on the edge of the Napoleon chair. "Do I go along with the wenches to New Orleans? I picked them. Can't I deliver them?"

"Of course, Jeff boy." Lafitte stood up and held out his hand across the desk. "You placed a lubricious lot and the customers are already panting for them. Right after I got word that the *Sainte-Claire* had docked, I ran into Gaspard Cosette at the bar of the St. George Hotel. I told him that you'd just brought the finest bevy of bright-skinned wenches that Havana had produced in ages. I thought old man Cosette would go off in his pants. Some of the other plantation bigwigs at the bar seemed equally interested. One young fellow was quite excited. He made the old man promise to let him know the minute you arrived with the wenches."

"Where do I make delivery?" Jeff asked.

Lafitte came around the desk to put his hand on Jeff's shoulder. "I've set up this procedure," he said. "As soon as the *Jerome* docks, Dominique You will come aboard. He will have carriages waiting to drive you and the trollops to Madame Hortense's Riding Academy. Then he'll get word to Gaspard Cosette, who will get first pick. I've promised him that. Then you can auction the rest off at Hortense's, or whatever Dominique decides. Once your business is concluded, you can rush into the arms of your Chloe. When will the *Jerome* sail, René?"

"At dawn tomorrow," Beluche answered, "to catch the flood tide at the mouth of the river."

Jeff rushed home to tell Vincente to pack his bag.

"Where we going, Mr. Jeff? Not Havana, I hope. New Orleans? Do I go, too? *Gracias a Dios*, Señor Jeff. I mean Mr. Jeff. You are finest *caballero* in whole world."

Gretchen, on the other hand, was desolate. "Oh, Jeff, you have just come home and again already you are leaving. I have such a fine dinner prepared."

"Don't worry, Gretchen, I'll eat it. And see if you can find a bottle of good wine in the commissary to go with it. I won't be gone long this time. You won't even have time to miss me. And don't forget—we have the whole night before us." He wrapped his arms around her plump yielding torso and gave her a brotherly kiss.

CHAPTER XXXII

A LIGHT rain fell through the night and the decks of the *Jerome* were wet as she sailed close to the wind along a westerly course on the approach to New Orleans. Dawn mists shrouded the Mississippi as the ketch tacked to enter the southerly reach of the great elbow that cuddled the city. Suddenly a flare blazed on the bank, painting an irised halo on the haze. A voice called faintly, "*Jerome,* ahoy!"

A dark craft pushed off from the bank, a single figure in the stern paddling furiously toward the ketch.

"*Jerome,* ahoy!" The shout came again, and the occupant of what appeared to be a pirogue gestured with his paddle between strokes.

"Ahoy, *Jerome*! I have a message from Captain Dominique You," cried the paddler.

"Come alongside then," called the mate on watch. A sailor threw the messenger a line, which he made fast to his canoe. A rope ladder was lowered and the man clambered aboard.

Jeff slept through the commotion on deck. He had spent a busy night saying goodbye to his dozen wenches, and he was exhausted, despite the fact that his farewells were restricted both by the time limitation and female reluctance to have coiffures mussed up so close to going ashore. He was fast asleep when Vincente pounded on his cabin door shouting, "Wake up, Mr. Jeff, please. Captain wants you on deck, pronto."

Rubbing his eyes, Jeff stumbled into his clothes and sleepily made his unsteady way on deck. He was surprised to see an odd-looking stranger standing beside the captain, clad only in a loincloth. His wet, naked torso glistened faintly in the half-light of dawn. His straight black hair fell to his shoulders.

"This man here," the captain said to Jeff, "brings a message from Captain Dominique You. Your plans have been changed. You are to accompany the messenger."

"Where to?" Jeff squinted suspiciously at the stranger.

"He does not say. He was told it was a secret," said the captain.

"M'sieur Lafitte instructed me to accompany the wenches to Condé Street."

"Yes, I know. But plans have been changed. Captain Dominique himself will meet the wenches and take them to Condé Street personally. You are to go with the messenger."

"Who is this character?" Jeff asked warily.

"I don't know exactly. We call him Pancho. He's a Houma Indian and he's been working for the Lafittes on the river for the last few years."

"Very well, since you vouch for him." Jeff turned to Vincente. "Get my bags."

"Sorry, Carson," said the captain, "but there'll be no room for your bags in the pirogue. Or for your boy either. He's got to stay with the wenches."

"Damn!" Jeff shook his head. "But there's one thing I've got to have. Vincente, go get—"

"I already got it, Mr. Jeff." Vincente beamed, proud of his prescience. "I knew you'd want that pistol. It's all loaded up with bullets, too." He handed Jeff the unwieldly weapon.

"Better push off now, Carson, so we can get underway," the captain said.

Jeff followed the young Indian down the rope ladder. He narrowly missed going into the water as the pirogue slid away from the side of the ketch. Pancho grabbed his arm and pushed him into the bow of the little craft. Jeff teetered, sat down abruptly, and waved nonchalantly to the skipper and Vincente while the Indian cast off the line and began paddling strenuously.

For half an hour Pancho paddled in silence. There was now sufficient daylight for Jeff to watch the play of supple muscles under the Houma brave's shoulders as he dug his paddle into the brown surface of the Mississippi. Jeff was increasingly uneasy about the mysterious change of plans. Was Pancho acting on behalf of some enemy of his?

Jeff squirmed in his seat and the pirogue mimicked his movement, shipping water from each side in turn.

"Have we got far to go?" he asked.

Pancho shrugged. He continued to paddle. Then with a few quick strokes he swung the pirogue around at right angles and nosed the craft against a sloping bank with such abruptness that Jeff was thrown backward. Pancho jumped out, pushed his boat further up the bank, and motioned to Jeff.

Jeff climbed out. Pancho dragged the pirogue through

the bushes and over an expanse of mud to what apparently was a bayou. As he nosed the pirogue into the water, an alligator rose to the surface before him and streaked away.

"In," said Pancho.

Jeff obeyed. Pancho gave the craft a final push and got in himself. He resumed paddling with long, slow strokes. Jeff got the impression that they were traveling across a green meadow studded with blue flowers; the bow of the boat slid through a floating mass of water hyacinths. After a few moments Pancho beached the boat again.

"Out," he said. He led Jeff for perhaps a quarter-mile through a grove of tall bearded swamp cypress until they came to a small clearing. In the middle of the clearing stood a log cabin. At the door of the cabin Pancho produced a key from the folds of his loincloth and handed it to Jeff.

"Inside you lock," he said. "Don't open for nobody. Bime-by man may come, but you don't unlock. Man have own key."

And the Indian disappeared into the trees.

Jeff stood staring at the cabin door for a long moment, fingering the heavy key, listening to the crescendo of his own heartbeat, wondering what kind of a trap he had been pushed into. Who was the man with the other key, the man who would come "bime-by"? If he were a Lafitte associate, why all this deviousness?

He tried looking through the single window that flanked the door, but could see nothing. For an instant he thought he glimpsed the flicker of a candle flame far in the back of the cabin, but it may have been an optical illusion. The first rays of the sun were filtering through the cypresses and making points of light on the window-panes.

Well, Jeff asked himself, are you going to stand here all day?

He shifted the key to his left hand. His right hand lifted his pistol tucked inside his belt. The feel of his grip on the butt of the gun restored his composure. The instinct of survival had never failed him yet.

Jeff turned the key in the lock, put his foot against the door, and pushed. When the door swung inward, he jumped to one side—stupidly, he decided on second thought. Anyone laying for him inside would certainly let him walk into an ambush. He cocked his pistol, stepped boldly through the door—and stopped.

No doubt about it. There was certainly a candle or some sort of flickering oil lamp in a back room. He advanced cautiously, step by step, his finger on the trigger of his gun. At the threshold he paused.

The small room was carpeted with mattresses. On a mattress, in one corner, a pile of blankets appeared to be roughly molded in human form. For an instant he thought he detected movement, but decided it was another illusion caused by the conflict of the brightening daylight with the wavering glow of the guttering candle. To be sure he raised his pistol as he moved to the edge of the blanket mound. He held his breath.

"Who's there?" he challenged.

Instantly the blanket fell away and a head and torso popped up.

Jeff gasped. There was no mistaking the long black hair streaming over the full breasts to the waist. Nowhere in the world could there be luminous eyes and silken lashes like those, nothing to match the rose-petal pink and ivory of the cheeks, the dazzling teeth between the parted red lips. He could not believe his eyes.

"Chloe!" He dropped his pistol and fell to his knees. "Chloe, Chloe, Chloe my darling!" He gathered her in his arms. "I must be dreaming. Don't let me wake up."

"Oh, Jeff dearest," she said when she could free her lips. "I've been waiting for you all night. I must have just fallen asleep."

"Chloe, my love." Never had Jeff been so expansive with a woman. "I've been waiting for months. Let's wait no longer." He was unbuttoning his fly when she stopped him with a frantic gesture.

"Jeff, the door is open. Go quickly and lock it. We are in real danger."

"We?"

"Yes." Fear swirled in her dark eyes. "Go quickly."

Jeff ran to the door, retrieved the key from the outside lock, and fastened the door from inside. He hurried back to the girl, a thousand questions churning in his head. They would have to wait. Wordlessly he dropped to the pile of blankets. She was ready for him, clothes and all.

His clothes. She herself was naked except for a flimsy negligee, which he easily whisked away. Chloe was the ultimate, the pinnacle of aphrodisia. The dozens of women he had made love to, the exotic wenches of Havana, were all fun and games. He had never really known true ecstasy except with Chloe. The emotion was so strong that he was whirling to a soaring climax before he was fairly buried in her warmth. He cried out. She echoed him. Strangely, his desire did not abate with the exquisite acme of his rapture. Neither did his male rigidity. He drove deeper with each stroke. He felt he could go on forever, having orgasm after orgasm, exploding like a string of firecrackers. She kept pace with him, moaning as she clasped him to her bosom.

Suddenly she pushed him off and sat up, listening.

"We're mad," she said. "Here we go on as though there were nobody in the world but us. And the world may end at any minute. Our world."

"But our world has just begun, my Chloe."

"Maybe. We can hope." She shook her head sadly. "But you must believe we are both in terrible danger."

He got to his knees. "I believe you," he said. "But there is so much I don't know. Where does the danger lie? What is it? How did you get here? What made Hortense let you go? Why—?"

Chloe laid a finger across his lips. "There's a road runs only a hundred meters behind this cabin," she interrupted. "We're not far outside the city. Lancer drove me here in a closed carriage with shades drawn."

Jeff's eyebrows went up. "What made Hortense let you out of the house?"

"She likes you. She detests the man who wants to buy my way out of the Riding Academy. And she wants to keep you alive so you can go on working for Captain Dominique and the Lafittes. It's as simple as that. Hortense is really a very kind woman."

"But not that kind. She knows how to squeeze a dollar. Somebody must have put up the five thousand."

"Six thousand."

"She promised me I could have your freedom for five thousand."

"But this other man offered her six."

"And who paid Hortense the six thousand?"

"Nobody paid."

"I can't believe that." Jeff shook his head. "Hortense wouldn't let you go just out of the goodness of her heart, any more than she'd send me her right hand wrapped in silk. You're one of her most valuable assets. Who paid?"

"Nobody paid. But Hortense had Captain Dominique send word to a rich widow they both knew. They thought she should know that you were in trouble, partly because of me, and she promised to put up the money."

A warm feeling of gratitude flowed through him. "Was this rich widow Helen Latimer?"

Chloe nodded and colored slightly. "I think my mother is in love with you," she said. "I don't blame her. I understand, but I've been terribly jealous of her. I suppose I can't be jealous of her anymore, can I, darling? She's given me to you, and with me out of the way, she may have saved your life."

Jeff leaned over and put his arms around Chloe. He kissed her. "What's the danger? Who wants to kill me?"

"The man who offered Hortense six thousand."

"And who the hell is he? And why does he want to kill me?"

"Because he wants to take me away with him, and Hortense won't let him because she promised me to you." Chloe did not look at Jeff as she spoke. Her voice was scarcely more than a whisper.

"Why does he want to kill me?" Jeff insisted. He didn't believe it was because of Chloe alone.

"Because he hates you." She avoided his eyes.

Jeff stood up. Chloe also got to her feet. At last she looked him squarely in the eyes. Then she reached up to draw his head down so she could press her cheek against his. "Because, darling," she said, "he says he hates all mustees who try to pass as white. He says you are not Jeff Carson at all, but a mustee called Bricktop."

"Bax Simon. The bastard."

"Yes."

"That bastard!" After all his precautions, despite his trust in the anonymity of the city, that son-of-a-bitch Bax Simon had run him to earth.

"Is it true, darling? Are you really Bricktop, a mustee?"

"Yes, I'm a mustee. But I'll never be Bricktop again. Never! As long as I live I'll fight to be Jeff Carson. I *am* Jeff Carson."

Chloe kissed him. "But if you really are a mustee, we can get married, can't we?"

"No."

The brusque monosyllable affected Chloe like a slap. She winced. "Don't you want to?"

"Wanting has nothing to do with it. Bricktop is a runaway slave, and a runaway slave not only can't get married but has to keep running to stay free. And now that Bax Simon has established the link between Bricktop and Jeff Carson . . ."

"It doesn't make any difference, darling, whether we're married or not." Chloe managed a smile. "As long as we can stay together."

"How long can we stay together? How long will he let us?"

"I hate him!" Chloe's white teeth gleamed in a fierce grimace. "He came to see me with a coiled blacksnake whip in his pocket. He lashed out with it to knock over a vase across the room to show how accurate he was.

He said he could decapitate a man with it." She shuddered.

"And would gladly." Jeff gently disentangled his arms and walked into the front room. He peered through the window a moment, then, noting there were no shades or shutters, returned to the back room.

"Nobody knows where we are," Chloe said reassuringly, "except Madame Hortense, Captain Dominique, and Lancer."

"There's also a Houma Indian named Pancho," Jeff said. "He brought me here."

"I don't know about him. He must be one of Captain Dominique's men."

"The captain seems to have plotted this thing down to the last detail." Jeff admired the efficient staff work of the jovial You. He did not know that Captain Dominique You had been an artillery officer with Napoleon. "What's next? Where's he taking us from here? And when?"

"As soon as feasible, the captain said, he will have us picked up. Probably not until dark, but you can never tell. Stop pacing, darling. Don't be so nervous. There's nothing we can do to hurry matters. Don't you trust the captain?"

"I have to." Jeff was on his knees again, groping for his pistol, which he had dropped when he first saw Chloe. He found it and stuck it under his belt.

CHAPTER XXXIII

BAXTER SIMON turned off St. Louis Street and walked into Pierre Maspero's Exchange through the Charles Street entrance. As he strode across the sanded floor, his gaze swept the block-long bar. Just beyond the noisy journalists' table he spotted the man he was looking for.

Gaspard Cosette stood at the bar dripping water into a spoon that held the tiny tip of a sugar loaf. The sweetened water overflowed the spoon to drip into a glass of greenish absinthe. A dandified old Frenchman, his long black hair and close-cropped beard were obviously dyed, and his pale lavender stock was wrapped tightly to hide his wrinkled neck. His écru linen coat, his tight fawn-colored trousers, his many-buttoned waistcoat of the same color, and his shiny high boots made an appropriate costume for a wealthy sugar planter and rum distiller, even if it was not exactly suited to the New Orleans climate. He was so intent on watching the absinthe gradually turn opalescent as the water dripped into the glass that he was unaware of Simon's presence until the man spoke.

"M'sieur Cosette, I gotta thank yo' fer sendin' word 'bout that boat from Barataria," Bax said.

"Ah, M'sieur Simon." Cosette put down the water jug but continued to hold the spoon over the glass of absinthe. "I'm sorry I could not get to the dock myself. Did she arrive on schedule?"

"Jes' a little late," Bax said.

"Allow me to offer you something to drink." Cosette slid the sugar bit into his glass and stirred. "Some absinthe, perhaps? Or a Sazerac?"

"Don' cotton much to these fancy tipples," Simon said. "Could use a toddy, though."

"Of course. Jules," Cosette addressed the mustachioed barman, "can you make a toddy for this gentleman?"

"If I can get some hot water from the kitchen." The bartender's eyebrows rose at the idea of a hot toddy in the noonday heat.

"Don' fuss none," Simon said. "Jes' pour me a slug o' corn 'n' splash in some spring water."

"Did you see the wenches?" Cosette asked.

"They purty secretive 'bout gettin' 'em ashore," Simon said, "but I got a look while they loadin' 'em in carriages. Mighty fine lot o' cunt, I'd say."

"Then you got the first look. You are lucky. *A votre santé, m'sieur*. To your very good health." Cossette raised his opalescent drink.

"Same to yo', *m'sieur*." Bax Simon downed his whisky in two gulps. "But yo' get first pick so yore luckier'n me. Hope yo' don' take all the hottes' pieces."

"There will be plenty to go around, I'm sure, M'sieur Simon. Plenty."

"Got a frien' who'd like a little new quiff, too, if'n any's left," Baxter said. "Mayhap yo' know him. He own The Georgics Plantation up in Mississippi. Name o' Walter George. Came to N'Orleans along with me to buy some buck niggers, but he'll look at yore fancies, too."

"Don't believe I know him," Cosette said.

"Yo'll meet him here," Simon said. "He due soon to have a toddy wi' me."

"I'd like to meet your friend, m'sieur, but . . ." Cosette tugged at a gold chain across the front of his vest and produced a thick gold repeater watch. He pressed a small spring on the rim and the watch gave off two slow-spaced pings and two quick ones. "Unless he arrives very shortly, I shall miss him. I have promised Captain You that I will call at Condé Street to examine the imported beauties at three o'clock." He pocketed the watch.

"I'll be there myself at three-thirty," said Simon. "Mayhap yo' still be there an' meet Mr. George."

"I hope so, m'sieur." Cosette drained his glass.

"Yo' don' be too greedy, yo' hear," said Simon. He winked. "Be sure yo' leave a couple o' wenches fer us."

"Don't worry, m'sieur." Cosette paid for the drinks, shook hands with Simon, and departed.

Bax Simon ordered another drink of corn while he waited for Walter George. It was not true that George had come to New Orleans to buy slaves. The Georgics was not too prosperous. He was still trying to make a living planting cotton, and the soil was about played out.

After Bax had revealed Jeff Carson as Bricktop, the mustee had gotten away. Two weeks ago Mrs. George had packed her three daughters into a carriage and driven off on a visit to her sister in Natchez. Inasmuch as Mrs. George had never been particularly friendly with her sister and hadn't seen her in years, George couldn't get rid of the awful suspicion that Minnie was pregnant.

Minnie and her mother denied it vehemently, of course, but Bricktop had been such a handsome devil, and Minnie had been so crazy about him before she found out that he was a mustee, that George supposed the skunk had seduced her. The idea that Minnie, one of the real belles of Mississippi and the daughter of a highly respectable plantation family, might give birth to a black baby was too horrible to contemplate. George would never be able to hold his head up again. The family would be disgraced. He would have to sell The Georgics and move away. But where? It would be hard to pull up roots. George had ridden down to Willow Oaks Plantation to seek advice from Bax Simon.

Bax was delighted to join George in running down the varmint. He had heard from the storekeeper at the crossroads that the so-called Jeff had been last seen riding off in the direction of New Orleans. Since Bax was taking a coffle of niggers to New Orleans that week, he invited George to come along. Together they would find Bricktop and avenge the honor of the George family.

George was a gray little man, an eminently respectable and unprepossessing person, who looked out of place among the flamboyant characters lining the bar at Maspero's Exchange, but he downed the corn whiskey with great gusto when he joined Bax Simon. He looked a little less harassed as he set his glass down.

"Well." He looked hopefully at Simon. "Have you found him?"

"Not yet," said Simon.

"I was afraid of that." George shook his head sadly and pushed his empty glass toward the waiting barman.

"But I ain' lost him," Simon continued. "I talk to the crew. He on the boat leavin' Barataria. They sneak him off somewheres las' night."

"So I've come all the way here for nothing." George was dejected.

"Don' believe it." Simon signaled the barman. "Yo' don' know Bax Simon, Mistah George. Ole Bax, he git what he start after."

"How are you going to find him?"

"Easy." Simon glanced about him to make sure none of his fellow drinkers were listening. "I spot this Cuban kid on the dock. Cain' hardly talk English but he herdin' these fancy cunts to they carriages. Damn, they fine-lookin' wenches! Got to hand it to the mustee bastard, he kin shore pick 'em. Great cocksman. Shoulda known he a nigger the way he hung. Never saw the like, black or white. No wonner gals spread they legs fr'im. Prob'ly screwin' any woman gits near him—white or black."

George looked ill. "About this Cuban boy."

"Oh, yes. I ast aroun' 'n' he come up from Havana with the mustee. Name of Vincente. He go right to Miz Hortense's with the wenches, 'n' I folla. I figger soon'r or late he gonna join up with Bricktop. Then we got Bricktop by the balls."

"How so?" George was skeptical.

"Jes' trust Bax Simon." Bax winked with the whole left side of his face. "I tol' yo' ole Bax know how to git what he want. When I go to Condé Street this mornin' I go roun' to Miz Hortense's stable. She got a groom used to be Willow Oaks nigger name o' Neptune. Neptune, he like me, 'n' he like my money even better. When this Cuba kid go fin' Bricktop, Neptune, he gonna folla so he kin tell me whereat he hidin'."

Simon didn't mention the fact that he also hoped to find Chloe wherever Bricktop was. He had called at Madame Hortense's the night before and had tried unsuccessfully to spend the night with the beautiful octoroon. Madame Hortense had said that Chloe was occupied with an all-night customer, but Simon was sure she was lying. Just wait, he promised himself, ole Bax git what ole Bax want. . . .

"I swear I'll kill that imposter," George was saying. "I should have killed him the night we discovered his masquerade, as I wanted to."

"Shootin's too quick for that polecat," Simon said. "Don' go shootin' him 'fore I whop some meat off his back." He patted his pocket. "Don' forget my black-snake here."

CHAPTER XXXIV

JEFF had no idea how long he had been dozing. First thing he noticed was that daylight was fading. When he finally realized where he was, and that he was naked, he sat up abruptly and looked around. Chloe was propped up on one elbow, adoring him with those luminous eyes.

"Do you know what I was just thinking?" she said.

"No. Maybe about when we are going to get out of this place?"

"Not at all," she said, with a toss of her head. "I was thinking about how I knew from the first time I saw you that you were one of us folks."

"You knew I was a mustee when you first saw me?"

"Not when I first saw you," she admitted, "but when I first felt you."

"Oh come now, Chloe. I know that I'm better endowed than most men, but that has nothing to do with the fact that one of my distant ancestors came from Africa. There are plenty of thoroughbred whites just as well hung. And in my experience as a slave buyer, I've seen puny blacks, too."

"Jeff darling." She put her arms around his neck. "You know that I've been working for Hortense ever since I've had things growing between my legs and on my chest. But all my men were white—every one of them—until you came along. That made it very simple for me, because I could watch myself. I did my job well—after all, I know my business—but without taking part. Oh, sometimes I enjoyed it physically. But rarely. Too often it was physically inadequate, even repulsive, like with your owner Simon. The moment you touched me, I felt something I had never felt before, something new and different and wonderful."

"That's because we loved each other from the start," Jeff said. "It has nothing to do with whatever Negro blood we may have in our veins. I never felt that sleeping with a black wench was any different from humping a white woman."

"What we have together is more than just love," Chloe said. She unwound her arms, took his hand, and drew him down beside her on the mattress. "A professor who used to come to Madame Hortense's occasionally, a Frenchman, had a name for it. He called it *négritude*. You say you are a slave dealer—yet I'm sure you have compassion. You are not cruel to your brothers. You would not kill."

"I've killed two men," Jeff interrupted.

"They were white, I'm sure. You killed to save yourself, didn't you?"

Jeff did not reply at once. It had not occurred to him that he might have shown more compassion for blacks than for whites. No, it was nonsense. He felt badly when Ramon had been killed, but he did not eat his heart out. And it was too bad about Trafalgar, too, but he himself might have killed Trafalgar—in self-defense—and it would have made no difference that he was black.

"That's all nonsense," he said at last. "No use trying to turn me back to Bricktop after I've decided I'm going to remain white Jeff Carson. In spite of Bax Simon." He kissed Chloe. "Let's stop this silly talk. Maybe I'm hungry, after all. And how about some light?"

The candle that had been glowing when Jeff had arrived had long since burned itself out, but they found some tallow stubs in the closet.

They ate bread and ham and drank wine out of a jug. They talked of their future—as if they had one—after Captain Dominique You had gotten them away from this place. Jeff supposed they would be going to Barataria. He remembered what Jean Lafitte had said before the start of the Havana venture—the fast schooner *Seraphine* was being readied to rescue Napoleon from Saint Helena and Jeff might be assigned to accompany Captain You on the expedition.

Chloe was sitting very straight, listening to sounds outside. She had paled slightly. Suddenly she leaned forward and extinguished the candle.

"What's the matter?"

Chloe laid a finger across his lips. "Horses," she whispered. "Or at least a horse. I'm sure I heard a carriage stop."

Jeff listened intently. The darkness appeared to grow more opaque. He could hear nothing except his own breathing for what seemed like several minutes but was probably only a few seconds. Then he detected the faint rhythm of footsteps. He groped for his pistol, found it, and got to his knees to peer out the window.

He saw a tiny point of blue light that expanded into a yellow flame, then went out—probably a defective sulphur match. He cocked his pistol.

The footsteps grew louder and more distinct as they approached the rear of the cabin. Jeff felt cold sweat bead on his forehead and in the palms of his hands. His grip on his pistol butt tightened.

There was a knock on the back door. Chloe's fingers again covered his lips. The knock came again, louder. Silence. Jeff held his breath.

The knock now became a tattoo, and above it a voice whimpered, "Let me in, Señor Jeff. I know you're there. It's me, Vincente."

Jeff breathed again.

"Don't open," Chloe whispered. "He may not be alone."

"Who's with you, Vincente?"

"Nobody, *señor*. I alone. I bring things for you. Very important, I think."

Jeff said, "Light the candle. I'm going to open for him."

"You're taking a terrible chance," Chloe said.

A friction match sputtered into flame and the candle flared. Jeff unlocked the door but held his foot against it as he opened it a crack wide enough for the muzzle of his pistol. When he was convinced that Vincente was alone, he let the lad in, closing and locking the door after him.

Chloe looked Vincente over. She frowned. "I think

335

you'd better find out how this boy knew where you were," she said.

Jeff nodded. "How about it, Vincente? Have you an explanation?"

"Sure." Vincente made a gesture with upturned palms. *"El Captain Domingo*, he fix everything."

It was a long and complicated story, Vincente said. First of all, he was so busy getting the wenches settled and taking care of the baggage Jeff had left aboard the *Jerome* that he hadn't had a chance to approach Captain Dominique You about the problem of locating Jeff. But when You had finished licking his lips over the goodies Jeff had brought from Cuba, he told Vincente that there was no way of communicating with Mr. Carson. However, when Vincente pleaded, Captain You's whole attitude had changed. "So I am here," Vincente concluded.

"Who brought you?" Jeff asked. "Not Captain You, surely?"

"No, no," said Vincente. "One of Señora Hortense's *estableros. Establero.* You know. He take care of horses. He drive me. A black man. Very nice. Name is Neptune."

CHAPTER XXXV

"ARE you sure we're on the right road, Baxter?" Walter George asked as the carriage rattled through the outskirts of New Orleans. His slurred speech was due to his having consumed more than his usual quota of alcoholic stimulants. After the few early afternoon corn whiskies at Prospero's Exchange, they had enjoyed Madame Hortense's hospitality while they were making their token appearance at the first showing of the new girls from Cuba. They had then dined at the St. Louis Hotel and George had gone on to French wines and brandy (Simon had begun to ration his intake of corn) while they were awaiting the closed carriage whose driver had been briefed by Neptune.

"Shore am," Bax replied. "Trust Neptune, I do," he added, " 'cause I not payin' him that other dollar till we get back."

"I can hardly wait to get my hands on that . . . nigger. That despoiler of southern womanhoood," Walter George said.

"Been athinkin' 'bout that Bricktop," said Simon. "Been athinkin' how we best do it—so it slow."

George said, "The idea that that bastard nigger impregnated my daughter is enough to drive me mad. I want him dead, Simon."

"Course, Mr. George." Simon saw that he would have to humor George's drunken indignation. He had been having second thoughts. On reflection, he had decided that he would get much more satisfaction if he could return Bricktop to Willow Oaks. He could think of many delightful ways to humiliate and torture him for the rest of his life—such as forcing him to watch him in bed with Chloe. In the end, Bax was sure, he would get Chloe. "I jes' think yo' better let me whop him good, then we take him back to Willow Oaks like any other runner."

The carriage stopped and the coachman was opening the door. " 'Scuse me fer interruptin', mastah," he said, "but this yere's far's we go. You gotta walk down that there path to Cap'n Dominique's cabin, mastah."

"Wait fer us here, driver," Simon said as he steadied George getting out. "We be right back—with two more fares."

Simon patted his hip pocket to make sure he still carried his coiled blacksnake whip.

Jeff paced the floor nervously.

"What time did Captain You say he would come for us?" he asked Vincente.

"Didn't say exactly, Mr. Jeff," Vincente replied. "But coming very soon now, I think."

"Wonder what's holding him up," said Jeff.

"Don't be impatient, darling," was Chloe's comment. "You don't even know where we'll be going next."

"Maybe Havana," said Vincente.

Jeff snorted. "You were so anxious to get away from Havana. Now you talk about going back. What's got into you?"

"This afternoon," said Vincente, "I have good look at whorehouse of Madame Hortense. I get great ideas. Maybe we open new place in Havana to steal customers from La Casa de Josefina. My sister Perla—"

Chloe said, "Vincente, Captain You will not need a light in the window to guide him to his secret lair, so it might be a good idea to move that candle into the other room or put it out."

"You heard her, Vincente," Jeff said.

"Sure, Mr. Jeff." Vincente's response was not entirely enthusiastic. He took the candle and walked into the front room. The faint shadows of Jeff and Chloe projected on the back wall made giant silhouettes that grew gradually smaller as the light source moved away. Jeff put his arm around Chloe's shoulders. She suddenly stiffened. "Listen," she murmured.

Jeff held his breath. He heard confused sounds beyond the entrance. "Must be You," he said.

At that moment there was a crash and the tinkle of broken glass. Jeff glimpsed a black streak, like the tail of a serpent, flick through the jagged hole and disappear. He heard a torrent of indistinct profanity, of which he could recognize only a few phrases: "son-of-a-bitch of a mustee . . . goddamn filthy nigger . . ."

He snatched his pistol from his waistband as an ugly black gun muzzle poked through the broken window, spewing flame and thunder.

Something struck Jeff in the chest and the impact knocked him down. He dropped his pistol as he sprawled backward. The bullet ricocheted off the golden cross at his breast and ripped across the throat of the girl beside him. With a little cry she fell against him. Her cry diminished to a whimper, which became a horrid gurgle. Her blood spurted over him in ebbing jets.

Vincente dropped the candle. He rushed from the front room, grabbed up Jeff's pistol, and fired through

338

the broken window. The first shot made a frightening roar. He turned the cylinder and fired again. And again. And again. . . .

"Get down, you fool!" Bax Simon growled at George. He gave him a sharp shove. George, sprawled on the ground, tried to reload his pistol. "Cain' you see he's got a bodyguard in there?"

"Horse shit, Mr. Simon," said George. "He's alone. Think I got him. Saw him go down. Got to finish him off."

Two more shots blasted through the broken window.

"Get up!" Simon clutched George's arm and dragged him to his feet. "No man kin reload 'n' start a-shootin' ag'in that fast. We gotta git back to the buggy afore that coachman hear the shootin' 'n' run off 'thout us."

"But I must make sure I got that nigger bastard," George protested as Simon elbowed him into the path leading to the road.

Another shot rang out.

"Cain' do nothin' more tonight if'n they gang up on us liken this," Simon insisted. "Need help, we do. But if'n he still alive tomorra, we git a legal paper 'n' take 'im back to Willow Oaks."

When Vincente had reloaded Jeff's revolving pistol with the bullets from his own pocket, he crept out the back door to carry on his one-man battle. The unknown enemy had disappeared but Vincente fired two more shots just to make his presence known. When he heard the sound of retreating hoofbeats on the New Orleans road, he returned to the cabin.

The candle had gone out. Vincente found and relighted it.

The yellow glow revealed Jeff, his chest covered with blood, kneeling beside Chloe, trying to coax her to speak to him. Vincente shook his head.

"She stop bleeding," the lad said. "*Qué lástima*! She dead, I think."

"She can't be dead! We've just begun to live!" Jeff's

was a child's voice, pleading, protesting against what he knew to be true but refused to accept. "She can't be dead."

"*Pobrecita*," said Vincente softly. He set the candle gently on the floor beside Chloe's head. "*Lo siento mucho. I am very sorry.*"

Jeff did not hear him. He went on staring in disbelief at the dead girl. She seemed to stare back at him, eyes fixed wide open. There was an ugly gaping wound at the base of her neck. She was beautiful, Jeff thought. That was all he could think. The waxen pallor spreading across her face gave her profile the classic lines of a fine carving.

"Chloe, Chloe, Chloe," Jeff whispered, tears hot on his cheek. He shook his head. He had died with her. Though he breathed, never again would he commit himself to love anyone so much that he could be hurt like this. Desolated. Empty. Doomed to live. To remember her. No. Once was enough.

"Mr. Jeff!" Vincente whispered. He approached and lifted the candle. He held it close to the cross around Jeff's neck. There was a dent in the center of the cross and a furrow bent one of the Savior's arms. "This lucky *cruz talismánica* sure save your life, I think. The bullet bounce right off."

"And killed Chloe." Jeff couldn't keep his eyes from Chloe's dead face, now more and more assuming the impersonal beauty of a perfect piece of sculpture. He was fascinated, even while the person of Chloe, the embodiment of the ultimate in sensual delight and of that imaginary state of mind called love, was rapidly fading away from him. Temporarily deranged, Jeff was as dead as she was.

Captain Dominique You pushed open the back door which Vincente had left ajar.

"*Nom de Dieu!*" he roared, standing in the doorway bareheaded, candlelight gleaming faintly on his fringe of white hair. His round face was flushed. He kicked the door shut behind him. "Who leaves the door unlocked when I say lock it always? What fool—?" He stopped with his mouth agape. He stared at the candlelit dead girl on the floor. He gazed at the blood on Jeff's clothes. He glanced again at the corpse and crossed himself. "You hurt, boy?"

Jeff shook his head. "There was just one shot fired. The ricochet killed Chloe."

"But I heard half-a-dozen shots as we came along the road."

"That was me," Vincente said, "with this new-fangled pistol."

"A fiacre rushed past on the road back to New Orleans, going like mad. Almost forced me off the road. Come on, Carson." Captain Dominique touched Jeff's arm, firmly yet with an odd gentleness. "You've got to get out of here. Simon has already got the sheriff of the parish looking for a runaway slave named Bricktop. There's a fiacre outside to take you on the road to Chalmette. Jean Desfarge will see you to the waiting pirogue. You've got to travel to Barataria through the bayous and the marshes. *Allez! Vite!*"

"But I can't go off and leave Chloe like this," Jeff said. "She—"

"You can't do a thing for the poor girl now. She's dead. Leave everything to me. Hortense will see that she is properly remembered. Come, Carson."

Jeff knelt beside Chloe, took her mother's cross from around his neck, and placed it on her breast.

"All right, captain." He got to his feet. "Let's go."

"Leave the candle," Captain Dominique said. "I'll be back, when I have made sure you are in the carriage."

Outside the cabin, Jeff realized Vincente was not with him. He turned and called, "Vincente, where the hell are you?"

"Coming pronto," answered the boy. He knelt and took up the golden cross Jeff had left on Chloe's breast and dropped it into one of his voluminous pockets. He groped over the floor for the jewel case Chloe had dropped when she fell.

"Vincente, damnit, I'm going off without you."

"Right there, Mr. Jeff," said Vincente, as he added Chloe's earrings to the salvage in his pocket.

CHAPTER XXXVI

RENÉ BELUCHE sat across the desk from Jean Lafitte and made a helpless gesture with both hands.

"That man from New Orleans insists on seeing you personally," he said. "Can't put him off much longer without feeding him to the crocks. He talks of sending the militia to Grande-Terre to burn the place down."

Lafitte touched the ends of his black cavalryman's mustache with two fingers. After a pensive moment he asked, "Is there any danger of Carson's walking in on us while the man is here?"

"Hardly," Beluche replied. "From all reports he has a hard time walking at all, the shape he's in."

"How long is Jeff overdue?"

"About a week."

"And you think he can't get here before tomorrow?"

"At the earliest," Beluche said.

"Make sure that he doesn't." Lafitte slapped his desk. "See that Carson's intercepted in the bay before he reaches Grande-Terre. Have him put directly aboard the schooner *Marengo*. I want to be able to say truthfully that we have nobody with his name or description on the island."

"And the man outside?"

"Let him wait another five minutes, then send him in."

When Beluche had left, Lafitte arose, came out from behind his desk, and crossed to the opposite wall to admire himself in an ornate gilt-framed Louis Quinze mirror. He had been warned that a man of the law would be down from New Orleans and he wanted to be dressed in a manner befitting the Lord of Barataria when he arrived. He ran his fingers through his dark curly hair and nodded his strong pointed chin in approval of his favorite costume —a lightweight blue cutaway jacket with wide lapels and brass buttons. He adjusted the embossed leather sword belt and drew his saber an inch from the scabbard before clicking it back. He was standing in front of his desk when the man from New Orleans was ushered in. The newcomer was a husky six-footer in civilian clothes.

"M'sieur Lafitte, my name is Petit," he announced. "I have a warrant signed by Governor Clairborne of the state of Louisiana calling for the arrest of a fugitive slave by the name of Bricktop, alias Jeff Carson. Where is he?"

"I don't know, Mr. Petit," said Lafitte, giving the name the French pronunciation while reflecting that it was a misnomer for a men of such burly proportions. "But if I did know, I am not sure I would tell you. We in Barataria do not recognize the authority of the state of Louisiana. Many of us have lived here under French rule, and some of us since the land belonged to Spain. We have our own laws here."

"Ah?" Petit unrolled an official-looking document. "Do they tolerate murder, M'sieur Lafitte?"

"In certain circumstances." Lafitte smiled, remembering the time he had shot one of Vincent Gambi's lieutenants for questioning his authority. "Is your runaway slave —what's his name?—a murderer?"

"The so-called Jeff Carson killed a prostitute," Petit said.

"In what brothel was this?" Lafitte was still smiling.

"No brothel." Petit was grim. "In a cabin belonging to the brothers Lafitte on the outskirts of New Orleans."

"Well! That brings the matter to my doorstep, n'est-ce pas? There are witnesses, of course?"

"Of course. Two gentlemen from Mississippi. One of them formerly owned this so-called Carson. They were looking for him to return him to his plantation when they witnessed the killing. They had to flee for their own lives when he and four of his accomplices opened fire on them. I have information that he and his accomplices are here in Grande-Terre."

"Please sit down, Mr. Petit." Lafitte waved to a chair

and resumed his own seat behind the desk. He stopped smiling. "I give you my word, Mr. Petit, that your man Carson is not on this island, or Grand Isle either. I know that you and your people call me Lafitte the Pirate, and therefore regard my solemn word as worth no more than . . . than . . . *une crotte de chien.* A dog turd. Therefore, Mr. Petit, we want you to assure yourself that your man is not here. M'sieur Beluche will go with you to show you around and to open any door that is locked. Or, if you had rather, go alone. Satisfy yourself. Take several days, if you like. Be our guest. We rather pride ourselves on our food here, and we have recently received some vintage wines from France. I will furnish you transportation to New Orleans whenever you are sure that I am not harboring a criminal."

"Thank you, M'sieur Lafitte, you are very kind," said Petit, looking very glum. "I accept your invitation. But I think I should like to look around by myself for a while."

When Jeff's pirogue slid into the upper end of Barataria Bay near Pointe à la Hache he should have felt elated, but he did not have the strength. He was still some twenty miles from the end of his journey, and the last lap would be smooth paddling for only a few hours. He didn't care. He was exhausted physically and listless mentally. He lay back on the boughs with which Vincente had lined the canoe and tried to remember all that had happened during the past . . . how many days had it been?

The phantasmagoria had begun shortly after he had said goodbye to Captain Dominique. The first thirty-six hours had been nasty but bearable—a constant change from waterborne transport to portage across knee-deep mud and slush, through clouds of fierce mosquitos, down creeks squirming with water snakes. He slept only in snatches while the pirogue was crossing the comparative quiet of alligator-infested bayous.

The fever began rising at the end of the first day. The second morning he was burning up. His face and arms were so flushed that Vincente commented, "You don't look so good, Mr. Jeff, I think."

Jeff had never had a sick day in his life. But he had to admit that something was dreadfully wrong with him now. Still, he kept up with the progress of his relentless guides—until the pain struck his joints. The shoulders and elbows were not so bad, as he was carrying nothing. But when the agony seemed to cut off his legs at the knees, he could go no further. Walking was excruciating torture. He sank down in the mud and wept from sheer anguish.

Vincente and one of the guides carried him across the swamp to a trapper's cabin, where they left him with some hardtack, a slab of sow belly, a canteen of drinking water—and Vincente. The guides would proceed to Barataria, report the situation, and return when they had new instructions. Vincente shouldn't worry about the trapper if he came back. He was a friend of the Lafittes.

Jeff lay on a stinking pile of untanned muscrat hides and drifted into delirious sleep. He dreamed of the first wench he had ever had—a mulatto that Baxter Simon had bought when he was Bax's slave playboy at Willow Oaks. Then the wench turned into Minnie George, and Bax killed her because she had borne a black baby, who turned into Jean Lafitte, who refused to give Jeff five thousand dollars to buy Chloe from Madame Hortense. So he got his self-loading pistol and killed Chloe and Lafitte and Madame Hortense and Trafalgar and Cugino. But he couldn't kill Bax Simon because there were no bullets left. He woke up screaming.

"You still hurt, Mr. Jeff?" Vincente knelt beside him, wiping sweat from his face.

"I'm going to die, Vincente."

"No you ain't, Mr. Jeff. You still got your lucky piece. I brought it along. See?" The lad produced the dented golden cross and slipped it over Jeff's head. "You get well now."

Jeff stared at the cross. It looked double. He couldn't remember where he had lost it. It didn't matter now.

"I've got *la plaga*, haven't I, Vincente?"

"No, Mr. Jeff. You don't shit right for *la plaga*. You don't even shit at all, so you don't got it."

"But Vincente, I've never had such pain." Jeff closed his eyes. "In my head, in my legs, my back, all over."

"Sure. You got the dengue." Vincente nodded wisely. He was proud of his diagnosis. There were epidemics of dengue in Cuba sometimes. It was very painful— *muy doloroso*—with high fever, but people didn't usually die of *el dengue*. After a few days they felt better and got red spots on their hands and arms and sometimes on chest and back. . . .

The spots had already started to appear on Jeff's hands by the time the boatsmen came back for them. As Vincente had predicted, he was in full bloom with the dengue rash by the time his pirogue was approaching Grande-Terre. Good thing he wasn't planning a new feminine conquest. He wouldn't be up to much anyhow; he felt completely washed out. He must be a rare sight with his spots and a week's growth of beard. He hoped that Lafitte or René or whoever got word of his imminent arrival would tell Gretchen so she could have a hot bath waiting for him.

Gretchen opened the door to the knock and stared at the tall stranger standing there.

"Is this Mr. Jeff Carson's house?" the stranger asked.

"Yes, it is," Gretchen replied.

"Could I speak to him, please? I'm a friend of his from New Orleans."

"Mr. Carson is not home just now. Didn't you see him in New Orleans? He is there now."

"I must have missed him," said the stranger. "I understand he is due back today, though."

"Oh, I hope so." Gretchen clasped her hands in front of her apron. "He was away in Cuba for such a long time."

"But when he comes back, you would see him before he left again, wouldn't you, miss?"

"Oh sure, sure. He would have to come here for clean linen. He didn't take much with him." Gretchen's face clouded. "But he wouldn't leave again so soon, I hope. Or have you heard something I don't know? Tell me, sir. Why do you say he is leaving again?"

"I merely wanted to be sure I didn't miss him," said the tall stranger. "I understand there's a ship sailing today, and I was afraid he might be on it."

"Today? You mean maybe the schooner *Wagram*. She sails tomorrow only."

"Then I'll have time in case Mr. Carson should show up." The stranger turned to go. "I'll be here for several days. M'sieur Lafitte has invited me. So I'll see you again."

"Won't you come in and have a cup of coffee, sir?"

"No, thank you."

"Could you tell me your name, sir, so I can let Mr. Carson know who has been looking for him?"

"I'd rather surprise him," said the stranger. "He doesn't know I'm here."

Gretchen watched him go down the few steps from the stoop. Mr. Jeff has such distinguished-looking friends, she mused.

CHAPTER XXXVII

MR. PETIT had a big night on the town. Everything was *"aux fraise de la princesse,"* according to Jean Lafitte, who added, "Or, as you Americans say, on the house." Jean and René Beluche were determined to get him drunk. With the quail on toast and *pâté de foie gras au porto*, Petit drank Napoleon's favorite red Burgandy, Chambertin. With the breast of pheasant he drank champagne. And all during the evening he drank Napoleon's favorite brandy while he played trente-et-quarante —and won, not being confused by the cognac or the six packs of cards. When he said good night in the small hours of the morning, he had done very well in keeping his feet—and his head.

He was up at dawn to make sure the schooner *Wagram* had not sailed. He had seen preliminary preparations

347

the day before when she was being fitted for sea. He haunted the docks all morning, and when he saw the water casks and sacks of flour being taken aboard, he made his move. He walked up the gangplank to board the schooner, but was stopped before he could step on deck. The watchman summoned the bo's'n, a French half-caste from Martinique named LeMay.

"You cannot come aboard," said the bo's'n. "*C'est défiendu.*"

Petit showed his papers and explained that Jean Lafitte had promised him free access to everything on the island. The bo's'n sent a messenger to get advice from René Beluche. Beluche came aboard himself and confirmed the statement.

"Show him everything," he said.

And when Petit had disappeared into a companionway, he added, "Go with him. Keep him below at all costs for at least half an hour."

Before the half-hour was up, a long pirogue came alongside the *Wagram* from the offshore direction. One of the boatmen shipped his paddle and helped Vincente disentangle Jeff from his bed of boughs. They seized a line dangling over the side of the schooner. They propped him up and looped the end of the rope under his arms and around his shoulders. Then they lifted him from the pirogue and lowered him into the water. He sank to his chin.

"Hey!" he protested. "How long—?"

Vincente clasped one hand over Jeff's mouth, then removed it and reached above Jeff's head to grasp the rope firmly with both hands.

Jeff was too weak to struggle. The water was warm enough not to be disagreeable, but he looked around anxiously for sharks. One of the boatmen passed his paddle behind the rope, holding the little craft close to the ship's side. Jeff heard sounds of running feet out of sight on the deck above him. There were shouts of men in the rigging, and the creak of tackle as sails were being hoisted.

"You must go ashore now," said the bo's'n at the head of the gangway.

"Who says so?" demanded Petit, wiping sweat from his forehead.

"M'sieur Beluche say so before he leave ship," said the bo's'n. "We are sailing now."

"And if I refuse to go?"

"Overboard." The bo's'n made a throwing motion with both arms. "I hope you can swim."

Petit looked at the two bruisers standing behind the bo's'n and opted for the better part of valor. The gangplank dropped. Several minutes after the schooner got underway, the pirogue pushed away at a signal from above, and Jeff and Vincente were hauled aboard.

The minute his feet touched the deck Jeff collapsed from sheer physical weakness and pent-up emotions of the past week. He fell asleep before he could pick himself up. Vincente and a sailor carried him into a cabin that had been set aside for him. He snored while Vincente pulled off his wet clothes and rubbed his naked body with coconut oil he had found in the galley.

By the time he awoke, the schooner had cleared the Grand Pass and was well into the Gulf. He sat up and yawned. Vincente tossed him a pair of denim trousers and asked, "Think you can walk now, Mr. Jeff? The captain wants to see you."

Jeff frowned at the trousers. "These aren't mine," he said. "Where are my trogs? Why didn't somebody have Gretchen bring my own stuff aboard?"

"Sure don't know, Mr. Jeff. Can you walk?"

"I can try." Jeff slipped into the trousers and stood up. He took a few barefoot steps and nodded. "Lead the way," he said.

As soon as he stepped through the wheelhouse door he recognized the faded uniform cap and the biblike gray beard.

"Captain MacFarland!" Jeff shook his head. "Am I going to spend the rest of my life in your lap?"

"Ye'll be doin' me no favor, that I'll tell ye." MacFarland scowled. "Ye look a bloody mess wi' all that seaweed on yer face an' the wrath of God tattooed on yer arms an' belly like a murderin' red Indian. What's been happenin' to ye, lad?"

"I've been through hell, skipper."

"This time ye'll not be makin' holes in my hull to build bunks fer yer niggers," the captain said. "This schooner is big enough to hold a king's phalanx o' blacks without yer fancy contraptions."

"What happened to the *Sainte-Claire*?" Jeff asked.

"The bark's been careened on the beach fer repairs. That storm opened up a few seams an' she's bein' recaulked. An' since I've always been a schooner man, they've given me the *Wagram*."

"But why am I being rushed away like this without even being allowed to go home for clean clothes?" A worried frown creased Jeff's brow. "Am I being exiled? Don't I get any bonus pay? Wasn't M'sieur Lafitte pleased with my Havana job?"

"Aye, that he was, lad," said the skipper, "an' ye'll get yer shares o' the *Sainte-Claire* profits when we return. The boss has left instructions wi' me, together wi' letters of credit an' some petty cash fer fun and sundries. He wants ye to bring back another two or three hundred niggers."

"Really?" The frown disappeared. "From Cuba?"

"Aye, from Havana eventually. But first we're bound fer Saint Domingue to pick up some o' our men. One o' our ships foundered an' the crew's marooned there."

"Where's San Domang?"

"An island in the Caribbean, lad. Some call it Haiti, but on my charts it's marked Saint Domingue."

Haiti! That was where one of his octoroon Fancies came from. What was her name? Antoinette? Yes, Antoinette, Duchess of Limbé. Not a bad little trick. In fact, he remembered she was damned good. She was the one with the big tits and very busy little hands . . . Haiti might very well merit further exploration.

Things began to look up. Life might turn out to be worth living after all. Funny how rapidly Chloe's image was fading. Oh, he felt a little stab whenever he thought of her, and he remembered their last hours together with pleasure and gratitude. Yes, he had really loved her, whatever love was—the only woman he had ever felt that way about. But she was gone now, and life went on. Life was a little like the sea, he mused as he felt the deck rise to the easy swell of the Gulf—unpredictable, beckoning, and teeming with fish just waiting to be caught.

"It's sort of nice to be sailing with you again, after all, skipper," Jeff said.

New York, N.Y.
St. Petersburg, Fla.
Falls Church, Va.

From Fawcett Gold Medal . . .

Great Adventures in Reading

Fiction

GOLDEN STUD
by Lance Horner   X3236 $1.75

DARK LABYRINTH
by Susannah Leigh   P3255 $1.25

A LESSON IN LOVING
by Mollie Chappell   M3256   95¢

THE ONLY GIRL
by Jeanne Judson   M3257   95¢

Non-Fiction

GET MORE FOR YOUR MONEY
by Tom Philbin   P3259 $1.25

Humor

RISE & SHINE, ANDY CAPP!
by Smythe   M3258   95¢

FAWCETT

Wherever Paperbacks Are Sold